A
Nightingale
Christmas Promise

Donna Douglas

arrow books

1 3 5 7 9 10 8 6 4 2

Arrow Books
20 Vauxhall Bridge Road
London SW1V 2SA

Arrow Books is part of the Penguin Random House group of companies
whose addresses can be found at global.penguinrandomhouse.com.

Penguin
Random House
UK

First published in Great Britain by Arrow Books in 2018

www.penguin.co.uk

A CIP catalogue record for this book is available from the British Library

ISBN 9781784757144

Typeset in 10.75/13.5 pt Palatino by Jouve (UK), Milton Keynes
Printed and bound in Great Britain by Clays Ltd, Elcograf S.p.A.

MIX
Paper from
responsible sources
FSC® C018179
www.fsc.org

Penguin Random House is committed to a
sustainable future for our business, our readers
and our planet. This book is made from Forest
Stewardship Council® certified paper.

Acknowledgements

As ever, a massive thanks to the team at Arrow, especially my editors Emily Griffin and Cassandra Di Bello, the design team for coming up with another great cover, and the brilliant sales and marketing guys for making the Nightingale series such a success. I literally couldn't have done it without you all.

Thanks also to my wonderful and ever-patient agent Caroline Sheldon for listening to (and trying to make sense of) all my wild and crazy ideas. And to my even more long-suffering family, especially my husband Ken, for doing the same for so many years.

A huge thank you to my readers, who have supported me throughout the Nightingale series, and who have written to tell me how much they've enjoyed the books. I hope you take the next intake of Nightingales to your hearts as much as you have the old!

Finally, I'd like to take a moment to remember Marjorie Lilian Riche, the extraordinary woman who took on a kid no one else wanted. She would have been 100 years old this year. She went through life never thinking she was anyone special. But her humour and her down-to-earth London warmth is at the heart and soul of every story I tell. As ever, this one's for you, Mum.

To Jacqui and Brian Quennell,
with much love

Chapter One

Christmas Eve 1913

'*Verdammt!*' Anna muttered under her breath.

'I heard that,' her sister Liesel said from the other side of the bakery kitchen. 'I'm going to tell Mother you said a bad word.'

'I couldn't help it.' Anna put down her piping bag and scowled at the blob of icing on the pristine surface of the Christmas cake. It had taken her hours to create the delicate tracery of intertwined holly and ivy leaves, and now it was ruined.

'Let's have a look.' Her father's apprentice Edward Stanning abandoned the mound of dough he was kneading and came across the kitchen to inspect the damage. 'It's not too bad,' he said. 'Nothing that can't be put right, anyway.'

Anna bent over the cake, smoothing out the blob with the tip of her finger. 'But I really wanted it to be perfect. Papa said it's for a special customer.'

'Anna made a mista-ake,' Liesel taunted her in a sing-song voice. 'Papa won't ever trust you to help him again.'

'Oh, shut up, Liesel!' Anna snapped. 'No wonder I can't concentrate, with you chattering away all the time!'

Liesel stuck out her tongue. 'I can't help it if I'm cheerful, can I? It's Christmas Eve.'

'As if I didn't know!' Anna straightened up and mopped her brow with the hem of her apron. Outside the steamed-up kitchen window, flurries of snow were swirling in the icy wind, but Anna could feel rivulets of perspiration trickling down between her shoulder blades. 'I've been up since

1

the early hours, helping Papa light the ovens and get the first batches of loaves ready. While you were still snoring in bed,' she accused.

'I do not snore!' Liesel turned pink. 'Anyway, I barely had a wink of sleep, with you two banging about down here, clattering trays and singing at the top of your voices.'

'Papa likes to sing Christmas carols as he works.' '*Stille Nacht*' and '*Ir Kinderlein Kommet*' were his favourites at this time of year.

' "*Ir Kinderlein, kommet. O kommet doch all*," ' Edward sang a few bars.

' "*Zur Krippe her kommet in Bethlehems Stall*," ' Anna joined in.

'Stop it, you two. You sound like a pair of cats fighting in the alley.' Liesel clamped her hands over her ears. 'You're supposed to be working, remember?'

'So are you,' Anna said. 'Have you checked those loaves in the oven? They should be done by now.' She glanced up at the clock on the wall. It was nearly three o'clock, just an hour until closing time, but the bell over the shop door hadn't stopped ringing since their father opened up first thing that morning.

'I know what I'm doing, thank you,' Liesel said huffily. 'Just because you're the eldest doesn't mean you can boss me about.'

'I'm not bossing you about, I'm just reminding you. You can be careless, you know.'

'Speak for yourself! You're the one who's just ruined Papa's cake!'

Anna turned her attention mournfully back to the cake on the pedestal in front of her. She had managed to smooth the blob of icing down to barely a smudge, but she could still see it.

'Anyway, I don't even know why I have to help out in the

kitchen,' Liesel went on sulkily. 'I should be behind the counter with Mother as usual.'

'You know Papa likes to be in the shop himself at Christmas.' Anna could hear her father, beyond the doors that led to the shop, laughing and joking with his customers. He would be handing out marzipan treats to all the children, and teaching them to say *'Frohe Weihnachten'*. Besides, you only want to be out there so you can flirt with all the boys.'

'That's not true!' Liesel blushed furiously to the roots of her blonde hair.

'Don't tease your sister.' Edward grinned at Anna. 'She's sixteen, she's allowed to flirt with whoever she likes.'

'That's right.' Liesel preened herself. 'Anyway, Papa says it cheers the customers up to see a pretty face behind the counter. Which is probably why he makes you stay in the kitchen!' she laughed.

'I stay in the kitchen because I'm the only one Papa can teach!' Anna snapped back, but she was stung. She was only too aware that Liesel was the one who had inherited their mother's fair hair and blue eyes, while Anna herself was slight and auburn-haired like their father. At sixteen, Liesel was all soft curves, while Anna at twenty-one was still waiting for her boyish figure to blossom. When she looked in the mirror, all she saw were her faults; dark eyes that were too small, skin that was too sallow, and a chin that was far too pointed ever to be called pretty.

'Anyway, I like being in the kitchen,' Anna said defiantly. Especially at this time of year, with it so warm against the bitterly cold weather outside, and the air rich with the fragrance of cinnamon, cloves, almonds, sugar and freshly baked bread.

Every surface was covered by trays of cooling loaves and pies. And then there were the Christmas specialities from

3

her father's native Germany: spiced ginger *Lebkuchen*, sugary biscuits so delicate they melted in your mouth, and his favourite *Stollen*, fruit loaves with a thick dusting of snowy powdered sugar and a heart of rich marzipan.

And finally there were the Christmas cakes, carefully packed away in their boxes and tied with ribbon. Each one was unique, beautifully decorated with delicate traceries of sugarwork that sparkled like frost. 'A labour of love,' her father always called them.

'And if Anna had been stuck in the shop we might never have spent any time together. And then we might never have fallen in love.' Edward put his arms around her and nuzzled her neck.

Liesel scowled. 'I'll tell Papa—'

At that moment the door to the kitchen opened and Friedrich Beck came in, followed closely by their mother.

'All I'm saying is you shouldn't have let her have it,' Dorothy Beck was protesting. 'She hasn't paid us for last month yet.'

'It's Christmas, my dear. Was I supposed to turn the poor woman away?' Even after twenty-five years, Friedrich's accent was still laced with German.

'Poor woman!' Dorothy replied scornfully. 'We'll be the poor ones, if you keep letting everyone have things on tick. You know we'll never see that money, don't you?'

Anna and Liesel exchanged knowing looks across the kitchen.

'She has been coming to my shop for ten years,' Friedrich said. 'Mrs Jarvis is one of my best customers.'

'When she pays her bill!'

Friedrich stepped smartly towards his wife, trapping her face between his hands and planting a kiss on her brow.

'It will be all right, I promise. Now, don't be cross. It's Christmas.'

4

She pushed him away, blushing. 'Your father's a fool, girls,' she said, but she was smiling in spite of herself as she said it. 'He thinks he's Father Christmas, giving away gifts to everyone!'

'And your mother is – what is his name? The man in the English book, by your Charles Dickens?' Friedrich frowned, trying to remember.

'Ebenezer Scrooge, sir?' Edward supplied helpfully.

'Yes! Yes, Mr Scrooge!' Friedrich laughed. 'You see, my dear, young Edward knew exactly who I was speaking about. He must think the same as me.'

'Oh, no, I don't . . . I didn't mean . . .' Edward looked mortified, tripping over his words.

'Take no notice,' Anna whispered. 'He's just teasing you, Edward. You should know what Father's like by now.'

'Yes, yes, I was only teasing, my boy. Pay no attention to me.' Friedrich beamed. He was a neat, dapper little man, with bright brown eyes and hair slicked back from his angular face. 'Now, how are you getting on with my cake, *Liebling*?' he said, turning to Anna. 'I am expecting to see a masterpiece.'

Anna glanced anxiously at Edward. 'It's finished, Papa.'

'Let me see.'

Anna bit her lip as her father bent low to inspect her work, his sharp eyes narrowed as he turned his head this way and that, looking at the cake from every angle. Friedrich Beck would never tolerate sloppy work leaving his kitchen.

Finally, he finished his inspection and straightened up.

'Perfect,' he declared.

Anna's shoulders relaxed, and she let out the breath she had been holding. 'Thank you, Papa.'

'You have a very delicate touch. I will make a master confectioner of you yet.' He smiled at her. 'Now we must get it packed up. Fetch a box, please, Liesel. And the silk ribbons. A cake like this deserves to be shown off.'

'Who is it for?' Anna asked. 'You said it was for a special customer.'

'Oh, yes, a very special customer indeed. Your grandmother.'

A tense silence fell over the kitchen. Anna shot a quick look over her shoulder at her mother's frozen face.

'In that case you might as well throw it straight in the bin,' Dorothy snapped.

'You don't know that, my dear,' Friedrich reasoned with her. 'Perhaps this year she will be ready to forgive us.'

'There's more chance of Mrs Jarvis paying her bill! Why do you think this year will be different from the past twenty five?'

'Because I believe no one can stay angry forever,' Friedrich said.

'Then you don't know my mother!'

'No, my dear. I do not. She never gave me the chance.'

Anna looked at her father's sorrowful expression and wondered how her grandmother could be so hard-hearted towards such a wonderful, kind man. His only fault, as far as she could tell, was not being the man her daughter had been supposed to marry.

They had heard the story many times. How their mother had been engaged to a promising young accountant from her wealthy father's company. But then she had been swept off her feet by a penniless young baker from Stuttgart. When her parents refused to accept the match, she had jilted her fiancé and run off with Friedrich Beck.

Her parents had cut her off ever since. Even when her father, Anna's grandfather, died ten years earlier, Grandmother Grey had refused to allow Dorothy to attend the funeral.

Anna glanced at her mother's taut expression. She knew that behind the mask of anger, Dorothy was still very hurt by her parents' rejection of her.

'It's a pity you've wasted all your time and effort,' she said shortly.

'Creating a thing of such beauty is never a waste of time,' Friedrich replied. 'Besides, I have a feeling that things might change for us next year. What do you say, Edward, my boy?' He winked at his apprentice.

'You're too optimistic, that's your trouble.' Dorothy snatched up a cloth and started rubbing furiously at an invisible spot on the counter top.

'Indeed I am,' her husband said. 'But think of it, my dear. If I had not been optimistic, I would never have come over to this country. I would never have opened up a baker's shop in Bethnal Green, and I would never have dared to believe such a beautiful girl as Miss Dorothy Grey would ever fall in love with me.'

'I don't know which of us is the bigger fool, in that case,' Dorothy muttered, still furiously scrubbing. 'What are you doing?' she protested, as her husband slid his arms around her waist, pulling her round to face him. 'Let me go, we haven't got time for this nonsense—'

The bell rang over the shop doorway.

'Saved by the bell,' Friedrich grinned, releasing her. 'Very well, let us go. You come too, Liesel. We need your smile to charm the customers.'

'Yes, Papa.' Liesel followed her parents through into the shop, with one last triumphant smirk over her shoulder at her sister.

'Thank goodness she's gone,' Anna said, as the door closed behind them. 'Liesel is more trouble than she's worth in this kitchen.' She wiped her hands on her apron. 'I'd best check on those loaves . . .'

'They'll be all right for another minute.' Edward stepped in front of her, barring her way. 'There's something I want to do first.'

Anna frowned. 'But I'll just—' He pulled her into his arms and kissed her, stopping the words in her throat.

She drew back in surprise. 'What's that for?'

'It's Christmas. Why shouldn't I kiss the girl I love?'

Anna looked away, pushing a damp strand of hair off her face. 'But I must look such a mess.'

'You look beautiful to me.' He kissed her, long and hard. Anna felt her resistance melting under the warm insistence of his mouth on hers, every thought chased from her mind . . .

The sound of a cough behind her shocked her back to her senses. Anna sprang away from Edward and turned to face the young man who stood in the doorway. He was shabbily dressed, tall and lean, his shoulders stooped. His face was narrow and hawkish, his dark eyes fixed on them.

'Tom!' Scalding colour flooded her face. 'I – I didn't know you were there.'

'You should have knocked,' Edward said gruffly.

The young man took off his cap and ran his hand through his thick dark hair. 'I didn't know you'd be messing about with the boss' daughter, did I?'

Anna looked away.

'How dare you speak to me like that!' Edward snapped. 'You're just the errand boy, remember?'

'And you're just the hired help.'

Edward's eyes narrowed. 'What did you say?'

'You heard.'

'It's time you learnt some manners!'

'Go on, then. Try it.' Tom's voice was low and taunting.

Anna looked up at Edward, saw the muscles bunching in his jaw. 'Don't, Edward. Please!' she begged, but he was already moving towards the delivery boy, his fists clenched.

8

Tom straightened slowly, drawing himself up to his full height. Anna saw his narrow face darkening, his eyes black with a stone-cold intent that terrified her.

She grabbed Edward's arm, drawing him back to her with all her strength.

'Don't!' she pleaded. 'Leave it, please. He isn't worth it.'

To her relief, Edward stopped in his tracks. 'You're right,' he muttered. 'I've got better things to do with my time than brawling with some street dog!'

Anna turned to face Tom. 'What was it you wanted?' she asked, in as neutral a voice as she could manage.

'Mr Beck said there was a special delivery to go up West.' Tom glared at Edward's turned back.

'Oh, he must mean this cake.' Anna hurried to fetch the box. 'The address is on the label,' she said as she handed it to him. 'Be careful with it, the icing's still not quite set –.'

But Tom was already gone, slamming the door behind him so hard it rattled in its frame.

Edward watched him go. 'Insolent swine!' he muttered. 'One day I'll knock some manners into him.'

'You shouldn't provoke him.'

'I'm not afraid of him.'

You should be, Anna thought. She had seen the way Tom had looked at him, the raw hatred in his face. Edward might be a tough East End boy, but there was something about Tom Franklin that was truly menacing.

'I don't know why your father ever took him on,' Edward said. 'Everyone knows the Franklins are all criminals.'

'Papa likes him.'

The Franklin family were well known locally. Four motherless boys and a drunken father, all living in squalor in the area between Bethnal Green and Shoreditch known as the Hatcheries. Anna had never been there, but she had heard tell of the dark warren of narrow alleyways and overcrowded hovels, infested with rats, bugs and diseases. It had a terrible reputation, and so did the Franklins. They had all spent time in jail, father and sons, and there were rumours that one of them had killed a man. But for some reason her father had taken pity on Tom, the youngest of the boys, and offered him a job.

'How can a man ever hope to change if no one helps him?' he had said when his wife protested. 'People can surprise you, if you give them a chance.'

'Your father's too trusting,' Edward said.

'He's been right so far,' Anna pointed out. A year after her father had given him the job, Tom Franklin was still turning up for work at the crack of dawn every morning, going off on his bicycle in all weathers, with never a word of complaint. He barely spoke to anyone, but he had the rough, guarded loyalty of a dog that had unexpectedly found itself in the hands of a kind new master after years of cruelty.

'You mark my words,' Edward said. 'One day he'll turn round and bite the hand that feeds him. His sort always does.'

'Must we talk about him?' Anna pleaded. The truth was, Tom made her feel uneasy. She didn't like the way he looked at her sometimes.

'You're right.' The tension left Edward's face, and his handsome, easy smile was back in place. 'We can't let him spoil this moment.'

'What moment?' Anna frowned.

Edward reached for her hands. 'Anna, there's something I want to ask you—'

'The loaves!' she cried out.

'What?'

'They're burning! Can't you smell them?' Anna pulled away from him and rushed to the oven.

'Can't you leave them a minute? They're probably ruined anyway.'

'But we might be able to save some.' Anna threw open the heavy oven door and stepped back, coughing and choking as a cloud of acrid smoke engulfed her.

'Anna—'

'Quick, open a window, let some of this smoke out.' She pushed past him, stumbling to throw open the back door.

'Anna, please—'

'That's better.' She breathed in the cold, fresh night air. From beyond the yard wall she could hear the rumble of barrow wheels on the cobbles as the hawkers and costermongers packed up their wares in nearby Columbia Road. 'It's a shame about those loaves, though. All your hard work spoilt.'

'Never mind the loaves.'

'But it's such a waste . . .'

'Anna, for God's sake! I'm trying to ask you to marry me!'

She turned slowly to face him. 'What?'

Edward let out an exasperated sigh. 'This is not how I meant to do it,' he said. 'I had it all planned. I was going to go down on one knee. I even had a ring, look!'

He pulled the small box from his apron pocket and held it out to her. 'I wanted it to be special,' he said. 'Because I know how much you love Christmas.'

Anna couldn't speak. She stared at the ring, sparkling in its box, then back up to his face.

Then the door opened and her father, mother and Liesel trooped in.

'We heard shouting,' said Friedrich. 'Have you asked her yet?' Edward nodded. 'And?'

Dorothy sniffed the air. 'Did those loaves catch fire?'

'Never mind the loaves!' Friedrich dismissed impatiently. 'Our daughter is getting married!'

'I don't know if she is,' Edward said. 'She hasn't answered me yet.' He looked at Anna. 'Well?' he said. 'What do you say?'

Anna stared back at him. He looked genuinely anxious, as if he could ever have doubted the answer to his question.

'I say yes!' she said.

Much to Anna's mortification, her father insisted on telling every customer who came into the shop that she was getting married. Not only that, he dragged her out of the kitchen and paraded her in front of everyone, so she could hear their congratulations.

She could just imagine what they must have made of her, standing there looking so thin and bedraggled in her stained apron, next to Edward. He looked so handsome, tall and well-built, with his fair hair, blue eyes and dazzling smile, she was sure they must all have been wondering how she ended up with someone like him. She could hardly fathom it herself.

As soon as the last customer had gone, Friedrich closed up the shop and invited all the neighbours round to celebrate. There were the Hudsons who ran the butcher's next door, and the Wheelers who owned the café on the corner and always brought their bread and cakes from her father. Then there was Mr Gold who had just opened a clothing manufacturer's with his daughter Rachel. They crowded into the tiny shop, and Mr Hudson brought a jug of beer from the Angel and Crown on the corner and they all toasted the happy couple.

Anna stood among them, engulfed by their good wishes but too dazed to take them in. She kept looking at the ring on her finger, expecting it not to be there.

Then her father made a speech. 'Thank you, my friends, for coming to celebrate our special day,' he said, beaming round at them all. 'I am so happy to welcome Edward into our family. Ever since I took him on as my apprentice, he has become like a son to me. And I hope he has come to look on me as a father.'

Anna stole a sideways glance at Edward's profile. He had grown up in the Barnardo's boys' home in Stepney Causeway after his mother died and his own father abandoned him. He never talked about it; she could only guess how difficult and painful his childhood had been.

'And now he will be part of our family,' Friedrich went on. 'And I cannot tell you, my friends, how proud and happy I—'

The back door slammed then, startling them all. A moment later Tom appeared in the kitchen doorway, a cake box in his hands.

Edward let out an angry sigh. 'Trust him to turn up and ruin everything,' he whispered.

The delivery boy glared round at the assembled company, his body taut, instantly on the defensive.

'She sent it back,' he blurted, holding out the cake box.

Anna glanced at her mother. Dorothy Beck's face was a blank mask, but her lips were white with anger.

'No matter.' Friedrich moved towards Tom, smiling in greeting, his hands outstretched. 'You must join us, my boy. We're celebrating. Anna and Edward are engaged, isn't that wonderful?'

Tom shot a dark look at Edward but said nothing.

'You must have a glass of beer . . .' Friedrich started to say, but Tom cut him off.

'I can't stop.'

'Then you must take the cake with you, as a Christmas gift from our family to yours.'

Tom's dark eyes narrowed warily, as if he was not sure whether Friedrich was making fun of him or not.

'Look at him,' Edward muttered. 'And to think, all your hard work will be wasted on that bunch of savages!'

Anna didn't reply. There was something almost pitiful about the young man as he stood there in his shabby clothes, so out of place in the middle of the party.

But then he looked up and caught her eye, and the cold, implacable contempt she saw in his face chilled her.

Tom Franklin didn't need or want her pity, she could tell.

Anna left the party as soon as she had a chance and slipped up to her room to catch her breath. Everything was happening so fast, she needed a moment to stop and take it all in.

It was dark, and as she went to light the gas lamp beside the bed, a voice came out of the shadows, making her jump.

'Leave it. I like the dark.'

Anna swung round. As her eyes grew used to the darkness, she could make out her sister's shape, curled up on the double bed they shared.

'Liesel? What are you doing up here? I thought you'd be enjoying the party.'

'It's your party, not mine.' Her sister's voice was sulky. 'No one would even notice if I was there or not.'

Anna stifled a sigh. There was no talking to her when she was in one of her moods.

'Don't be so dramatic.' She lit the lamp and turned it up, filling the room with a soft glow. She crossed the room to the mirror and examined her reflection. She looked even worse than she'd imagined, her hair hanging in lank strands around her pale, tired face.

'The belle of the ball,' Liesel said sarcastically.

'Don't.' Anna tried to pull her hair back into the nape of her neck, but that only drew attention to her odd, bony face.

'Here, let me,' Liesel sighed. She clambered across the bed to where Anna stood. 'You need to make it softer, like this . . .'

Anna watched her sister artfully twisting, combing and pinning, gradually shaping her hopeless hair into something that looked almost pretty.

'When are you going to marry him?' Liesel asked suddenly. Anna looked at her sister's reflection. She was still combing away, her expression intent.

'I don't know,' she said. 'Not for a while, I suppose. We'll have to save up, find somewhere to live –'

Liesel was silent, tugging the comb through her hair. Then she suddenly blurted out, 'I don't want you to go.'

Anna smiled. 'But you're always telling me how you can't wait for me to leave home, so you can have this room to yourself!'

'Yes, but I didn't mean it.' Liesel threw down the comb and wrapped her arms around her sister's waist in a fierce, sudden hug. 'Why do things always have to change?' she whispered. 'I like it here, with you and Mother and Papa.'

'So do I.' Anna stroked Liesel's soft curls. Her hair smelt of baking spices from the kitchen. 'They won't change,' she said. 'Edward and I won't get married for a long time. And even when we do, we'll still be working here at the bakery every day.'

'Yes, but it won't be the same, will it? You'll be married.'

'I'll still be your sister, Li. And even if things do change, it will be for the better.'

'Do you promise?'

Anna thought for a moment. She was perfectly content, she realised. She had everything she wanted. Edward loved her and wanted to marry her, she had a close family around her, a comfortable home and work that she enjoyed.

When she looked into the future, all she could see was more love and happiness coming her way.

She only wished she could have bottled this moment, so she could treasure it forever.

'I promise,' she said.

Chapter Two

September 1914

But Anna couldn't keep her promise. As the hot, sultry days of summer passed, the mood seemed to darken and grow heavy, like the sky before a thunderstorm.

Around the world, alliances were made, promises given and treaties sent back and forth. The talk of war spread like a contagion, as an old, long-buried hostility and mistrust towards Germany resurfaced. It was all anyone seemed to talk about, in the bakery and on every street corner. Every day the newspapers urged the government to take action and purge their old enemy. Music hall performers sang patriotic songs, and it was impossible to walk through Victoria Park without seeing kids acting out imaginary invasions, taking it in turns to play the dreaded Hun.

It all made Anna feel very uncomfortable, especially when she heard rumours of how Mr Speer's pork butchers in Gossett Street had been attacked by vandals. But she knew her father was too well known and well loved in the area to suffer a similar fate. So she went on working in the bakery kitchen every day, kneading dough and shaping loaves and doing her best not to think about what was going on beyond the back door. Edward read the newspapers and avidly devoured every word. Anna refused to listen when he talked about things he had read.

'Don't,' she said. 'The way everyone's going on, anyone would think it had already happened.'

'It's only a matter of time.'

Anna shook her head. 'Papa says it's all nonsense. We won't go to war.'

'But after what they did to Archduke Franz Ferdinand—'

'Why should we start fighting over a place we know nothing about?' Anna cut him off. 'Half the people in Bethnal Green have never been further than Shoreditch, and yet they're talking about the Balkans as if they're next-door neighbours!'

'That ain't the point. We promised Russia—'

'I don't want to hear about it,' Anna snapped. 'Please, Edward. Can't we just be happy while we have the chance?'

Their chance didn't last long. On a grey day at the beginning of August, the storm finally broke. Germany invaded Belgium, and the following day Britain declared war.

'They say huge crowds gathered outside Buckingham Palace to see the King and Queen,' Anna told her father, as he slashed the tops of a row of loaves waiting to be baked. 'There was so much shouting and cheering when they came out on the balcony, you could hear it halfway up the Strand.'

'It is wrong, all wrong.' Her father shook his head. 'Imagine cheering because you are going to war. And what is the King thinking? The Kaiser is his cousin, for God's sake!'

'The Kaiser is also cousin to the Czar,' Edward pointed out over the clatter of the tins he was emptying into the sink. 'But that didn't stop him declaring war on Russia.'

Within days of war being declared, her father was ordered to go down to the town hall and register as a foreigner. Anna's mother had to go too. When she returned, her face was flushed with anger.

'Do you know, the man behind the desk had the cheek to ask me why I married a German!' she said. 'I told him, if it's good enough for Queen Victoria then it's good enough for me. That shut him up!'

She was trying to make light of it, but Anna could tell she was shaken by the experience.

Then Edward joined the queue of eager young men down at the recruiting office. He was most dejected when they turned him away.

'They're sending trained reservists and experienced soldiers first,' he said to Anna while they worked in the kitchen together. 'They said I'm to turn up for weekly drill practice, and they'd call me for training when they needed me. But I daresay the war will be over long before then.' He looked gloomy at the prospect.

'I'm sorry, Edward.' Anna did her best to hide her relief. 'I know how much you wanted to go.'

'It's not that,' he said. 'I don't want anyone thinking I'm a coward.'

'No one would think that.'

'I don't know about that,' Liesel said from by the sink where she was running the tap over some tins. 'I saw a woman give a boy a white feather on the bus yesterday. She told him he should be ashamed of himself for not fighting for his country.'

Anna gasped. 'What a horrible thing to do!'

'You don't know what it's like,' Liesel said over the rush of running water. 'It feels as if the world is going mad. War, war, war, it's all everyone talks about.'

'Not here.' Edward smiled across the counter at his fiancée. 'Anna doesn't like talking about the war, do you, my love?'

'I know,' Liesel said, turning off the tap. 'She pretends it's not happening because she's safe in this kitchen.'

'I do know what's happening, thank you very much,' Anna snapped back, stung. For a moment she went on beating the cake mixture she was preparing, then said, 'As a matter of fact, I was thinking of volunteering myself.'

She looked up at them. They were both staring at her in disbelief.

'You?' Edward said.

'Why not? Mary Hudson next-door has started working in a munitions factory. And a few of the girls down at the church are taking first aid lessons so they can join the Voluntary Aid Detachment. I feel as if I should do something.'

'And what are you going to do?' Edward asked. 'Bake cakes for the soldiers?'

'Her cakes are so heavy they could use them as weapons!' Liesel said.

Anna stared back at their smirking expressions. 'Actually, I was thinking of becoming a nurse.'

Edward and Liesel looked at each other, then they both burst out laughing.

'What's so funny?' Anna demanded, her voice rising to be heard over their laughter.

'You!' Liesel wiped her streaming eyes on the hem of her apron. 'How could you be a nurse? You don't know one end of a bandage from another.'

'I know, but I'm sure they'd be able to train me.' She turned to Edward. 'I don't understand. I thought you'd be happy that I'd want to do something for my country?'

'I am, my love. It's just—' Edward paused, searching for the words. 'I can't imagine it, that's all.'

'Why not?'

'Because you're such a homebody!' Liesel put in. 'Honestly, Anna, could you imagine yourself tending wounded soldiers on the battlefield? You get nervous if Mother sends you to the market, and that's only round the corner!'

'I do not!' Anna turned on her. 'Besides, I wouldn't have to go far from home. I was thinking of applying to the Florence Nightingale Hospital, and that's just around the corner.'

Liesel hooted. 'You? A Nightingale girl!'

'Why not?' She stared in frustration at her sister's laughing face and fought the urge to slap her. 'I could do it, you know!' she said.

'I'm sure you could, sweetheart,' Edward said kindly, his hand on her shoulder. 'But I expect your father will need you in the bakery once I'm called up. And besides, there are lots of other ways you can help with the war effort.'

'You can knit socks for the soldiers with the rest of the old church ladies!' Liesel mocked.

Anna stared from one to the other. They didn't believe she could do it, she thought. At least Edward was trying to be kind about it, unlike her sister.

I'll show you, thought Anna.

And so, on a dull, wet morning in September, she presented herself at the Florence Nightingale Hospital in Bethnal Green to begin her nursing training.

Her nerve started to fail her as she stepped through the wide wrought-iron gates with her parents. Ahead of them, at the far end of the gravel drive, was the main hospital building, with its imposing Georgian façade. Beyond that lay a sprawl of outbuildings, clinics and laboratories.

'It's like a village in itself,' her mother said. 'How will you ever find your way around?'

'I'm sure she will get used to it, in time,' her father replied, giving Anna's shoulder a bracing squeeze. 'It will be quite an adventure for you, won't it, *Liebling*?'

Anna scowled down at her feet and said nothing. What was she thinking? she wondered. Liesel was right, she was a homebody. This was far too big an adventure for her.

They finally found Porthleven House, a tall, dark stone building whose square bay windows and gothic crenellations did nothing to soften its austere appearance. The middle-aged woman who answered the door to them was as bleak-looking as the house: tall, thin and upright in her grey uniform.

'Yes?' She looked at them all down her sharp blade of a nose.

Anna shrank back from her forbidding face, and it was all she could do not to hide behind her mother's skirts. But her father stepped forward, holding out his hand with his usual cheerful smile.

'Good afternoon, madam. My daughter—'

'Name?' The woman looked straight past him, her gaze fixed on Anna.

She cleared her throat nervously. 'Anna Beck, miss.'

The woman drew herself up straighter. Her jet-black hair was pulled back in a tight knot, emphasising her long face. She looked down at Anna with disdainful grey eyes.

'You will address me as Sister or Miss Noonan,' she said. She took a notebook from the pocket of her starched white apron and consulted it. 'Let me see . . . ah, yes. Beck.' She closed the notebook with a snap. 'Bring your bag and I'll show you to your room.'

She turned on her heel and disappeared inside the house. Anna and her parents went to follow, but no sooner had they stepped inside the hall than Miss Noonan turned on them.

'And where do you think you're going?' she snapped. 'Families are not allowed inside the probationers' home at any time.'

Anna saw her mother's shoulders stiffen. 'But surely we should be allowed to help her settle in.'

'Families are not allowed inside the building,' Miss Noonan insisted. For a moment the two women faced each other, and Anna felt sure her mother was going to put the Home Sister in her place. But then her father laid his hand on Dorothy's arm.

'It's all right, my dear,' he said gently. 'If those are the rules then we must abide by them. And I am sure it will be easier for Anna to settle in if we are not here fussing over her.' He turned to his daughter with an encouraging smile. 'This is where we must say goodbye, *Liebling*.'

Anna looked from him to her mother and back again. She felt as if all her insides had disappeared, to be replaced by one enormous ball of roiling fear. She didn't dare speak for fear of crying.

Anna could see her mother biting her lip, also fighting back tears. Only her father remained smiling, albeit rather fixedly.

He took Anna's hands in his, his touch warm and reassuring. 'I am so proud of what you are doing, going out in the world and doing your duty for your country.'

'Yes, Papa.' Anna fought an urge to rush into his arms, to beg him to take her home. If she had, she knew her parents would have given in without another thought. It took every bit of self-control she had to hold herself steady and silent.

'Take care of yourself, my love.' Her mother's voice was choked with emotion as she embraced Anna. 'You will come and see us soon, won't you? Let us know how you're getting on.'

'Of course she will,' her father said. 'And she will bring all the new friends she has made. Isn't that right, *Liebling*?'

'Yes, Papa.'

A moment later, Miss Noonan had ushered them out. Anna stood in the hall, her bags at her feet, staring at the front door for a long moment after the Home Sister had closed it.

'Good God, what a fuss!' Miss Noonan exclaimed. 'Anyone would think we were sending you to Constantinople.' She headed towards the stairs, then paused and looked back at Anna. 'Well, come along,' she said. 'You've taken up far too much of my time already. I have several other probationers arriving this afternoon, not just you!'

Anna followed her up the stairs, doing her best to listen to all the instructions the Home Sister threw over her shoulder.

'This is where you'll stay for the six weeks of your pre-liminary training,' she said. 'You will take your meals here, and attend lectures and practical sessions in the class-rooms downstairs or the main hospital block. When you have passed your first examination – if you pass it –' she threw a doubtful look over her shoulder at Anna '– you will move next-door to Lennox House to live with the other first-year students, or probationers as we call them. But that's a long way off for you.'

She reached the landing, and turned to head up another flight of stairs. The bunch of keys at her belt jangled with every step. 'There's no maid here, so you'll be expected to clean your own room and to do your share of keeping the common areas swept and polished. Beds need to be stripped once a week, on a Friday, and linen is to be left out on the landing by half-past six in the morning. Clean linen will be left outside your room, and your mattress will need to be turned and the bed made up by the time I carry out my Friday evening inspection. Any personal laundry will be done on a Tuesday. You'll need to leave it on the landing in a laundry bag marked with your name . . . I will not tol-erate squabbles over lost items, do you understand?'

'Yes, Sister,' Anna replied, her head reeling.

By the time they had gone up a third flight of stairs, Miss Noonan had delivered another lecture on specific times for bathing and washing, and warned her about making sure to leave hot water for the other girls.

Finally, just when Anna didn't think she could take in

another instruction, the Home Sister reached the top landing. She unhooked the bunch of keys from her leather belt, selected one and unlocked the door.

As she threw it open, Anna was caught by a gust of cold and damp air. But Miss Noonan didn't seem to notice as she led the way into the room.

'This is your room. You're fortunate here that you don't have to share with anyone. They're two or three to a room in Lennox House.'

Fortunate wasn't the word Anna would have used, looking around at the sparsely furnished room, with its bare floorboards, narrow iron bedstead and cheerless, empty fireplace. She thought with a pang of the cosy room at home that she shared with Liesel.

She barely listened as Miss Noonan issued yet more instructions, telling her to change into her uniform and be ready for tea in the dining room at four o'clock sharp. Then, finally, the Home Sister left, and Anna was alone.

Alone.

She couldn't remember the last time she was by herself. At the bakery there were always her parents, or Edward, or customers coming in and out. Even when she went to bed at night, she had Liesel snuggled in beside her, chattering in the dark.

She busied herself, unpacking her belongings. She quickly stuffed the photographs she had brought from home into her bedside drawer without looking at them, afraid they would make her cry. Then she hung up her uniform, smoothing out the creases in the thick blue-striped cotton. This was the first time she'd been able to bring herself to look at it since her mother brought it home from the dressmaker's a week earlier, and it still made her stomach flip with nervous anticipation.

As she was making up her bed, she heard Miss Noonan

showing another girl to the room next-door, reciting her usual litany of instructions. Anna paused for a moment, listening. But the door closed and the Home Sister's footsteps receded down the stairs.

Aware of the time inching steadily towards four o'clock, Anna put on her uniform. The calico-lined dress felt heavy, even in the coolness of the room, and the scratchy black wool stockings made her legs itch. It took a long time to attach her high collar and cuffs, fiddling to push the studs through the thick, starched cotton.

She brushed her hair and tried to twist it up under her cap, but it slipped out of the pins and fell in strands around her face. Anna stared despairingly at her reflection in the mirror. Where was Liesel when she was needed? And what kind of nurse was Anna going to make if she couldn't even pin up her own hair properly?

She turned away from the mirror and sat down on the bed. The flat horsehair mattress barely yielded under her. Out of the small window, she could see a landscape of rooftops and the trees in the park, and beyond that the factory chimneys, belching their dirty yellow smoke into the grey sky.

She thought longingly about the bakery. Her parents would have returned home by now. As it was late afternoon, her mother would be cleaning the kitchen, scrubbing down the floors and sinks and surfaces with carbolic soap. Her father would be in the shop, packing up the last of the bread and cakes. A small crowd would have gathered hopefully around the door, knowing that he sold off goods cheaply at this time of day, hoping for a stale loaf or a leftover pie for their tea. But he would always keep some aside to send a package home with Edward, and one for Tom, too.

A tear splashed on to the back of her hand, then another, until Anna finally gave in to the torrent of misery that had been threatening to engulf her since her parents said good-bye to her. She cried and cried, mopping her tears on the corner of her stiff white apron. The unfamiliar scent of starch made her cry even more. Everything here was so strange, so foreign to her. Her heart ached for home, and the comfort of her family – and Edward.

She was crying so hard, she hardly heard the tapping on her door at first. She looked round, startled. There it was again. She hastily dried her face on her apron and went to answer the door.

Standing there in front of her was the prettiest girl Anna had ever seen, with wide green eyes and flawless porcelain skin. Her blonde hair tumbled in glorious waves over her plump shoulders.

She smiled at Anna. 'Sorry to trouble you, but I wondered if you had any hairpins I could borrow?' she asked, in a cheerful cockney accent. 'Silly me, I've left all mine at home. Now I've got to try and tame this.' She pushed her hand through her hair.

'Oh. Yes, of course. Come in.' Anna sniffed back her tears and stepped aside to let the girl enter.

'Ta. You're a life saver.' The girl stepped inside the room, looking about her. 'I could have sworn I'd packed mine. Honest to God, I reckon I'd forget my own head if it wasn't on my shoulders!'

Anna glanced at her face in the dressing-table mirror as she gathered up the pins. She looked so blotchy, her eyes red-rimmed, it was impossible to miss the fact that she had been crying.

'Will these do?' She kept her head down, carefully averting her face as she handed the girl the pins.

'Lovely, ta very much.' The girl paused. 'I'm Sadie Sedgewick, by the way. From next door.'

'Anna Beck.'

'Pleased to meet you, Anna. Come far, have you?'

Anna shook her head. 'Just down the road. Chambord Street.'

Sadie looked at her curiously. 'Hang on a minute . . . Did you say your name was Beck? Of Beck's Bakery?'

Anna looked up sharply. 'Yes, that's right. Why? Have you heard of it?'

'You're joking, ain't you? Everyone's heard of Beck's Bakery!' Sadie smiled, her cheeks dimpling. 'My landlady used to catch the bus from Hackney Wick every Saturday morning to buy bread there. It's the best bakery in London, so she said.'

'Yes, it is.' The words lodged painfully in Anna's throat.

'Anyway, I'd better not keep you chatting,' Sadie said. 'I've got to sort out my hair and I can see you haven't done yours, either.'

Anna glanced away, towards the dressing table. 'I'm having a bit of trouble with it,' she admitted. 'My sister always does – did – it for me.'

'Can I help you?' Sadie offered. 'As it happens, I'm a dab hand with a hairbrush.'

'Oh, no, I don't want to put you to any trouble.'

'It's no trouble. Have a seat in front of the mirror.' Sadie picked up the brush and started to pull it through Anna's hair. 'You're lucky,' she said, 'your hair's lovely and silky, not a thatch like mine . . .'

Anna smiled back at her reflection. It was the first time anyone had ever said anything nice about her hair. Liesel always said it reminded her of rats' tails.

Anna studied Sadie's reflection. The girl reminded her of her sister, so fair and pretty. For a moment she could almost convince herself it was Liesel standing there . . .

Anna felt the tears welling in her eyes again and looked away sharply.

'It's a rum old place, ain't it?' Sadie said, twisting a lock of hair and pinning it deftly into place. 'All those rules and regulations, I can hardly remember them all. And that Miss Noonan!' She shook her head. 'She's even worse than the landlady at my old lodgings!'

'You were in lodgings?' Anna said.

'Mrs Stainsby's boarding house for respectable young ladies in Hackney Wick.' Sadie recited the words, eyes sparkling with mirth. 'She thought she was so proper. She didn't know the half of what went on there!' She laughed. 'I daresay it'll be the same here, once we get used to it.'

Anna looked down at her hands bunched together in her lap. 'I don't know if I'll ever get used to it.'

''Course you will, just give it time. And we can always help each other out, if we get stuck.'

'I suppose so.'

Sadie finished her work and stepped back, the brush in her hand. 'There, what do you think?'

'It looks lovely. Thank you.' Anna turned her head this way and that, admiring the neatness of the bun at the nape of her neck. Sadie's handiwork was just as good as Liesel's, and she didn't pull and yank at the hair nearly so much. Anna's scalp was usually sore by the time Liesel had finished with her.

'I'm glad to help. Now, I'd best go and get myself ready, or I'll be in Miss Noonan's bad books before we've even started!' Sadie grinned. 'Thanks for the pins. I'll bring them back when I get some of my own.'

'There's no hurry. I've got plenty.'

'Ta.' Sadie paused for a moment, then said, 'Don't forget what I said. If you need help, or someone to talk to . . .'

'Thank you. And the same to you.'

When Sadie had gone, Anna went to the window and stared out over the rooftops, silhouetted against the gathering dusk. Even though her family were just across Victoria Park, they felt like a million miles away.

Oh, Anna, she thought. *What have you done?*

Chapter Three

Oh, Sadie, what have you done?

Sadie Sedgewick gazed around at the five other girls gathered around the dining table, their hands clasped and eyes closed as they listened to Miss Noonan saying Grace.

They all looked so fresh and polished, with their shiny hair, clean nails and bright, smiling faces. Sadie knew she would never fit in here, not in a million years.

'And we pray, O Lord, that you will bless this food before us . . .'

As Miss Noonan droned on Sadie's stomach began to grumble. She hadn't eaten all day. But hungry as she was, she wasn't sure she could manage anything. Even the food here seemed strange to her: wafer-thin cucumber sandwiches with the crusts cut off, and dainty little cakes that looked as if they would disappear in one mouthful.

She caught the eye of a curly-haired girl at the far end of the table, who had one eye open over her clasped hands. She grinned conspiratorially back, just as Miss Noonan said a very loud 'Amen'.

Sadie watched the girls helping themselves to the food, all so polite, saying 'please' and 'thank you' and 'would you mind awfully . . . ?' in their posh voices. No one had ever taught her proper manners. Even Mrs Stainsby, who fancied herself a cut above, didn't seem to mind her lodgers reaching across each other or putting their elbows on the table, or holding their forks the wrong way.

Sadie had a feeling Miss Noonan would not be quite so

easy to please. She had chosen a seat as far away from the Home Sister as she could get, but she could still sense her hawk-like gaze from the head of the table, just waiting to swoop on a scattered crumb or an awkwardly held teacup.

Why had she come here? she wondered. This wasn't where she belonged. She should be back at Barlow's, sticking flowers on hats. It was all she was good for.

Come on, Sadie girl, this ain't like you. She forced herself to lift her chin as she sipped from her teacup. She had as much right to be here as any of these other girls. She had passed her Matriculation, same as them, even if she did have to go to night school to get it.

And she had faced worse than Miss Noonan, too.

'Would you like a cake, Sadie?' She looked up sharply at the sound of her name. Anna Beck was holding out the plate to her, smiling. She was about to reply when Miss Noonan barked out,

'You will address each other by your surnames, if you please!'

'Yes, Sister. Sorry, Sister.' Poor Anna looked so crestfallen, Sadie could have throttled Miss Noonan for shouting at her. Couldn't the Home Sister see how the girl was struggling?

Don't get involved, she reminded herself. She had already broken that rule when she knocked on Anna Beck's door. She had made up her mind to keep herself to herself, but how could she ignore the poor kid sobbing her heart out in the next room? In the end, Sadie had pretended to forget her hairpins just so she could make sure her neighbour was all right.

At least she looked more cheerful now she had washed her face. But Sadie could still see the red rims around her eyes where she had been crying.

She's not your problem, Sadie reminded herself, looking away. If she can't toughen up, that's her look out, not yours.

As they ate, Miss Noonan gave them all another lecture, this time about their daily timetable.

'You will be called at quarter-past six in the morning,' she intoned. 'Breakfast and prayers will follow at seven, then from half-past seven there will be an hour's housework . . .' Sadie noticed several of the girls looking askance at each other. 'After that, you will return to your room to change into a clean uniform, ready for your first lecture at half-past nine. Lunch is at half-past ten, followed by a cookery class, then you will have dinner at half-past one. After that you are off duty.'

There were a few sighs of relief from around the table, but Miss Noonan had not finished. 'Tea is prompt at four o'clock, followed by a practical nursing class at five. After that, you will have time in the evening for writing out your notes and private study, until supper at eight-thirty, then prayers. You will return to your rooms by ten, and lights are to be out by ten-thirty. Is that understood?'

'Yes, Sister,' they all chorused. Out of the corner of her eye, Sadie caught the mutinous expression of the curly-haired girl at the other end of the table.

'Your classes will vary each day,' Miss Noonan went on. 'You will find a full list on the timetable in the hall. You will be expected to arrive at each class promptly, and fully prepared. Each class will be conducted by Matron, the Assistant Matron Miss Swann, or Miss Pascoe the Sister Tutor. Your first lessons will be in basic nursing skills, followed by—'

She was interrupted by a noisy clatter as the gawky girl beside Sadie dropped her teacup. They all watched in horror as a brown stain spread over the snowy white tablecloth.

'I – I'm so sorry!' The girl blundered to her feet, upsetting her bone china plate and sending it crashing to the floor.

'You clumsy girl!' Miss Noonan roared.

'Here, let me help you.' Sadie crouched down to pick up the fragments of shattered china, while the other girl towered over her, stammering apologies.

'I – I couldn't help it,' she said. 'It just sort of fell out of my hand . . .'

'It was an accident,' Sadie reassured her.

'But your uniform . . .'

Sadie looked down at herself. She hadn't noticed until that moment that her starched dress was spattered with tea stains too.

'Here, let me help.'

'It's all right.' Sadie ducked away as the other girl came at her, wielding a linen napkin in her fist, narrowly missing her jaw. 'I daresay it'll come out in the wash.'

She glanced at Miss Noonan, who was watching them, tight-lipped with fury.

Thankfully, they were dismissed shortly afterwards. Miss Noonan told them that as it was their first day there would be no classes, and they could go to the common room.

'Thank you for your help,' the tall girl whispered to Sadie as they left the dining room. 'My mother's always telling me off for being clumsy, but I can't seem to help it.'

'As I said, it was an accident.' Sadie smiled back at her. 'I'm Sadie, by the way. What's your name?'

The girl's long, pale face flushed bright pink. 'Grace,' she mumbled.

Sadie looked up at her, with her big hands and feet, and loose, flailing limbs, and felt a smile twitching the corners of her lips.

Grace grinned back at her. 'It's all right, I don't mind if you laugh. I'm used to it!'

The common room overlooked the garden, with French windows leading out on to a paved terrace. Beyond it was a small square of lawn lined with neat flowerbeds, and a couple of apple trees at the far end.

The room itself was shabby but comfortable, with a sofa, a chaise-longue and a couple of worn leather armchairs flanking the fireplace. There was a piano in one corner, and a bookshelf in the other.

One of the girls, a sharp-featured little creature with thin brown hair and a beaky nose, headed over to peruse the books, while the others found seats for themselves.

'Well, I don't know about anyone else, but I came here to get away from rules.' The curly-haired girl flopped down on the sofa beside Sadie. 'I wanted a bit of fun, and this is worse than school!'

'Fun?' An earnest-looking girl with brown hair stared back at her. Her name was Eleanor Copeland, and her room was on the same floor as Sadie's. She had heard her moving in earlier, bumping her heavy trunk up the stairs behind her. 'We're here to learn, not to have fun.'

'Speak for yourself,' the curly girl muttered under her breath. 'I'm Dulcie, by the way,' she said to Sadie. 'Dulcie Moore.'

'And I'm Miriam Trott. But I want to be called Mimi from now on,' announced the beaky girl from over by the bookshelves where she was still perusing the books.

'My aunt had a poodle called Mimi,' Dulcie said.

'Mimi is the tragic heroine of Puccini's opera, *La Bohème*,' Miriam announced loftily.

'It doesn't matter who she is,' Eleanor Copeland said. 'Didn't you hear what Miss Noonan said? We have to call each other by our surnames.'

'I'm sure we can call each other whatever we want in private,' Miriam muttered, looking mutinous.

'Yes, but rules are rules,' Eleanor replied.

'And rules are made to be broken,' Dulcie said. 'I'm certainly not going to be tucked up in bed by half-past ten. I want to see the bright lights of London!'

Eleanor pursed her lips. 'My mother says only fast girls stay out late.'

Dulcie giggled. 'Fast? Chance would be a fine thing, with that old witch watching over us!' She narrowed her eyes and tightened her mouth in a very good impression of Miss Noonan's hawk-like features. Everyone laughed except for Eleanor, who looked disapproving.

'Well, I don't want to see any bright lights,' Grace declared. 'I think I shall be utterly terrified to set foot outside this hospital. Everything seems so big and noisy here. I got on the wrong bus coming from the station. I thought I'd be lost forever.' She gazed longingly out of the window. 'I shall miss looking out of my bedroom and seeing nothing but rolling fields.'

'You can always have a stroll in Victoria Park,' Sadie suggested.

'And the local dairy off Columbia Road keeps a few cows,' Anna added.

'Perhaps they'd let you milk them!' Dulcie joked.

'And I know of a family down near the river who keep a donkey and a couple of pigs,' Sadie said.

Grace looked hopeful. 'Do they have a farm?'

'No, they just keep them in their back yard. Mind you, they let them in the house when it gets too cold for them outside. In winter the kids and the pigs all sit round the fire together!' Sadie laughed, until she looked round the room and saw the others all staring at her. She retreated quickly into silence, annoyed with herself for letting her guard down. The less she told these girls about where she came from, the better.

'Why did you apply to come to London, if you wanted to stay in the country?' Dulcie asked Grace.

Grace lowered her gaze. 'My mother said the Nightingale was the best hospital for nursing training. I've always wanted to be a nurse, ever since I was a little girl. I took care of all the orphaned lambs on the farm, and the runt piglets. No one thought they would survive, but I nursed them back to life.'

'I daresay nursing people will be a bit different from nursing piglets!' Miriam scoffed.

'I'll tell you why I wanted to come here,' Eleanor said, even though no one had asked her. She was solid and heavy-jawed, with straight brown hair that did nothing to soften the square lines of her face. 'My brother Harry has joined up, and I thought it was only right that I did my bit too.'

'My young man has enlisted too,' Anna said. 'But I'm hoping he won't be called up.'

'Harry is in the reserves, so he was taken straight away,' Eleanor said. 'I'm glad he's gone. I'm proud he's fighting for his country. I have no time for boys who don't want to get into khaki.'

'Listen to her,' Dulcie whispered to Sadie. 'She sounds like one of those daft women who go round handing out white feathers to all and sundry!'

Eleanor's broad face flushed. 'Actually, my mother is one of the Order of the White Feather, and I see nothing wrong in it. It is every young man's duty to serve his country. And every young woman's, too,' she added with feeling.

Silence fell in the room as they all looked round at each other. Then Dulcie Moore said, 'Well, I don't know about doing my duty. All I want is to marry a doctor,' she said.

Everyone laughed. Dulcie looked back at them blankly. 'I'm serious,' she said. 'I've set my heart on marrying a handsome, rich young consultant. Preferably one with a practice in Harley Street, so I'll never have to go and live in the country again. No offence,' she said to Grace, 'but I really can't think of anything worse than being a farmer's wife.'

'My mother says I'll be lucky to find anyone to marry me,' Grace said mournfully.

'How about you?' Anna asked Sadie. 'What made you decide to start nursing?'

Sadie shrugged. 'I had no choice. The hat factory where I was working closed down, and I had to find something else to do. And nursing seemed as good a job as any.'

The others stared at her. Then Miriam said, 'You were a – factory girl?'

Sadie lifted her chin. 'What's wrong with that?' She stared hard at Miriam until the other girl looked away.

Then Grace accidentally knocked the coal scuttle over with a clatter. Sadie watched as they all rushed to help her. She had given away too much, she thought. It was all very well trying to be friendly, but she had to learn to play her cards closer to her chest in future.

Chapter Four

The first of the wounded soldiers arrived from France at the end of October. Anna and the other girls saw the stretchers being unloaded from the ambulances as they headed back to Porthleven House for dinner after their afternoon Invalid Cookery class in the main hospital block.

They weren't the only ones watching. A crowd had formed outside the grounds. They threw chocolate bars and cigarettes through the fence for the wounded men.

'Look at them all,' Grace Duffield said. 'Anyone would think it was the Coronation all over again!'

'It's because they're heroes,' Eleanor said.

'I wonder why they've started bringing them here?' Anna said.

'I daresay the military hospitals can't cope with all the casualties,' Sadie Sedgewick replied in her usual direct manner.

'It makes it seem real, doesn't it?' Miriam Trott sighed. 'I mean, you read about all those poor men in the papers, but when you actually see them –'

Anna glanced at Eleanor. Her expression was stoical, as usual, but Anna could only imagine how worried she must be about her brother Harry. The newspapers were full of stories about how the British and French had been driven back in Ypres with so many thousands killed and injured.

Once again, Anna breathed a sigh of relief that her Edward was not in danger. He was still in London, going for drill practice three times a week, intensely frustrated that he could not do more.

'I wish I was fighting for my country and not just charging at sandbags in Victoria Park,' he moaned to Anna. She tried to be sympathetic, but deep down she was relieved that he had not yet been called up. Seeing the stretchers being unloaded from the ambulances made her wonder how she would cope with the worry when it was Edward's turn to go.

But at least she knew if the time came she would have the other girls in her set to support her. They had only been training together for three weeks, but Anna already felt as if they were her second family.

They were all in the same boat, so they kept each other going. If one of them was homesick, the others would rally round to cheer her up. If one of them had had a telling off from one of the Sister Tutors, the others would reassure her and dry her tears. They laughed together, and cried together. They practised dressings on each other, bandaging arms and heads and putting splints on legs. They took each other's pulses and temperatures, and endlessly drilled each other on the various bones of the body and the Latin abbreviations doctors scrawled on patients' notes.

Eleanor was at the heart of their set. She was forever organising trips and days out for the girls. She was the one who got them together to study, and if one of them was feeling low, it was Eleanor who helped to cheer her up.

And she had singled out Anna to be her best friend. Their rooms were on the same landing, and Eleanor was forever popping round to chat or revise. Anna was sure she would have missed her family a lot more if Eleanor had not been there to help her.

Eleanor fell in beside Anna now as they trooped back to Porthleven House.

'You haven't forgotten about the Sewing Drive down at the Red Cross Centre this afternoon?' she asked. Then, without waiting for an answer, went on, 'We're meeting downstairs after dinner. We can walk through the park together, as it's a nice day.'

Anna nodded. 'I'll be there. Are the other girls coming?'

'All except Moore. She wants to go up West – again!' Eleanor's mouth tightened in disapproval.

'Oh, well, I'm sure there'll be more than enough of us anyway,' Anna said.

'I don't know about that.' Eleanor frowned. 'Mrs Jennings the District Organiser did say there's a lot of work to be done . . .'

'We'll all have to sew twice as fast then, won't we?' Anna smiled. Poor Eleanor, she took her responsibilities so seriously. Within a week of starting at the Nightingale, she had managed to attach herself to all kinds of committees and fundraising organisations involved with the war effort. Now, if she wasn't unravelling jumpers to re-knit into socks for soldiers, she was collecting money, organising raffles and making up food parcels.

Her friend looked fretful. 'I don't want to let anyone down,' she said. 'Mother says our boys are relying on us to do our bit.'

'You're doing more than your fair share,' Anna said. 'You'll wear yourself out.'

'I'm doing it for Harry,' Eleanor told her firmly. 'And you'll do the same for your Edward, when the time comes.'

Anna was silent. She didn't think she could ever be like Eleanor Copeland. She was a force of nature, a whirlwind that flattened everything in its path. Anna always felt weak and lazy beside her.

41

When they arrived back at Porthleven House, Miss Noonan was waiting for them. They all jumped to attention automatically, and Anna prayed silently that the Home Sister wouldn't notice the scuffed shoes that she hadn't had time to polish that morning.

But for once Miss Noonan did not single her out. Nor did she notice Grace Duffield, even though her cap was askew and the hem of her dress had come undone.

'This note came for you, Sedgewick.' She handed Sadie an envelope.

'Thank you, Sister.' Sadie took it from her, and slid it into her apron pocket.

'I wonder what that's about?' Eleanor whispered to Anna as they followed her upstairs.

'I don't know. I hope it isn't bad news?'

'Strange she didn't open it. Don't you think that's odd?'

'Perhaps she already knew what it would say?' Anna wasn't sure anyone else had noticed the way Sadie's face had paled when she saw the letter in Miss Noonan's hand.

'Well, I still think it's strange,' Eleanor said. 'If someone sent me a note I'd jolly well want to read it straight away.'

As they passed Sadie's room, the door was open. She was standing by her bed, reading. Anna would have passed by, but Eleanor stopped and said, 'Is everything all right?'

Sadie looked up, startled. 'What?'

'The note?'

'Oh. No, it's nothing.' Sadie crumpled the piece of paper into a ball and shoved it in her pocket.

'So you're still coming to the Red Cross Centre this afternoon, I hope? The Sewing Drive?' Eleanor prompted when Sadie looked blank.

'Sorry, I can't.' She tore off her cap, scattering pins. 'That note – was from a sick friend. I have to go and visit her.'

Eleanor folded her arms across her chest. 'I thought you said it wasn't bad news?'

'She's not seriously ill. But I still have to go.'

Anna went to move on, hoping Eleanor would follow her, but she stood her ground.

'In that case, surely you can spare an hour or two?' she said. 'It's for the boys—'

'Look,' Sadie turned on her. 'I've already told you, I can't come.'

'But—'

'You'll have to find someone else to pack your food parcels or darn your socks, or whatever else it is you're doing today!' Sadie slammed the door in Eleanor's face with a resounding crash.

'Well!' Eleanor stood still, staring at the door. The shocked expression on her face was so priceless Anna had to stifle a smile with the back of her hand.

Eleanor was still fuming about it later as they set off across the park with the other girls. She strode in front, Anna hurrying to keep up with her. Miriam and Grace trailed along at the back, as Grace had somehow managed to twist her ankle coming down the stairs.

'Sick friend indeed!' Eleanor huffed. 'I don't believe a word of it!'

'But why would she lie about it?' Anna asked.

'Because lying is second nature to her sort,' Miriam said.

Anna looked over her shoulder at her. 'And what sort is that?'

Miriam and Eleanor looked at each other.

'Common,' Miriam said.

'That's a bit unfair, don't you think?' Grace cried. 'She seems nice to me.'

'And me,' Anna said.

'I didn't say she wasn't, did I?' Miriam snapped. 'I just

43

said she doesn't have the same manners as the rest of us. She's not been brought up the way we have.'

'Don't forget she's a factory girl,' Eleanor put in. 'She told me she'd got her Matric at night school. Can you imagine?'

She made it sound like a criticism. Anna couldn't understand why.

'If you ask me, there's a man involved,' Miriam said.

'She doesn't have a young man,' Grace said. 'I've asked her.'

'It might be a secret admirer?' Miriam said.

'But why would she need to keep it a secret?' Anna wondered.

'Perhaps he's married?'

Anna gasped. 'No!'

She looked at Eleanor but her friend merely nodded, lips pursed. 'I shouldn't be at all surprised,' she said. 'As I said, there's a reason she hasn't come with us, and it's got nothing to do with visiting a sick friend.'

Anna was silent for a moment, taking it all in. She looked around at the other girls. They all seemed so certain about it. 'I can't believe it,' she said.

'That's because you're a good person, and you like to think the best of people,' Eleanor said. 'But you mark my words – Sadie Sedgewick is hiding something.'

Chapter Five

The police station was dark and shabby, the air rank with stale sweat and alcohol from the drunks sleeping it off in the cells.

Sadie looked up at the clock ticking ponderously on the wall above the desk. It was nearly four o'clock. She would not be back for tea at Porthleven House. Her backside felt numb from sitting for so long on the hard wooden bench. In her hand she still clutched the note her mother's friend Belle had sent her.

'How much longer?' she asked the desk sergeant for the third time.

Sergeant Lomax looked up from his ledger. He was a wiry man, his narrow, foxy face half- obscured by gingery whiskers. Sadie knew him well from all her previous visits to the police station. 'In a hurry, are you?'

'I am, as a matter of fact.'

'Well, I beg your pardon, I'm sure. But perhaps if that mother of yours didn't go plying her trade down the docks in broad daylight, you wouldn't be so inconvenienced!'

Sadie ignored his contemptuous sneer. She had no time for Sergeant Lomax. Most of the Old Bill at Bethnal Green nick were decent enough, but there was something about Lomax that repulsed her. Belle had told her none of the dock girls liked him. He was too fond of a free grope, they said.

She thought about the other girls back at the hospital. No doubt Eleanor Copeland would have something to say about her not helping out at the Red Cross Sewing Drive. Sadie could just imagine them all gossiping about her, wondering why she had disappeared so suddenly.

She crumpled the note in her fist. She had to smile, wondering what Eleanor would say if she could see her now, waiting at the nick to bail out her mother yet again.

She looked back at the clock. Nearly twenty past four. She had been waiting long enough, she decided.

'And where do you think you're going?' Sergeant Lomax said as Sadie got to her feet.

'I've had enough of waiting. I told you, I'm in a hurry.'

'What about your mother?'

'Keep her here as long as you like. You can throw away the key as far as I'm concerned.'

Sergeant Lomax's mouth curled. 'You're a fine daughter, ain't you?'

'She's a fine mother, too.'

'All right, then.' The desk sergeant closed his ledger with a thud. 'Machin?' he summoned one of the young PCs with a nod over his shoulder. 'Go down to the cells and fetch Lily Sedgewick, would you? I reckon she's had enough time to cool off by now.'

Sadie frowned. 'I thought you said she had to wait for the superintendent?'

Lomax laughed. 'As if the superintendent would want to be bothered with a scabby old dock dolly! No, she tried to sink her teeth into PC Brennan's arm while he was arresting her, so I thought I'd give her a bit of time to consider her actions.'

'You mean you've kept me here all this time for nothing?'

'Maybe I just like your company?' He leered across the desk at her.

The suggestive way he looked her up and down made

Sadie's skin crawl, but she was determined not to show it. Squaring her shoulders, she faced him boldly. 'Go on, then. Have a look. It's as far as you'll ever get.'

'I dunno about that. You're your mother's daughter, ain't you? And I know for a fact Lily Sedgewick ain't fussy!'

Sadie stared back at him with contempt. 'I wouldn't let you lay a finger on me even if you was paying for it!'

Before he had a chance to reply, PC Machin came up the steps from the cells with Sadie's mother in tow. Lily Sedgewick looked even more of a mess than usual. Her heavy make-up made her look older than her forty years, thick powder settling into the careworn folds of her face, her scarlet lipstick fanning out in the tiny lines around her thin lips. Her artfully teased hair was as dry and brittle as straw. Even across the reception hall, Sadie could smell the stale drink coming off her as she wriggled in PC Machin's grasp.

'Get off me, Peter Machin!' she hissed. 'I can walk by myself, thank you very much.' She looked the picture of injured dignity, in spite of her unkempt appearance.

PC Machin mumbled something Sadie couldn't hear.

'Don't you come it with me, boy,' Lily Sedgewick snapped back. 'I knew you when you was a little kid on the streets, wetting your trousers 'cos the bigger lads were chucking stones at you!'

Peter Machin blushed so deeply, Sadie couldn't help smiling in spite of herself. She had grown up with Peter, sat in front of him at primary school. They'd played out together until his mother decided she didn't want her son associating with a dock dolly's daughter.

He caught Sadie's eye and his blush deepened, his ears turning scarlet beneath his neatly cropped dark hair.

'She's all yours,' he mumbled.

'Until she goes to court on Friday,' Sergeant Lomax chimed in.

Sadie's mother glared at him. 'You'll be wasting the judge's time. I was only waiting for a bus.'

'And I s'pose that sailor was just keeping you company?'

Lily Sedgewick looked huffy. 'Ain't no law against talking, is there?'

Sensing her mother was squaring up for another fight, Sadie said, 'Let's go, shall we?'

Lily marched out ahead of her, making a rude gesture at Sergeant Lomax as she went. Fortunately, the desk sergeant had gone back to consulting his ledger and didn't notice. But Peter Machin did. Sadie saw him shake his head, his cheeks growing even more scarlet.

'Where's Belle?' her mother demanded, as soon as they were outside.

'She didn't have the cash to bail you out, so she sent me instead. It's all right, you don't have to thank me,' Sadie called out as Lily marched off down the road.

'I didn't ask you to come.'

'In that case, I won't bother next time!'

'Please yourself.'

Sadie followed her down the street. 'What were you doing down the docks, anyway?'

'Have a guess.'

'I thought you'd stopped all that?'

'Yes, well, I needed the money, didn't I?'

'What about Mr Wonderful? Keeping you short again, is he?'

Her mother's face coloured under its thick coating of powder. 'If you must know, Jimmy's gone,' she muttered.

Sadie's heart lifted. 'Gone? Gone where?'

'How should I know?' Lily couldn't meet her eyes. 'He's had to make himself scarce.'

'So he's in trouble with the police again?'

'I wouldn't know anything about that.'

You never do, Sadie thought. Her mother could give the three wise monkeys a run for their money when she felt like it.

'How long has he been gone?'

'I dunno, do I?' Lily shrugged. 'About a week.'

'Let's hope he doesn't come back.'

Her mother gave her a sombre look. 'You mustn't say that,' she warned. 'If he ever found out you'd been talking about him like that—'

Sadie's chin lifted. 'I ain't afraid of him.'

'You should be,' her mother said quietly.

Lily Sedgewick lodged in a squalid, rundown tenement house close to the docks. The window frames were rotten, and the paint on the front door had peeled so much it was hard to tell what colour it had once been.

As she lifted the latch on the front door, Lily threw over her shoulder, 'Are you coming in, or what?'

'I might, since you've asked so nicely.'

Inside it stank of boiled cabbage and cat's pee. Damp bloomed on the faded wallpaper. From somewhere deep in the house a baby was wailing.

Belle was waiting for them in her mother's two rooms on the top floor. She was kneeling on the threadbare rug, making up the fire.

'All right, girl? I was wondering when you'd turn up,' she greeted Lily cheerfully. 'Thought I'd pop round and get a fire going, give you a nice welcome.'

'Thanks, mate.' Lily sat down in the solitary armchair and held her hands out to the flames to warm them. Even in her heavy coat, she looked painfully thin. Sadie wondered when she had last eaten. 'That cell was bloody cold. Played hell with my rheumatism, it did.'

'I'm not surprised. There's no meat on you. The cold'll go straight through to your bones. Here, put this blanket round you, warm you up a bit.' Sadie watched Belle fussing over her friend. She was only a few years older than Lily Sedgewick, but she looked after her like a mother. In spite of her kindness, though, Sadie knew there was nothing soft about Belle. She had a reputation for being hard as nails. Sadie had seen her pull another dock girl's hair out by the roots in a cat fight.

'Who collared you?' Belle asked.

'That new bloke – what's his name? Brennan. He's a bit keen. Most of them know to turn a blind eye, but not him.'

'I suppose he just wants to make a name for himself,' Belle said.

'He'll think twice about collaring me next time, I reckon,' Lily cackled. 'Took a bite out of his arm, I did. Nearly went through to the bone!'

'No! Blimey, Lil, you don't know your own strength!'

Sadie listened to them talk, wondering once again what Eleanor Copeland would make of it all. Those big eyes of hers would pop out of her head, she decided.

'It's lucky your Sadie was there to help out,' Belle said. 'I'm boracic myself.'

Lily grunted in response.

'You're welcome,' Sadie said to her mother, her voice heavy with sarcasm.

There was a long silence. Her mother kept her face averted, gazing into the sputtering flames.

Belle rose to her feet. 'Tell you what, why don't I put the kettle on? I reckon we could all do with a nice cuppa.'

'Sod that. I need something stronger.' Lily got up and went to the cupboard where she kept her gin bottle. Sadie watched her tipping it into a chipped china cup.

'That'll do you a lot of good,' she remarked.

Lily spared her a glowering look. 'I've had a shock, all right?'

'A shock!' Sadie mocked her. 'I would have thought you'd be used to it by now. You sleep in that cell more often than you do your own bed.'

'Listen to her! So high and mighty. Far too good for the likes of us, Belle.'

'That wouldn't be difficult,' Sadie murmured.

Belle sent her a reproachful look then turned back to Lily, who was already refilling her glass. Her hands were shaking so much the neck of the bottle clashed against the china.

'Steady on, Lil.' Belle looked nervous. 'Maybe you should lay off for now?'

'Don't you start!' Lily waved the bottle at her. 'I have enough earache from that one, without you getting on at me. You're supposed to be my mate!'

Sadie sighed. 'Let her be, Belle. If she wants to drink herself to death then that's her look out. Don't tell her off on my account. I've spent half my life watching her getting pie-eyed!'

'Oh, haven't *you* had a hard life!' her mother sneered.

'I have, as a matter of fact,' Sadie replied quietly.

Lily turned away, downing her gin.

'Any word from Jimmy, Lil?' Belle changed the subject.

She shook her head. 'Not a dicky bird.'

'Old Bill has been round to see me. Wanted to see if I knew anything.'

'And what did you say?'

'Same as always. I didn't see or hear anything.' Lily paused for a moment, then said, 'You know he died – the old man from the post office? A stroke, so they say, brought on by the shock.'

'So I heard.'

Sadie looked from one to the other of them. 'What's this?'

She saw the warning look Lily shot at Belle over the rim of her cup.

'Nothing,' Belle said. 'It's nothing. Just a bit of gossip, that's all.'

But Sadie had already guessed the truth. 'So that's why Jimmy's disappeared,' she said. 'He killed someone.'

'It wasn't like that,' her mother answered quickly. 'That old man should never have fought back. If he'd just done as he was told . . . there was no need for anyone to get hurt.'

Sadie looked at her with contempt. 'That's never stopped Jimmy giving you a beating, has it?'

Lily stared down into her drink. 'You know nothing about it,' she muttered.

'I reckon I do,' Sadie fired back. 'I lived with you both long enough. I've been watching him giving you hidings since I was ten years old!'

Her mother said nothing. Her mouth was a tight line, the way it always was when Sadie spoke up against her precious Jimmy Clyde.

'I'll go and make that tea.'

Belle started to get up, but Sadie said, 'Don't bother, I ain't stopping.'

Belle looked disappointed. 'But I was looking forward to having a good chinwag. We wanted to hear all about how you've been getting on at the hospital, didn't we, Lil?'

Sadie caught the pleading look Belle gave her mother. Lily's face remained blank, indifferent.

'It's all right,' she said to Belle. 'I know she ain't interested in me.'

'Don't be like that, love,' Belle pleaded, but Sadie was already on her feet, putting on her coat.

'Let her go.' Lily's voice was dulled by gin. 'I don't need her here, looking down on me.'

'It ain't difficult, the state of you!' Sadie snapped back.

She took some money out of her purse and laid it on the table. 'Here,' she said. 'Save you earning it down the docks.'

'I don't want your money.'

'Go on, take it. Or are you only interested in cash that's come from robbing old men?'

'Cheeky cow!' her mother muttered as Sadie left.

Belle followed her out, clattering down the stairs after her.

'I'm sorry about your mum,' she said. 'She's just in a bit of a state, that's all.'

'Stop making excuses for her, Belle. We both know what my mother's like.' Sadie took some more coins out of her purse and handed them over. 'Here, take these. Look after her. Make sure she eats something, and stick some pennies in the meter. She'll only drink away what I've left for her.'

'Thanks, love. I'll take care of her, I promise.'

'I know you will, Belle.' The other woman had been looking after Lily for years, ever since she first found her as a frightened young girl by the docks. Belle had watched over the newcomer then, showed her the ropes, taught her how to stay alive. And she had been doing it ever since.

But Belle couldn't save Lily from herself, any more than Sadie could.

As she left, Belle said, 'You're a good girl, Sadie.'

'Tell that to my mother.'

'She already knows.'

'Funny she never says it, then.'

'You know what your mum's like. She's proud.'

'Proud!' Sadie laughed bitterly. 'What's she got to be proud about? Anyway,' she shrugged, 'I don't care what she thinks of me.'

Belle smiled. 'You two are as bad as each other. You're too alike, that's your trouble.'

You're wrong about that, Sadie thought as she made her way up the narrow, damp alleyway outside. The tenements rose up on either side of her, forming a dank canyon, illuminated only by a narrow strip of dusky sky.

She thought about the pathetic woman sitting hunched by the fire, her face heavily powdered over yellowing bruises, swigging gin to help her carry on with her mess of a life.

No, Sadie would never, ever be like her mother.

Chapter Six

A month later, on a damp day in November, the results of the preliminary training exams were announced.

The students made a gloomy group at breakfast that morning. Anna looked down the length of the table at the bleary-eyed faces. Everyone looked as if they'd had the same sleepless night she'd had. They stared down at their empty plates, too tense to eat. Only Eleanor seemed unconcerned, buttering her toast with the complacent attitude of someone who had spent the past fortnight swotting.

Miss Noonan didn't help matters. She lingered even longer than usual over morning prayers, then sent them off to their rooms for their daily chores. Usually they managed these quite cheerfully, but this morning they bickered and snapped at each other as they made their beds and swept their rooms. Even Anna found herself turning on poor Grace Duffield when she accidentally emptied the contents of the dustpan onto the landing.

As Anna polished the banister rail she saw the Home Sister pinning up a piece of paper on the noticeboard by the front door.

'I wish I could see the names from here,' she whispered to Eleanor beside her.

'You've got nothing to worry about,' her friend said soothingly. 'I'm certain you've passed.'

'I'm not.' At first, Anna had felt she might have done enough to scrape through the examination. Then, as the days went by, her confidence faded and she became just as convinced she had failed dismally. Since then she had flipped from one extreme to the other. One minute she thought she had done well, the next she could see herself packing up her belongings.

'You've worked hard,' Eleanor said. 'You deserve to get through.' She smiled. 'Just think, this time next month we'll be on the wards!'

'Don't.' Anna felt queasy at the thought. She wasn't sure which prospect daunted her more, being sent home in disgrace or having to nurse real patients.

When they had finished their chores, Miss Noonan insisted on holding one of her bedroom inspections.

'She's doing it on purpose, I swear,' Miriam Trott muttered as they headed to their rooms. 'It's just cruel.'

Anna's knees nearly gave way beneath her as the Home Sister prowled around her room, running a finger along the tops of doors and cupboards and frowning at the turn-down on her top sheet.

Then, finally, Miss Noonan dismissed them.

'You may go and check the noticeboard. Quietly, if you please!' she instructed, but her words were drowned out by the sound of ten pairs of feet thundering down the stairs.

Anna fought her way past jostling elbows to get a glimpse of the list. At first she couldn't see her name, but the next thing she knew, Eleanor was hugging her fiercely and saying,

'We passed! We both passed!'

'Did we?' Anna stared at the list. She couldn't allow herself to believe it until she saw her name written down. And there it was, right in the middle – not a spectacular result, but good enough to get her to the next two years of training.

Around her, the other girls were laughing with relief too.

'Look who's top of the class,' Grace Duffield was saying. 'You're a dark horse, Sedgewick!'

Anna looked sideways at Sadie Sedgewick, who said nothing. She was staring at her name with a dazed expression on her face.

Miriam peered at the noticeboard, counting the names. 'One . . . two . . . three . . . Someone's missing.'

'Me,' Dulcie Moore said in a small voice.

'Oh, no! Poor you!' The other girls immediately gathered round her, offering sympathy. 'That's such bad luck.'

'Perhaps they'll let you stay on anyway?' Grace said hopefully.

Eleanor turned on her. 'Don't be silly, Duffield. Why on earth would they do that?'

'I don't know, do I?' Grace looked helpless. 'If she didn't fail too badly—'

'Failed means failed,' Eleanor said, in such a sharp way that Anna was surprised.

Before she could say anything, Miss Noonan appeared.

'Well done, girls. Please return to your rooms and pack up your belongings. You will be moving over to Lennox House before tea this evening. Moore, you must go and see Matron straight away to discuss what is to be done.'

'Yes, Sister.' Dulcie stood there meekly until the Home Sister had gone. Only when the office door had closed did she allow her shoulders to slump.

'Oh, Lord,' she groaned. 'This is it, girls.'

'Perhaps you should throw yourself on Matron's mercy?' Sadie said. 'I'm sure she'll be decent about it.'

The other girls exchanged wary looks. Anna had only met Matron a couple of times, but she didn't strike her as the type to be merciful or decent.

'Oh, well, I suppose I'd best get it over with.' Dulcie managed a weak smile. 'Wish me luck.'

'Here.' Sadie stepped forward and put Dulcie's cap straight on her curly head. 'That's better. I don't suppose you've got any other cuffs, have you? Those are a bit grubby.'

'Here, have mine.' Anna unfastened her cuffs and gave them to Dulcie. 'I'll put a fresh pair on later.'

'Thank you.' Dulcie fastened on the cuffs and faced them all. 'Well, just in case Matron tells me never to darken her door again, it's been nice knowing you all.'

As they watched her walk away, Miriam said, 'I can't say I'm surprised. If she'd spent more time with her books and less dreaming about men, she might have passed the examination.'

Sadie turned on her. 'You're a fine one to talk, Trott! We've all seen you, reading those romance novels when you're supposed to be studying.'

Miriam blushed deeply. 'At least I passed!'

'Stop arguing, you two,' Anna said. 'We should be celebrating, not falling out with each other.'

'She's right,' Eleanor said. 'This is a big day for us, and we should do something special.'

'What shall we do?' Anna asked.

'Have tea and cakes,' Grace said promptly.

'That's what you always say!' Eleanor said.

Grace shrugged. 'I like tea and cakes.'

'We could go to my father's bakery?' Anna ventured. 'I was going this afternoon anyway, to tell them my examination results . . .'

'What a good idea.' Eleanor nodded her approval. 'It's about time we visited this bakery you're always talking about.'

'Are you sure your father wouldn't mind?' Grace asked.

'Oh, no, Papa loves company. He's always asking when he's going to meet my new friends.'

'Then it's settled,' Eleanor said. 'We're all going to visit Beck's Bakery!'

'Count me out.' Sadie spoke up. 'I want to wait for Moore, see what Matron has said to her.'

'We all know what Matron will say,' Eleanor dismissed.

'Then I want to make sure Moore's all right,' Sadie replied. 'She's bound to be feeling wretched, and I don't think it's very nice to go out celebrating and leave her on her own. We are supposed to be a set after all.' She looked around at them reproachfully as she said it.

Anna blushed and looked at the others. 'Perhaps we should all stay and help cheer her up?'

'Nonsense,' Eleanor cut across her. 'We've made plans now, and we should stick to them.' She looked around the group. 'We deserve a day out after all our hard work. And besides, we won't be getting as much time off once we're all working on different wards.' She turned to Sadie. 'You don't have to come.'

Sadie's chin lifted. 'I've already told you, I'm not.'

'Me neither,' Grace said. 'I think I'll stay and keep Moore company too. Besides, I get too nervous going out in the city.'

Anna glanced at Eleanor. Her teeth were clenched together, her square jaw working, a sure sign that she was vexed.

'You don't know what you're missing,' she said. Then, to Anna's relief, she smiled. 'We'll just have to eat their share of the cake, won't we, girls?'

It was a damp day and a dull canopy of dirty grey cloud hung over Bethnal Green. The streets were alive with the cries of the costermongers – hawkers pushing barrows laden with boots, rolls of cloth, pots and pans and old furniture. Women carrying bundles of matchboxes passed by, huddled under thick shawls, their breath curling in the cold air. The smell of onion bread, garlic sausage and pickled fish drifted from the Jewish grocers, mingling with the acrid stench of factory smoke.

It was her London but Anna barely noticed it as she trudged along, her gloved hands thrust deep into her coat pockets.

Eleanor fell into step beside her. 'Cheer up,' she said. 'You're not still thinking about what Sedgewick said, are you?'

'She's got a point, hasn't she?' Anna said. 'It doesn't seem right for us to be out having fun when Moore's so upset. We are supposed to be a set, after all.'

Eleanor's lips tightened. 'Moore should have thought about that, shouldn't she? It's hardly our fault she's failed. Why should we suffer because she decided to go gadding about instead of working like the rest of us?'

'I suppose you're right,' Anna sighed.

'I know I am.' Eleanor linked an arm through hers. 'Now do cheer up,' she ordered. 'We're having a good day, and you're not to spoil it!'

Columbia Road market was bustling with stalls and people, but the other girls barely seemed to notice. Miriam complained constantly about how dirty everything was, and how much her feet hurt, while Eleanor couldn't stop going on about Sadie coming top in the examination.

'I have no idea why I only came second,' she said for the fourth time. 'I know I answered every question correctly, because I checked them in the textbook afterwards. And the examiner said mine was the tidiest many-tailed bandage she'd ever seen. And to come second to Sedgewick, of all people,' she went on. 'I might not have felt so bad if it had been any of you girls, but her . . .' She shook her head. 'Have you heard the way she speaks? So uneducated . . .'

'We're here now,' Anna cut her off. 'Just around this corner—'

She turned into Chambord Street and stopped in her tracks at the sight of what lay ahead of her.

Chapter Seven

'What is it?' Eleanor asked. 'What's happened?'

But Anna did not answer. She was already running down the street to where Edward was standing on the pavement outside the shop, watching Tom pick shards of glass from the broken window.

He turned at the sound of running footsteps. 'Anna! What are you doing here?'

She ignored the question, fighting for breath. 'What happened?'

'Someone put a brick through the window just now.'

'Did you see who did it?'

'No. They were gone by the time I came out.' He looked up and down the street, his expression grim.

'Was anyone hurt?'

'Your father got some glass in his hand, but he's all right. He's inside, with your mother.' Edward nodded towards the shop.

Anna asked the other girls to wait outside, then went to find her father. He was in the kitchen, sitting on a chair while her mother bandaged his hand.

'Stop fussing,' he was saying. 'I told you, it's nothing more than a scratch.' He saw Anna come in and his face brightened. '*Liebling!* What a surprise. What are you doing here?'

'I thought I'd come to visit. I wanted to tell you I'd passed my preliminary training. I brought some of the other girls . . .' Her voice trailed off as she looked at his wounded hand.

'But that is wonderful!' Friedrich Beck stood up, shrugging off his wife's ministrations. 'Did you hear that, my dear? Our daughter has passed her exams. Such a clever girl.' He beamed at Anna, his brown eyes twinkling. 'But where are your friends?'

'I left them outside. I could tell them to go? '

'Nonsense, I will not hear of it! They are our guests, you must bring them inside.' He was already heading through the door leading to the shop.

Anna turned to her mother, who shrugged helplessly.

'But, Papa, your hand,' Anna called after him.

'It is nothing. My fault for being careless, that is all.' Friedrich flung open the shop door. The girls stood huddled outside where Anna had left them, looking uncertain.

'Come in, my dears, please,' Friedrich Beck greeted them. 'I do not know what my daughter is thinking, leaving you outside on such a cold day.'

They hung back, still uncertain.

'Are you sure, Mr Beck?' Miriam spoke up. 'We could come back another day, if it isn't convenient.' She glanced towards the shattered remains of the shop window.

'I am afraid we are not looking our best,' Friedrich said ruefully, 'but guests are always welcome here, particularly if they are friends of my daughter. Please,' he ushered them inside, 'go upstairs to the parlour, you will be more comfortable there. Anna will show you the way. *Liebling*, take your friends' coats, *bitte*. We will have tea and cake, yes? I have some apple cake, fresh from the oven.'

Anna took the girls up to the cosy parlour, where the fire was roaring. It was a comfortable room, but she could sense her friends' unease as she took their coats and got them settled.

'Perhaps we should go?' Eleanor looked very uncomfortable.

'No, please stay. Papa will be upset if you leave now.'

'So long as we're not in the way?' Miriam said, settling herself on the sofa. 'I must say, that cake does smell delicious.'

'I'll bring it straight in to you.' Anna hurried back downstairs to the kitchen.

She could tell right away her mother and father had been having words. They shut up as soon as Anna walked in, her mother turning away to watch the kettle boil. She looked as if she had been crying.

'What's going on, Papa?' Anna asked. 'Edward said someone threw a brick.'

'It was just children messing about,' her father dismissed the question. 'Nothing to worry about.'

'Have you called the police?'

She saw the look that passed between her parents. 'Your father doesn't think it's worth troubling them,' Dorothy replied, tight-lipped.

'It was a prank, that is all. Nothing serious.'

'But you were hurt.'

'It was my own silly fault.'

'What if that brick had hit you? Or me? Would you think it was serious then?'

Anna stared from one to the other of her parents. She had never heard her mother speak to her father like that. They would often bicker in a joking way, but she had never seen them argue openly.

'Calm down,' Friedrich said. 'Anna's friends will hear you.'

'I don't care!' Dorothy dismissed. 'What if whoever threw that brick comes back?' she demanded.

'They won't.'

'How can you say that? You don't know. After everything that's been going on around here lately—' She stopped talking suddenly, her mouth closing like a trap.

'What?' Anna said. 'What's been going on, Papa?'

'It's nothing,' he replied. 'Just a few fools causing trouble, that is all. But I have been here for more than twenty years, everyone knows me. They like me. No one would allow any harm to come to us.'

'So where were they when someone smashed our shop window?' Dorothy asked quietly.

A long silence followed. Then Friedrich stirred himself and said, 'I do not want to think of this today. Anna has brought her friends to see us, we should be celebrating with them, not walking around with long faces.' He beamed at Anna. 'Come, *Liebling*. Help me with the cake.'

In spite of her father's efforts to be cheerful, tea was a sombre affair. Anna picked at her sliver of cake, too upset to eat. The other girls made polite conversation, but Anna could see the sidelong looks that passed between them. Eleanor was utterly silent, her face pale.

It was a relief when it was time to leave. While Eleanor and Miriam put on their coats and said their polite good-byes, Anna sneaked back down to the kitchen to see Edward.

She nearly cried with relief to see him there, scrubbing down tins at the sink. At least something had stayed the same, even though the rest of the world seemed to be tilting crazily on its axis.

'Oh, Edward!' She rushed to him, throwing herself against the solid, comforting wall of his chest. His arms came up to embrace her.

'My hands are wet,' he murmured into her hair.

'I don't care. I just want you to hold me.' Anna clung to him. 'Hold me and tell me everything will be all right.'

'I hope so, my love,' was all he could say.

Anna pulled away from him. 'What's happening?' she said. 'Do you know why someone broke that window? My father says it was just kids messing about, but it wasn't, was it?'

Edward turned away from her, plunging his arms back into the sink. 'No,' he said.

'Then who was it?'

'I don't know. But there's been a lot of trouble around here lately with German shops and businesses being vandalised. You know that German barber's on Roman Road? They had paint thrown at their windows last week. And two days ago Mr Shulman the tailor was burgled. They ripped up all his stock.'

'No!' Hans Shulman often came to play cards with her father. Anna could hardly imagine why anyone would want to hurt such a pleasant old man.

'But I don't understand,' she said. 'How can someone throw a brick in broad daylight and no one see them?'

'I don't know. I asked the neighbours, but no one noticed anything. Or so they said,' he added in a low voice.

Anna stared at him. 'Why would they lie to you?'

'Perhaps they might not want to be next?'

'Don't. It's too horrible to think about.' Anna shuddered and Edward reached for the towel to dry his hands before pulling her close again.

'It'll be all right,' he murmured into her hair.

'I hope so.' She pulled away from him. 'I'd better go. You will look after them all, won't you?'

'Of course,' he promised, his blue eyes solemn. 'I'll make sure no harm comes to them, I promise.'

'And you'll let me know – if anything else happens?'

'It won't,' Edward assured her.

Anna looked up into his handsome face. How she wished she could believe him, but the world had turned so upside down lately, she couldn't be sure of anything anymore.

*

The other girls were very subdued on the way back to the hospital. Their silence made Anna uneasy.

'I'm sorry,' she said. 'If I'd known there was so much trouble going on, I would never have asked you to come.'

'We're just sorry for your family,' Miriam said. 'Whoever put that brick through their window should be ashamed of themselves. Isn't that right, Copeland?'

Eleanor said nothing. She had barely spoken a word since they had arrived at the bakery, Anna realised.

They returned to Porthleven House, where Miss Noonan was waiting to hurry them along.

'Go upstairs to your rooms and collect your belongings,' she instructed. 'You must take them over to Lennox House and unpack before tea at four o'clock.' She clapped her hands. 'Well? Don't just stand there, girls. Be quick about it!'

'I won't miss her, barking her orders all the time,' Miriam muttered, as they hurried up the stairs.

'Let's hope the new Home Sister isn't even worse!' Anna whispered back.

At first sight, Lennox House seemed a lot more welcoming than Porthleven. It looked more like a graceful country house, with its large bay windows and mellow sandstone walls. Gas lamps cast a welcoming glow from behind heavy lace curtains.

Miss Westcombe the Home Sister was very different from Miss Noonan, too. She was surprisingly young, in her thirties, rounded and motherly-looking, with a soft, smiling face and gentle hazel eyes.

'Welcome, girls,' she greeted them with a smile. 'You are not all here. Who is missing?'

'Sedgewick and Duffield, Sister,' Miriam said.

A small frown creased the Home Sister's soft features.

'That's rather a nuisance. Oh, well, never mind. I shall have to attend to them when they arrive.' She consulted a list in her hand. 'Now, I have your room allocations here. You will be sharing rooms, since we have a great many probationers at Lennox House. Trott, you will be sharing room three with Duffield when she arrives.'

Miriam sighed. 'Lord, I'll have to lock all my valuables away in case she accidentally smashes them.'

Alice smiled at Eleanor. Her profile was expressionless.

'Sedgewick was supposed to be sharing a room with Moore, but I understand she will not be joining us, so Sedgewick will be on her own for the time being. Which leaves . . .' Miss Westcombe's gaze ran down the list. 'Beck and Copeland in room four.'

They went upstairs, dragging their suitcases. 'I'm sure it wasn't this heavy when I arrived,' Anna said, leading the way along the landing. 'Now what number did she say? Four, wasn't it? Oh, here we are. Home sweet home!'

She threw open the door to a large, airy room. Anna dumped her suitcase on the floor and looked around. 'Well, at least it doesn't smell of damp like Porthleven. And there's no draught coming up through the floorboards. And there's a nice view, too.' She went over to the window. 'Look, you can see over the front lawn, almost to the main building. Would you like the bed nearest the window, or over in the corner? I don't mind, you can choose.'

She turned round. Eleanor stood rigid in the doorway, her suitcase still in her hand.

'Copeland? Are you all right?'

Eleanor looked as if she might cry. 'I can't,' she blurted out.

Anna stared at her. 'Can't what?'

'I can't share a room with you.'

'What are you talking about? We wanted to share, didn't we? You said . . .'

68

'That was before,' Eleanor mumbled.

'Before what?'

'Before I knew who you were.' Eleanor looked up suddenly, her eyes blazing. 'Why didn't you tell me your father was German?' she cried.

Anna sank down on the bed, dazed. 'Is that what this is about?'

'I would never have – if I'd known . . .' Eleanor appealed to her. 'You must see it makes things difficult?'

'No, I don't. I don't understand what this has to do with us.'

Eleanor looked down at her hands. 'My father says the Germans are our enemies,' she said quietly.

'But I'm your friend,' Anna said.

'No!' Eleanor stared at her. 'I – I can't be your friend,' she said.

'Eleanor—'

'My father wouldn't like it.' She shook her head. 'It wouldn't be right, not with my brother in France, fighting for his country. I'd feel like – a traitor.'

'A traitor?' Anna repeated coldly.

'I'll speak to the Home Sister,' Eleanor said. 'I'm sure she'll be able to change things round, find someone else to share with you.'

'Eleanor!' Anna called after her. But she had already gone, slamming the door behind her.

Chapter Eight

'Well, girls, it looks as if I might not be cut out for nursing after all!'

Dulcie managed a bright smile, but Sadie could tell how miserable she was feeling under her brave face.

They were in her room at Porthleven House, watching her pack before she caught her train back to Devon. Poor Dulcie was in such a daze, she barely seemed to know what she was doing. She kept taking things out of her drawer, folding them and putting them back in again.

'Don't say that!' Sadie said. 'You'll be back. Matron said you could try again, didn't she?'

'If I'm lucky. She said if I apply again, I'll be considered along with everyone else – "Although I do hope, Miss Moore, that if you are selected you will work a little harder next time",' she perfectly mimicked Matron's haughty tone.

'And what did you say to that?' Grace asked.

'I promised I would, of course,' Dulcie said. 'Believe me, I'll be a bigger swot than Eleanor Copeland if they give me another chance!'

'I'll believe that when I see it!' Sadie grinned.

'Copeland isn't the biggest swot in the set now,' Grace pointed out, her eyes glinting with mischief. Sadie felt herself blushing.

'Oh, yes, I'd forgotten about that.' Dulcie paused in rolling up a stocking. 'Honestly, Copeland's face when she saw your name at the top of the list. It was priceless!'

'It was a fluke,' Sadie muttered.

'No, it wasn't.' Dulcie threw the stocking at her so it bounced in her lap. 'You're very good, Sadie Sedgewick.'

Sadie tossed back the balled-up stocking. 'We'll see how good I am after another two years' studying. I expect I'll be back at the bottom of the class by then.'

'Nonsense,' Dulcie said. 'What was it Miss Pascoe called you last week? A natural.'

Sadie felt her blush deepening. 'I don't know about that,' she mumbled.

Dulcie went back to her packing, pushing the stocking into a corner of her suitcase. 'Even if I do manage to get past Matron and come back, you lot will all be proper nurses long before me. I'll be left behind!'

'Not that far behind,' Grace said. 'And anyway, you'll soon catch up.'

'I don't know . . .' Dulcie stared down at the pile of silky petticoats in her hands as if she didn't know quite what to do with them.

'Here, let me help you.' Sadie took them from her and put them in the suitcase. 'Tell you what, why don't you fetch everything from your cupboards and I'll fold and pack things for you?'

'Thank you.' Dulcie smiled gratefully, tears shining in her brown eyes. The poor girl was in a dreadful state, Sadie thought. She was glad she and Grace had stayed behind to be with her. 'I don't know what I'm doing,' Dulcie said in a choked voice. 'I keep thinking about having to go home and tell my parents I've failed . . .'

'I'm sure they'll be all right about it,' Grace said kindly.

'I suppose so.' Dulcie gazed out of the window, over the rooftops. 'Just think,' she sighed, 'this time tomorrow I'll be bringing the cows in!' She looked forlorn at the prospect.

They walked down the long drive towards the main gates, carrying the suitcase between them.

'You'll have to write to us and tell us all your news,' Sadie said.

'I will. Although I don't suppose there'll be much to tell, being stuck in the country.'

Sadie grinned at her. 'I told you, you'll be back.'

'Perhaps.' Dulcie smiled. 'I just hope all the handsome young doctors haven't been sent off to war by then!' She clutched Sadie's hands, her eyes glistening with tears. 'Say goodbye to the others for me, won't you?'

'Of course.'

They said their final goodbyes at the Tube station, then Sadie and Grace trudged back to the hospital together.

'It's such a shame the others weren't here to wish her well,' Grace said.

'They might have been, if it hadn't been for Copeland.' There was little love lost between Sadie and Eleanor Copeland. She found the other girl too bossy and overbearing. She was sure Eleanor looked down on her, too. For whatever reason, they tried to stay out of each other's way.

But she was surprised when Grace suddenly blurted out, 'She would probably be a lot nicer if it wasn't for her father.'

Sadie turned to stare at her.

'It's all that *John Bull* nonsense he spouts in her ear,' Grace went on. 'He believes every word, and he makes sure she does, too.'

She was right, Sadie thought. Eleanor was forever quoting her father's opinions, which in turn he had taken from the *John Bull*, a rabble-rousing newspaper which called openly for a vendetta against every German in Britain. It constantly urged its readers to attack 'The Hun' wherever they found them.

'I loathe Horatio Bottomley and his wretched newspaper,' Grace muttered. 'He's a cruel, evil man, and all he wants to do is spread hatred.'

Sadie glanced sideways at her. Grace Duffield was a quiet, even-tempered soul who rarely raised her voice to anyone. It was a shock to see her so angry now.

'They should send him to the Front, see how much he likes war then,' Grace went on. 'It's all very well him—'

'Look out!'

Sadie swung round as a runaway coal wagon came thundering out of nowhere, careening wildly from side to side across the road, shedding sacks of coal as it went. Without thinking, she grabbed Grace's arm and managed to yank her back from under the horse's flailing hooves. They both tumbled to the pavement, inches away from the cart's wheels. Sadie looked up and caught a glimpse of the driver's face, eyes bulging in terror, every sinew straining as he fought for control.

The cart disappeared around the corner and Grace struggled to sit up.

'What the—' she started to say. But no sooner had she opened her mouth than there was a terrible, splintering crash, followed a second later by the sound of screaming.

Before they knew what they were doing, they were on their feet and running towards the source of the commotion.

Sadie rounded the corner first. For a moment she could only stare, trying to work out what she was seeing. The cart was upturned in the middle of the road, sacks of coal spilling out all around it. A few men had got hold of the horse and fought to calm it as it bucked and reared, ears flattened, eyes rolling. They ducked as its mighty hooves pawed the air, narrowly missing their heads.

Yet more people were gathered around the rear of the wagon. As they drew closer, Sadie caught a glimpse of the driver on the pavement, blood pooling in a crimson halo around him. She could only see his top half; the rest of him was buried under the cart.

'Is he dead?' Grace whispered.

'I don't know,' Sadie said grimly.

'Should we do something?'

'What can we do?'

'I don't know. We are supposed to be nurses, aren't we?'

'Hardly!'

'All the same, we should do something.'

Sadie swallowed hard. 'Run to the hospital,' she said to Grace. 'Go and get help.' Then she started to push her way through the gathering crowd.

The driver was sprawled in the gutter, the lower half of his body under the cart. Two strong men were lifting the cart, while another had the injured drayman under the arms, trying to pull him free.

'One, two, three . . . lift!'

The cart was raised an inch, enough to shift the man slightly. As he moved, Sadie caught a glimpse of blood pumping from raw, mangled flesh. So much blood, soaking the sacks of coals, rivers of it running in the gutters.

Think, Sadie. Think!

She wanted to look away, but she couldn't. She was too mesmerised by the blood. And the smell . . . coppery, metallic.

Nausea rose up, clogging her throat.

Think, Sadie.

Suddenly it came to her, out of nowhere. A distant memory of two weeks earlier, a misty October morning, the leaves turning on the oak tree outside the classroom. Sadie's attention wandering, listening to Miss Pascoe explaining the principles of the tourniquet . . .

She unwound the scarf from around her neck and stepped forward on legs that barely held her up.

'Here,' she said. 'You need to tie this around his leg, to stop it bleeding. Between the wound and his heart.'

The men looked up at her, and for a moment she thought they were going to tell her to go away.

'You a nurse or something?'

'Yes,' she said, her throat dry. 'Yes, I – I'm a nurse.'

One of the men stood up. 'You do it then,' he said.

Sadie's head swam as she forced herself to kneel down. Why was she doing this? It wasn't what she was used to. So far she had only dressed wounds on a nice clean dummy in the practice room. This was a real man, stinking of dirt and sweat and blood.

She knelt down beside him. The stench of the blood made her feel sick; she recoiled from the hot stickiness of it flowing over her shaking hands as she tried to apply the tourniquet.

Between the wound and the heart. The wound and the heart, she told herself, over and over again. But there was nothing there. Just a crushed, bloodied mass of flesh and shattered bone, like nothing she had ever seen before . . .

'Don't bother with that.' Suddenly someone was at her side. A smartly dressed young woman knelt beside her, blood soaking through her skirt.

Sadie stared at her, dazed. But the young woman barely seemed aware of her as she shrugged off her jacket and examined the man.

'Put him flat on his back,' she ordered the onlookers.

Sadie stepped back as they wrestled the man over, his limbs flopping like a rag doll's. She could see from his livid blue lips that the life had already almost gone from him.

She watched as the young woman rolled up the sleeves

of her blouse, exposing a slim white forearm, then drew herself up on to her knees over the man's apparently lifeless body.

'What are you doing?' Sadie whispered, but the young woman ignored her. She made her right arm rigid then drove her fist hard into the man's belly, leaning down on it with all her weight. Locks of dark hair escaped from under her hat, falling around her face.

'How's the bleeding?' she asked through gritted teeth.

Sadie checked the wound. 'It's stopped!' She stared down at the ruined pulp, where only seconds before blood had flowed over her hands and into her lap.

The young woman nodded. 'Good. I'll just have to hold him like this until the ambulance arrives.' She sent Sadie a sidelong look. 'The tourniquet was a good idea,' she said.

Sadie nodded, unable to speak. She suddenly felt very hot, in spite of the cold November weather.

'Are you all right?' The young woman's voice sounded strange, as if she was underwater.

Sadie nodded. 'I'm fine.'

'No, you're not.' The young woman sighed impatiently. 'Can someone take this girl away please, before she faints?'

Sadie struggled to her feet. 'I – I'm all right,' honestly—'
The last thing she saw was the young woman's face turning fuzzy in front of her, before her knees buckled and she slid to the ground.

Chapter Nine

Kate Carlyle ran a practised eye over the rows of benches in the Casualty Hall. There was a woman with a crying baby, a small boy who wouldn't stop scratching, a sprained wrist, two burns and a rather fat man who kept clutching his chest and grimacing.

Dyspepsia, she thought. He had too much colour in his florid face for there to be anything wrong with his heart, no matter what he might think. All he needed was an aperient.

The small boy had scabies and needed sulphur treatment, and the baby was simply miserable. Its mother gave Kate more concern. She was pale and tired-looking, and in desperate need of a tonic.

She sat back, bored. She had been waiting for nearly an hour, and in that time had mentally diagnosed everyone who came in, treated them and sent them home again. And yet no Casualty doctor had appeared for at least twenty minutes. Even the Casualty nurse, seated on her dais at the far end of the hall, seemed to be asleep at her desk.

Kate shook her head. Lazy and inefficient. If she was working here, there would never be a queue.

If she was working here . . .

The door opened and a doctor appeared, a stocky young man in his late twenties, with a shock of wavy brown hair brushed back off his high forehead. He spotted Kate and headed for her.

'You came in with the driver of the coal wagon?'

'That's right.' Kate stood up. 'How is he?'

The young man looked grave. 'He's alive,' he said. 'But as you know, he suffered a serious injury in the accident.' He reached out and took her hands. 'I'm afraid we've had to amputate his leg.'

Kate looked down at the man's hands, holding hers. 'I should jolly well hope so,' she said. 'There wasn't a lot of the limb left from what I could tell.'

The young man looked startled. 'Well, quite. But I have to assure you, your husband is quite comfortable, and we're expecting him to make a full recovery.'

Realisation dawned. 'Oh, but you've made a mistake. I'm not his wife!' Kate said, drawing her hands away.

'Oh!' The man coloured. 'Well, I'm sure your marital arrangements are nothing to do with me—'

Now it was Kate's turn to blush. 'You've got it wrong,' she said. 'I happened to be passing when the accident happened. I went to help.'

'Ah.' The doctor looked sheepish. 'Oh, Lord, I'm sorry. You get so used to breaking bad news to sobbing relatives, you don't really stop to think . . .' He paused, then said, 'You mean, you're the one who stopped the bleeding?' Kate nodded. 'That's rather impressive. How did you know what to do?'

Kate shrugged. 'The wound was too high inside the iliac to apply a tourniquet, so I cut off the blood supply by applying pressure to the descending aorta. Anyone with a basic knowledge of anatomy could do it.'

'Which you clearly have?'

'Of course.' Kate saw the young man's puzzled face and said, 'I'm sorry, I should have explained. I'm a medical student. Fourth year.'

'Are you indeed?'

There it was, that look of amusement and slight disbelief. Kate was used to it by now, but it still irritated her.

She waited for him to laugh. They usually did, sooner or later.

But this one didn't. 'Well, it's a lucky thing for our man that you happened to be passing by,' he said. 'You saved his life, without a doubt.' He held out his hand. 'I'm Rufus French. Senior houseman.'

'Katherine – Kate – Carlyle.'

'Pleased to meet you.' His handshake was steady and firm. He had an odd face, Kate thought. His features were too irregular to be called handsome, but his engaging smile and the warmth in his brown eyes made up for it. 'Where are you studying?'

'Hampstead Women's Hospital. But I'm hoping to transfer here.'

'Really?' His brows rose. 'I heard they were letting women in now. I daresay you'll be the first?'

'The first of many, I hope. Actually, I was on my way to see the Dean of the medical school when the accident happened.'

'You're not going to see him like that, I hope?'

Kate looked down at herself. Her skirt was stiff with dried blood. It was on her hands, too, caked between her fingers and blackening under her nails. How had she not noticed before?

'I don't suppose I'd make a very good impression, would I?' she said ruefully.

'Hardly. The Dean gets upset over a badly starched shirt, so heaven knows what he'd make of you.'

'Probably a good idea to go home and change first, then.'

'I would.'

At that moment the Casualty nurse stirred herself behind her desk and called out, 'Dr French?'

Rufus looked over his shoulder. 'I'd better go,' he said. 'But I daresay we'll meet again, Miss Carlyle.'

'I hope so, Dr French.'

As Kate turned to go, he called after her, 'Carlyle . . . You wouldn't be related to Sir Philip Carlyle, I suppose?'

Kate smiled. 'He's my father.'

'Ah.' Dr French nodded, his face suddenly serious. 'In that case, I wouldn't bother going home to change, Miss Carlyle. I daresay you'll have no trouble getting in to this medical school whatever you look like!'

'You did it, then?' her brother Leo said, over dinner that evening.

'Yes.'

Kate looked at their father across the dinner table, waiting for him to speak. But he remained implacably silent, his gaze fixed on his plate, cutting his meat with his usual neat, precise movements.

She longed for him to speak. She wanted him to be pleased for her, to welcome her to the Nightingale the way he had welcomed all her brothers.

'Well, I must say, it's jolly unfair of you,' Leo laughed. 'I was enjoying being the bright one for a change, but once you come along you'll put me straight back in the shade!'

'A bit of friendly competition never hurt anyone.'

'I still don't understand why you couldn't have stayed at the Women's Hospital?' her mother said. 'I thought you were happy there?'

'I was, when it was all that was available to me. But now I've been given the chance of finishing my studies at the Nightingale. That's what I've always wanted, to study there like Ollie, and Clive and Leo.'

'She wants to prove she's as good as a man,' Leo said.

Kate turned on him. 'And why shouldn't I? I'm the best student in my year.'

Leo's mouth twisted. 'Such modesty!'

'That isn't what I meant, and you know it.' Kate glared at her brother across the table. 'I want the chance to prove myself. Not just against other women students, but against men, too. Otherwise how will I ever know how good I could be?'

Her father cleared his throat, preparing to speak, and all eyes turned towards him. Sir Philip Carlyle was a powerful presence even in his own home. Kate could only imagine what kind of fear he struck into the young physicians working under him.

'You are aware, are you not, that you will only be permitted to treat women and children?'

'For now,' Kate said. 'But that may change in the future. If more men are called up—'

She saw her mother's pained expression and stopped talking. Kate's eldest brother Oliver had signed up in the Royal Army Medical Corps, and her middle brother Clive was a ship's surgeon. Kate knew her mother worried endlessly about them both.

'Not if I have anything to do with it!' her father replied angrily. 'There's been far too much change for my liking as it is. This war has a great deal to answer for!'

For once Kate managed to keep her mouth closed. Her father was right; if it hadn't been for the war then she would never have been allowed to study at the Nightingale. So many young men had enlisted that many of the leading medical schools had been forced to open their doors to women just to make up the numbers.

But it hurt to know that her own father had voted against the Nightingale taking on female students.

'I don't know,' her mother sighed. 'Don't you think it's rather – unseemly? I should hate to think of you becoming an embarrassment to your father or your brother?'

'How could I embarrass them?'

She stared at her mother until she looked away.

'I'm only thinking of you,' Marjorie Carlyle murmured. 'No man wants to marry a bluestocking.'

'Then perhaps I won't get married?'

'Kate!'

'Well, why should I? Ollie and Clive aren't married yet, but I don't see anyone fretting over their marital prospects. And what about Leo? If he said he wanted to devote his life to his medical career, you'd probably say what a wonderful, dedicated young man he was. But if I said the same, you'd worry that I would end my days as an old maid.'

'Leave me out of this,' Leo muttered.

'But, Kate, you must see—'

'Oh, leave her be, Marjorie,' her father snapped. 'She clearly needs to get this nonsense out of her system, and there'll be no talking to her otherwise. But I'm warning you now, if you persist with this plan of yours, you can expect no help from me, Kate.'

'No, Father.'

'I mean it. As far as I'm concerned, once you step into that hospital you are on your own!'

They finished their meal in tense silence. Her father ignored Kate and refused to meet her gaze. Her mother was clearly still agitated at the prospect of her only daughter not being married at the age of twenty-three. Even Leo's sense of humour seemed to have failed him. He kept his head down, desperately trying to avoid their father's simmering wrath.

Kate did not speak to her brother again until after dinner, once their father had retired to his study.

'You shouldn't provoke them, you know,' he said.

'I can't seem to help it, can I?' Kate sighed. 'Everything I do is wrong. I really thought Father would be proud at the idea of another Carlyle at the Nightingale.'

Leo looked sympathetic. He was two years older than Kate, and already a senior houseman. 'You should know by now, trying to win Father's approval is like asking for the moon!'

'It is for me. I don't understand it. I work so hard, I do well in my studies—'

'I know. You've already told us how clever you are,' Leo said dryly.

'But Father insists on treating this as some kind of silly fad that I need to get out of my system.'

'Before you come to your senses and get married?'

'Always assuming anyone will have a sour old blue-stocking like me.'

'Never!' Leo grinned. 'Believe me, Mother will have her work cut out trying to marry *you* off.'

'That's because all the men she chooses are idiots,' Kate dismissed.

'You're far too clever for any man. That's your trouble. Men like to be flattered and made to feel powerful. You make them feel small and insignificant.'

'Do I make you feel small and insignificant?' Kate teased.

'All the time.' Leo shook his head. 'Seriously, sis, are you sure you wouldn't rather stay at the Women's Hospital?'

'Leo!'

'No, hear me out. I'm thinking of you. You won't find it easy at the Nightingale.'

Kate pulled a face. 'You think it will be too taxing for my poor female brain?'

'Not at all. I daresay you'll run rings round the lot of them, as usual. But I'm warning you now, it isn't as easy you might think, being a Carlyle at the Nightingale.'

Kate's mouth twisted. 'It can't be harder than being a female medical student, surely?'

'I don't know about that. There's certainly a lot to live up to, being Sir Philip's offspring.'

'Yes, well, I'll never know about that, will I? Not since Father has made it clear he'll never acknowledge me,' Kate said bitterly. 'I'm surprised he hasn't ordered me to change my name!'

Leo regarded her, his grey eyes serious.

'You know, sometimes I think that might not be such a bad idea,' he said.

Chapter Ten

Sadie wasn't surprised when Eleanor Copeland pushed her way in behind her in the queue for the bathroom the following morning. She had heard the others talking in the probationers' common room the previous evening, and had a feeling it wouldn't be long before she was approached.

Neither of them gave any greeting. Sadie simply kept her back turned and waited for Eleanor to speak.

It didn't take her long. 'I want to ask you a favour,' she said. Sadie smiled to herself. How this must be hurting her!

'Oh, yes?' she said innocently. 'What's that?'

'I want to swap rooms with you.'

Sadie feigned surprise. 'Why?'

Eleanor lowered her voice. 'It's personal.'

Sadie looked back at Anna, standing alone further down the queue. The poor girl looked utterly forlorn. 'Why don't you want to share with Beck? I thought you two were good friends.'

'We were.' Eleanor was tight-lipped.

'Have you had a falling out?'

'You could say that. Look, will you do it or won't you?' Eleanor burst out impatiently.

Sadie stared back into the other girl's face, her jaw clenched so tight she could see the muscles bunching around her square chin. She must be desperate if she was asking for Sadie's help.

'And why should I do you any favours?' she replied.

'You've never done anything for me. You've never had a good word to say about me, as far as I know.'

Eleanor's cheeks reddened. 'That's not true.'

'Isn't it? What is it you and Trott call me? Common – that's it. You think I don't hear you whispering about me, laughing about my manners, saying I don't deserve to be here?'

Eleanor opened and closed her mouth, but no sound came out.

'But that ain't the reason I won't change rooms with you,' Sadie went on. 'I don't really care what you and your mates think of me, if I'm honest. No, the reason I ain't doing what you ask is because I reckon what you're doing is cruel and wrong.' She nodded towards Anna. 'Look at that kid. What's she ever done to you? All she wanted was to be your mate, and you're treating her like dirt.' She looked at Eleanor with contempt. 'If that's the way you treat your friends, then I'm glad I ain't one of them!'

Eleanor glared, and for a moment Sadie thought the other girl might try to hit her. Then she turned and fled in a blaze of fury.

Grace Duffield sidled up to Sadie at the basins. 'Well said,' she murmured. 'Trott's been on at me this morning too, trying to get me to change places with Copeland so they can share together. I said no.'

Sadie glanced at Miriam Trott, who was scowling at her from the other side of the bathroom. 'They're as bad as each other.'

'I daresay she and Copeland will be as thick as thieves now,' Grace said. 'Trott's always been jealous of her friendship with Beck. Poor Beck,' she sighed. 'She doesn't deserve any of this.'

Sadie glanced across at Anna, standing by herself at the far basin. She looked so bewildered and forlorn.

Sadie finished washing, and picked up her towel from the rack. As she passed Anna, she thought about saying something to her, then thought better of it. It was none of her business.

The girls had been given the weekend off after the examination results were announced. Most were taking advantage of their three days of freedom to go home to their families. Against her better judgement, Sadie decided to visit her mother, too.

All the way to Lily's lodging house, she kept up an argument with herself. This was a fool's errand. She must be going soft, there was no other explanation for it. Why else would she be doing this, letting herself get her hopes up when she knew it would all be for nothing?

But she had seen the other girls' excitement as they packed to go, how they couldn't wait to tell their families they had passed the PTS examination, and somehow Sadie had convinced herself that her own mother might give a damn that she had come top of the class.

She knew she was wrong, of course. Lily Sedgewick barely knew what day it was most of the time. But perhaps Sadie could drop in on Belle and tell her? She would be interested, even if Lily wasn't.

As Sadie stood on the narrow landing outside her mother's door, she heard a commotion coming from inside the room that stopped her in her tracks.

'Where is it?' she heard Jimmy Clyde roar. Sadie's heart sank like a stone in her chest. So he was back. She should have known the respite was too good to last.

She stood there, her hand on the doorknob, listening.

'It's safe, Jimmy. I promise.' Her mother's voice sounded shaky.

'Then why ain't you wearing it? I told you to wear it.'

'I – I was worried. It's so precious, I didn't want it to get lost . . .'

'Maybe I should give it to someone else,' Jimmy said. 'I can think of plenty of women who would be only too happy to wear it if you won't, you ungrateful mare!'

'I know that, Jimmy. I – I'll fetch it. Please, let go. You're hurting me . . .'

Sadie could stand no more. She threw open the door and walked in.

Jimmy had her mother pinned against the wall, one arm twisted in his powerful grasp. Her mother was squirming, trying desperately to free herself. When she saw Sadie she froze, panic and dismay in her eyes.

'Sadie!'

Jimmy glanced over his shoulder. 'Oh, it's you,' he said casually.

Sadie ignored him, looking at her mother. 'What's going on?'

'I—' Lily started to reply, but Jimmy cut in.

'It's private, between your mother and me.' He released Lily, who stepped away from him, massaging her arm. Even from across the room, Sadie could see the red welts encircling her thin wrist.

'Well?' Jimmy said. 'Ain't you going to fetch it?'

Lily Sedgewick scuttled out. Jimmy threw himself down at the kitchen table and poured himself a glass of beer from the stone jug on the table.

'And to what do we owe this honour?' he said.

Sadie stared back at him. Jimmy Clyde might have been a good-looking man once, tall and well-built with black hair and blue eyes. But now his muscular body was softened by fat, his eyes bloodshot from too much booze, and his hair hung in thin, greasy strands around his bloated face.

'I came to see my mother.'

His mouth twisted into an ugly sneer. 'And there was me, thinking you'd come to welcome your old dad back home.'

'If I'd known you were here I would have stayed well away. And you ain't my dad.'

'No, but I put clothes on your back and food on the table, which is more than your real father ever did – whoever he was!'

'Is that why my mother had to go out working down the docks every night?' Sadie said. 'As I recall it was her who put food on the table. You were too busy spending all your earnings at the pub.'

Jimmy fixed her with his cold blue eyes. 'You want to watch yourself,' he muttered. 'That mouth of yours could get you into trouble one of these days.'

Before Sadie could reply her mother returned.

'Everything all right?' Lily's face was bright and desperate-looking.

'Oh, yes. Your daughter was telling me what a waste of space I am.'

'I'm sure that's not right. You didn't mean it, did you, Sadie?' Sadie heard the plea in her voice.

'If I'm that bad, how come I treat your mum to expensive presents?' Jimmy said. He jerked his head at Lily. 'Go on, show her.'

Her mother glanced at Sadie, then at Jimmy. Sadie could sense her reluctance. 'Show me what?'

'Go on, show her!' Jimmy barked.

Her mother's smile was even more strained as she fished inside her blouse and drew out a small locket on the end of a thin chain.

'Jimmy gave this to me. Pretty, ain't it?' She spoke with a pride that didn't match the mute desperation in her eyes.

Sadie looked at the locket. 'Where did it come from?'

'She just told you, didn't she? Have you got cloth ears or what? I gave it to her.'

'It looks like gold.'

'That's right. Nothing but the best for my Lil.' Jimmy smiled, pleased with himself.

Sadie examined the locket more closely. It was engraved, leaves and flowers encircling what looked to be initials.'

'AR,' she read them aloud.

Her mother turned away, tucking it hastily back inside her blouse.

'Where did you get it?'

'The pawn shop, if you must know.'

'You sure it wasn't nicked?'

'Of course it wasn't!' Lily flashed a nervous glance sideways at Jimmy. 'You should know better than to say such things.'

But Jimmy seemed unconcerned, smirking as he helped himself to another glass of beer. 'Call it my reward for a job well done.'

As he lifted his glass, Sadie caught the glint of a gold signet ring on one fat finger. A dim memory stirred at the back of her mind.

'Ronson,' she said. 'Maurice Ronson.'

Jimmy's expression darkened. 'Eh?'

'That was the old man's name. The one who ran the post office. The one who got killed. It was in the newspaper. Maurice Ronson. He was a widower, seventy years old. His wife was called Annie.'

Her mother's face paled. 'Now, we'll have no talk about that in this house. We don't know anything about any robbery, do we, Jimmy?'

'No,' he said. 'No, we don't.' He stared moodily into the depths of his glass.

Sadie kept her eyes fixed on him. 'It wasn't enough for you to rob the post office, was it? You had to go upstairs and steal his valuables while he lay dying.'

'That's enough!' her mother snapped.

Sadie turned on her. 'You're just as bad, turning a blind eye. You really think he bought that locket for you? Why are you hiding it, in that case?' She shook her head. 'You know the truth as well as I do. Make you proud, does it, knowing you're wearing a stolen locket? I wouldn't be surprised if that old man died trying to protect it.'

'That's enough!' Jimmy brought his fist crashing down on the table. 'You'd better shut your mouth if you know what's good for you, young lady!'

Sadie looked at him. 'What's the matter? Touched a nerve, did I?'

'Stop it, Sadie!' her mother jumped in. 'Take no notice of her, Jimmy,' she pleaded. 'She's talking nonsense, you know she is.'

'That's right. You stick up for him as usual.' Sadie curled her lip in disgust. 'Why's he been in hiding all this time if he didn't have anything to do with it?'

'He hasn't been hiding,' Lily insisted stubbornly. 'He's been away on business.'

'What kind of business?'

'My bloody business!' Jimmy snapped. He pointed his finger in Sadie's face. 'And if you know what's good for you, you'll stop asking questions. You don't want Billy Willis to find out you're sticking your nose in where it's not wanted.'

Billy Willis . . . Sadie had grown up hearing that name, usually whispered in fear. Billy Willis ruled most of the East End, from Hackney Marsh back towards the city beyond Clerkenwell. Nothing illegal went on in Bethnal Green without Billy having a hand in it.

Jimmy worked for him, collecting rents and money from the girls he ran and the businesses he protected. For a while her mother had worked in one of Billy's brothels, which was how she and Jimmy had first met. Although the way Lily told it, anyone would think it had been some kind of fairy tale, with Jimmy as her Prince Charming.

'I ain't scared of Billy Willis,' Sadie said.

'You should be.' Jimmy looked her up and down insultingly. 'Billy's always had an eye for a pretty girl. Maybe I should introduce you to him, see what he makes of you.'

'Don't!' Lily spoke up. 'Leave her out of this, Jimmy, please.' She turned to Sadie. 'You've got to be careful,' she said. 'He's right, you don't want to get on the wrong side of the Willis family. Jimmy won't be able to protect you if you go making trouble.'

'Protect me?' Sadie laughed. 'Look at him, he's more frightened of Billy Willis than the rest of us put together!'

'I ain't afraid of no one!' Jimmy pulled himself up to his full height. 'Besides, me and Billy are mates.'

'Is that why he sent you away?' Sadie said.

'He was looking after me.' Jimmy looked defensive. 'Billy looks after his own.'

'Billy looks after himself,' Sadie said. 'You think he sent you into hiding for your own protection? It was for his own sake, not yours. He didn't want you around him, not after you got too heavy-handed at that post office. God knows what he must think of you, getting careless and killing someone. I expect the last thing Willis needs is Old Bill sniffing around. And you brought them straight to his door.' She looked at the ring on his finger. 'Does he know you've got that? I wouldn't go around flaunting it in front of him if I were you, or you'll be dead next.'

'You dunno what you're talking about. I told you, Billy looks after his mates.' But she noticed Jimmy twisting the ring off his finger and slipping it into his pocket as he said it.

'But you ain't his mate, are you? You're just a dogsbody, doing his dirty work for him.'

'Stop it!' Lily begged. 'Take no notice of her, Jimmy, she don't know what she's saying.'

'And you can shut up, an' all!' Jimmy snarled, turning on her. 'I don't need some old brass sticking up for me. I know where I stand with Billy. We're like brothers. I could have been part of the family, if I'd married one of his sisters. He gave me his blessing, you know that? But instead I had to go and saddle myself with an old whore!'

'I know, Jimmy.' Lily stared down at the bare boards, her hands twisting together.

Sadie stared at her. 'Are you really going to let him talk to you like that?'

'He's right,' Lily said humbly. 'I know he could have done a lot better for himself than me.'

'Too right I could!' Jimmy's pride had reasserted himself. He strutted around the room like a fat, greasy-haired peacock. 'I should never have let myself get tied down. I should have taken up with a decent woman. Someone like Billy's wife, Mollie. Now there's a proper lady. You'd never see her plying her trade down the docks, lifting up her skirts for sailors without even knowing their names.'

'How dare you—' Sadie started to say, but Lily silenced her.

'Leave it, Sadie,' she pleaded. 'He's right. He could have had any woman he wanted. I dunno why he ended up with me, truly I don't.'

Sadie stared at her mother, furious and frustrated. Stand up for yourself, she pleaded silently. Put him in his place for once. Perhaps if Lily spoke up, Sadie might be able to stop despising her . . .

A picture came into her mind of another Lily Sedgewick, a pretty, sparky young woman, singing with Belle as they painted up their faces. Sadie had been very young then, when she and her mother shared lodgings with Belle. The two women had brought her up together. There was little money in their household, but a lot of love and laughter.

How had Jimmy Clyde managed to turn that lively young woman into the sorry, downtrodden creature who stood before them now, wringing her hands?

'I'm sorry,' Sadie said. 'I can't stand to stay around and listen to this, even if you can.'

'Go on then,' Jimmy said. 'No one's asking you to stay.'

Sadie looked over at her mother. All her adoring attention was fixed on Jimmy, as usual. Her Jimmy, her man, returning like a conquering hero with his stolen spoils.

It was only when Sadie was walking away from the building minutes later that she realised she hadn't told her mother the good news about her examination.

She shrugged it off. Lily probably wouldn't be interested, anyway.

Chapter Eleven

Sir Philip Carlyle was true to his word about not helping his daughter. Kate was mortified when her father refused to allow her to join his firm. Instead she was placed under the direction of another of the hospital's consulting physicians, William Ormerod.

'Don't be so despondent, sis. Ormerod has an excellent reputation,' Leo tried to console her.

'That's not the point,' Kate said bitterly. 'Everyone in the hospital will know Father has turned me down, and they'll all wonder why. I bet he's done this on purpose to humiliate me, hoping I'll run off back to Hampstead.'

Leo pulled a wry face. 'Then he doesn't know you very well, does he?'

'No,' Kate said. 'No, he doesn't.'

In spite of her disappointment, she was determined to put on a brave face when she joined her fellow students for her first morning of hospital practice. The students were due to meet outside the Female Medical ward at nine o'clock for Dr Ormerod's morning round, but Kate was early as usual. She had hardly been able to sleep for excitement.

This was what she had always wanted. She had enjoyed her time at the Hampstead, but at the back of her mind there was always the nagging feeling that she could do more, if she was only given the chance. Now she had been given that chance, and she intended to make the most of it.

Pride swelled in her bosom as she made her way through

the warren of green-painted passageways. Her three brothers had walked these same corridors when they were medical students. Now it was her turn to make her mark on the Nightingale, to make her father proud . . .

She arrived outside Everett, the Female Medical ward, and peered in through the glass-paned double doors. The ward was bigger than those at the Hampstead, a cavernous, high-ceilinged space with tall windows running the length of one wall. Forty beds were arranged in two long rows, with the ward sister's desk in the middle. The scene was a hive of activity, with nurses bustling to and fro, pushing trolleys and putting up screens.

She looked up and down the empty corridor. It was five minutes to nine. At the Hampstead, the students would all be waiting at least ten minutes before the consultant was due, just in case he was early.

As the clock ticked towards nine, she heard footsteps and the sound of voices approaching. Kate took a moment to tidy herself, smoothing down her skirt and blouse and tucking loose strands of hair back into the knot at the nape of her neck, then turned back as two doctors came around the corner, their white coats flapping.

She recognised Rufus French's stocky figure immediately. With him was a taller, sandy-haired young man.

The other man saw her first. 'Well, well, who have we here? Looks like you owe me half a crown, French.' He smiled and held out his hand. 'You must be Miss Carlyle? I'm Charlie Latimer, senior houseman with Ormerod's firm.'

'Pleased to meet you,' Kate greeted him, then turned to Rufus. 'Hello again, Dr French.'

Rufus nodded tersely. He seemed very different from the jovial young man she had encountered in the Casualty Hall the previous week.

'French told me you'd met,' Charlie Latimer went on. 'An accident, wasn't it? Chap with his leg hanging off?'

Kate winced at his casual tone. 'How is the patient?' she asked Rufus.

'Surviving, just about. He's recovering on Blake ward.'

'I heard you saved his life,' Charlie Latimer said. 'French was most impressed. Weren't you, old boy?'

Kate looked at Rufus French's scowling face. He didn't look very impressed.

'It was a nasty accident, by all accounts,' Charlie went on. 'I'm surprised you managed to keep such a cool head, Miss Carlyle.'

'Because I'm a woman?' Kate turned on him. 'You expect me to have a fit of the vapours at the first sight of blood?'

'No! No, indeed not.' Charlie Latimer looked taken aback. 'I just meant – well, as I said, it was a nasty accident. I reckon it would have turned the strongest stomach. It would have turned mine,' he said.

His face coloured, and Kate felt sorry that she had snapped at him. She had to stop being so prickly, she decided.

Just then, the other students came round the corner. Half a dozen young men, talking amongst themselves. They stopped dead in their tracks when they saw Kate.

'You'll have to excuse them,' Charlie Latimer laughed. 'They're all utterly terrified of ladies, I'm afraid. Especially Randall here.' He slapped the back of a nervous-looking young man, so hard that his spectacles slipped down his nose. The boy pushed them back in place, his face scarlet.

'That's half a crown you owe us, French!' said another of the students, a ginger-haired boy with a freckled face. 'Pay up!'

'I'm afraid you've cost our friend French here rather dear,' Charlie Latimer explained to Kate. 'We all had a bet with him about whose firm you'd be with. He was adamant you'd be with your father.'

'So was I,' a handsome, dark-haired young man piped up. 'I assumed you Carlyles would stick together.'

Kate glanced away. 'My father didn't want to show any favouritism,' she said.

'God forbid,' Rufus murmured under his breath.

Kate looked at him sharply. 'I beg your pardon?'

'The drinks will be on French and Talbot in the Students' Union bar this evening!' Charlie Latimer said, before Rufus could reply.

Kate ignored him. 'What did you mean—' she started to ask Dr French, but the ginger-haired student cut her off.

'Watch out, here comes The Dragon!' he hissed.

The double doors opened and Sister Everett appeared, flanked by her staff nurses, with the students trailing at the rear. Kate noticed the keen looks and smiles that passed between them and the medical students. A few of them sent curious glances her way, too, as the ward sister arranged them in a line outside the door.

'I say, Sister, have you met our newest recruit, Miss Carlyle?' the ginger-haired boy spoke up.

The ward sister turned slowly. She was a squat, bulky woman in her forties. 'No, I have not.' She fixed her gaze on Kate, her eyes like tiny raisins lost in the doughy folds of her face.

'This is Miss Sutton,' the young man introduced her. 'Stay on the right side of her and she will make sure you don't go astray. Isn't that right, Sister?'

'I'm afraid it might be too late for you, Mr Wallace,' said Miss Sutton, eyes still fixed on Kate.

Kate dragged her own eyes away from the ward sister's unnerving scrutiny. 'Is Dr Ormerod always this late?' she whispered to Charlie Latimer.

'Oh, God, yes. This is nothing. Sometimes we can wait an hour for him. He has a huge number of private patients to see before he ever graces us with his presence.' He turned to the short, stocky student at his side. 'Go up to the end and keep watch for him, will you, Evans?'

'It's always me!' Evans grumbled as he stomped off.

'What's Dr Ormerod like?' Kate asked.

'The Great Man? He's quite a character.' Charlie turned to her. 'Not sure what he'll make of you, though.'

Kate frowned. 'I don't understand what you mean?'

'Well – you're a girl for a start!' Wallace said.

'Dr Ormerod disapproves of the decision to allow female medical students to study here,' Dr Latimer explained.

'He's not the only one,' a serious-looking boy at the back muttered.

'I don't think any of Ormerod's previous students was ever as pretty as you,' Charlie Latimer said. 'Apart from Talbot, of course!' He nodded towards the dark-haired young man.

The other students laughed. Kate looked round at them all, grinning and so pleased with themselves. 'I don't see what that has to do with anything,' she said, raising her voice over their laughter.

'Don't you?' Latimer looked her up and down.

Kate lowered her eyes. 'I just want to be treated the same as everyone else.'

'Yes, but you're not like everyone else, are you?' Wallace said. 'You're a girl.'

Kate swung round to face him. 'Well spotted. I'm glad your three years at medical school haven't been wasted!' she snapped.

'You heard her. She wants to be treated the same as everyone else.' Rufus French spoke up, silencing them all. 'We should all respect that, don't you think?'

He turned to Kate. 'You wanted to know what

Dr Ormerod is like?' he said. 'Well, let me tell you. The Great Man appreciates plain speaking. He can't abide mumblers and shufflers. If you have something to say, you should say it. Be bold.'

Kate looked around at the other students. They were all nodding in agreement.

'French—' Charlie Latimer started to speak, but Rufus ignored him.

'And he likes a good argument,' he went on. 'Make a good impression on him from the start and you won't have too much trouble.'

'He's coming!' Evans plodded back down the passageway towards them.

'Thank goodness for that!' Miss Sutton sighed with relief and turned away to give her nurses one final scrutiny.

'Thank you,' Kate whispered to Rufus.

'Don't mention it.'

A moment later, the Great Man appeared, barrelling down the passage towards them. He didn't seem that great at all to Kate. He was a small man, bespectacled, with a perfectly round, smooth bald head. His physical presence was not nearly as imposing as her father's, Kate decided.

Dr Ormerod's brows rose when he saw her. 'Well, gentlemen, I see we have a new member of our happy band this morning.' His voice was high-pitched, almost nervous.

Kate saw her cue, and went straight in, one hand stuck out.

'Good morning, sir. I'm Kate Carlyle.'

He ignored her outstretched hand. 'We all know who you are, young woman.' He turned to address the other students. 'Gentlemen, we are privileged to have the daughter of one of our consulting physicians with us. I'm sure you all feel, as I do, we are truly in the presence of greatness.'

Kate's smile wavered as she let her hand fall back to her side. She didn't like the way the other students all smirked at her.

'Right, let us begin. We are already late.' Dr Ormerod pushed open the double doors and marched through, leaving the rest of them to scurry after him.

They went around each of the consultant's patients in turn, followed by a retinue of nurses. As they reached each bed, Dr Ormerod would pause while one of his senior housemen presented the case, then he would turn to the students and ask their opinion.

The students all jostled each other, hoping to catch the Great Man's eye. For the first three patients, Kate found herself at the back, lost among the nurses. She could barely see past the wall of white coats in front of her. By the time they had reached the end of the ward, she had managed to elbow her way through to a position where she could at least see the patient, a pale middle-aged woman, who wore a lacy bed jacket and a lot of cheap scent.

Kate sniffed the air. The scent was overpowering and unpleasant. It had a curious, pungent undercurrent, like pine trees.

Dr Latimer read aloud from his notes. 'New patient admitted yesterday,' he quoted. 'Complaining of fever, which started with a chill, followed by pain and swelling, which migrates from joint to joint. Inflamed joints are painful to the touch. Temperature ranges around one hundred and two degrees, and the pulse is rapid and irregular.'

'Thank you, Latimer.' Dr Ormerod looked around at the students. 'What are we seeing here?'

'Um – scarlet fever?' Evans suggested cautiously.

Dr Ormerod fixed him with a beady stare. 'Do you think

we would have her lying here in the middle of the ward if she were suffering from an infectious disease? Good grief, man! Think before you speak!'

'Influenza?' someone else suggested, and was rewarded with another baleful glare from the Great Man.

Dr Ormerod sighed. 'Very well, what if I were to tell you the patient sweats freely, and that this sweat is acid and possessed of a sour and foul odour?' He looked around at them. 'Tongue is coated, appetite lost, bowels are constipated. Urine scanty and concentrated, and she has anaemia.'

Kate looked at the woman. She was looking quite dismayed:

'Acute arthritis,' Kate said.

A silence followed her words. Dr Ormerod's gaze skimmed briefly over her, then settled on the young men around her.

'And can anyone tell me the most common complication of acute arthritis?' he asked.

'Endocarditis,' someone said.

'Correct. Any others?'

'Periocarditis.'

'Meningitis.'

'Convulsions, chorea and nephritis.'

'Very good,' said Dr Ormerod. 'Although fortunately this case appears to be rather more straightforward.'

The woman's face relaxed. 'I'm glad to hear it,' she said. 'For a minute there I thought I was a goner for sure!'

Dr Ormerod turned back to his students. 'Treatment?' he said.

'Absolute rest and the application of heat to the affected joints,' said the serious-looking young man whose name was Gibson.

'And?' The students looked at each other. Dr Ormerod sighed impatiently. 'Come on, what else?'

Kate wiped her watering eyes. The woman's perfume was truly unpleasant, almost overpowering.

And then it came to her. The pungent pine aroma the woman was trying to disguise with her cheap scent was wintergreen.

'Salicylic acid,' she said.

Dr Ormerod glanced at her. 'Quite.'

'There is also the possibility of alkaline treatment,' Gibson put in.

'Indeed, Mr Gibson.' The Great Man bestowed a smile on him. 'Well done.'

They started to move away from the woman's bed. For a moment Kate hesitated, wondering if she should speak up. Then she remembered Dr French's advice.

'There's also vaccine treatment,' she said.

Dr Ormerod stopped and turned slowly to face her. 'I beg your pardon? Did you speak?'

Kate glanced around at the other students. They were all watching her, mouths gaping. Then she caught Rufus French's eye as he stood behind Dr Ormerod. He gave her a nod of encouragement.

'Vaccine treatment,' she repeated. 'It's—'

'I know what it is, thank you very much!' Dr Ormerod cut her off. 'However, the treatment is unproved.'

He likes a good argument. Kate cleared her throat.

'The treatment might be in its infancy, but it shows a great deal of promise, especially in long drawn out cases where the disease will not yield to ordinary measures—'

As she spoke, she could see the eyes of her fellow students widen. Even the nurses were looking at her in astonishment. But it was only when she caught Latimer shaking his head and Rufus trying hard not to laugh that she realised she had been taken in.

She stopped speaking abruptly, but the damage had already been done. She hardly dared look at Dr Ormerod.

'You know, Miss Carlyle, you remind me of your father,' the consultant said at last. 'He always likes to have the last word too!'

Several of the students tittered appreciatively at the joke.

'I – I'm sorry, sir,' Kate started to say, but Dr Ormerod held up his hand.

'No, no, Miss Carlyle, please don't apologise. It's quite clear you believe you have very little to learn from me. I should be honoured that you have even bothered to attend today, although I suppose you thought you might be able to teach me a thing or two?'

Kate cringed, but Dr Ormerod still had not finished with her. 'I daresay you considered yourself to be quite bright at the Women's Hospital,' he said. 'No doubt you young women were allowed to chatter like parakeets, all giving your opinion and expecting everyone else to listen to it. But let me tell you something, Miss Carlyle. Just because our medical school has made the woeful decision to admit female medical practitioners to the Nightingale, that does not mean you can march in here and take charge of everything. This is *my* firm. Here I am the physician and you are the student. And when I want an opinion from you, I will ask for it. Is that clear?'

'Yes, sir,' Kate whispered.

After that she kept silent and stayed at the back of the group for the rest of the round. But she could see the patients whispering with each other, all craning to get a look at her.

She forced herself to keep her chin up, determined to show the others she could take a joke with the best of them. But she couldn't bring herself to look at Rufus French.

At last the round ended. They headed to Male Medical

next, and Dr Ormerod announced loudly, 'This is where you leave us, Miss Carlyle. I'm afraid we will have to do without the benefit of your great wisdom.'

The other students sniggered. Kate forced herself not to look away, even though she could feel herself blushing. 'Yes, sir,' she said.

As Dr Ormerod led the way through the doors to Male Medical, Kate heard him saying, 'Thank God some doors are still closed to women. Eh, gentlemen?'

'That was a low trick you pulled, French. You should be thoroughly ashamed of yourself.'

Latimer faced him across the billiard table in the Students' Union recreation room. He had a cue in one hand, and a glass of brandy in the other.

Rufus laughed. 'You heard what she said. She wants to be treated the same as everyone else. You've never minded when we've done it to any of the other students.'

'This is different. You shouldn't do that sort of thing to a lady.'

'Since when have you been so chivalrous?' Rufus mocked. 'Could it be because she's a Carlyle?'

Latimer leant over to pot his shot. 'The poor girl looked utterly mortified,' he said.

'Then she'll have to develop a thicker skin, won't she?'

Charlie Latimer shook his head. 'You know, you really should think about what you're doing, French. Our Miss Carlyle would make a far better friend than she would an enemy. You should be cultivating her.'

'Is that what you're doing? Cultivating her?'

'I was only being polite and welcoming, dear boy.'

'Of course you were.' Rufus took his shot. The cue ball swerved past the red without hitting it.

'Foul shot, old boy.' Latimer put down his glass and

prepared to take his shot. 'Look, I'll admit, it doesn't hurt to have friends in high places.'

'And Miss Carlyle clearly does, or she wouldn't be here.'

Latimer smirked across the table at him. 'I know what this is about,' he said. 'You're still harping on about that business with Leo Carlyle, aren't you?'

'No.'

'Yes, you are.' Latimer sighed. 'Look, I told you. Let it go. So the old man took his son onto his firm instead of you. So what?'

'But it should have been my place,' Rufus burst out. 'I was recommended for it. I worked hard, I deserved it—'

Latimer shook his head pityingly. 'That's not the way the world works, is it, old boy? Not our world, anyway. It's not enough to win scholarships and be top of the class.'

'Obviously.' Rattled, Rufus took his next shot. It skidded past the cue ball and tumbled straight into the corner pocket.

'Oh, dear. Another foul shot. You're rather off your game tonight.' Latimer bent down, studying the formation on the table before taking his own shot. 'Look, if you want to get on, you have to know the right people. You think old Ormerod got his nice private practice in Harley Street by working hard and being an all round good egg?'

'Who says I want a private practice?'

'Who doesn't?' Latimer laughed. 'Are you seriously telling me you want to spend the rest of your life here, tending to people's aches and pains?'

'I rather thought that was the point of becoming a doctor?'

'Oh, it is. But there's a difference between the great unwashed that comes through these doors, and the wealthy patients who'll pay a fortune for your time and talents, don't you think?' He straightened up. 'Your shot. Try to make it a good one this time.'

Rufus whacked the ball with such force it ricocheted off the end cushion and rolled backwards, taking Latimer's cue ball with it.

'Look at that. You're too emotional, that's your trouble.' Latimer sighed. 'You need to start thinking with your head, old boy, and not that heart of yours. You might be the brightest student in our year, but you really are a duffer when it comes to the ways of the world. We're senior housemen, we need to start making our mark, impressing the right people.'

'Starting with Miss Carlyle, I suppose?'

'Why not?'

Latimer slapped him on the shoulder. 'You stick with your Uncle Charlie, old boy. You won't go far wrong.'

'No, thanks,' Rufus said.

'Then you're making a big mistake.' Latimer shook his head. 'Typical Rufus,' he said. 'Always having to do things the hard way. Must be that Spartan Northern upbringing of yours, eh?'

He neatly pocketed the final ball and straightened up. 'That's another half a crown you owe me.' He grinned, setting down his cue. 'At this rate you'll have to win another bursary just to pay me back!'

He sauntered off, hands in pockets, whistling to himself.

Rufus watched him go. Latimer would never understand, he thought. He'd had all the advantages life could offer. His father was a high court judge, he had gone to all the right schools, mixed in all the right circles.

And it wasn't just him. All the other students here were cut from the same cloth, their lives stretching ahead of them like a golden carpet.

But there had been no golden carpet for Rufus French. Latimer liked to tease him about his humble roots, but he didn't know the half of it. He didn't know how much Rufus' widowed mother had struggled, the sacrifices she had made for him and his three sisters. There had been no expensive private schools for Rufus, just the local grammar school in Leeds, and even that had been on a scholarship.

And he had been a scholarship boy ever since. No matter how hard he worked, how many examinations he passed or how many awards and prizes he was given, he never quite felt good enough.

He wasn't good enough for Sir Philip Carlyle, that was for sure.

Rufus couldn't help feeling bitter. He had so desperately wanted to join Sir Philip's firm, he deserved it. But the Appointments Committee had given the place to Leo instead. Lazy Leo, who was more charming than gifted.

It was the unfairness of it that kept Rufus awake at night and filled him with fury.

Latimer was right, he thought. All the hard work and ability in the world didn't matter a damn if you didn't have the right name, the right background, the right friends.

And now there was another Carlyle to contend with. Would Kate have been admitted to the Nightingale if she hadn't been a Carlyle? He doubted it. No, she had ridden in on her father's coat-tails. Rufus had no doubt she would be every bit as lazy and feckless as her wretched brother.

Chapter Twelve

Eleanor was going home to Hampshire for a few days before the probationers began work on the wards, and Anna couldn't have been more relieved.

Anna sat before the dressing-table mirror, trying to pin up her hair as she watched Eleanor sullenly packing her suitcase on the other side of the room. They had only been sharing for two weeks, but she could already hardly bear the strain of the silence. It was so hard to believe that only a few days before Eleanor had been her friend, and now she could hardly bear to look at her.

'It'll be nice for you to be able to spend more than a weekend with your family for once?' Anna broke the awkward silence. Eleanor did not reply. 'I'm going home myself this afternoon,' Anna tried again. 'But then, I'm lucky, aren't I? I can go home for a couple of hours. Not everyone is so fortunate. Poor Duffield has hardly been home at all since we started training.'

Eleanor grunted a non-committal response as she turned away to struggle with the latch on her suitcase.

'Would you like some help?' Anna stood up, but Eleanor waved her away.

'Leave it. I can manage.'

'But—'

'I said leave it!' Eleanor glared at her.

Anna sat down again with a sigh. Eleanor seemed to blame her for their situation, even though she had gone to Miss Westcombe herself and asked if she could be moved.

The Home Sister had sent her away with a brisk telling-off.

'I have far better things to do than sort out your silly squabbles,' she had told her. 'I know you girls. I'll go to all the trouble of sorting out a new room, only to find you've made up again and want to stay,' She must have seen Anna's look of distress because her face softened and she said, 'Look, whatever you've fallen out about, I'm sure it will all blow over soon.'

I doubt it, Anna thought, seeing Eleanor's set expression reflected in the mirror.

She set down her brush. 'Can't we just be friends?' she pleaded. 'It seems such a shame to be like this when we were so looking forward to sharing a room together. I can't help who my father is, any more than you can.'

Eleanor scowled at her. 'I'm proud of my father,' she snapped. She left the room, dragging her suitcase behind her.

'So am I,' Anna said. But the door had already slammed shut.

Anna could hardly wait to get home. She longed for the comfort of her family around her, to be surrounded by people she loved. She could help her father in the bakery for a couple of hours, spend time with Edward . . . Everything would be just as it used to be.

She was surprised to find the closed sign up in the bakery window. Anna peered in through the doorway, but all was in darkness.

Strange, she thought, Friday morning was generally a busy time at the bakery, with people coming to pick up their orders for the weekend.

She went around to the alleyway that ran along the back of the parade of shops and let herself in through the gate. The yard was empty, and Tom's bicycle was gone.

The back door was unlocked as usual. But the kitchen was empty.

'Papa?' she called out. 'Mother?'

She sniffed the air. There was no smell of baking, and the ovens were stone cold when she touched them.

'Papa?' She called out again, her apprehension growing.

'Anna?' She swung round to face the door as Liesel appeared. She looked wretched, her face ravaged by tears.

'Liesel? What are you doing home from school?'

'Oh, Anna!' Liesel launched herself into her sister's arms, sobbing.

'Liesel, what is it? What's happened?' Panic rose in Anna's chest. She disentangled herself from her sister's fierce embrace so she could look into her red-rimmed eyes. 'Tell me!'

Liesel wiped her face with her sleeve. 'Oh, Anna, they've taken Papa away!'

'They came first thing this morning,' Liesel told her. 'They said they had orders to round up any man with German nationality. They think they might be spies.'

'But that's nonsense! Papa's no spy. He loves this country.'

'That's what he tried to tell them, but they wouldn't listen.' Liesel sniffed back her tears. 'Oh, Anna, it was so horrible, the way they bundled him into the back of a motor car and took him away. They were pushing and pulling him about as if he was a – a criminal, or something. And he was being so brave, telling us not to worry . . .' She started sobbing again, and Anna handed her a handkerchief.

'Where's Mother?' she asked.

'She's gone down to the police station, to find out where they've taken him.'

'And Edward?'

Liesel blew her nose noisily. 'He didn't come in this morning.'

'Why not?'

'I don't know, do I?' Liesel snapped. 'Honestly, Anna, can't you stop thinking about your precious Edward for a minute and worry about Papa instead?'

'I am worried about him.'

'It doesn't seem like it. Anyway, Edward wasn't here, but Tom was. He tried to stop them taking Papa away, but the men pushed him about. I think they hurt him, actually. His nose was bleeding, so Mother sent him home.'

'What about the neighbours? Didn't they try to help?'

'Oh, them!' Liesel's mouth curled. 'They all came out to watch, but they did nothing. Not that I'm surprised,' she added.

'What do you mean?'

Before Liesel could reply, the back door opened and Edward came in, the cold air blowing in around him.

'Edward!' Anna ran to him. 'Where have you been?'

He didn't reply. 'Is it true what they're saying? That they've taken all the Germans away?' he asked, shrugging off his overcoat. His handsome face was tinged red from the cold.

Anna nodded. 'Liesel says they took Papa this morning. Mother's gone to look for him. Oh, Edward! I don't understand. Why are they doing this to us?'

'I don't know, sweetheart.' He pulled her into his arms. 'There's been a mistake, I'm sure,' he said softly, holding her close. 'But it'll be all right. Your mother will sort it out. She'll bring him home.'

But when Dorothy Beck returned to the bakery an hour later, she was alone. She looked grey-faced, drained and utterly exhausted.

Anna shot to her feet. 'Mother! What's happened? Where's Papa?'

'Anna.' Her mother smiled wanly at her. 'I'm glad you're here. I was going to send word to the hospital, as soon as I heard something.'

'What's going on, Mrs Beck?' Edward asked.

'Mr Beck has been taken to an internment camp.' Dorothy Beck's voice was steady, but her hands were shaking as she took off her hat.

'What's that?' Liesel asked.

'It's like a prison,' Anna told her. 'For people who haven't done anything wrong.'

'I'm sure it's not that bad.' Her mother sent her a warning look. 'And we mustn't despair, girls. Your father has been sent to a place in North London, near Alexandra Palace, so we'll be able to visit him often. It could have been worse – some of the men are being sent a long way away.'

'How long will they keep him for?' Edward asked.

'No one seems to know. It might be weeks, months . . .' She took a deep breath. 'We can only hope they'll come to their senses and let him come home soon.'

Anna rose to her feet. 'I'll make some tea.'

'I think your mother might need a brandy,' Edward said. He was right, Anna realised. Dorothy Beck had aged twenty years in just a few hours, her blue eyes drooping in the down-drawn lines of her face.

Edward fetched the brandy from the cupboard, and poured one for each of them. Anna sipped her drink with a grimace, while Liesel downed hers in one fiery gulp that left her coughing and gasping for breath.

'What are we going to do?' Anna said.

'I don't know.' Her mother was silent for a moment. 'I suppose we must do our best to carry on and keep the business running. It's what your father would want.'

'How can we?' Liesel said.

'Of course we can,' Anna said. 'We still have Edward. He

can take over the baking.' She saw the look that passed between Edward and her mother then. 'What is it?' she said.

'You haven't told her?' Dorothy said.

'I haven't had a chance, with everything else that's going on.'

Anna looked from one to the other. 'Told me what? What's going on?'

Edward turned to her. 'I've been called up,' he said. 'I had to go and register this morning. I leave for training next month.'

She took another sip of her brandy to steady herself. 'Where are they sending you?' she asked at last.

He lowered his gaze. 'Scotland.'

'Scotland!'

Beside her, Liesel started to wail. 'You see?' she said. 'We'll never be able to manage with Papa and Edward both gone!'

'We'll sort something out,' her mother assured her.

'I'll give up nursing and come home,' Anna said.

Dorothy shook her head. 'No, I won't hear of it. Your father wouldn't want that.'

'But Liesel's right. How will you cope by yourselves?'

'I don't know, but we'll have to try, won't we?' Her mother looked determined.

'I don't know why we don't just shut up shop,' Liesel said, dabbing her eyes with the handkerchief. 'After all, it's not as if we have any customers anymore!'

'Liesel!' Dorothy sent her a warning look.

'It's true,' Liesel persisted. 'Everyone wants to buy British bread these days. Even the Wheelers go to Freeman's on Roman Road now. Haven't you seen the sign on their door? "No business transacted with Germans". They think Papa will poison them!' she said bitterly.

Anna remembered Eleanor's apple cake, left untouched on her plate. 'I can't believe it. The Wheelers are our friends.'

'The same friends who stood and watched while Papa was taken away,' Liesel said.

The atmosphere in the bakery was so sombre, it was a relief to go out for a walk with Edward later. But even the cold afternoon air did nothing to clear the dazed jumble of thoughts in Anna's head.

Edward seemed just as distracted as they walked in silence through Victoria Park. Anna couldn't blame him. He was probably thinking about his own future, and what awaited him far away on the battlefields of France.

A sudden picture of stretchers being unloaded from the back of a string of ambulances filled her mind, and she pushed it away with a shudder.

As if he knew what she was thinking, Edward put his arm around her shoulders. 'It will be all right,' he said softly.

'But it won't, will it? Everything's changing, falling apart. And it's happening so fast. How long before it's all gone?'

'It won't.'

'How can you say that? A few months ago we were so happy. We could never have imagined that people would turn on us, that they would arrest Papa, that you would have to go away and fight.'

'Things will get better, I promise. They'll release your father, and everything will go back to the way it was.'

'And what about you? You'll still be gone.'

'I know.' Edward's handsome profile was sombre. 'But you won't lose me, I promise.'

How do I know that? Anna thought again about the

military wards. They had had to open another one this week, to cope with all the casualties sent back to England.

And that was only one hospital. How many more boats and ambulance trains were there, bringing wounded men home every day?

She turned her thoughts away determinedly. No, she could not allow herself to think like that, to torture herself with what might be. She owed it to Edward to have faith.

She forced herself to smile at him. 'I know,' she said. 'When this war is over, everything will go back to the way it was, and you'll come home safely and then we'll be married.'

'Why do we have to wait?'

Anna stared at him. 'What are you saying?'

'Why can't we do it now, before I leave for Scotland?' He turned to her, holding on to her hands. 'It would mean so much to me, to go away knowing you were my wife. That I had someone of my own, waiting for me.'

'But you know I'll wait for you.'

'It's not the same.' He lowered his gaze. 'You're all I've got,' he whispered. 'Growing up in the orphanage, I've never had a family of my own. I'd like to feel as if I belong somewhere. That someone might care if I didn't come home . . .'

'Don't!' Anna cut him off. 'Don't talk like that, Edward, please. Of course you'll come home.'

'I know.' The next moment he was smiling again, taking her gloved hands in his. 'So what do you say? Will you do it?'

'But there's so much to organise. The church, my dress . . .'

'Oh, we could do without all that, surely?'

Anna hesitated. She had dreamt of her wedding for so long, of walking down the aisle in a beautiful white gown.

But she was just being selfish. What did all that matter, as long as they were together?

But there was someone else who did matter, very much. 'What about Papa?' she said. 'It wouldn't be right without him there to give me away.'

'If I know your father, he'd be more worried about making sure you were looked after.' Edward squeezed her hands tighter, his strong fingers encircling hers. 'He'd want you to be happy, don't you think?'

'I suppose so. But it still doesn't seem right . . .' Friedrich had been looking forward to his daughter's wedding day almost as much as Anna had. He'd be so proud to walk her down the aisle. 'At least let me ask him,' she said.

Edward frowned. 'How can you ask him when he's locked up?'

'I'm sure we'll be allowed to visit him soon. I'll ask him then. Please, Edward?'

His frown deepened. 'You know he'll say yes,' he muttered.

'I know, but I'd still like to ask him.'

Her heart was beating fast in her chest. Edward was such a strong, determined man, she knew how quickly his attitude could harden if he didn't get his own way. She didn't think she could bear it if he sank into one of his cold, dark moods now, not when they had so little time left together.

But then Edward smiled again, and it was like the sun emerging from behind a storm cloud.

'Very well, if you must. I suppose I can wait another few days. After all, we'll have the rest of our lives together, won't we?'

Chapter Thirteen

Nearly a month after they had passed their examinations, the probationers were finally given their ward allocations. On Monday morning, Sadie reported to Everett, the Female Medical ward. She had been assigned there, with Miriam Trott and Grace Duffield, much to Miriam's dismay.

Sadie had heard her discussing it with Eleanor Copeland at breakfast in the hospital dining room that morning.

'It's going to be awful,' Miriam was saying fretfully to her friend. 'I wish we could have been assigned together.'

'Me too,' Eleanor had replied, shooting a sideways look towards Anna, who sat alone at the end of the table, her head down. 'It's bad enough that I'm stuck sharing a room with her, without having to work on the wards with her every day,' she said in a loud whisper. Sadie could have slapped her.

After breakfast, Sadie made her way up to the main hospital building with Grace. Miriam insisted on walking to the hospital with Eleanor, determined not to be parted from her a moment before she had to be.

'What do you think Miss Sutton will be like?' Grace chewed her lip. 'I've heard the other nurses call her The Dragon. Why do you think that is?'

'I don't know.' Sadie shrugged. 'But don't look so worried, I doubt she breathes fire!'

'I hope she's not too awful,' Grace said. 'I get even more clumsy when I'm nervous.'

Sadie smiled to herself. Was that possible? she wondered.

They had already had to go back to Lennox House once so Grace could change her uniform after she'd tipped a pot of jam into her lap at breakfast.

Miss Sutton was not on the ward when they arrived at seven o'clock. They walked into the middle of a very busy scene, with nurses hurrying to and fro, serving breakfast to the patients.

'What do we do?' Grace fretted, looking around nervously. 'Should we speak to someone, do you think?'

'I'll speak for us,' Miriam announced. She stepped forward as a staff nurse in a blue uniform approached them. 'Excuse me, we're—'

'Here, take this.' The staff nurse thrust a bedpan into Miriam hands. It was covered in a cloth, but Sadie could still smell it.

Miriam held it at arms' length. 'What shall I do with it?'

The nurse stared at her. 'Take it away and empty it, of course.' She turned to Grace and Sadie. 'And you two can lend a hand with the breakfasts. We're all behind this morning.'

Miriam cleared her throat. 'We're supposed to report to Miss Sutton.'

Once again the staff nurse looked at her. 'Sister doesn't come on duty until eight. And we've got a lot to do before then, so hurry up!'

For the next hour, Sadie was kept busy serving the patients their breakfast. She lost count of how many times she ran up and down the cavernous ward, handing out plates, then serving up cups of tea, then running up and down again to gather up the plates and get them back to the kitchen.

'Where's Duffield?' Sadie asked, when she saw Miriam up to her elbows in soapy water at the sink. 'I thought she was supposed to be helping me with the washing up?'

Miriam looked smug. 'She's in the sluice doing the bed-pans. Don't look at me like that, it was her idea. She said she'd only end up smashing all the plates if she tried to wash them up.'

At precisely eight o'clock, the double doors swung open and the ward sister Miss Sutton swept in. She had a queenly presence for such a short, squat woman. Her starched apron crackled like paper as she walked. She stood at the end of the ward, looking around, taking in everything with her tiny dark eyes.

Her gaze came to rest on Sadie and Miriam. 'You!' she beckoned them forward. 'You are the new probationers, I take it?' Her eyes narrowed, nearly disappearing into the fleshy folds of her face. 'I thought there were supposed to be three of you?'

At that moment there was an almighty clatter of metal from the sluice as a cascade of bedpans crashed to the ground.

Sadie cringed as the ward sister turned sharply towards the sound. 'I take it that is the third new arrival?' she said.

'Yes, Sister.'

'I will speak to her later,' Miss Sutton said ominously. 'And you.' She turned to Sadie. 'Make sure your sleeves are rolled down and your cuffs properly fastened when you address me in future.'

'Yes, Sister.'

At that moment the night sister arrived and Miss Sutton went over to her desk to take report from her. Sadie took her stiff white cuffs from her pocket and rolled down her sleeves. How could she have made such a foolish mistake on her first day? But she had been so busy putting the dishes away she hadn't stopped to think.

The senior staff nurse, a young woman called Gifford, smiled at her. 'Don't worry about it,' she said. 'We all forget sometimes. Just try not to do it too often. You don't want to end up in the ward book.'

'The ward book?'

'You see that ledger on her desk?' Gifford nodded towards it. 'Everything that happens on the ward has to be written down for Matron's inspection. Good and bad,' she said. 'And don't think you can get away with anything, because nothing gets past Sister.'

Sadie glanced at Miriam. Even she looked nervous.

Gifford grinned. 'You'll be all right. Just do everything you're told straight away. Follow all the instructions you're given, and do it all as quickly and as quietly as possible.'

There was another crash from the sluice.

Staff Nurse Gifford flinched. 'You had better warn your friend, too,' she said.

Miss Sutton finished taking report from the night sister, then went up and down the ward, talking to all the patients and making sure they were comfortable. She turned her attention to the nurses next, pointing out a crooked cap here and a hole in a stocking there.

In Sadie's case, it was a missing cuff stud. 'Really, Nurse, this is the second time I have had to talk to you about your uniform,' she said. 'If I have to mention it again then I will report you to Matron.'

'Yes, Sister.' Sadie eyed the ledger on the desk.

Miss Sutton gave them each a list of jobs that needed to be done. Once again, Sadie was kept busy, rushing up and down the ward, making beds and sorting dirty linen for the laundry, wiping bedside lockers and damp dusting bed frames.

At nine o'clock, it was time for the consultant's round. They all had to stop what they were doing and line up outside the ward with Miss Sutton and the staff nurses.

'Anyone would think we were expecting the King himself!' Grace whispered.

'The hospital consultants are like kings here,' Gifford said. 'Everything stops when they are on the ward.'

'But what if a patient needs something?' Sadie asked.

Gifford stared at her. 'You'd best make sure they don't,' she said. 'It's the same when Matron does her round. But the patients know what to expect, so they generally behave themselves.'

At that moment, a group of around a dozen young men in white coats came rushing round the corner. Sadie, Miriam and Grace immediately stood to attention, but Gifford said,

'It's only the students and the housemen. We don't have to bow and scrape to them – yet!' She looked at her watch. 'I do hope the Great Man's on time today. Sometimes he keeps us waiting so long everything's late and we have to rush about to get it all done. Then Sister gets in a furious mood about it.'

Some of the young men smiled at them, trying to catch their attention.

'Pretend you haven't noticed them,' Gifford advised. 'If Sister catches you flirting on the ward she will have something to say about it and you don't want that, do you?'

'No, Staff,' Miriam said, but Sadie noticed her keen eyes did not leave the young men's faces.

But there was one person in the group who wasn't looking at them. A serious-looking young woman with dark hair and colouring stood slightly apart from the other students, reading through the pile of notes she carried.

'Who's that girl with them?' Grace whispered.

'Oh, that's Miss Carlyle. She's just started here.'

'She's a medical student?' Miriam looked scandalised.

'I know.' Gifford's mouth tightened. 'Being a nurse isn't good enough for some people.'

Sadie stared at the young woman. The last time she had seen her, she was kneeling beside her, saving a man's life.

As if she knew she was being watched, Miss Carlyle suddenly looked up. She saw Sadie and gave a puzzled frown, as if trying to place her.

Before she had a chance to react Dr Ormerod arrived, and it was time to begin the round. As they all filed back on to the ward behind the Great Man, Sadie lagged behind deliberately, still fiddling with her cuff stud. The wretched thing would not fasten. She only hoped Miss Sutton would not notice.

They reached the first patient.

'Mrs Ada Dixon,' Dr Ormerod recited from her notes. 'Age forty-five, wife and mother of four children.'

'I dunno about children,' the woman butted in. 'My George is nearly twenty-five.' She looked around proudly at the faces assembled around her bed. She was a big, blowsy woman, her lacy bed jacket barely covering her ample curves. She reminded Sadie of Belle, with her scarlet-painted lips and bold, cockney manner.

'Patient has a history of dyspepsia over several months,' Dr Ormerod went on, ignoring her. 'She complains of pain in the middle of the epigastrium, which is aggravated by taking food.'

'I've barely been able to eat for a week,' Mrs Dixon said.

'More recently, there has been vomiting and haematemesis,' Dr Ormerod continued.

'Bringing up blood,' Mrs Dixon explained helpfully. 'Gave me quite a fright, it did.'

Dr Ormerod gave her a hard stare over his spectacles. He clearly wasn't used to being interrupted. 'Surgery was considered,' he said, 'but given that this is the patient's first incidence and tests have shown no suspicion of malignancy, nor any sign of perforation, it was decided that a medical treatment would be preferable.'

'I don't want anyone cutting me about,' the woman said. 'Besides, it'll be nice to put my feet up for a few weeks.' She settled back comfortably against the pillows.

A couple of the nurses giggled, but Miss Sutton sent them a silencing look.

Dr Ormerod turned to the students. 'Can anyone tell me the most important aspects of treating a gastric ulcer?'

Miss Carlyle's hand went up straight away. Dr Ormerod looked straight past her.

'Rest, the removal of all foci of infection, the provision of a bland, non-irritating diet and continuous neutralisation of the gastric contents,' a young man with bright red hair and a freckled face spoke up.

Dr Ormerod turned his piercing gaze on him. 'What kind of infection?'

The young man faltered. 'Er – blood-borne?'

'Yes? And what else?'

The student looked near to tears. Miss Carlyle stepped in, her voice clear and calm.

'Diseases of the mouth and teeth,' she said.

Dr Ormerod rolled his eyes. 'I was asking young Wallace here, but as usual Miss Carlyle has to have her say.' The other students chuckled appreciatively. Sadie saw a tinge of red in the young woman's cheeks.

'Very well, Miss Carlyle, since you're so determined to give us the benefit of your great knowledge.' Dr Ormerod paused, playing up to his audience. 'To which diseases are you referring?'

Miss Carlyle did not flinch. Holding her head high, she said, 'Pyorrhoea, periodontitis and apical abscess, and infection of the accessory nasal sinuses. Infected tonsils and chronic nasal catarrh—'

'Yes, yes, I think we've heard enough. We're all very impressed, I'm sure.' Dr Ormerod dismissed her with a wave of his hand. 'Now, as to the neutralisation of the gastric contents, can anyone suggest ways in which this could be achieved? Anyone except Miss Carlyle, that is,' he added, as she opened her mouth to speak.

Afterwards, they advanced slowly down the ward, stopping to consider several other patients. Some were missed because, as Gifford explained, they were under the care of another consultant or a specialist.

At each bed the routine was the same. One of the doctors would list the patient's symptoms, note her progress or otherwise, then Dr Ormerod would ask the students questions. Every time Miss Carlyle would put up her hand, and every time the consultant would ignore her.

Then, as they reached the far end of the ward, disaster struck. Sadie's cuff stud came loose and dropped to the ground. She watched helplessly as it rolled across the polished wooden floor towards Miss Sutton . . .

Miss Carlyle stepped forward, as if to get a better look at the patient, and trapped the stud under her foot, hiding it from the ward sister's sight.

As they moved on to the next patient, Miss Carlyle bent down, picked up the stud and slipped it into Sadie's hand.

'Yours, I think?' she muttered out of the side of her mouth.

'Thank you,' Sadie whispered back.

Miss Carlyle gave her a quick smile and then she was gone, following the other students as they crowded around the bed of a heart patient. Later, the probationers discussed Miss Carlyle as they prepared lunch in the kitchen.

'Did you hear the way Dr Ormerod spoke to her? He certainly put her in her place.' Miriam Trott looked pleased.

'I thought he was very unfair,' Sadie said. 'He didn't speak to the other students like that.'

'He's probably sick of her,' Miriam replied. 'She never stops trying to show off, have you noticed?'

Sadie looked at her. It takes one to know one, she thought.

When Sadie returned from her break at ten o'clock, Gifford was waiting for her.

'I need you to take a bedpan to Miss Maslow in room two,' she said.

'Room two, Staff?'

'One of the private rooms, up the corridor.' Gifford pointed the way. 'Hurry up about it, please. The poor woman's dying to go.'

'Yes, Staff.'

Sadie hurried straight off to the cupboard to collect a bedpan, remembering what she'd been told. She didn't want to end up in the ward book.

Miss Maslow was obviously not that desperate because she was asleep when Sadie crept into her room a moment later, carrying the bedpan carefully under a cloth.

'Miss Maslow?' she called out softly. 'You wanted a bedpan, love?'

The woman went on sleeping peacefully. Sadie tucked the pan under her arm and reached out to wake her. Her skin felt clammy and cold.

'Miss Maslow?' As Sadie touched her, the old woman's head suddenly lolled to one side, and Sadie found herself staring into a lifeless face the colour of marble.

Sadie let out a scream and sprang back, dropping the bedpan with a clatter. It rolled across the floor and landed at the feet of Miss Sutton as she flung open the door.

'Whatever is the matter, Nurse?' She looked down at the bedpan at her feet, then back at Sadie.

Sadie pointed to the woman in the bed. 'She – she's dead, Sister.'

'Of course she's dead. She died an hour ago.' Sister stooped and picked up the bedpan. 'She certainly won't be needing this. What were you thinking, girl? Who sent you here?'

Sadie glanced past the ward sister's shoulder to where Gifford and two of the other staff nurses were watching from the passageway, their hands over their mouths to muffle their laughter.

She straightened her shoulders. 'No one sent me, Sister.'

'So you just decided to wander around the private rooms with a bedpan, in case someone wanted one?' Miss Sutton thrust the pan back at her. 'Take this away, and don't let me catch you being so foolish again.'

'Yes, Sister.'

'And don't make such a fuss in future,' Miss Sutton called after her. 'I can assure you, this is not the last dead body you are going to see!'

'Sorry,' Gifford said, as Sadie emerged, still shaking, from the room. 'We like to play a trick on the new girls, help them settle in. Thanks for not giving us away,' she added.

Sadie was still shaking when she returned the bedpan to the cupboard.

'What was it like?' Grace was agog, wanting all the details. 'Did you touch it? Was it cold and stiff?'

'I don't want to talk about it.' Sadie shuddered. 'I feel sick thinking about it, if you want to know.'

By the time they came to serve lunch to the patients at midday, she had recovered from her shock enough to see the funny side. So when Gifford told her to prepare some peptonised milk for the gastric ulcer patient, she was able to say, 'I hope this one's alive?'

Ada Dixon was very much alive.

'And what's this when it's at home?' She stared down in

disgust at the cup Sadie had placed on the bed tray in front of her.

'Peptonised milk, Mrs Dixon. It's easy for you to digest.'

Ada Dixon peered dubiously into the contents, then looked away, her nose wrinkling. 'And if I drink all this I can have my proper dinner?'

Sadie shook her head. 'I'm afraid that's all you can have until your ulcer settles down. Solid food will only aggravate it.'

Mrs Dixon took a reluctant sip, then grimaced at the taste. 'Blimey, that's horrible! Can I at least have a nice cup of tea to help wash it down?'

'I'm sorry, Mrs Dixon. It's more than my job's worth.'

Mrs Dixon took another sip of her drink and pulled a face. 'And I thought it was going to be like a holiday, being in here. Some bleeding holiday! It's worse than a wet weekend in Clacton!'

'I know, it's awful, ain't it? They made us try it in training.' Sadie looked sympathetic. 'But once your ulcer improves, you can have a poached egg and some steamed fish.'

Mrs Dixon laughed. 'I never thought the day would come when I'd look forward to a bloody poached egg!'

Sadie laughed too. But the next minute Sister's voice rang out down the ward.

'Sedgewick!'

Sadie glanced over her shoulder at Miss Sutton, who was watching her keenly from the kitchen doorway.

'Oops, Sister's watching. I'd better look busy.' Sadie quickly made a show of tucking in Mrs Dixon's bedclothes. 'I've already been in her bad books twice today.'

'Why? What have you done?'

Sadie told her about the missing cuffs and Miss Maslow in room two. Ada Dixon roared with laughter. 'I ain't surprised you had a fit, love!'

'And it's my first day, too,' Sadie said ruefully.

'What a rotten trick to play. You should have reported them to Sister.'

Sadie shook her head. 'Oh, no, I'd never tell. It was only a bit of fun.'

Mrs Dixon looked thoughtful. 'You're a local girl, ain't you? You sound local. Where are you from, love?'

'I—' Just at that moment Gifford appeared.

'I've come to warn you, Sister's got her beady eye on you,' she whispered. 'Better not let her catch you chatting.'

Mrs Dixon gulped down the rest of her milk and handed the empty cup back to Sadie. 'There you are,' she said. 'You can tell that old bag I finished every drop.'

'Sister will be very pleased, I'm sure,' Sadie said primly. 'Now, is there anything else I can do for you?'

'No, ta, love. You've got enough to do without fussing over me.'

It was a long day. By the time Sadie came off duty at six o'clock her feet were sore, her back and head ached, and all she wanted to do was to go back to her room, lie down and sleep.

As she returned to Lennox House, Miss Westcombe came out of her office.

'Ah, Sedgewick, I've been waiting for you.' She took an envelope from her pocket. 'This came for you an hour ago.'

Sadie looked at her name written in Belle's childish scrawl on the envelope, and her heart sank. Not again!

'Thank you, Sister.' Sadie slipped the note into her pocket and headed for the stairs.

'The woman who brought it seemed very agitated,' Miss Westcombe called after her.

I'll bet she did.

In her room, Sadie put the note on the bedside table and pulled off her shoes, then fell back on the bed. Pain throbbed through her feet, and weariness consumed her. Would every day be this bad? she wondered. She thought if she closed her eyes she would sleep forever . . .

She opened one eye and there was the note, propped on the bedside table.

What was it this time? Drunk and disorderly? Fighting in the street? Or had her mother been caught with a sailor down by the docks again?

No, she thought. Not this time. She wasn't going to traipse all the way down to the police station and suffer that humiliation, not again. Whatever it was, she didn't want to know about it. Let someone else pick up the pieces for a change.

She took off her uniform. Her arms ached so much she could barely lift the heavy dress to hang it up in the wardrobe. She carefully folded up her apron, ready for the laundry.

But all the time the note sat in the corner of her vision, nagging away at her . . .

All right, she would read it. But that didn't mean she had to do anything about it. She would read it and then she would throw it away and forget all about it . . .

She picked up the envelope and tore it open.

Chapter Fourteen

'What's she doing here?' were her mother's first words when Sadie walked into the room. Lily Sedgewick sat on the bed with her back to the door, a flannel pressed to her cheek. As she turned, Sadie caught a glimpse of a swollen, blood-encrusted lip.

'She's your daughter, Lil,' Belle said. 'She's got a right to know what's going on.' She turned to Sadie. 'She was curled up on the floor when I came in. Right mess, she was.'

Lily dabbed the flannel against the puffy flesh of her cheekbone. 'It ain't as bad as it looks,' she muttered.

Sadie looked around. 'Where is he?'

'Long gone.' Belle looked grim. 'I doubt he'll be back for a while. Probably scared himself.'

'It was nothing,' Lily insisted. 'Just a misunderstanding, that's all.' She went to stand up, then hissed in pain and sat down again.

'What is it?' Sadie said.

'It's nothing.'

'Let me see.'

'Stop fussing – ow!' Lily cried out as she tried to shrug her daughter off.

'Let her have a look, mate,' Belle said.

Lily looked sullen as she reluctantly unbuttoned her blouse. Sadie caught a glimpse of a patchwork of blue-black bruises blossoming like a girdle against her white skin.

Belle let out a gasp behind her. 'Sweet Jesus! What's he done to you, girl?' she whispered.

Sadie bent and gently pressed the area around her mother's abdomen. She was so thin Sadie could almost count the ribs protruding through her skin.

She pressed again, and her mother jerked away, hissing with pain. 'Does that hurt?' Sadie asked.

'What do you think?' Lily said through gritted teeth.

'Is it bad?' Belle looked anxious.

'I reckon she's cracked a couple of ribs.' Sadie straightened up and faced her mother. 'You need to go to the hospital.'

'No. No hospitals.'

'But you need to see a doctor.'

'And have them ask me all kinds of questions?' Lily turned away to fasten her blouse. 'I don't want anyone knowing my business.'

'Someone should know what he's done.' Sadie looked at Belle. 'Talk some sense into her, please. Tell her she needs to go to hospital.'

Belle stared at Lily for a long time, and Sadie could see some unspoken message passing between them. When Belle turned back to her she already knew what the answer would be.

'Can't you do something, love? You're a nurse, ain't you? You could patch her up.'

Sadie looked at her mother. Lily's battered face was set in determination. 'Looks like I'll have to, don't it?'

'Don't do me any favours, will you?' Lily snapped.

'Shut up, Lil! Can't you see she's trying to help?' Belle turned back to Sadie. 'What do you need, love?'

'Something to strap up her chest – about ten inches wide, and this long.' Sadie held her hands wide apart. 'A torn up sheet will do. And a needle and thread.'

'I'll find something, love. Don't you worry.' Belle hurried off, glad to be useful. Sadie turned back to her mother.

'You really should go to the hospital,' she tried again. 'The broken ends of the bone might damage your lung . . .'

'I'll be all right,' Lily insisted. Sadie watched her mother lowering herself on to the bed, wincing at the movement. Sadie could only imagine the pain she was in, and yet she went on protecting Jimmy.

'What happened?' she said. Lily was silent. 'I suppose he was drunk again?'

'I already told you, it was a misunderstanding. He'd had a falling out with Billy Willis. He said Billy disrespected him.'

'So Jimmy came home and took it out on you?'

'He couldn't help it.'

'Listen to you, making excuses for him even now!' Sadie stared at her mother, her once pretty face ravaged and battered by endless beatings. 'When are you going to leave him?'

'You don't understand—'

'You love him, is that it?' Sadie's mouth curled in disgust. 'I don't know why I bother talking to you. You'll never do the right thing and walk out on him. You're too weak. Weak and pathetic.'

'That's enough!' Belle stood in the doorway, an old sheet in her hands. 'Leave her be, she's been through enough. You should be looking after her, not having a go.'

Sadie looked at Belle. Her eyes were hard, thin lips pressed tight together. 'Someone should talk some sense into her,' she insisted.

'Now ain't the time, all right?' Belle proffered the sheet. 'Tell me what you want done with this . . .'

Together, they helped Lily undress. Then Sadie carefully wound the dressing around her mother's painfully thin torso, afterwards stitching it into place. She could feel Belle behind her in the doorway, watching her every move.

133

'There,' she said, when Sadie had finished. 'That's better, ain't it? You'll be as right as rain now, Lily.'

'Until the next time,' Sadie muttered. Her gaze fell on the locket lying on the dressing table. 'I'm surprised he didn't take that with him.'

'It's mine.'

'But you never wear it, do you?'

Her mother looked away. 'He gave it to me,' she insisted stubbornly.

'And that makes it all right, does it? He gives you a stolen trinket, and that makes up for all the beatings?'

'Sadie!' Belle shot her a warning look.

She watched Belle putting Lily to bed, as gentle as a mother with her child, carefully tucking in the covers around her, brushing the hair from her face and murmuring endearments. No one who had seen Belle down at the docks, swearing at the sailors and brawling with the other girls, would ever have believed it.

'There, you rest now,' she said. 'I'll bring you in a nice cup of tea, how about that? Plenty of sugar, just the way you like it.'

Sadie followed her out of the bedroom, closing the door behind them.

'I dunno about tea. I reckon we need something stronger.' Belle fetched the gin bottle from the cupboard. She took out two cups, but Sadie shook her head.

'Not for me, thanks.'

'I forgot. You don't, do you?' Belle looked at her admiringly. 'You're a good girl, Sadie. Lucky you were here to patch your mum up.'

'I don't know about that. I've never had to bandage a broken rib before, I've only read about it in books.'

'You did a good job, from what I could tell.'

'I still think she should see a doctor.'

'You heard what she said.'

'Yes, but I don't understand it. Why would she want to protect Jimmy Clyde after what he did to her?'

'I daresay she has her reasons.' Belle filled her cup.

'Yes, I know. She loves him.' Sadie went to the window and looked out into the tiny cobbled yard. Below her, children played in the fading late-afternoon light.

Belle seemed to read her thoughts. 'Don't worry, he won't come back,' she said. 'Not tonight anyway.'

'How do you know that?'

'Because I know Jimmy Clyde. He'll lay low with some of his pals over the river, if he knows what's good for him.'

Sadie felt a black tide of hate rising inside her. She could imagine Jimmy, drinking and playing cards with his mates, his arms around another woman, while all the time her mother was suffering, too afraid to get help.

She half-turned away from the window. 'But if he does come back—'

'I'll be here waiting for him, don't you worry.' Belle gave a grim nod. 'And I'll give him more than a piece of my mind, I can tell you. I ain't afraid of that greasy little sod!'

Sadie looked at Belle's set, angry face. No one would dare take her on. She only wished her mother had her friend's fighting spirit.

In that moment she made up her mind. If Lily Sedgewick wouldn't stand up for herself, then Sadie would have to do it for her.

When she left her mother's lodgings later, instead of heading east towards Victoria Park and the Nightingale, Sadie turned down in the opposite direction, over the railway line to Seabright Street.

It was strange how she remembered the street so clearly, even though it had been many years since she'd returned. She had often played there as a kid, rattling over the cobbles in a cart made from old pram wheels and an orange crate they'd scrounged from Columbia Road market.

A middle-aged woman answered the door. Sadie recognised her, too, those narrowed eyes that missed nothing, mouth always pursed in disapproval.

'Yes?'

'Is Peter in?'

The woman folded her arms across her chest. 'Who wants to know?'

Before Sadie could reply, his voice came from inside. 'Who is it, Mum?'

'Some girl calling for you.'

Sadie heard footsteps coming down the stairs, then Peter Machin appeared. He looked even younger out of his policeman's uniform, tall and lanky, his hair cut short over clean ears.

He frowned when he saw her. 'Sadie?'

'All right, Peter?'

'Sadie Sedgewick.' His mother's eyes grew cold. 'It's you, is it?' She looked her up and down. 'You've changed, I must say. You're looking very smart.'

For a tart's daughter, Sadie finished for her silently and turned back to Peter. 'Can I have a word? In private, if you don't mind.' She glanced back at his mother.

Mrs Machin's chin lifted. 'If you've got anything to say, you can say it in front of me. We don't have secrets in this family.'

'Ain't you the lucky ones?' Sadie faced her boldly.

'Leave it, Ma.' Peter was already shrugging on his coat. 'We'll go outside,' he said to Sadie.

'Mind you don't stay too long,' his mother called out as Peter closed the door behind him. 'It's perishing out there.'

'No, Ma.' Sadie caught Peter's embarrassed expression

and tried not to smile. Peter Machin had always been a proper mummy's boy, doing as he was told.

They walked up to the corner of the street. 'What's this about?' he asked.

Sadie took a deep breath. 'Jimmy Clyde,' she said.

He stopped. 'What about him?'

'You're after him for that post office job?'

'Who told you?'

Sadie sighed impatiently. 'Are you or ain't you?'

He paused, then nodded. 'We can't get any evidence against him. He's got an alibi for that night.'

'But he did it.'

'We know that. Believe me, my inspector would like nothing more than to collar him for it. But three blokes have come forward to swear he was with them that night.'

'Then where did he get this?'

Sadie took the locket from her pocket and dangled it in front of Peter's eyes.

He stared at it, mesmerised. 'Where did you get it?'

'Where do you think?'

'Would you swear to that?'

'I'd swear to anything if it got him locked up.'

Peter looked back at the locket, then at her. 'You do realise this might mean trouble for you?' he said in a low voice. 'You're upsetting some dangerous people, Sadie. I wouldn't want any harm to come to you.'

Sadie lifted her chin. 'I ain't scared,' she said. 'I just want him locked up.'

Peter gave her an admiring look. 'In that case,' he said, 'I think we'd better go down to the station . . .'

Chapter Fifteen

'They've done what?' Kate stared at her brother.

'I'm sorry, Kate.' Leo looked apologetic. 'They'll be letting you know officially later on, but I thought I should warn you first.' He regarded her warily. 'I thought you'd be upset.'

'Upset?' Kate stared back at her brother. The word barely described the rage that burnt inside her. 'They can't do it,' she declared. 'I'm a medical student at this hospital. I should be afforded the same rights as every other student.'

'I'm afraid the SU committee don't agree,' Leo said. 'Look, it isn't that bad,' he tried to reason with her. 'You're only banned from the bar and the smoking room. You'll still be allowed to use the reading room and dining room.'

'For now,' Kate said. 'But how long before they decide to ban me from them, too?'

'They wouldn't.'

'Wouldn't they?' Kate shot back. She turned away from him, pacing across the courtyard in her agitation. The cold December wind swirled around her, shaking the bare branches of the plane trees. 'I know what they're doing,' she muttered. 'They want to squeeze me out, to make it as difficult for me as they can so I give up and leave.'

Leo sighed. 'You're being ridiculous.'

'Am I?' She turned on him. 'You haven't seen the way they look at me. I can't walk down a corridor without being jeered at.'

'I'm sure you're imagining it,' Leo said, but he couldn't meet her eyes.

'They go out of their way to exclude me, to make me feel uncomfortable,' Kate insisted. 'It's as if they resent me for being here. They're trying to drive me out, Leo.'

'They can't do that.'

'No, you're right. They can't. I won't let them. I've worked too hard to get here.' Kate shook her head. 'I'm going to fight this.'

Leo looked nervous. 'What are you going to do?'

'I don't know yet.' Kate paused, thinking. 'Perhaps I should talk to the chairman of the committee . . .'

'I wouldn't if I were you.'

'Why? Who is it?'

Leo lowered his gaze. 'Rufus French.'

'Ah.' Suddenly it all made sense to her.

'But it was the whole committee's decision,' Leo said quickly. 'You're not going to make a fuss, are you?' he pleaded.

'Why shouldn't I?'

'Because it would embarrass Father.' Leo tried to reason with her. 'Honestly, Kate, it isn't worth it. You're not missing much. You wouldn't want to go to the Students' Union bar anyway, would you? You don't even drink.'

'That's not the point,' Kate insisted. 'I'm a student at this hospital and I should be allowed to behave as every other student does.'

'But you don't have the same rights, do you? You're not allowed on the male wards.'

'And that's hardly fair, either! Don't you see, Leo? That's why this is so important to me. I've already had too many doors closed to me, I don't need another one.'

'Yes, but—'

The clock chimed noon. 'Look, I've got to go,' Kate cut him off. 'I'll be late for the post-mortem demonstration. I'll see you later.'

'Remember what I said, won't you?' Leo called after her. 'Please don't do anything to upset Father. You know what he's like . . .'

The theatre where the pathology demonstrations took place was a high-ceilinged room, pungent with the scent of antiseptic and formaldehyde. Tiered banks of seating were arranged in a semi-circle, looking down on a space in the middle where a solitary wooden operating table stood, illuminated by a beam of sunlight streaming down from the skylight overhead. On the operating table lay a figure, covered in a snowy white linen cloth.

As the students attended the daily post-mortem demonstrations on a voluntary basis, most of the time Kate was the only one who bothered to come. But this time there were three young men lounging on the back row together when she walked in. Kate could feel their gazes on her as she made her way down the steps to the front row, her notebook clutched tightly under her arm.

'There she goes. Old Werner's pet!' one of them muttered.

'Damned ghoulish, I call it. What kind of a girl wants a front row seat at a PM?'

'But she's a cold fish, isn't she?'

'I'd never allow my fiancée to see something like this. Not that she'd want to, of course. Far too much of a lady for that.'

Kate fought the urge to turn around and defend herself, concentrating instead on arranging her pencils in a neat line in front of her.

This was what Leo didn't understand, she thought. He had never had to live through the disapproving and obstructive behaviour she endured every day.

She opened her notebook at a fresh page just as the door below her opened and the Head of Pathology walked in, followed by his clerk, a tall, serious-looking young man.

Dr Werner was a cadaverous creature himself, thin-limbed, with sparse grey hair slicked back to reveal a fleshless face with deep-set eyes, a lipless mouth and stark cheekbones. Yet his bright blue eyes glinted merrily as he surveyed the near-empty benches before him.

'I see we have quite an audience today. Good afternoon, gentlemen.' Dr Werner greeted them formally, his voice gruff and with a foreign accent. 'And Miss Carlyle, of course.' He bowed his head in Kate's direction. He always sought her out, unlike most of the other lecturers, who wouldn't even look at her if they could help it.

For a moment the two men busied themselves, checking their instruments, putting on aprons and murmuring to each other. Then Dr Werner stood back while his clerk pulled away the cloth with an almost theatrical flourish, revealing the figure beneath. Kate leant forward, craning her neck to look.

She had seen a great many dead bodies, and this young man's ashen pallor did not alarm her. Indeed, she barely registered his face, all her attention fixed on the ugly blistering that covered his left thigh. The black bubbles looked obscene, some as large as her own hand. Kate took a deep breath to quell the nausea that rose in her throat.

'Twenty-year-old male, brought in by ambulance train from France yesterday morning.' Dr Werner looked up at them over his notes. 'Now, who would like to tell me the cause of death?'

He looked around at them all. Behind Kate, the young men had fallen silent.

'Well?' Dr Werner prompted them. 'Come, surely you do not need a post-mortem result to tell you? You can see the evidence with your own eyes.'

Kate raised her hand. 'Gas gangrene, sir,' she said.

'Indeed, gas gangrene. An almost uniformly fatal

suffusion of tissues with noxious gases from specific bacterial wound infections. You see the blistering here and here? This is typical of how the condition progresses. After forty-eight hours the edges of the wound begin to swell up and gape. The cut surface then takes on the curious balloon-like swelling you see before you here. This is because the tissues are being blown out with gas, and on pressing the fingers down on this swelling, a distinct crackling or bubbling sensation can be felt.' He looked up. 'Can you tell me, please, the type of bacteria that causes this?'

'Clostridia, sir,' a voice came from behind Kate.

'Indeed. Anaerobic bacteria found deep in soil. And we have trench warfare to thank for bringing this bacteria to the surface. Soldiers' clothing becomes saturated with mud, so that when they are wounded, pieces of bacteria-saturated uniform become lodged in the open tissue, leading to the condition you see before you. Clostridia works quickly and produces toxins which cause severe pain, gaseous swelling and myonecrosis.' Dr Werner picked up his scalpel. 'And now, we will perform the post-mortem . . .'

Kate watched the pathologist and his assistant at work, carefully removing the various organs, weighing and checking them and recording the results. She tried to concentrate as Werner pointed out the scarring, the fatty deposits, the state of the young man's liver and lungs, but couldn't stop her mind drifting back to her conversation with Leo.

It was so unfair. Her brother was right; she would probably quite willingly never set foot inside the students' bar or their wretched smoking room. But what he didn't understand was that there was a world of difference between choosing not to go and not being allowed.

It was all Rufus French's doing, of course. He had taken

against her for some reason she couldn't fathom. He never missed an opportunity to trip her up and make a fool of her. She could just imagine him turning the committee against her.

An hour later, the post-mortem was over. As the clerk set about stitching up the cadaver, Dr Werner said, 'Miss Carlyle? A word, if you please?'

He was at the sink in the corner, washing his hands under the tap. He looked over his shoulder at her. 'Do you have a moment?' he said.

'Of course, Doctor.' Kate gathered up her books.

Dr Werner turned off the tap and reached for a towel. Kate watched him carefully dry his hands.

At last he said, 'You are an excellent student, Miss Carlyle. Very dedicated.'

'Thank you, sir.'

'Now I wish to ask you something.' He nodded towards his clerk, the tall figure bent over the body he was stitching. 'Mr Chapman here has been called up, so now I find myself with a vacancy for a clerk in my department for three months. I wondered if you would be interested?'

'I—'

'I only ask because you seem very keen,' Dr Werner went on. 'I notice you come to my pathology demonstrations every day, not like the other students.'

Kate hesitated. She didn't want to admit that the only reason she came to the pathology demonstrations was because they were one of the few teaching resources in the hospital made available to her. She was excluded from watching any surgical demonstrations involving live male patients.

'But, of course, you do not have to answer me yet,' Dr Werner said. 'I am sure the vacancy will still be open for some time. Think about it, will you?'

'I will, Doctor. Thank you.'

Kate was heavy-hearted as she left the theatre. Dr Werner had been so kind to her. He was one of the few lecturers who had any time for her. He made no distinction because she was a young woman; indeed, he had told her that in the rest of Europe, women had been training and working as doctors for years.

But at the same time, she wondered if she had been his first choice. She doubted many of the other students would be keen to take the job. They all looked down their noses at Pathology, and at Dr Werner, because he was German. Kate wondered if he had asked her because she was an outsider, like himself.

As she was heading down the stairs towards the dining room, she spotted Rufus French sauntering along the corridor in her direction, Charlie Latimer at his side. Kate's first thought was to dart away down a side corridor to avoid him, but then she changed her mind. Why should she stay out of his way? She had done nothing wrong. It was he who should be embarrassed, not her.

She forced herself to walk towards him. 'Dr French?' she called out.

He didn't look surprised. Kate had the feeling he had seen her before she saw him.

'Miss Carlyle!' Charlie grinned. 'How—'

'May I have a word?' Kate cut across him, her gaze still fixed on Rufus French.

He folded his arms across his chest. 'What about?'

'I wanted to talk to you about the committee's decision to ban me from the Students' Union bar?'

'Oh, yes. Sorry about that.' He was smiling as he said it. Kate fought the urge to smack his smug face.

'I'm sure you are,' she said sweetly.

'Still, I'm sure it won't make much difference to you,' Rufus said. 'You don't strike me as the type to enjoy a drink.'

'I intend to appeal,' Kate said.

'Indeed?' Rufus' brows rose. 'Well, you'll be wasting your time. The vote was unanimous. No one wants you,' he added, as if she didn't quite understand.

Charlie Latimer laughed awkwardly. 'No need to be quite so blunt, old chap.'

'All the same, I will appeal,' Kate insisted.

'If you must.' Rufus shrugged. 'You can stamp your little foot all you like, but you can't have everything your own way.' His mouth twisted. 'Although I suppose you could always run off to your father and complain?'

'Now that's enough.' Charlie Latimer stepped in before Kate could reply. 'Really, French, you might remember your manners when you're speaking to a lady.'

Rufus sent him a sideways look. 'I leave the charm to you.'

He turned on his heel and walked off, leaving Charlie with Kate.

'Pay no attention to him,' Charlie said.

'I don't,' Kate replied coldly, her eyes still fixed on him as he disappeared around a corner.

'I did think it was a bad show by the committee,' Charlie went on. 'If I'd been there I would have voted against it.'

'Thank you.'

'French was wrong, you know,' Charlie said quietly. 'About no one wanting you. I for one am glad you're here.'

Kate glanced sideways at him. He stared back at her in a curiously intent way. She had noticed him looking at her like that before, as if there was some kind of secret message he wanted to convey. She knew she was supposed to understand, but it only confused her.

'He's right about one thing, though,' Charlie said. 'There's no point trying to win over the committee. French has them all firmly under his control.'

Kate looked back at him. 'Then I shall have to think of something else, won't I?' she said.

Chapter Sixteen

'You must be joking!'

Rufus glared at his friend. He should have known better than to expect any sympathy from Charlie Latimer. 'I am not. She went to see the Dean.'

Charlie roared with laughter. 'Good for her,' he said. 'I didn't think she'd take it lying down. Oh, don't look so sour, old man. You should never have tried to ban her in the first place.'

'The Students' Union committee voted,' Rufus insisted. 'We were unanimous.' He had tried to make the same point to the Dean, but the old man wouldn't listen. Rufus was still stinging from their encounter in his office. The Dean had humiliated him, treated him as if he were some foolish first-year student. 'Now she's come along and made him overturn our decision.'

'And why not?' Charlie shrugged. 'If you have friends in high places, why not use them?'

'That's the difference, isn't it? She has special privileges. Can you imagine what would happen if I went whining to the Dean every time things didn't go my way? He'd throw me out of his office!'

'That's because you're not pretty enough.' Charlie grinned at him.

'Or because my name isn't Carlyle,' Rufus said bitterly. 'Well, this isn't the end of it. It's unconstitutional, and I'm going to fight it.'

Charlie Latimer sighed. 'Must you? Personally, I'm rather

bored with the whole matter. And I'm sure the rest of the committee will agree with me. They only voted against because you got so hot under the collar about it.'

'That's not the point!'

'No, the point is you have a personal grudge against the girl and you're dragging everyone else in to it.' Charlie patted Rufus on the shoulder. 'You've already lost the battle, so why not just give in gracefully? You'll never win with all those big guns ranged against you, anyway.'

'All the more reason to go on fighting,' Rufus muttered.

Charlie gave him a pitying smile. 'Look, I understand,' he said. 'She's made a fool of you. But if you carry on like this you're going to make an even bigger fool of yourself. Why not just let the whole thing drop?'

Rufus stared back at his friend. Infuriating as it was, he knew it was right. He was waging a personal war that he could never win.

But that was what chafed so painfully at Rufus. He would never win against the likes of the Carlyles. They could do as they pleased, all doors automatically open to them. And when someone like Rufus French tried to close one, all they had to do was call on their big guns, as Charlie called them.

'It doesn't look as if I have much choice,' he muttered.

'That's the spirit!' Charlie looked relieved. 'I knew you'd see sense in the end, old boy. Tell you what, why don't I meet you in the bar later to celebrate the end of hostilities?' He smiled mischievously. 'Perhaps we could allow Miss Carlyle to buy us a drink, in the interests of equality?'

He was still chuckling to himself over his joke as he walked off. Rufus watched him go, still simmering with suppressed rage.

Kate Carlyle had humiliated him. Not just in front of the Dean, but before the rest of the committee, too. He was the one who had pushed hardest for her to be excluded from the SU bar. It had been his idea, and the others had fallen in with it, and now they would all know that she had beaten him.

Infuriatingly, Kate was the first person he saw when he walked through the double doors on to Everett ward ten minutes later. She was with one of his patients, a bronchiectasis case who had been brought in a week earlier. Staff Nurse Gifford was with her.

He watched Kate for a moment, dark head bent over her notes. Even the meticulous way she filled them in irked him.

He took a moment to compose himself, then went over to join her.

'Miss Carlyle.' He greeted her with a nod.

'Good morning, Dr French.' If she was crowing over her victory it didn't show in her cool expression.

'What are you doing?'

'I've prescribed an inhalation for this patient.'

Rufus snatched the notes from her. 'But I ordered postural drainage?'

'Yes, Doctor. But I checked the sputum levels for the past three days, and the measurement is just the same as it was before the treatment commenced. If you look at the figures—'

'Yes, yes, I see them.' Rufus wanted to argue with her, but there was nothing to say. He should have checked the sputum levels himself, then he would have known his treatment wasn't working. As it was, he found himself being corrected by a student. He could feel Staff Nurse Gifford's steady gaze on him.

'I see you've prescribed Iodoform and Eucalyptol?' he commented.

'That's right.'

'Not Creosote?'

'I thought I would try this first. Creosote is known to irritate—'

Rufus ignored her, crossing out her precise little notes to scrawl his own instructions. 'One part Carbolic Acid, three parts Creosote and six parts Spirit of Chloroform.' He thrust the notes to Nurse Gifford. 'And if that doesn't work, refer back to me.'

He waited for Kate to argue but she pressed her lips together and said nothing.

'In future you should consult me before you change my patients' treatment,' he said.

'I waited for you, but you were late.'

He looked up at her. Her face was a blank mask. 'Only ten minutes.'

'How was I to know how long you would be?'

'Nevertheless, you should have waited.'

'Of course, Doctor.' There was a distinct edge to her voice. 'In future I will certainly put your needs before those of the patient.'

As he walked away he noticed Staff Nurse Gifford's smile. In spite of his efforts, he sensed he hadn't come off best from the encounter.

He found the ward sister behind a screen at the end of the ward, bullying a young student nurse through her first application of leeches. The poor girl was doing her best, but she was obviously nervous. And Miss Sutton wasn't making it any easier, growling over her shoulder at her.

'No, no, hold it by its end. No, the other end . . . Now, direct the head . . . For heaven's sake, stop shaking, or you'll never get it in the right place!'

As Rufus pulled back the screen the girl looked up and promptly dropped the leech. The black, wriggling creature fell with a plop on to the starched white bed cover.

'Now look what you've done!' Miss Sutton sighed. 'Pick it up and put it back in the jar. And don't touch anything until I come back.'

Rufus gave the young student a sympathetic smile as he pulled the screen back around the bed. He knew her name was Sedgewick because he had heard Charlie Latimer mention her several times. Apparently his friend had been trying his luck with her, but she seemed to be one of the few girls who could resist his charms.

Rufus wasn't surprised Latimer was interested; she was extraordinarily pretty, with her green eyes and soft blonde curls escaping from beneath her cap.

'Do you have anything for me, Sister?' Rufus asked.

Miss Sutton looked up and down the ward. 'Not really, Doctor. Miss Carlyle has already seen most of the patients . . .' Then, just as Rufus' irritation began to rise, she added, 'But there is someone I thought you might want to see yourself. A new admission, sent up from Casualty half an hour ago. Paroxysmal auricular fibrillation, although she seems all right now.'

'It might have just settled down by itself. These things often do. Where is she?'

'Bed twelve.' Then, as Rufus turned away, Miss Sutton added, 'You might remember the patient, Doctor? Mrs Hopkins?'

Rufus looked back at her. 'Mrs Hopkins? Not the same one who—'

'Yes, Doctor.' Miss Sutton inclined her head. 'The very same.'

Rufus paused for a moment. 'I'll tell you what,' he said. 'Why don't we get Miss Carlyle to take a look at her?'

Sister frowned. 'Miss Carlyle?'

'Why not? I'd be fascinated to hear her opinion.'

Miss Sutton's tiny eyes narrowed. 'Very well,' she

said. 'I will tell the nurse to prepare Mrs Hopkins for examination.'

Kate Carlyle seemed very surprised to be summoned. Rufus watched her as she approached, smoothing down her white coat and tucking a stray lock of hair behind her ear.

'You wanted to see me, Doctor?'

'I thought you might like to see the new admission?'

'Me?'

'Why not? Mrs Hopkins is a most interesting case, and I'd like to know what you make of her. I think you could learn something.'

'Thank you, Doctor.' He saw Kate blush and felt a small stab of guilt. Then he remembered her visit to the Dean.

Mrs Hopkins was waiting for them behind the screen. She was in her forties, her plump face topped by a crown of brown curls. She looked at Kate, her face clouded with suspicion.

'Is this her? The student?'

'This is Miss Carlyle. As I explained, I'd like her to take a look at you.'

Mrs Hopkins looked at Kate dubiously. 'You didn't tell me she was a woman. Are you sure she knows what she's doing?'

Rufus saw Kate bristle out of the corner of his eye. 'Yes, indeed. Miss Carlyle is a very able student. And I've asked her to look at you specifically because you're such an interesting case.'

This appealed to Mrs Hopkins, as he knew it would. She smiled, pleased with herself.

'Well, in that case . . .' She preened herself, smoothing down the ruffled neckline of her nightdress. 'You carry on, love.'

Rufus turned to Kate. 'Proceed, Miss Carlyle.'

He was aware of Miss Sutton frowning at him from the other side of the bed as Kate Carlyle set about her examination. He had to admit she was very thorough, reading through the notes several times, taking the patient's pulse, checking her breathing and listening to her heart before reading through the notes again.

Finally she pulled her stethoscope from her ears. 'I can't find any sign of a fluttering heart now,' she declared.

'It's been on and off all day,' Mrs Hopkins said irritably.

'Any ideas, Miss Carlyle?' Rufus prompted her.

'I'm not sure . . .' Kate hesitated, looking thoughtful. 'I might have said thyrotoxicosis, but I've checked her throat and there's no sign of a goitre . . .' She consulted the notes again. 'I don't see any history of heart disease, either.' She looked up at Mrs Hopkins. 'Have you had any pain recently? Across here?' She laid her hand on her sternum.

'It's funny you should say that.' Mrs Hopkins nodded eagerly. 'I have been in a bit of pain over the past couple of hours.'

'What kind of pain?' Kate said. 'Was it very bad? Did it come and go? Any fainting or dizziness?'

'Well, yes. Now you come to mention it.'

'Which?'

'All of them.'

It was all Rufus could do not to burst out laughing. He glanced across at Sister Sutton, but her frown had only deepened.

Rufus read her expression and stifled a sigh. It was time to end the fun.

He gestured for Kate to follow him through the screens.

'Well?' he said. 'What do you think?'

Kate looked thoughtful. 'I'm still not sure,' she said. 'But I suspect it might be a case of early heart congestive failure.'

'Interesting.' Rufus nodded thoughtfully. 'And what would you suggest?'

'Complete rest, possibly followed by digitalis treatment later, if the symptoms persist.'

'You're certain of that? You would prescribe digitalis?'

'If the symptoms continued, yes.'

'What symptoms?'

Kate frowned uncertainly. 'You heard what she said—'

'Yes, I did.' Rufus paused, enjoying his moment. 'But what if I were to tell you, Miss Carlyle, that this patient also has a history of rheumatism, intestinal obstruction and suspected pleurisy? And this is just in the last six months. Lord only knows what she's had before that.'

'I – I don't understand.'

'Miss Carlyle, Irene Hopkins is suffering from nothing more than chronic hypochondria.'

He saw Kate's features tighten as realisation dawned. 'You mean—'

'There is no tachycardia or auricular fibrillation, paroxysmal or otherwise. Mrs Hopkins is quite well, in body at least. But she is a lonely, anxious woman, and she quite enjoys the attention of being in hospital. We usually just give her a night on the ward and a handful of sugar pills, and she's as right as rain. Until the next time, anyway.'

But Kate didn't seem to be listening to him. Two bright spots of colour lit up her cheekbones. 'And you didn't see fit to tell me this earlier?' she snapped.

'I rather hoped you'd have the common sense to work it out for yourself, since you're supposed to be a doctor,' Rufus said. 'Now, if you'll excuse me . . .'

He left her standing there, speechless, and went back inside the screens where Mrs Hopkins and Miss Sutton were waiting for him.

'Rather cruel of you, don't you think, Doctor?' Miss

Sutton murmured as he filled out the prescription for Mrs Hopkins' sugar pills.

'I don't see why. Dr Ormerod says that we should teach the new students wherever we can find the opportunity. And I think I've taught Miss Carlyle an important lesson today.'

Even if that lesson was not to try to get the better of him.

Chapter Seventeen

On a cold Saturday afternoon in early December, Anna went with her mother and Liesel to visit their father at the internment camp in Holloway.

As they joined the throng of other women and children waiting at the iron gateway to be searched by the guards, Liesel burst into tears.

'What an awful place. It's like a prison,' she sobbed.

'Pull yourself together,' Anna hissed. 'Papa won't want to see us upset.'

'I can't help it.' Liesel fumbled for her handkerchief. 'I'm not hard-hearted like you.'

'Anna's right,' their mother said. 'We must put on a brave face for your father. Here, take this.' She handed Liesel her own handkerchief. 'Now, the guards will want to search our bags. Just be quiet and let me speak for us. And, for heaven's sake, stop sniffing, Liesel!'

Beyond the gates lay the camp itself, an old army barracks consisting of rows of featureless single-storey blocks, surrounded by watch towers and high fences strung with barbed wire.

'Oh, God, I can't bear it!' Liesel's blue eyes filled with tears again.

'How do you think Papa feels?' Anna muttered.

Ahead of them the prisoners waited, at least two hundred men, watched over by more guards. Even as they stood to attention in their rows, they were craning their necks, looking out for their families.

Liesel spotted their father first.

'I can see Papa!' She waved. 'Papa! Over here! Oh, he looks so thin and ill!'

Anna barely recognised Friedrich as he hurried towards them, arms outstretched in greeting. He had lost so much weight, his shabby grey uniform hung from his shrunken frame. But she would have known his warm, loving smile anywhere.

'Remember to smile, girls,' her mother whispered as he came towards them.

'My family!' The next moment Friedrich was hugging them all fiercely to him. His rough serge uniform smelt of stale tobacco, even though Anna knew her father had never smoked. 'How wonderful to see you all.'

'We've missed you, Papa!' Liesel immediately burst into tears again, her face pressed into his chest.

'I've missed you too. Let me look at you all.' He released them, standing back to admire them. The brightness of his dark eyes lit up his thin, drawn face. 'How you've all grown!'

Anna managed a smile. 'It's only been a few weeks!'

'It feels like a lifetime.'

'We wanted to come and see you sooner,' Dorothy spoke up. 'But they wouldn't give us the right papers . . .'

'It doesn't matter. You're here now, and that's all I care about.' Friedrich put his arm around his wife's shoulders. 'Come, let's sit inside the recreation hut. It's warmer in there. Then I want to hear all your news.'

The recreation hut was crowded with other men and their families. It was thick with tobacco smoke and rank with the smell of sweat and stale cooking. But there was a welcoming fire burning in the stove, and friendly women serving tea, and they managed to find a quiet corner where they could hear themselves speak.

Friedrich sat in the middle, flanked by his family. Liesel

157

clung to him, still weeping. But Anna was determined to keep her emotions in check, for her father's sake. She sat quietly, smoothing out her leather gloves in her lap, almost too afraid to speak or even look at him in case she lost control.

'How are you keeping?' her mother asked. 'Are they treating you well?'

'Well enough. I cannot complain.' Friedrich managed a brave smile. 'Most of the guards are kind, and the other men are friendly. They keep us busy here, in the work-shops, but I do miss my kitchen.' He smiled wistfully.

'When are you coming home, Papa?' Liesel asked.

'Shush, Liesel!' Anna snapped, but Friedrich stroked his daughter's fair head and said,

'I wish I could tell you, my dear. No one has said any-thing about it, but I am sure they cannot keep me here for much longer.' He reached for Liesel's hand, holding it firmly in his own. 'You never know, perhaps I might be home in time to help with the Christmas orders. They must be starting to come in now?'

He looked around at them all, and they smiled bravely back but no one spoke. They had already agreed that they would try not to worry him unduly.

Dorothy changed the subject. 'I nearly forgot, I brought you something . . .' She rummaged in her bag and pulled out a cake wrapped in brown paper, some chocolate and a couple of oranges. 'The apple cake is not as good as the ones you make, but I did my best . . .'

'Oh, my dear! You have no idea how grateful I am.' Her father held the brown paper package in his hands as if it was the greatest treasure he had ever received. 'But how did you manage to bring them in?'

'Mother smuggled them!' Anna found her voice at last. 'You should have seen how she spoke to the guard.'

'She put on a posh voice and asked him if she looked like the kind of woman who would bring in contraband!' Liesel joined in.

'He was so embarrassed, he didn't dare ask her to empty her bag!' Anna said.

Friedrich raised his eyebrows. 'Is that so? I can scarcely believe it of you, my dear.'

His wife blushed. 'I learnt it from my mother. She used to speak to tradespeople like that all the time.'

Friedrich smiled. 'However you managed to smuggle it in, I thank you for it. I will share it with the other men later.' He wrapped up the cake and tucked it inside his jacket. 'But tell me, what is going on at the bakery? I have been thinking of you every day, wondering how you are managing.'

'We're doing our best.' Dorothy did not meet her husband's eye.

'It will be more difficult for you now with Christmas getting nearer,' Friedrich said. 'I was thinking perhaps you should look for someone to help Edward—'

'Edward has been called up,' Liesel blurted out.

'Liesel!' Anna shot her a warning look.

'What? Papa has a right to know what's going on.'

Friedrich turned to Anna. 'Edward is leaving? When?'

'In two weeks' time. Christmas Eve. But we'll have all the Christmas orders done by then, and I've asked if I can take two days' holiday from the hospital so I'll be able to help.'

'Anna, *Liebling*, I was not thinking about the shop!' He reached for her hand. 'You poor child, how worried you must be.'

Anna looked down at her father's fingers wrapped around hers. 'I try not to think about it,' she murmured.

'Edward wants to marry Anna before he goes.' Once again, Liesel spoke up.

159

Anna glared at her sister. Liesel stared back at her, the picture of injured innocence.

Her father sighed. 'Will someone please tell me what is going on?'

'Edward had the idea of getting married before he left for France,' Anna explained.

'I see. And what did you say?'

'I said I wanted to speak to you about it first.'

'And yet you have not mentioned it?'

Anna lowered her gaze. 'I – was waiting for the right moment.'

Her father sat back and regarded her thoughtfully. 'It seems like a sensible idea,' he said. 'I can understand why he would want to marry you before he goes . . .'

'But I want you to be there, Papa!' Anna broke in desperately. 'You won't be able to give me away.'

'I know, *Liebling*. But we mustn't stand in the way of your future happiness, if that is truly what you want?' Friedrich paused for a moment. 'You have my blessing,' he said at last.

'Thank you, Papa.' Anna searched her father's face, looking for clues to his real feelings. His smile gave nothing away.

For the next two hours they talked, played cards, and went for a stroll in the grounds. Her father pointed out the hut that had been given over to a small library, and the patch of ground where the prisoners grew vegetables. But Anna only saw the ugliness of it all, the dull grey stone blocks and the vicious tangle of barbed wire that surrounded them everywhere they walked. How could he bear it? she wondered.

All too soon, their time was up, and they had to leave. Of course Liesel made another fuss, weeping and clinging to him.

'I want you to come home!' she whimpered.

'I will come home soon, my love. I promise,' her father said. Anna heard the broken note in his voice and was furious with her sister.

He turned to her. 'Just think, you may be a married woman by the time I next see you!'

'Yes, Papa.'

Friedrich pulled her into his arms and kissed the top of her head. 'My strong girl. Look after them for me, won't you?'

'Yes, Papa. I promise.' And what about me? Anna wanted to say. Just because she didn't weep and wail like Liesel, it didn't mean her heart wasn't breaking, or that she didn't feel utterly lost.

'You're a good girl, *Liebling*.' Her father held her at arms' length and stared into her face. 'I know you will do the right thing,' he said, his brown gaze holding hers.

As he turned to say goodbye to his wife, Anna whispered to Liesel, 'Come on, we'll wait by the gate.'

'But I want to stay with Papa!' Liesel protested.

'For heaven's sake, do you always have to be so selfish?' Anna snapped. 'Let them have a few minutes together on their own.'

She looked over her shoulder at her parents, clinging to each other like young lovers. She pictured the day when she had to say goodbye to Edward, and turned determinedly away from the thought.

As they trudged back down the drive towards the gates, Liesel said, 'I hate that place. I don't think I ever want to come back.'

Anna stared at her, shocked. 'Don't you want to see Papa?'

'Of course I do, but I don't think I could bear it here again.'

'*You* can't bear it?' Anna turned on her, temper snapping. 'How do you think poor Papa feels, being locked up in this dreadful place every day? The only thing he has to look forward to is a visit from his family. We must keep coming, for his sake.'

Liesel pulled a face and fell into a sulk. They had reached the gate before she spoke again.

'I suppose you'll be getting married now you have Papa's blessing?'

'Perhaps.'

'Perhaps? Are you or aren't you?'

'I don't know.'

'Have you changed your mind?'

'It still doesn't seem right, Papa not being there.'

'But he said—'

'I know what he said.' She had also seen the look in his eyes when he'd said it. 'I just don't think I can do it.'

'So you'll tell Edward you can't marry him? I can't imagine he'll take kindly to that.'

'He'll understand.'

'Are you sure about that?'

'What's that supposed to mean?'

'Nothing.' Liesel's face was the picture of innocence. 'I just don't think Edward's the patient type, that's all.' A malicious smile crossed her face. 'If I were you I'd snap him up before some French mademoiselle does!'

'Liesel, stop teasing your sister!' her mother warned. 'Take no notice of her, Anna.'

'I don't,' Anna said. But her heart told a different story.

Chapter Eighteen

'Certainly not. I won't hear of it.'

Dr Ormerod threw Kate's letter back across the desk at her. His round face was pink with indignation.

'Even if I were in favour of such a proposal, I couldn't allow it,' he said. 'Hospital rules expressly forbid female doctors from treating male patients.'

'Yes, but surely under the circumstances—'

'It's against the rules, Miss Carlyle,' he insisted. 'There is nothing I can do about it. And frankly, even if I could, I wouldn't. As far as I'm concerned, the whole idea is absurd.'

Kate stared back at him across the desk. She could feel her anger rising, and fought to control it.

'What's absurd is that there is a shortage of doctors,' she said. 'Three more students left this week to join the Army Medical Reserve. We barely have enough medical staff to go around, and yet you refuse to allow a good doctor to work on the military ward, just because I'm a woman.'

Dr Ormerod's brows rose. 'A good doctor? You think rather a lot of yourself, Miss Carlyle, for someone with so little experience.'

And how can I gain experience, if I'm not allowed to treat patients? Kate pressed her lips together to hold back the comment.

'The military wards are overflowing, with more men arriving every day,' she persisted. 'We're closing the female wards and sending patients home to make room for them. Soon there will be no one left for me to treat!'

Dr Ormerod smiled over his steepled fingers. 'If you don't feel your – talents – are put to sufficient use here, you can always leave?'

Kate stared at him in frustration. That was all he wanted, all any of them wanted. How could they be so short-sighted? she wondered. It made no sense to her.

She shook her head. 'Oh, no, Dr Ormerod. I'm not going anywhere,' she said.

'Then I'm afraid you'll just have to put up with the situation. We've already changed enough rules to accommodate you.'

'Very well.' Kate got to her feet, picking up the letter he had thrown back at her. It had taken her ages to write it, and now she felt as if she had wasted her time. 'Thank you for seeing me, sir.'

As she walked away, Dr Ormerod said, 'I'm doing you a favour, you know.'

She turned slowly to look at him. 'Sir?'

'The military wards ... they're really no place for a woman. Some of the men are in a ghastly state.'

Kate lifted her chin. 'I know, sir,' she said. 'I attend the post-mortem demonstrations every day.'

Leo was waiting for her when Kate emerged into the wintry December sunshine. He fell into step with her as she walked back towards the main hospital building.

'Well?' he asked. 'How did it go?'

Kate shook her head. 'He barely listened to me.'

'I told you you'd be wasting your time, didn't I? Old Ormerod's not one for changing his mind, least of all on your account.' He gave her a sympathetic smile. 'Sorry, old girl. But you did try . . .'

'I'm not giving up,' Kate said.

Leo frowned. 'But you just said—'

'He'll change his mind,' she said confidently. 'He'll have to, sooner or later.'

'Kate—'

'He will,' she insisted. 'Look, two years ago no one ever imagined the Nightingale would allow women to study here. And yet I am. And now it's only a matter of time before we're allowed to treat male patients, too. I shall make sure of it.'

Leo looked at her admiringly. 'You're really not afraid of anything, are you? Father, Dr Ormerod, the Students' Union – you just take them all on.' He sighed. 'I wish I had your fighting spirit.'

'Be grateful you've never needed it.'

'Haven't I?'

Kate sent her brother a sidelong look. 'Since when have you had to fight for anything?'

'We all have our struggles, Kate,' Leo said quietly. He caught her eye and smiled. 'Oh, take no notice of me. I'm just tired, that's all.' He ran a hand over his eyes. 'I was up all last night on the military wards. Ormerod's right about one thing. It is pretty ghastly down there.'

'I'll never know, will I?' Kate murmured. 'I'm destined to be stuck on Female Medical with wretched Dr French.'

Leo frowned. 'I must say, I'm surprised,' he said. 'Everyone else seems to think very highly of him. I've never heard anyone say a bad word.'

'I know,' Kate said. She had seen for herself the effect he had on people. The nurses couldn't do enough for him, and neither could Miss Sutton, who never had a kind word for anyone else. All the patients adored him, too. Kate had never found it easy to deal with people, but Rufus had a kind of easiness around them that she couldn't help but envy. He reassured them, charmed them and even flirted with them sometimes, and always left them with a smile on their faces.

And unlike many of the other junior doctors, he was popular with the other students. He seemed to go out of his way to help them.

But not her.

He seemed to reserve all his contempt for her, and Kate didn't understand why.

'Perhaps you've done something to upset him?' Leo suggested.

'I can't think what.' All she had done was to try her best, but still Rufus did his utmost to make life difficult for her. He never seemed to miss a chance to belittle her, or to push her out.

Kate could only assume that, like so many others, he felt the doors of the Nightingale should have stayed closed to her.

Well, he would have to get used to her. As she had told Dr Ormerod, she was here to stay.

Typically, Rufus was the first person she met when she entered Everett. He was perched on the edge of Ada Dixon's bed. Kate could hear her raucous laughter ringing down the length of the ward.

'And the butcher said, "That's the first time anyone's ever called it that!"' Rufus delivered the punchline of his joke with a triumphant flourish.

Ada Dixon wiped the tears from her eyes with the hem of her bed jacket. 'Ooh, doctor, you're a caution!'

Kate went to pass them, but Rufus called out to her.

'Back again, Miss Carlyle? I thought you'd be on the military wards by now?'

Kate gritted her teeth into a smile. 'It seems my services are not needed, Dr French.'

His brows lifted. 'What's that? Don't tell me they didn't let you get your own way?' He shook his head. 'Good heavens, don't they know who you are?'

Kate ignored him, turning instead to Ada Dixon.

'Is there a problem with this patient?' she asked.

'Her name is Ada,' Rufus corrected her, 'and she's had a bad night.'

'Shocking,' Ada confirmed.

Kate picked up her chart. 'What seems to be the matter, *Mrs Dixon*?' she said, with a sideways glance at Rufus.

'Oh, don't worry about it, ducks. The doctor's sorted me out.' Ada Dixon beamed at him. 'I'm right as rain now.'

Kate consulted her notes. 'It says here you've been having some pain?'

'I'm afraid Ada has been rather a naughty girl.' Rufus sent her a reproachful look. 'Do you want to tell Miss Carlyle or shall I?'

Mrs Dixon looked shame-faced. 'I didn't think it would do any harm,' she said.

'Her sons have been smuggling in chocolate for her,' Dr French explained to Kate.

'And treacle toffee,' Mrs Dixon said. 'I'm very partial to a bit of treacle toffee.'

'Ada's been enjoying midnight feasts.' Dr French shook his head.

'I couldn't help it. I got so fed up with all that horrible milk and nothing else.'

'At any rate, I've confiscated all the offending items, given her a morphia shot for the pain, and Ada has promised to be a good girl in future. Isn't that right, my dear?'

'If you say so.' She sent him a coquettish look from under her lashes.

Kate stared from one to the other. They both seemed to think it was a big joke. 'That was a very foolish thing to do,' she said sternly.

'I know,' Rufus said. 'I've already told her that.'

Kate ignored him. 'You could have perforated your

ulcer,' she told Ada. 'Then we would have had no choice but to operate.'

Ada's smile faded. 'All right, you don't have to go on about it!'

Kate put down the notes. 'I think I should take a look at you.'

'There's no need,' said Rufus. 'I've already examined her.'

'But there might be something you've missed . . .'

'I think I'm competent to carry out an examination.' Rufus was smiling when he said it, but a muscle pulsed in his jaw.

For a moment they stared at each other. Kate was aware that the rest of the ward seemed to have fallen strangely silent, all eyes turned in their direction.

It was Ada Dixon who broke the tension between them.

'No offence, love, but I reckon the doctor knows what he's doing. He is qualified, after all.'

'Well said, Ada,' Dr French murmured, his stony gaze still fixed on Kate. The next moment he had turned away and was smiling again. 'Now, remember what I said. No more treacle toffee!'

Ada looked coy. 'I'll remember, Doctor.'

Kate followed him down the ward. 'May I speak to you?' she called out.

He turned back to her. 'Yes?'

His look of indifference infuriated Kate, pushing her to the limits of her self-control.

'I'd appreciate it if you didn't contradict me in front of the patients,' she said.

Rufus French straightened up, anger flaring in his eyes. 'I beg your pardon?' he said slowly. 'Are you telling me I'm not to question you?'

'Well, no, of course not, but—'

'I'm glad to hear it,' he cut her off abruptly. 'Because, may I remind you, *Miss* Carlyle, I am the senior doctor here? And I am not about to take orders from a medical student. No matter who they are!'

'I'm not giving—' Kate started to say, but he was already walking away from her, striding down the ward. As she stared after him, she was suddenly aware that once again the nurses had all paused in their work to listen and to watch. Even the patients had fallen silent. At the far end of the ward she could see Miss Sutton monitoring the scene from the doorway to the private rooms, a forbidding expression on her face.

Fortunately, Kate didn't have to meet Rufus French again for the rest of the morning. Monaghan, the other Female Medical ward, was due to be given over to military patients, and Kate had the job of helping to decide which of the patients needed to be moved to another ward, and which were well enough to be discharged.

Her last patient on the ward was another gastric ulcer.

'She was only admitted yesterday,' Staff Nurse Hanley, the acting ward sister, said. 'She should really have gone to Everett, but they didn't have a bed. I've already put her on the list to be moved . . .'

Kate recognised Irene Hopkins the minute she pulled aside the screens. She was sitting up in bed in a freshly laundered nightgown, looking pleased with herself.

But her face fell when she saw Kate.

'Where's the real doctor?' she demanded, looking past Kate's shoulder. 'Isn't he here?'

'I'm afraid you're stuck with me, Mrs Hopkins.' Kate spoke through gritted teeth. 'Now, what's this about abdominal pains?'

'Ooh, my belly's playing me up something shocking.' Mrs Hopkins remembered a little late in the day that she needed to look ill, and wrapped her arms around her abdomen. 'Awful, it is.'

'I see. Have you been sick?'

'Oh, yes. Terribly.'

'Any blood?'

'Yes. Yes.' Mrs Hopkins nodded vigorously.

'Hmm. We'd better have a look at you, then.'

Kate performed a cursory examination, having already made up her mind. She could almost hear Rufus French's mocking laughter.

'Arrange for her to be discharged,' she instructed Nurse Hanley.

'But – but—' Mrs Hopkins gasped. 'My stomach pains!'

'Your respiration, pulse rate and temperature are all perfectly normal,' Kate said.

Nurse Hanley looked anxious. 'Are you quite sure? She only came in yesterday. Perhaps we should keep her in, just for a couple of days?

'There's no need,' Kate said. 'This woman is quite well.'

'But I've been bringing up blood!' Mrs Hopkins protested.

'What colour is it?'

Mrs Hopkins looked blankly at her. 'Eh?'

'The blood. What colour is it?'

Mrs Hopkins eyed her suspiciously, sensing a trick. 'Red, what else?'

'There, you see?' Kate turned to Nurse Hanley. 'Blood from a gastric ulcer would be mixed with gastric fluids, giving it a darker colour.'

Mrs Hopkins looked affronted. 'Are you calling me a liar?'

'Yes, Mrs Hopkins, I am,' Kate said.

Nurse Hanley cleared her throat. 'Miss Carlyle, I really think it would be safer to get a second opinion.'

'We don't need a second opinion,' Kate cut in. 'I know a gastric ulcer when I see one. And I know a malingerer when I see one, too.'

'Well, of all the – I've never been so insulted in my life!' Mrs Hopkins gaped at her. 'And me an invalid.'

'Mrs Hopkins, you're as fit and well as I am.' Kate turned to Nurse Hanley. 'Please make arrangements to have this patient discharged.'

Nurse Hanley did not move. She was a big woman, as tall and broad as a man, and she kept her large feet firmly planted. 'I'm really not sure about this, Miss Carlyle,' she said quietly. 'Perhaps it might be better if Dr Ormerod or Dr French took a look?'

The sound of Dr French's name sent a fresh wave of rage through Kate. He would have a field day if she called him in to give a second opinion on Mrs Hopkins.

'Nurse Hanley, I am giving you an order,' she snapped. 'We are stretched to capacity as it is, with military patients coming in every day and not enough doctors and nurses to look after them. The last thing we need is to waste our time nursing someone who doesn't need our care.' Kate glared at Mrs Hopkins. 'You should be ashamed of yourself, taking up a bed that could be used by a wounded soldier!'

She walked away, still simmering.

Chapter Nineteen

Dear Mother,

I hope this letter finds you well. How is the Christmas Fundraising Drive going? I'm sure you and the committee have managed to make up lots of boxes to send out to our boys. I enclose some socks I've just finished knitting. Sorry they took such a long time, but the first pair I did was full of holes, so I doubt' they would have kept anyone warm! I also enclose some chocolate. I hope it will make a more cheerful Christmas for our brave boys.

Speaking of which, have you heard from Harry recently? I've written to him three times in the past month and I have yet to get a letter back from him. I know he was never the most dedicated of correspondents. Do you remember how you used to have to go on at him to write his thank you letters at Christmas? When he does write to you, please tell him to spare a thought for his poor sister. I do so long to hear from him.

You'll be pleased to learn I've finally been assigned to a military ward! Yesterday we spent the day moving the female medical patients out of Monaghan ward, and getting it ready for the soldiers to arrive. We had to take down all the beds, scrub the ward from top to bottom, clean the windows and polish the floors, then make up the beds again. We've had to line extra beds down the corridor that leads to the private rooms, as we're expecting so many casualties. Sister says we won't know what kind of injuries the men have until they arrive, so we've had to put in several fracture beds just in case.

She warned us the soldiers would be in a terrible state. I wasn't surprised, after what Father told us about the monstrous things the Huns have been doing to the poor people of Belgium. From what Sister said, it sounds as if Mr Bottomley was right about the special bullets they use, that tear the flesh and don't leave a clean wound like our guns. I daresay I shall find out soon enough. A few of the other girls looked rather nervous at the prospect of what was to come, but I don't mind. I'm very proud to be able to do something for the war effort at last. This is what I trained for, and I can't wait to get started.

On the other side of the room, Anna stirred in her sleep. Eleanor shielded the lamp with her hand and stayed very still, hoping the other girl wouldn't wake up. Outside the thin curtains, she could hear the world stirring into life in the darkness, the sound of footsteps on gravel, the voices of weary porters and delivery men. It must be nearly time to get up, she thought.

Anna turned over, pulling the covers close around her shoulders. Eleanor waited until she could hear the slow rhythmic breathing of sleep, then continued with her letter writing.

The only infuriating thing is that Beck is going to be on the ward, too. Personally, I think it's wrong that the daughter of a German should be allowed to nurse our boys, but Sister says we need all the help we can get. Working with her is bad enough, but it's intolerable that I have to go on sharing a room with her. I keep asking if I can move, but Sedgewick still refuses to change places with me, and the Home Sister says there's no space anywhere else.

Eleanor paused before continuing, her pen poised, looking across at Anna's slight, sleeping form.

I've taken to ignoring her, as Father said I should. She still tries to talk to me, but I simply cut her dead. The only time I speak to her is when we're on the ward, because I know Sister would not approve if I ignored her. She takes a dim view of 'silly spats', as she calls them. As if there is anything silly about this!

'Six o'clock, Nurses. Time to get up.'

Miss Westcombe's voice rang out from downstairs, followed by the sound of her stout shoes on the stairs.

'Come along now, girls. You'll be wanted on the wards in an hour.'

Anna rose sleepily from her bed, swinging her feet to the floor, still bleary-eyed.

'Good morning,' she mumbled, pushing the hair from her eyes.

Eleanor turned her face away to stare at the wall. She heard Anna sigh, then her slippered footsteps padded across the floor and the door closed behind her.

Eleanor slid her unfinished letter into the drawer of her bedside cupboard. It was so tiresome of Anna to continue trying to speak to her when she had made it obvious that she did not wish to talk.

By seven o'clock they were back on Monaghan ward, preparing dressings, padding splints and checking the linen and china cupboards were properly stocked. Just before midday, Miriam Trott and Sadie Sedgewick arrived from their wards to lend a hand.

'I hope Sister lets me stay here,' Miriam said. 'I'd much rather nurse wounded soldiers than women with ulcers.' She looked thoughtful. 'I wonder if any of them will be handsome?'

'You'll find out soon enough,' said Sadie, who had been standing at the window looking out. 'The first ambulances are just arriving.'

The next hour was chaotic. As the men were brought in all the medical staff were darting about, the nurses hurrying to get the patients settled as quickly as they could, while Dr Latimer, Dr French and three medical students rushed from bed to bed, assessing their injuries and giving orders about the treatment to be administered.

In the middle of it, Eleanor stood rooted to the spot, taking it all in. She thought she had prepared herself, but the scene still came as a terrible shock. It almost felt as if she was in the middle of a battlefield herself, surrounded by the stench of cordite and unwashed bodies, everything a blur of dirt and filth and torn uniforms, blood caked on hands and faces and limbs, or seeping through bandages, staining them dull brown.

And the noise . . . many boys, grown men, screaming out in agony, while others whimpered and sobbed like babies, and others still lay in absolute silence, already half-dead.

'Don't just stand there, Copeland. You're needed!' A brisk voice shook Eleanor from her reverie. The new ward sister Miss Parker was a small woman, whip-thin, a no-nonsense Scot with bright blue eyes that missed nothing.

They worked quickly: kneeling beside stretchers, carefully peeling blood-caked uniforms from wounded, shattered limbs, sponging the dirt from frightened faces. The doctors worked around them, examining the men, sending some straight down to the operating theatre and ordering treatment for others. Eleanor noticed how the medical students' hands shook as they wrote up their notes, their faces pale and tense. She knew what they were thinking; these boys, with their broken bodies, crying out for their mothers, could so easily be them.

Eleanor moved to help a young man. Both his legs were missing, bloodied stumps wrapped in stained dressings.

As she wiped away the dirt from his face, he clutched her arm tightly.

'Where am I?' he whispered urgently, the whites of his eyes bright against his blackened face.

Eleanor looked down at his hand gripping her arm, fingers biting through her sleeve. 'You're at the Nightingale Hospital.'

'In England?'

'Yes. London.'

'Thank God!' He released his grip and fell back against the pillows. Eleanor reached down to rinse out her flannel, but when she turned back he was lying very still, his eyes staring up at the ceiling.

Eleanor cried out and jumped to her feet, just as Miss Parker came along. She took one look at the young man and said, 'Call an orderly and have him moved to one of the side rooms, then finish washing him. I'll help you perform last offices.'

It took a long time for Eleanor to finish washing the young man. At first she could hardly bring herself to touch the pale flesh, already cooling and so strangely heavy and inert. She could scarcely believe that the life could have gone out of him so suddenly and completely.

She told Sister about the question he had asked before he died. Miss Parker did not seem at all surprised by it.

'I've seen this before,' she said. 'They hold on and hold on until they reach home. Then, once they know they're safe, the life just goes out of them.' She looked across the bed at Eleanor. 'For goodness' sake, girl, get the blood from underneath his fingernails. I know it's difficult, but this is our last act of respect for this young man. Don't you think he deserves it?'

Within a couple of hours, peace and order had been restored. All the men had been cleaned up and put to bed, their wounds dressed and broken limbs carefully splinted. Most were already asleep, lulled by the morphine they had been given.

Eleanor took the last lot of soiled dressings down to the basement for burning. She stood for a moment beside the stoke hole, feeling its heat on her face. She knew she should return to the ward as quickly as she could, but her limbs were too heavy with weariness to move.

She looked at the watch on her bib. It was past three o'clock, and she hadn't eaten since breakfast that morning.

As she returned to the ward, the first thing she heard was Miriam Trott's voice, coming from the kitchen.

'It's delicious . . . what did you say it was called?'

'*Stollen*,' Anna said. 'We make it every Christmas.'

Eleanor went to the doorway and looked in. 'What's going on?'

Miriam turned round to face her guiltily, a piece of cake in her hand.

'Beck has brought in some special Christmas cake for us to try,' Miriam explained, her mouth full. 'Here, have some. It's heavenly.'

Eleanor ignored the plate she was offered. 'Why have you brought that in?'

Anna's chin lifted. 'It's St Nicholas' Day.'

'In Germany the children don't put stockings out on Christmas Eve. They put boots outside their doors on the evening of the fifth of December,' Miriam said. 'Isn't that odd?'

Eleanor went on staring at Anna. 'Does Sister know about this?'

'Does Sister know about what?'

Eleanor swung round to face Miss Parker, who stood behind her.

'Beck has brought in cake, Sister,' she managed to find her voice.

'Has she? Let's see . . .' The girls fell silent as Eleanor stood aside to let Miss Parker into the kitchen. Eleanor caught sight of Anna's tense expression. Now she's for it, she thought.

Miss Parker examined the slices of cake on the place. 'It's *Stollen*, isn't it?'

'Yes, Sister.'

'I've heard of it, but I've never tried it. May I?'

'Of course, Sister.' Anna proffered the plate. Eleanor saw the smug glint in her eye as Miss Parker took a piece and tasted it.

'Very nice,' she declared. 'Tell me, is there much to go round? Perhaps the men might like to try some with their tea?'

Eleanor gasped. 'But – but it's German, Sister!'

Miss Parker turned to face her, her blue eyes sharp. 'So are Christmas trees, and carols, and nearly every other festive tradition we have,' she said. 'Are you proposing we should do away with those, too?'

Eleanor felt scalding colour flooding her face. Out of the corner of her eye she could see the other girls looking at her. She could only imagine how Anna Beck must be enjoying this moment.

'I thought not.' Miss Parker drew herself up to her full height. 'Now, go back to work and stop talking so much nonsense. There is more than enough misery in the world at the moment without you going around trying to stir up more. And change your apron, it's filthy,' she added.

Eleanor stood rooted to the spot as Miss Parker walked away. She could feel her ears burning with humiliation. The silence in the kitchen felt heavy with meaning.

What was Sister thinking? Eleanor wondered. She could only imagine what her father would say about this. He would think Miss Parker a traitor, she was sure of it.

'You don't have to help handing it out.' Anna's voice was soft. Eleanor swung round to look at her. Her expression was carefully neutral, but Eleanor fancied she could see the glint of triumph in those brown eyes.

'I have no intention of touching your wretched cake,' she said haughtily. 'If Sister wants it handed out she can do it herself!'

She turned on her heel and marched back to the ward. She expected the other girls to follow, but a moment later saw Anna pushing the tea trolley down the length of the ward while Sadie handed out cake to the men.

'I'm sure she meant well,' Miriam said quietly. 'It was meant as an act of kindness.'

'Kindness?' Eleanor turned on her. 'Do you think it's kind what the Germans have done to our boys?' She pointed a shaking finger towards the door. 'You've seen them, you've dressed their wounds. Does that look like an act of kindness to you?'

'Just because we're at war—' Miriam started to say, but Eleanor cut her off.

'They're monsters,' she said. 'All of them. You have no idea what they're doing out there – destroying villages and killing innocent people. My father told me they burnt down a convent last week, and laughed when the nuns were burning to death—'

She saw the startled look on Miriam's face and stopped speaking. What was the point? Eleanor thought. Miriam would never understand, because she didn't know what it was like to have someone she loved at the Front. She didn't know what it was like to lie awake at night, worrying . . .

Miriam left, and Eleanor stood for a moment in the sluice. She gripped the sink, pressing her forehead against the wall. The tiles felt cool against her aching head.

The Germans were the enemy, not just at the Front but wherever they were. They needed to be rooted out, locked up, shunned. To do anything else was a betrayal of King and country.

She went into the kitchen and found the rest of the *Stollen*, a few pieces lying on a plate where Anna had left them. Eleanor thought of the young man who had died earlier, so young, robbed of his life by a cruel German bullet.

Then she thought of her brother Harry, out there somewhere, awaiting his fate.

She snatched up the plate and threw the pieces of *Stollen* into the bin.

Chapter Twenty

'What exactly were you thinking, sending a very sick woman home?'

Kate cringed in the low chair before her father's desk, her hands knotted together in her lap to stop them from shaking. She had faced her father's wrath many times in her life, but she had never seen him as angry as he was now.

'I – I'm sorry, Father,' she whispered. 'I didn't know—'

'You didn't know? Good God, and you call yourself a doctor?'

Kate stared down at the patterned rug beneath her feet. She wanted to defend herself but she had nothing to say. She'd been wrong, and now all she could do was sit there and suffer her father's justified anger.

'How is she?'

'She'll live, no thanks to you!' A vein pulsed in Sir Philip's broad forehead. 'She had an emergency operation this afternoon. An operation she might not have needed if you were able to spot a near-ruptured gastric ulcer when you see one!'

Kate looked up at him. 'But Mrs Hopkins was a known malingerer,' she tried to explain. 'She had already been admitted at least three times in the last—'

'That doesn't matter!' her father cut her off. 'You should still have treated her as you would any other patient presenting with those symptoms. But, of course, you had to be clever, didn't you? You had to prove you knew best.'

'No, that's not it at all. I don't—'

'How do you think I felt when Ormerod told me what had happened?' her father raged on. 'To hear that my daughter nearly killed a patient with her negligence? And Ormerod, of all people. He tried to put on a show of concern, but I could see the ghastly little man was gloating . . .' Sir Philip Carlyle glared across the desk, his silvery eyes cold with anger. 'God help us both if the wretched woman does die. Ormerod will have an absolute field day.'

'Perhaps I could talk to him?'

'Are you quite mad? Believe me, that's the last thing you should do.' Her father shook his head. 'Better by far to stay out of his way.'

'How can I when I'm on his firm?'

Sir Philip gave a hollow laugh. 'You really don't understand, do you? Do you think he wants you on his firm after this? It was all I could do to convince him not to send you before the disciplinary committee.'

Blood rushed to Kate's head, making her feel faint. 'The disciplinary committee?'

'Dr Ormerod felt the situation serious enough to warrant it, and I must say I agree with him. The only reason I talked him out of it is because of the shame it would have brought to this family.' He leant back in his chair, the aged leather creaking under his weight. 'The Carlyles have a proud tradition at the Nightingale. I have no intention of letting you drag my name and that of your brothers through the mud.'

Kate hung her head. 'I'm sorry, Father.'

There was a long silence. She could feel his gaze on her. 'You're not entirely to blame,' he said eventually. 'I should never have allowed you to come here in the first place. I should have known the rigours of study would prove too much for you.' Then, as Kate opened her mouth to protest, he went on, 'Under the circumstances, I think the best course of action, for everyone's sake, is for you to return to the Hampstead.'

'No!'

'Thankfully you won't have the black mark of a disciplinary against your name,' her father continued, not listening to her protest. 'You should be able to resume your studies there without too much trouble.'

'I'm not going,' Kate declared.

Her father's eyes narrowed. 'I don't think you quite understand,' he said. 'I'm not asking you to leave. I'm telling you.'

'And I'm telling you, I'm not going.' Kate sat up straighter. 'I know I've made a mistake, and I'm sorry for it. But I won't slink away in shame, no matter how many people think I should.' She met his gaze across the desk. 'I want another chance,' she said. 'I'll work harder, I'll do better. I won't make another mistake or let you down in any way, I swear. Please, Father, let me stay.'

Sir Philip let out a heavy sigh. 'Good God, why do you always have to be so difficult? Are you intent on making a laughing stock of this family?'

'No, Father.'

'Well, you could have fooled me!'

Kate watched him drumming his fingers impatiently on the desk. He couldn't make her go, not if she refused. But she knew she wouldn't stay if she didn't have his permission, if not his blessing. His approval meant too much to her.

'Even if I did say yes, I can't think of anyone who would take you on,' he said finally. 'Ormerod only let you join his firm in the first place as a favour to me. A fact that he did not hesitate to throw back in my face!' he added bitterly. 'And once word of this lapse in judgement gets out, I shouldn't think anyone else would touch you with a barge pole.'

'What if I were to find a place for myself? Would you allow me to stay then?'

'As you've already pointed out, I can't force you to leave.' Her father smiled mirthlessly. 'But who in their right mind would ever take you on?'

'Have you heard? Our Miss Carlyle is moving to Pathology.'

Rufus looked up from his hand of cards to a group of students standing at the bar. Wallace was holding forth as usual, a pint glass in his freckled hand.

'Good,' Gibson muttered into his drink. 'About time she moved on.'

'What's the matter, Gibson? Tired of not being the cleverest in the class anymore?' Talbot slapped him on the shoulder.

'It has nothing to do with that,' Gibson defended himself. 'She doesn't fit in here, that's all. And there's nothing clever about nearly killing a patient,' he added.

'At least she won't be able to kill anyone in Pathology!' Evans laughed.

'She won't have to be nice to them, either,' Talbot muttered into his pint.

'That'll be a relief to her, I daresay,' Wallace joined in 'It'd be easier to get a smile from a cadaver than the Ice Maiden!'

'Your turn, old man.' Charlie Latimer's voice called for Rufus' attention. He looked back, blinking.

'I'm sorry – what?'

'Ten of diamonds.' Latimer nodded at the card he had just laid on the table. 'Trump that if you can,' he said, looking pleased with himself.

Rufus pulled a random card from his hand and laid it down.

Charlie looked down at it. 'Five of hearts? Good god, man, you're not even trying, are you?' He collected up the cards. 'Or are you letting me win for once?'

'Got to give you a sporting chance, haven't I?' Rufus smiled, his gaze drifting back to the students at the bar.

Charlie sent him a shrewd look. 'I take it you hadn't heard about Miss Carlyle?'

Rufus shrugged, feigning indifference. 'I heard what happened.'

'I had the misfortune to be there when Ormerod found out. My God, he went apoplectic with rage. I thought he was going to have a cerebral haemorrhage himself, the way he was going on.' Charlie laughed.

'But it was an easy enough mistake to make, surely?'

'Not as far as Ormerod was concerned. Although I reckon he was just looking for a reason to dismiss her. Between you and me, I think Miss Carlyle's days here are numbered. Which is rather a pity, since I was just getting somewhere with her,' Charlie sighed.

Rufus smiled at him. 'Of course you were!'

'I was, I swear. A couple of times I caught her almost smiling at me.'

'I wouldn't be calling the banns just yet.' Rufus laid down a card, which Charlie promptly trumped.

'You may mock, but the Latimer charm will win her over in the end.' He scooped up the cards and added them to his pile. 'I daresay you'll be delighted she's going, at any rate.'

'Why should I care?'

'One less overprivileged Carlyle for you to loathe?' Charlie laughed. 'Oh, come on, dear boy, you never had any time for her.'

'I wouldn't say that,' Rufus began, then he caught Charlie's expression of disbelief. 'All right, perhaps it's true,' he conceded. 'But only because I believe in fairness. And actually, I don't think it's entirely fair that she should be treated so severely over one mistake.'

'What's this?' Charlie laughed. 'You've changed your tune, haven't you? Excuse me, but weren't you the one who introduced her to Mrs Hopkins in the first place?'

'I didn't tell her to discharge the woman, did I?' Rufus stared down at his cards. The truth was, he did feel guilty for what he had done. Perhaps if he hadn't tried to humiliate Kate for initially being so cautious with Mrs Hopkins' diagnosis, she wouldn't have been so rash with the patient's welfare later.

Charlie Latimer seemed to guess his thoughts. 'Look, I wouldn't chastise yourself too much, old man. Between you and me, I think Ormerod was looking for an excuse to get rid of her.'

They were interrupted by loud laughter from over by the bar.

'Sounds like they're happy about Ormerod's decision, at any rate.' Charlie commented dryly.

Rufus cocked his head to listen.

'Of course, you know why old Werner's taken her on?' Wallace was saying. 'No one else would work with him.'

'I'm not surprised,' Randall spoke up. 'Pathology's a grim old place.'

'It's nothing to do with Pathology,' Wallace said. 'It's Werner that's the problem, not his department.'

'If it weren't for the Dean he'd be in an internment camp by now, with the rest of his Hun friends,' Gibson said.

'Quite appropriate Carlyle's going to work with him – no one wants either of them,' Randall said, and they all laughed.

186

Rufus threw down his hand of cards. Charlie looked at him. 'Giving up already? I was just getting into my stride.'

'It's too noisy to concentrate.' Rufus shot a dark look towards the young men at the bar. 'Besides, I need some rest. I'm on call again from midnight.'

'Back on Monaghan? It's grim, isn't it?' Charlie sent him a sympathetic look. 'I'm on call tonight myself, but fortunately I'm only supervising the Midder boys.'

Rufus frowned at the glass in Charlie's hand. 'Should you be drinking, in that case?'

Charlie waved away his concern. 'Sister Maternity assures me that none of the mothers will be giving birth tonight.' He reached for his pint and held it up in salute. 'And besides, I'm only wetting the babies' heads in advance.'

Rufus shook his head. Charlie Latimer was incorrigible in every way.

On his way back to the doctors' lodging house, he thought about Kate Carlyle. It was very strange, the way she had been treated. He would have bet money on her getting away with anything, but she seemed to have been disciplined far more harshly than any of the other students.

He wondered if Ormerod would have been so severe if it had been a male student who had made the wrong diagnosis. Last winter Talbot had diagnosed huge doses of liquid paraffin for what turned out to be a spastic colon, and got nothing worse than a slap on the wrist for his mistake.

Then, as if he had somehow conjured her out of his imagination, he suddenly saw Kate Carlyle coming down the steps of the main hospital block, her coat collar turned up, hat pulled down against the rain.

Rufus froze, at a loss. She looked so unhappy, head bowed, shoulders slumped inside her heavy coat.

It was none of his business, he told himself. He should

ignore her, walk on. He was still telling himself the same thing when he heard his own voice calling out to her.

She turned round. Rufus saw the look of dismay on her face, and felt a stab of guilt.

Kate Carlyle stood her ground at the foot of the hospital steps and waited for him to cross the courtyard towards her. She looked as if she wanted to run away, but politeness was forcing her to stay.

'I heard about what happened . . . about Mrs Hopkins,' he said.

'Have you seen her? How is she?' Kate asked.

'Recovering well, I understand. Well enough to be complaining that she thinks she has the beginnings of appendicitis!' Rufus smiled, but Kate's woebegone expression did not alter.

'I'm glad to hear it,' she said shortly and started to walk away, but Rufus called after her.

'Anyone can make a mistake, you know.'

Kate stopped and looked back over her shoulder at him. It was difficult to work out what was going on behind those cool grey eyes of hers.

'Any of the students could have done the same as you,' Rufus went on, filling the charged silence.

Kate smiled sadly at him. 'Yes, but there's a difference, isn't there?'

'What's that?'

'They can afford to make mistakes. I can't.'

She walked away, leaving him standing in the rain.

Chapter Twenty-One

'And I used to think the hat factory was hard work!'

Sadie straightened up, massaging the small of her back. It was barely eight o'clock in the morning, but her spine was already aching from making beds. Now she and Grace Duffield had the job of getting the soiled linen ready for the laundry. A wintry draught blew in through the grille above their heads in the sluice room.

'I don't know why we even bother having a laundry, since we have to do all the hard work ourselves!' Grace grumbled as she bent low, scrubbing away at a nasty brown stain.

'You know what Sister Tutor says. "Stains must not be allowed to dry on the linen, because it makes them harder to remove." ' Sadie recited the words they had heard repeated so often during Preliminary Training.

Grace groaned. 'Don't! You sound just like Copeland.' She flexed her fingers. 'I wouldn't be surprised if I ended up with chilblains, you know.'

Just then Staff Nurse Gifford appeared in the doorway. 'I need help doing last offices for a patient,' she announced. 'Duffield, you can come with me.'

Grace grimaced. 'Just my luck,' she murmured under her breath.

Sadie grinned back at her. 'Scrubbing stains off sheets doesn't seem too bad now, does it?'

But Sadie stopped smiling when Grace had left and she was by herself. She scrubbed until her arms ached and her fingers were sore, all the time aware of the minutes ticking by. Half-past eight inched towards nine, when the porters came to take the linen down to the laundry. If it wasn't ready, there would be a black mark by Sadie's name in the ward book.

She was still wrestling the last wet, flapping sheet from the stone sink to the laundry basket when she heard the door open behind her.

Sadie glanced at the clock on the wall. Ten minutes to nine. Sometimes the porters liked to turn up early just to catch them out.

'Nearly finished,' she said, without looking round. 'Give me a hand with this, will you?'

'Look here, Sedgewick. You may be senior to me, but there's no need to think you can go around dishing out orders!'

Sadie swung round. There, in the doorway, stood Dulcie Moore, looking smart in the blue-striped uniform of a probationer, her cheeky face framed by the severe lines of her cap.

'Moore!' Sadie let the wet sheet drop from her hands and rushed to hug her friend. 'Where did you spring from?'

'This is my first morning on the ward.' Dulcie looked pleased with herself. 'I told you I'd be back, didn't I?'

'You managed to get through the examination this time, then?'

'Just about.' Dulcie rolled her eyes. 'It was touch and go, especially when I sprayed the examiner with a soap and water enema!'

'You didn't?'

'I did. I nearly died. I couldn't even look at her in case I burst out laughing.' Dulcie grinned. 'Lucky she saw the funny side, too! But, to be honest, I reckon they would have passed me anyway, they're so desperate for nurses.'

'Well, I'm certainly glad to see you.'

'Me too. I was afraid I might end up on a ward with Eleanor Copeland!' Dulcie smiled. 'Is she still a know all?'

'Worse, if anything!' Sadie said. She looked down at the wet sheet pooling at her feet. 'Here, help me get this into the laundry basket, would you? Sister will have a fit if it ain't ready by the time the porters come.'

They finished with the linen, and then went back to the ward. Sister had instructed Sadie to look after Dulcie and show her the ropes, so they were able to keep up a conversation in hushed voices as they went about their work.

'I need to hear all the gossip,' Dulcie whispered as they made the patients' mid-morning tea in the kitchen. 'How's Duffield? Still as clumsy as ever?'

'I'm afraid so. She dropped a whole jar of leeches the other day. And she managed to step on a few and squash them while she was picking them up.'

Dulcie shook her head. 'I'm amazed that girl has kept all her limbs. And what about Beck and Copeland? I expect they're still as thick as thieves?'

'Hardly!' Sadie arranged the cups on the tray. 'Oh, I forgot. You left before they fell out, didn't you?'

'They fell out?'

'Well, Copeland fell out with poor Beck.' Sadie explained how Eleanor had taken against Anna.

Dulcie looked outraged. 'I hope you told her she was being daft?' she said.

'Duffield and I did,' Sadie said. 'Trott's still sucking up to her.'

Dulcie's lip curled. 'I'm not surprised. She's so desperate!'

'Moore!' Sadie said, but couldn't help giggling. She hadn't realised how much she'd missed Dulcie.

As they took the patients' tea round, Sadie introduced Dulcie to all of them.

'How do you remember them all?' Dulcie whispered. 'I'll never keep their names in my head, let alone what's wrong with them and how they like their tea!'

'You'll soon get used to it.' Sadie pushed the trolley to the next bed. 'Cup of tea, Ada?'

'Yes, please, ducks.' Ada Dixon looked up at her over her knitting. Her gaze rested on Dulcie. 'Who's this, then?'

'This is Nurse Moore, our new probationer. This is Mrs Dixon. She prefers us to call her Ada,' she whispered. 'But not when Sister's around because she doesn't approve.'

Dulcie was all smiles as she placed Ada's cup of tea on the bedside locker. 'That knitting's coming along nicely,' she commented. 'What are you making?'

'It's supposed to be a jumper for Frank, my youngest. Except it's more holes than knitting.' Ada looked at it, her mouth pursed. 'I ain't really got the patience for all this lark, but my sister-in-law reckoned it would give me something to do, save me going mad with boredom in here. I ain't one for sitting still in the usual run of things.'

'Never mind, you'll be going home soon,' Sadie reminded her.

Ada grinned, showing a wide gap where her front teeth had once been. 'Christmas Eve,' she said. 'I can't wait. Although Gawd knows what state my house will be in when I get home, with my old man and the boys there, and no woman to keep an eye on 'em.'

'You don't have a daughter, then?'

Ada shook her head. 'No, love. Just me and a houseful of men.' She grimaced. 'I'd have liked a little girl, but the Good Lord saw fit to send me four boys instead.' She shook her head. 'And a right handful they've been at times, I can tell you.'

Dulcie's eyes twinkled. 'Are they handsome?'

'Moore!'

Ada's mouth twisted. 'I'm their mother, I'd be bound to think they're handsome, wouldn't I?' She looked at Dulcie. 'Why? You looking for a young man, are you?'

'I might be.' Dulcie smiled, her cheeks dimpling. 'Although I've really set my sights on marrying a doctor,' she added.

Sadie looked away, feeling a blush rising in her face at Dulcie's shamelessness.

'Have you now? You sound like a girl who knows what she wants?'

'Oh, I do,' Dulcie said.

'Well, if it's a doctor you're after, I don't s'pose you'd be interested in any of my boys.' Ada sighed. 'It's a shame. I wouldn't mind marrying a couple of 'em off.' She looked at Sadie. 'I don't s'pose you'd be interested? I wouldn't mind you as a daughter-in-law.'

Sadie laughed. 'I don't suppose they'd thank you for picking their wives for them, Ada!'

Ada Dixon's mouth firmed. 'They'll do as they're told and like it!'

At that moment Miss Sutton summoned Dulcie to help Miriam make up a bed. She went off, humming to herself. Ada watched her go.

'You two seem very thick together?' she commented.

'We met in Preliminary Training,' Sadie said. 'We really hit it off.'

'She seems like trouble to me.'

'I know she might seem a bit lively but she's got a heart of gold.'

'I didn't say otherwise.' Ada looked huffy. 'I just said, she seems like trouble. I've met a few girls like her in my time, believe me!'

'A minute ago you were trying to marry her off to one of your sons!'

'A girl would need to have a bit about her, to put up with them. You know, someone who didn't take any nonsense from anyone.' Ada cocked her head. 'That's why I reckon you'd be perfect.'

Sadie sighed. 'Don't start that again! I told you, I ain't interested in getting married.'

'I don't believe you,' Ada said flatly. 'You just ain't met the right man yet, that's all. Now I'm telling you, when you meet my Frank or my Ronnie or my Nick . . .'

Sadie shook her head. 'Sorry, Ada.'

She sighed in frustration. 'You ain't telling me a pretty young girl like you wants to spend the rest of her life an old maid?'

A picture of Jimmy Clyde came into her mind. 'I can think of much worse fates than that.'

At two o'clock, Sadie went off duty, leaving Dulcie to the tender mercies of Miriam Trott. Dulcie was soon consigned to the sluice, surrounded by a mountain of dirty bedpans and looking very sorry for herself. Miriam had wasted no time in pulling rank, Sadie thought.

It was a dull, wet December day, and the light was already fading from the sky. Outside the main doors, two porters were struggling to put up an enormous Christmas tree. Sadie had stopped to watch them for a moment when she heard someone calling her name. She turned to see PC Machin hurrying towards her, his dark waterproof cape around his shoulders.

'That's a bit of luck,' he said. 'I was just coming to the nurses' home to drop off a note for you.'

There was something in his sombre expression that made Sadie's chest tighten. 'Why? What is it? What's wrong?'

'We've arrested Jimmy Clyde.'

She breathed out in relief. 'About time,' she muttered.

'He's been on the run long enough.' All these weeks she had been living in dread, expecting him to turn up at her mother's lodgings again as if nothing had happened. She had been so preoccupied she couldn't even enjoy the fragile peace that his absence had brought them.

'Has he admitted to the robbery?'

Peter shook his head. Rain dripped steadily off the brim of his helmet. 'He reckons he knows nothing about it. Says he was nowhere near the place when it happened, just like the last time we questioned him.'

'But it's different this time, ain't it? You've got my evidence.'

'Have we?'

Sadie stared at him. 'What do you mean?'

'I mean you don't have to testify against him.' Peter's eyes met hers, dark and full of meaning. 'You can change your mind. No one would blame you for it.'

Sadie frowned. 'Why would I want to do that?'

'Because Jimmy Clyde has a lot of dangerous friends.'

'You don't need to tell me that.' How many years had she listened to him boasting about Billy Willis and his mates? She had grown up with horror stories of enemies having their hands and feet chopped off, or thrown into the river in sacks filled with bricks.

'If I do this . . . are you sure he'll be locked up?' she said.

Peter nodded. 'He'll be charged with armed robbery and probably with manslaughter too. But he ain't the only one you need to—'

'Then I'll do it.'

She saw the colour draining from Peter's face. 'Sadie . . .'

'For Gawd's sake, Peter, call yourself a policeman or what? I'm offering to help you put Jimmy Clyde behind bars, and you're trying to talk me out of it!' Sadie forced a laugh. 'Now, are we going down to that nick or what?'

Chapter Twenty-Two

The station platform was a sea of khaki.

A group of carol singers had gathered outside the ticket office, singing 'God Rest Ye, Merry Gentlemen'. The merry tune was a bitter contrast to the mood on the platform, as wives, mothers, fathers and sweethearts all said goodbye to their loved ones.

Anna looked around her at the young men, laughing and joking. She thought of the wounded men who had arrived at the hospital the previous morning, their faces burnt and scarred, shattered limbs held together with tattered, bloody bandages.

It wouldn't happen to Edward, she told herself. He would be one of the lucky ones, the ones who came home safely. He had to come home. She couldn't bear to lose someone else, not after her father . . .

'All right?'

She looked up. Edward was smiling down at her. He looked so proud and handsome in his uniform, his cap pulled low over his blue eyes.

Anna forced herself to smile back at him. Poor Edward, he was the one who was going into the unknown. She had to try to be strong, for his sake.

As if he could read her thoughts, Edward said, 'You don't have to worry, you know. I'll be back.'

Anna thought of all the young men on the ward who cried out in their sleep, and yet more who never slept at all.

'I know,' she said.

He lifted her hand to his lips, then looked down at the engagement ring on her finger. 'Just think,' he said, 'it was exactly a year ago that I proposed to you.'

Anna nodded, not trusting herself to speak. She couldn't bear to think of that day, how happy they had all been, how certain she was that her perfect world would go on forever . . .

He sighed. 'I had hoped you'd be wearing a wedding ring by now.'

'I know. I'm sorry.' She remembered what Liesel had said, how she should have snapped him up before some French mademoiselle had the chance. 'I wish I'd said yes when I still had the chance.'

'You had your reasons.'

She looked up at him, saw the wistful expression in his eyes. 'I was just being silly.'

'You wanted your father there to give you away. I understand that.'

But her father had understood, too. He had wanted the wedding to go ahead, even without him. This was all Anna's doing, and now she bitterly regretted it.

'Anyway, it's probably for the best,' Edward went on. 'I mean, if I come home wounded and can't work anymore . . . I wouldn't want to be a burden on you.'

'Don't! Don't talk like that.' Anna had a terrifying image of another young man on the ward, the same age as Edward, an arm and a leg blown off during a recce in no-man's-land. He was one of the lucky ones, so they said. By rights he should never have survived his injuries. But Anna had seen the despair in his eyes, and she understood how much he wished he had died out there in the freezing mud.

She reached up and kissed Edward fiercely, clinging to

him. 'I'll wait for you,' she promised, pressing her cheek against the rough wool of his tunic. 'Whatever happens, I'll always wait for you.'

He tilted her chin up so that she was looking at him. 'And I'll come home,' he promised.

Anna gazed around the crowded platform, at all the young men comforting their wives and mothers with the same words. How many of them would keep their promises? she wondered.

She realised Edward was speaking to her and turned back to him.

'I'm sorry I can't stay to look after you and your family,' he was saying. 'I feel as if I'm letting your father down . . .'

'You can't help that. It isn't your choice to go, is it?' Anna reached for his hand. 'Anyway, we'll be all right.'

'Will you?' His hands tightened around hers. For a moment he hesitated, then he said, 'Anna, I want you to promise me something.'

'What?'

'Don't trust Tom Franklin.'

Anna frowned. 'What makes you say that?'

Edward's gaze dropped. 'It doesn't matter. Forget I said anything.'

'Edward, what is it? What's wrong?'

For a long time he stared at her, his blue eyes searching her face. Then he took a deep, steadying breath.

'There are some things I've never told you – about myself,' he said slowly.

Apprehension crawled up her spine. 'What kind of things?'

He looked away from her, up and down the platform. 'Now isn't the right time,' he muttered. 'Not just as we're about to be parted. I don't want to go away and leave you with the wrong idea about me . . .'

'Edward, please. You're scaring me. Whatever it is, you know you can tell me.'

'Even if they make you hate me?'

She stared up at him. She had never seen him looking so nervous. 'I love you,' she said quietly. 'Nothing could change that.'

'Couldn't it?' He paused, and Anna could see him weighing up the words in his mind. Then he took another deep breath.

'When I was young,' he said, 'after I came out of the orphanage, I fell in with a bad crowd and got into trouble.'

'What kind of trouble?'

'Theft. Nothing serious, just stealing from shops, pick-pocketing.' He glanced away from her. 'God, I'm so ashamed, I can hardly talk about it.'

Anna stroked his hands with her thumbs. 'It's all right,' she said soothingly.

'Is it? You do understand, don't you?' There was an urgency in his voice. 'It's all in the past, I swear. Since I started working for your father, well – it's been like a new life for me.'

'Of course.'

'But back then I was so young – and scared.' He swallowed hard. 'As soon as I got involved I realised it was wrong. I wanted to get out, but they wouldn't let me.'

'They?'

'The Franklin boys.'

Anna stared at him. 'Tom's brothers?'

Edward nodded. 'I joined their gang when I came out of the orphanage. You must understand, I had no one – I just wanted somewhere to belong . . .' He looked at her, his blue eyes appealing. 'But when I tried to get out, they threatened me. Said I was part of their family, and they'd kill me if I betrayed them.'

Anna paused for a moment, taking this in. 'What happened then?'

He smiled. 'You did.'

'Me?'

'You – and your family. Your father made me his apprentice, and it was like a second chance for me. A chance to start a new life, the life I should have had.' Edward straightened his shoulders. 'So I stood up to the Franklins. I told them to do their worst, to kill me if they wanted. But I swore I would never do another dishonest thing, not as long as I lived.'

'And did they come after you?'

He shook his head. 'They were angry and they warned me to keep my mouth shut, but after a while they stopped bothering me. And then Tom Franklin came to work at the bakery.' His mouth curled in contempt.

Anna stared at him, taking it all in. No wonder the two of them had never got on. 'I always wondered why you hated him so much,' she murmured.

'Can you imagine how I felt when your father took him on? From that moment I've lived in fear that he might tell your father about my shameful past, that I'd lose everything . . .'

'Father would never do that,' Anna said. 'He believes everyone deserves a second chance.'

'And what about you?' Edward said. 'Will you give me a second chance too, now you know my secrets?'

He looked so uncertain, Anna put her arms around him.

'I don't know why you even have to ask that,' she said. 'You said yourself, you were young and scared. You took the wrong path, but at least you found your way back.'

'Thanks to you and your family.' He smiled down at her.

'Papa would say that is the mark of a real man,' Anna said. 'To be able to recognise mistakes and put them right.'

'Your father is a good man,' Edward said. 'If it hadn't been for him, God knows what my life would have become.' He held her at arms' length. 'But now do you see why I'm asking you not to trust Tom? I know the kind of family he comes from, what they're capable of. I'm worried he'll try to take advantage of you when you're all alone.'

The train came in then, belching steam and filling the air with the smell of burning coal. The people on the platform started to shift uneasily, saying their last goodbyes, arms around each other, tears flowing. Men in uniform lifted their children in the air, swinging them round, trying to coax smiles even while their own eyes were filled with tears.

Edward picked up his kit bag and swung it over his shoulder. 'Well, here we go.' He forced a grin.

Anna clutched his sleeve, suddenly not wanting to let go. 'Promise you'll come home safe?' she whispered.

'I promise.' He leant down and gave her one last delicate kiss. And then he was gone, piling on to the train with the other men, all jostling to wave out of the windows as the guard blew his shrill whistle.

Anna stood on the platform long after the train had pulled out and all the other families had gone. She stood all alone, watching the plume of steam as it disappeared from view.

Thankfully, she had the afternoon off so she didn't have to return to the hospital. She didn't think she could bear to look into the faces of the wounded soldiers, not so soon after seeing Edward off. All she really wanted was to go home to the bakery, to the comfort of her family.

The first person she saw as she entered the back yard was Tom Franklin. He emerged from the wood store as she let herself in through the gate. He started when he saw her, stopping in his tracks. He had a brown paper package under his arm.

'Miss Anna! I didn't know you was coming home.' He

jerked his head towards the shed. 'Your mother asked me to chop some wood to see her through Christmas. I was just putting it away.'

Anna stared at him, wondering if she'd imagined the shifty look on his face. 'Thank you, Tom,' she said.

For a moment neither of them spoke. 'I daresay you'll want to get home as it's Christmas Eve?' Anna broke the silence.

Tom's mouth curled. 'I s'pose,' he grunted. 'Unless you want anything else doing . . .'

'No,' she said, too quickly. She saw his dark brows lift a fraction.

Anna watched as he retrieved the bicycle from behind the shed and placed the brown paper package in the front basket.

'What's that?' she asked.

Tom looked at it. 'Leftover bread and cake. Your mother said I could take it home.' He raised his chin defiantly.

'Of course.' She should have remembered. Last Christmas Eve her father had piled his delivery basket high with bread and pies, and given him a whole iced cake to take home.

Usually she would have gone inside and left him, but this time she stood by the back door, watching as he shouldered open the yard gate and wheeled his bicycle through it.

Don't trust Tom Franklin.

'Happy Christmas, Tom,' she called after him. He looked up, his eyes meeting hers for the first time. He opened his mouth to speak, but the gate slammed shut on his reply.

Usually Anna loved Christmas Eve. They would put up the Christmas tree and light candles, and her mother would cook fish with potato fritters and sauerkraut, and then they would all gather around the warm glow of the fire to open their presents amid lots of laughter and excitement.

But tonight, putting up the Christmas tree only reminded Anna painfully that her father wouldn't be there to see it. She thought of him and the other men in their dismal bunk room at the internment camp. Her father so loved Christmas. She could imagine him, humming 'Ir Kinderlein Kommet', trying to bring some festive cheer to the other men. Last time Anna had visited, he had told her that he was going to teach the camp cook to make *Lebkuchen*. That was so typical of him, she thought, always trying to make the best of his situation, never allowing anything to get him down.

She looked at her mother, standing beside her as she hung a wooden ornament on the tree. From her faraway expression, Anna guessed she was having similar thoughts.

Only Liesel seemed to be thinking of herself, as usual. She was in one of her sulky moods, in spite of Anna's and her mother's best efforts to make everything happy and cheerful. She refused to help decorate the tree, and pushed her dinner around her plate in moody silence.

'Try to eat something, my dear, please,' her mother pleaded, while Anna fumed quietly. That was just typical of Liesel! Anna was the one who had just said goodbye to her fiancé, the one in desperate need of comfort, but instead they all had to fuss around her spoilt younger sister.

As soon as Dorothy went out of the room to fetch the pudding, Anna turned on her sister.

'Why do you have to be so selfish all the time?' she snapped. 'Don't you think this is hard on all of us, without you trying to make it worse? And you can stop that, too,' she said, as Liesel promptly burst into tears. 'You're not a baby. Crying might work on Mother and Papa, but I know—'

'Oh, shut up, Anna!' Liesel wiped her nose on her sleeve. 'I'm not crying because I'm upset. I'm crying because I'm – I'm scared.'

Anna frowned. 'Scared? What have you got to be scared about?'

Liesel cast a quick glance towards the door. 'I can't say in front of Mother,' she said in a low voice. 'But I have something to show you . . .'

Anna stared down at the crumpled piece of paper in her hands.

'Where did you get this?'

'I found it on the mat this morning. It must have been pushed under the back door during the night.' Liesel wiped her face. Her tears had dried, but her eyes were still puffy from crying.

'Did you show it to Mother?'

'Of course I did!' Liesel snapped. 'But she said it was all nonsense and we shouldn't mention it to you. Then she threw it away, but I got it out of the fire before she lit it.'

Anna read the words again. It was hard to make out the thick pencil scrawl.

'GET OUT,' the note said. 'THEY ARE COMING FOR YOU ON CHRISTMAS DAY.' It was ominously signed, 'FROM A FRIEND'.

'Who do you think it could be from?' Liesel whispered.

'I don't know.' Anna looked up at her sister's worried face. Liesel was watching her closely, waiting for her reaction. She forced herself to screw up the note. 'Mother's right, it's nothing to worry about. Just someone's idea of a nasty joke, I expect.'

'What if it isn't?' Liesel said. 'What if someone is going to come and murder us?'

Anna put her arm around her sister's shoulders. Liesel

was shivering like a frightened animal. 'Now who would want to do that?'

'The same people who put bricks through our windows and spit at us on the street.' Liesel's blue eyes were wide with fear. 'You're not here every day, you don't know what it's like. They want to drive us out, Anna!'

She started to cry again, and Anna pulled her closer. 'Don't worry,' she whispered into her sister's hair. 'I'll be staying here over Christmas. I'll look after you.'

'I wish Papa were here,' Liesel sobbed into her shoulder.

'I know, love.' So do I, Anna thought.

Chapter Twenty-Three

Late on the afternoon of Christmas Eve, and just as everyone was beginning to give up hope, Miss Sutton finally allowed the porters to set up the Christmas tree on Everett ward. Dulcie and Miriam set about decorating it, assisted by a couple of the medical students who happened to be on the ward.

Sadie, who was busy helping Ada Dixon pack her belongings, watched with amusement as Dulcie flirted with a particularly good-looking student called Talbot.

'I told you she was trouble, didn't I?' Ada commented behind her.

'She's harmless.' Sadie smiled and packed Ada's nightgown in her suitcase. 'Now, is that everything?'

'I think so.' Ada paused in powdering her face to look around. It was strange to see the bedside locker so empty after it had been strewn with her bits and pieces for so long.

'It's a shame you won't see the ward all decorated for Christmas,' Sadie said.

Ada grinned. 'I reckon I can live without it, ta very much. All I want now is to go home.' She dusted her face with the powder puff, sending clouds of it into the air. 'No offence, ducks, you've all been very good to me. But you can't beat your own bed, can you?'

'I suppose not.' Sadie eyed the drifts of pink powder settling on the white bedcover. 'I bet you're looking forward to a nice family Christmas?'

'I can't wait!' Ada cackled. 'We always have a big knees-up round our house on Christmas Day.'

'Don't forget what the doctor said, will you? You're not to overdo it.'

''Course not. I'll be as good as gold.' Ada sent her a mischievous look as she twisted the top off her scarlet lipstick. Sadie smiled back. If she knew Ada, she would be dancing and singing with the rest of them by tomorrow afternoon. 'How about you? Will you be seeing your mum on Christmas Day?'

Sadie shook her head. 'I'm working all day. It depends when Sister tells me I can go off duty.'

'That's a shame. I'll bet she'll miss you?'

I doubt it, Sadie thought. Lily would probably start on the gin first thing and be too blind drunk to notice anything by teatime.

'I'm sure I'll pop in sometime,' she said. 'Anyway, we have a good time on the ward, so Nurse Gifford tells me. We sing carols, and give out presents, and have a Christmas dinner.'

Ada pulled a face. 'Yes, but you can't beat a proper family Christmas, can you?'

I wouldn't know, Sadie thought. Perhaps if she had been born into a family as warm and loving as Ada's, she would feel more bereft at missing the festivities.

'No,' she said. 'I suppose not.'

Just then two of Ada's sons arrived. They were both big, hulking slabs of men, with thick necks and broken noses.

'And what time do you call this?' Ada turned on them. 'I thought I told you to be here half an hour ago?'

'Sorry, Ma,' they mumbled.

'And take your hats off when you're indoors.' Ada sighed. 'Blimey, Nurse Sedgewick will think you've got no manners.'

They snatched their caps off their heads, both blushing

like schoolboys. 'Look at them,' Ada said to Sadie. 'See how bashful they turn when there's a pretty girl present? No wonder they ain't married!' She shook her head, but the smile she gave them was full of maternal pride.

Sadie fastened Ada's suitcase and went to move it. At once one of the boys – the youngest, Frank – moved to take it from her.

'Now, you mustn't allow your mother to do too much,' Sadie warned them.

The other son, Ronnie, laughed. 'You try stopping her, Nurse!'

'Quite right,' Ada said. 'Once I get back in that house, I'm in charge.' She sent them a severe look. 'I hope you boys ain't turned the place into a pigsty while I've been away?'

'It's a palace, Ma.'

'Is it, now? I s'pose there's a first time for everything.' Ada stood up and enveloped Sadie in a pillowy, perfumed embrace. 'I'll miss you, ducks,' she said.

'I'll miss you too, Ada. Take care of yourself, won't you?'

They were interrupted by the arrival of Miss Sutton, followed by a porter with a wheelchair. She glared at Sadie as she extricated herself from Ada's arms. 'All ready to go, Mrs Dixon?'

Ada looked askance at the wheelchair. 'What's this for?'

'It's hospital rules, Mrs Dixon. Patients must be wheeled down to the main doors.'

Frank grinned and swept into a low bow. 'Your carriage awaits, Milady!'

'Daft bugger!' Ada shook her head.

Sadie watched the procession leaving, Ada waving regally to the other patients as she was wheeled the length of the ward. Everett wouldn't be the same without Ada Dixon, she thought.

*

Christmas Day on the ward was just as pleasant as Staff Nurse Gifford had promised it would be. After breakfast, Miss Sutton invited them all into her sitting room for coffee and a tot of the brandy she kept locked in the medicine cupboard. She handed out the boxes of chocolates she had bought for everybody, and they presented her with the small Staffordshire figurine they had clubbed together to buy for her. Then there were more presents to be handed out to the patients on the ward, and the ward sisters came round to sing some rousing Christmas carols, followed by the medical students, who sang some rather risqué songs and acted out comic scenes, which made everyone laugh except Miss Sutton, who glared throughout.

And then it was time for dinner to be served. The porter brought a roast turkey to the long table in the middle of the ward, amid much pomp and ceremony, and the Chief Surgical Officer appeared to carve it, wielding his knife with a flourish that made some of the women on the ward wince.

Later in the afternoon, once the dinner was cleared away and the last Christmas cracker had been pulled, it was time for the visitors to arrive. To Sadie's relief, Miss Sutton told her she could finally go off duty.

Dulcie came with her. As they walked back to Lennox House, she said, 'Some of the medical students are having a party in the Students' Union later on. Would you like to come?'

'I'm not sure . . . I thought I might go and visit my mother.'

'Oh, do come!' Dulcie pleaded. 'So far Trott's the only one who's said yes, and I don't really fancy spending the whole evening watching her batting her eyelashes at all the young men.'

'You're a fine one to talk! I saw you flirting with Mr Talbot yesterday. Right under Sister's nose, too!'

'So what if I did? It's Christmas, isn't it? A time of

goodwill to all men.' Dulcie sent Sadie a coy sideways look. 'Between you and me, Sam Wallace has asked me to invite you 'specially. I think he's got his eye on you.'

'In that case, I'm definitely not coming!' Sadie laughed.

Dulcie pouted. 'You're no fun.' She let out a martyred sigh. 'Oh, well, I suppose I shall just have to put up with Trott.'

As she trudged off to her mother's lodgings through the cold, dark streets, Sadie almost wished she had accepted Dulcie's invitation. She was bound to have a better time with her friend than she would with her mother.

She couldn't remember a time when she had enjoyed Christmas. As a child, she recalled bleak holidays spent alone in cold, dark lodgings because her mother was out working on the streets and she didn't have any money for the gas. Later on, Christmas was usually spent in fear, waiting for Jimmy Clyde's temper to give way. He could be the life and soul of the party one minute, then clutching her mother by the throat the next, depending on how the drink took him. Sadie shuddered at the memory of all the times she had hidden away, holding her breath, listening to him giving her mother another beating.

At least she knew he wouldn't be there today. He was still safely behind bars in Wormwood Scrubs, awaiting trial.

As she climbed the narrow staircase to her mother's lodgings, she heard the sound of women's laughter drifting down from above. Sadie stopped for a moment to listen, her heart sinking. The only time her mother laughed was when she was drunk.

But today Lily Sedgewick didn't look drunk. Sadie barely recognised the smiling woman who sat opposite Belle, warming her hands in front of the fire.

She rose to her feet when she saw Sadie. 'Oh, good. You came. I wasn't sure you'd find the time.'

'Sister let me go early.' Sadie stared at her mother. Lily was clear-eyed, her hair and clothes spotlessly clean. Even the grim little room smelt of polish and disinfectant.

'I told you she'd be here, didn't I?' Belle winked at Sadie. 'Your mum's been on pins all day, waiting for you.'

Lily blushed. 'I have not!' She looked shyly at Sadie. 'I kept you some Christmas dinner, if you want it?'

Christmas dinner? Sadie glanced at Belle in confusion. She had rarely known her mother cook anything.

'No, thanks, I had my dinner at the—' She saw her mother's crestfallen expression. 'Oh, go on, then. I reckon I could manage a bit more.'

'It's in the oven. I'll fetch it. You take your coat off and sit down. I'll put the kettle on too, while I'm at it.'

Her mother picked up the kettle from the stove and hurried out on to the landing to fill it. Belle grinned at Sadie. 'I'm glad you came,' she said. 'She's been fussing about all day, trying to make it all nice for you.'

'So I see.' Sadie ran her hand over the polished surface of the table. She looked up at Belle. 'What's going on?'

'She's changed, ain't she?' Belle looked pleased. 'She's a new woman, I reckon. And no prizes for guessing why, either.'

Sadie fetched a knife and fork from the dresser and sat down at the table. A moment later her mother returned, carefully carrying a plate of food.

'Sorry, it dried up a bit in the oven,' she said as she placed it down in front of Sadie.

'It looks lovely.'

'I dunno about that. I ain't much of a cook . . .'

Sadie picked up her knife and fork and started to eat, conscious of her mother standing the other side of the table, watching her.

'Is it all right?' Lily asked, her face creased with anxiety. 'I know it's dry . . . you don't have to eat it if you don't like it . . .'

'For Gawd's sake, Lil, let the poor girl have it in peace!' Belle cried.

'Sorry.' Lily smiled apologetically. 'I'll go and pour that tea, shall I?'

Sadie watched her mother as she busied herself at the stove, humming while she worked. She couldn't remember a time Lily had looked or sounded so happy.

After dinner, Sadie gave her mother and Belle the tin of talcum powder she had bought for each of them.

'It's lily-of-the-valley,' she said. 'I thought you'd like it, as it's named after you, Mum?'

'I hope it smells better than your mother does!' Belle cackled.

'Shut up, you!' Lily nudged her, laughing. A smile lit up her face. 'It's lovely, Sadie. Thank you.' She turned the tin around in her hands, as if she had never seen anything so wonderful in her life. 'And I've got something for you, too.' She nodded to Belle. 'Fetch it for me, would you, ducks? It's over there, on the dresser.'

'For me?' Sadie stared at her.

'Don't look so surprised,' Lily said. 'It's Christmas, ain't it?'

Sadie said nothing. She couldn't remember the last time her mother had bought her anything, Christmas or birthday.

Belle returned and handed her a small package, about the size of a pack of cards but flat. Sadie stared down at it. 'What's this?'

'Best open it and find out, hadn't you? It ain't much,' Lily said. 'Just something I got off the market. But I thought you might like it.'

'It – it's lovely.' Sadie stared down at the gift in her hands, a delicate framed picture made up of tiny dried flowers.

'Like I said, it ain't much. But I thought it might do to cheer up that room of yours at the nurses' home?'

Sadie looked up into her mother's face, bright with hope. Suddenly she felt tears pricking her eyes.

'What is it, love? What's wrong?' Lily Sedgewick stared back at her in concern. 'If you don't like it . . .'

'I do.' Sadie dashed away the tears with the back of her hand. 'Take no notice of me,' she muttered.

'I expect she's tired, ain't you, mate?' Belle looked sympathetic.

'Yes. Yes, that's it.' Sadie smiled back at her. There was so much she wanted to say, but she was too afraid. It felt as if they were in a delicate little bubble of Christmas magic, just the three of them, and she wanted it to go on and on.

In the end, it was Belle who broke the spell.

'I wonder how Jimmy Clyde's enjoying his Christmas in the nick!' she mused.

Lily's face fell. 'Don't, Lil,' she said.

Sadie noticed her mother's hands were shaking as she reached for the teapot to refill their cups.

'It'll be a good thing if they keep him locked up,' Belle said. 'But knowing that little worm, I expect he'll find a way to wriggle his way out.'

'Not this time.'

Sadie hadn't realised she had spoken out loud until she looked up and saw both women staring at her.

'And what makes you so sure of that?' Belle said.

'Because I'm going to testify against him.'

Her mother set down the teapot with a clatter, splashing hot tea all over the lace tablecloth.

'I'd better wipe that up.' She hurried away as Belle turned to face Sadie.

'You what?' Her voice was low and flat.

'I went down to the police station and told them what

213

he'd done,' Sadie said. Her mother returned and started dabbing at the cloth with agitated little movements. 'And I took them that locket. The one he stole.'

Lily's hand went to her bare throat, her fingers trembling.

'Oh, Sadie, what have you done?' Belle shook her head.

'I had to do something,' she snapped. 'You saw what he did to Mum!'

'You shouldn't have done it,' Belle said. 'You don't go running to the police, you should know that. God only knows where it might lead.'

Peter Machin's warning came back to her then. 'Jimmy can't hurt anyone if he's locked up,' Sadie said.

'He's got mates though, hasn't he? Some very important mates.'

'If they're that important they won't concern themselves with a nobody like Jimmy.'

'You know nothing about it.'

Lily Sedgewick spoke up. She turned to Sadie, eyes burning in her pale face. 'You should never have done it,' she said. 'You should have stayed out of my business.'

'And watched you being used as a punchbag?' Sadie shot back at her.

Lily started pacing, twisting the tea-stained cloth between her hands.

'You must go down to the police station and take back your statement,' she muttered, almost to herself. 'Tell them you made a mistake.'

'No!' Sadie said. 'Besides, they've got the evidence.'

'You've got to do something!' Her mother looked at her, face desperate. 'You've got to save him . . .'

Sadie saw the despair in her eyes and realisation dawned. Her mother wasn't afraid of Jimmy. She loved him. She was too hopelessly in thrall to him ever to save herself.

Sadie's chin lifted. 'I'm going to stand up in that court and tell everyone what he did.'

For a moment they faced each other in silence.

'Then you're no longer welcome in my home,' Lily said coldly.

Belle gasped. 'Now, Lily, you know you don't mean that!'

'I do.' Lily Sedgewick's face was calm. 'This is between me and Jimmy, it's nothing to do with her.'

'All right, if that's how you feel . . .' As Sadie went to fetch her coat, she heard Belle whispering urgently to her mother, and Lily's voice saying, 'No, Belle, it's for the best. If she can't mind her own business, then I don't want her around.'

'But, Lil—'

'It's all right, Belle. You heard her, she's made her choice.' Sadie reached into her bag and pulled out the dried flower picture. 'And you can keep this. I don't want anything from you!'

For a moment, her mother hesitated. Then she reached out and snatched the picture back.

Chapter Twenty-Four

There was a riot going on in the Students' Union on Christmas night.

Charlie Latimer was standing on top of the bar, flanked by Talbot and Evans, all three of them dressed in blue-striped nurses' uniforms that exposed inches of pale, hairy ankle. Their caps sat askew on their heads as they threw their arms around each other, murdering a Gilbert and Sullivan chorus they had adapted.

Three little student nurses are we, come from a class on anatomy . . .

Rufus winced into his pint at their flat, high voices. But the student nurses they had invited to be their audience seemed to enjoy it. They clapped along, cheering encouragement and roaring with laughter.

'I wonder you aren't up there with them?' Joan Gifford said. She sat across the table from Rufus, nursing a pink gin.

He smiled ruefully. 'My voice isn't up to it.'

'Neither are theirs.' She sized him up over the rim of her glass. 'You could borrow my uniform,' she said. 'I reckon you'd look a treat in one of my aprons!'

'I daresay I would.'

Her eyes sparkled with mischief. 'Go on, then. Do it. I dare you!'

'No, thanks. I'm not in the mood for cavorting around.'

'I can see that.' Joan sat back in her seat and sipped her gin moodily.

Rufus sighed. This was a mistake. He should never have invited Staff Nurse Gifford out tonight.

He could tell she was disappointed, and he didn't blame her. Any other night and he would have been up there with Latimer, singing along and showing off his ankles. But tonight . . .

He glanced across to the next table, where Leo Carlyle sat, his arm draped around the shoulders of a pretty young nurse. He had been on the military ward today too, but he looked as if he didn't have a care in the world.

Across the table, Joan Gifford gave a dissatisfied sigh. 'Well, this is great fun, I'm sure,' she muttered. 'I would have had a better time playing whist with Miss Sutton.'

'I'm sorry,' Rufus said. 'I've had a hard day, that's all. We lost three men on the ward today.'

Joan Gifford shrugged. 'Patients die all the time. You should be used to it by now.'

'Yes, but they were only boys. One was barely eighteen.' He caught Joan's blank expression and stopped. 'You're right,' he said. 'Being miserable about it won't bring them back, will it?' He held up his glass to her. 'Cheers.'

She held up her own. 'Here's to not being miserable.'

Rufus downed his pint and stood up. 'Another?'

'Why not?' She smiled.

He found himself standing next to Leo Carlyle at the bar. They nodded to each other.

'Where's your sister?' Rufus asked.

Leo cupped his hand over his ear. 'Who?'

'Your sister,' Rufus shouted over the din.

Leo shrugged. 'Probably still at work, knowing Kate.'

Rufus looked at his watch. 'At this time? It's nearly ten o'clock.'

'You know how dedicated she is.' Leo turned to the barman. 'Port and lemon and a whisky. A double,' he added.

For the next half an hour Rufus did his best to be entertaining. He determinedly sank another pint and listened to Joan Gifford complaining about Miss Sutton and her fellow staff nurses.

He watched her mouth moving and tried hard to concentrate, but her voice turned into an annoying buzz in his head.

He looked at Latimer and the others, still cavorting on the bar. Maybe Joan was right. He should put on an apron and a cap and join them. He could forget his troubles, forget those young men who had died before their time. He wasn't going to bring them back by being miserable, was he?

Charlie Latimer and the other medical students finally clambered down from the bar, helped by the laughing student nurses. A moment later Charlie joined Rufus, still dressed in his nurse's uniform. He had lost a stud and his starched collar was half hanging off.

'You're a picture!' laughed Joan. 'I'm not sure what Sister would make of you.'

'Mincemeat, probably!' Charlie grimaced and reached for Rufus' glass to take a gulp of beer.

He went to put it back in front of him, but Rufus pushed it away. 'Have it,' he said, standing up.

Charlie and Joan both looked at him. 'Are you off already, old man?' Charlie said.

'I've just remembered, there's something I need to do.'

'And what about me?' Joan looked put out.

'Charlie will see you safely back to the nurses' home. That's all right, isn't it?' he asked Latimer.

'Well, I—'

'It's not all right with me!' Joan huffed. 'You were the one who asked me to come out with you tonight.'

'Latimer here is far better company than I am,' Rufus said, already shrugging on his coat.

But Joan Gifford clearly wasn't satisfied. 'What is it you've forgotten anyway?' she demanded.

'I need to take some samples down to Pathology for testing.'

'At this time of night?' Joan snorted. 'There won't be anyone there. It's Christmas Day.'

Rufus glanced at Leo.

'I think I know someone who'll be there,' he said.

A crack of light spilt from the pane of glass in the door to Pathology, illuminating the dark section of passageway outside. Rufus stood looking in for a moment, watching Kate at her bench. Her dark hair was caught up in pins on top of her head, and there was something oddly vulnerable about the slender arch of her neck as she bent over a microscope. She didn't look like the tense, hostile young woman he had seen on the ward. Here, she seemed peaceful, content.

And then she looked up and caught him watching her, and her scowl was suddenly back in place.

'What do you want?' she snapped as Rufus walked in, letting the door swing shut behind him.

'I have a couple of tissue samples for you to examine.'

She glanced at the clock. 'Couldn't they wait?'

'I'd like them done as soon as possible, if you don't mind.'

'Don't you have juniors to do that for you?'

'They're all too busy flirting with nurses in the SU bar, I'm afraid.' He paused. 'I'm surprised you aren't there too?'

'Flirting with the nurses?'

He smiled. 'Was that a joke, Miss Carlyle?'

She took the samples from him and crossed the lab to prepare the slides.

'There's no need to do it straight away,' he said. 'It's just a couple of lung lesions, nothing serious.'

She glanced over her shoulder at him. 'I thought you said they were needed as soon as possible?'

Rufus looked down at his feet, caught out in the lie. 'I don't want you to miss the party,' he mumbled.

'I'm sure I'm not missing much.'

'Oh, I don't know. Latimer was dressed up as a nurse.'

'It sounds rather puerile to me.'

Rufus watched her as she selected a glass slide from a box, her back turned to him. She was so cool and dismissive, he felt his old resentment against her resurfacing.

'You made such a fuss about being allowed in to the SU bar and yet I've never seen you there,' he remarked.

Kate took a pipette of fluid, holding it up to the light. 'I only wanted the door kept open. I didn't necessarily want to go through it.'

He stared at her dark head, bent over the slide she was preparing, and suddenly he understood. He knew only too well what it was like to have doors closed on him.

He pulled his attention away from her and glanced around the laboratory, with its rows of glass jars, each filled with ominous-looking organ specimens. The strong smell of formaldehyde hung in the air.

He turned away with a shudder. 'How can you bear this place?'

Kate looked up from her work. 'It suits me very well,' she said. 'And Dr Werner is very good. He's taught me a lot.'

'I've never cared for the work myself. I much prefer dealing with the living, not the dead.' He paused then confessed, 'I passed out during my first post-mortem.'

He told her the story of how he had woken up in the middle of the Pathology demonstration theatre with Dr Werner staring down at him, a bone saw in his hand, and how he had somehow got the idea that he was to be the subject of the doctor's post-mortem.

It was an amusing tale, and usually made the nurses laugh when he told it to them. But Kate listened to him with an expression of strained politeness on her face, as if she was watching a child reciting a poem badly. A look that made Rufus wonder why he was even telling her the story in the first place.

'Sorry, I'm rambling.' He stopped talking abruptly. He was nervous, he realised. There was something about Kate's cool aloofness that made him feel like a humble grammar school boy again. 'I'll let you get on with your work. I'll leave the notes here, shall I?' He placed the file down on the bench and headed for the door, then turned back to look at her. 'Are you sure you won't come to the bar?'

'I don't think I'd be very welcome.'

'Since when has that stopped you?'

She glanced up at him. A lock of dark hair had escaped from its pins and fallen across her face, but behind it he thought he could detect the slightest hint of a smile.

Kate was studying the slide under the microscope half an hour later when the door opened behind her.

Thinking it was Rufus French, she said, 'I'm glad you've come back. I have something to show you.'

'Sounds promising.'

She looked up sharply. Charlie Latimer stood in the doorway, grinning wolfishly. He was wearing a suit but his tie hung loose about his neck.

'What are you doing here?' she asked.

'Looking for you.'

'Why aren't you at the party?'

221

'It was no fun without you there.'

Kate turned back to her microscope. 'I find that difficult to believe.'

'It was no fun for me, put it that way.'

As he came towards her, Kate could smell the waves of alcohol coming off him. 'That's not what I heard,' she said. 'Dr French said you were the life and soul of the party.'

'Dr French is rapidly turning into a miserable old bore.' He pulled a hip flask from his pocket and put it down on the bench next to her. Kate stared at it.

'What's that?'

'What does it look like? I thought if you wouldn't come to the party, I'd bring the party to you.' He pulled off the top of the flask and took a swig.

'Put it away!' Kate said, appalled. 'You know you're not supposed to drink in the lab.'

'And who's going to tell?' Charlie looked around at the rows of jars. 'Go on,' he said, thrusting the flask at her. 'Live dangerously for once.'

'No, thank you.' Kate turned away from him, back to her microscope. 'Take a look at this slide, would you?'

Charlie Latimer squinted at her, clearly taken aback. 'What?'

'This sample Dr French gave me. I'd like you to look at it.'

'Now?'

'If you wouldn't mind?' Kate slid from her stool to allow Charlie to take her place.

It took him a moment to get his balance, and even longer to stare down the lens. 'What am I supposed to be looking at?

She said, 'Do they look like tubercles to you?'

'Yes, I suppose so.'

'Are you sure? Look again.'

'I think I know a tubercle bacillus when I see one, Kate.'

'That's what I thought.' She looked down at the scrawled notes Rufus French had left with her. 'You were wrong,' she murmured.

Charlie Latimer frowned. 'I beg your pardon?'

'It doesn't matter,' Kate dismissed the question. 'But if you'll excuse me, I have to write up my notes.'

'Can't it wait?'

She shook her head. 'I need to get them written up as soon as possible.'

Charlie stumbled from the stool and she took his place, pulling her notebook towards her. She could feel him standing there, inches away from her, watching as she peered into the microscope again.

She looked up at him. 'Was there something else?'

He cleared his throat. 'I must say, you're looking very lovely this evening.'

Kate studied his flushed face. 'Are you drunk?'

'Perhaps I am.' Charlie's chin lifted defiantly. 'Perhaps I needed some Dutch courage.'

'Whatever for?'

'This . . .' Before Kate had time to register the sprig of mistletoe he had pulled from his pocket it was too late. He lunged at her, nearly knocking her off the stool as his mouth came down on hers, wet and sloppy and tasting of beer.

Kate jumped to her feet, pushing him away so hard he staggered backwards, his legs buckling under him. He sprawled on the floor at her feet, staring up at her with a stunned expression.

'It was only a Christmas kiss,' he mumbled.

Kate turned away from him, shaken. 'I think you'd better go,' she said.

She heard him stumbling to his feet. 'I'm sorry,' he mumbled. 'I thought you liked me . . . I've been waiting weeks to do it . . .'

'Just go, will you?'

'I'm sorry . . .'

She held herself rigid until she heard the door close behind him.

Chapter Twenty-Five

For once Liesel didn't mind sharing a room with Anna. She huddled up in bed, the covers pulled up to her chin, while Anna sat at the dressing table, brushing her hair.

'This is the night the note said they'd come,' Liesel whimpered.

'I told you, no one's coming.'

'How do you know?'

'Because I know.'

'But the note said—'

'Liesel, will you shut up about the note?' Anna scowled at her sister's reflection in the mirror. 'It's just nonsense, that's all.'

'Then why is Mother so afraid?' Liesel asked.

'She isn't.' But Anna knew this was a lie. She had seen Dorothy Beck struggling to put on a brave face for her daughters all day. Every time the wind howled outside her mother would look up sharply, as if she expected the door to crash off its hinges any second.

When they went to bed, Anna had watched her carefully locking the windows and bolting the doors.

'It's to keep out the draughts,' she had said. 'It's such a cold, windy night.'

Anna couldn't see how a bolt could keep out a draught, but she said nothing. Nor did she argue when her mother said she was going to sit up for a while, after the girls had gone to bed. Anna had left her in the parlour, bent over some sewing by the light of the gas lamp.

Anna laid down her brush and went to turn down the lamp, but Liesel said, 'Leave it for a while. Please?'

Anna was about to argue but then she looked into her sister's blue eyes, wide with fear.

'Just for a few minutes, then,' she sighed. 'We don't want to waste it.'

She clambered into bed. Liesel immediately huddled against her, limbs caught in a tangle of flannel nightgown.

'Will you keep talking to me until I go to sleep?'

'What shall I talk about?'

'Anything. I don't mind. I can't sleep if it's too quiet.'

Anna smiled. 'You're usually telling me to shut up!'

'I know.' Then, before Anna could say any more, Liesel suddenly burst out, 'We won't be murdered in our beds, will we?'

'Liesel!'

'Promise?'

'I promise. Now go to sleep.'

'I can't.' Liesel's voice trembled. 'I'm too scared to sleep.'

'Oh, Liesel.' Anna put her arm around her sister, pulling her close. 'What if I stayed awake and kept watch?'

Liesel lifted her head from the pillow. 'And what good would that do? You'd be no good against a murderer, would you?'

Anna smiled. Now she sounded more like the old Liesel. 'Go to sleep,' she ordered. 'Or I'll be the one committing murders!'

She turned down the lamp and lay in the darkness, her arm around Liesel's slim shoulders, stroking her hair. It was comforting, like being a child again. At first the sound of the wind whistling through the eaves made her jump, but as her eyelids grew heavy, soon the sound became almost soothing.

'Christmas Day is over, and no one came to get us,' were

the last words she murmured to herself, as she drifted off to sleep.

The next thing, she was sitting bolt upright, shaken out of sleep by a cry in the darkness.

She sat there listening hard. Somewhere in the distance she could hear a faint crackling sound, and a smell, acrid, burning . . .

'Fire!'

Anna shot out of bed, tripping over the hem of her nightgown.

'Liesel!' She shook her sister roughly, half dragging her out of bed. 'Liesel, wake up!'

Her sister stirred blearily. 'What is it?'

'There's a fire. We've got to get out.' Anna ran to the window and threw it open, letting in the cold night air. She looked down at the ground below. It was too far to jump, and the drainpipe was out of reach.

'A fire?' Liesel was instantly awake, throwing off the bedclothes and springing out of bed. 'Where's Mother?'

'We'll find her.' Anna pulled a blanket off the bed and draped it around both of them, pulling it over their hands. 'Come on.'

The landing was thick with swirling black smoke. Anna felt it filling her lungs, choking her. She doubled up, coughing. Liesel screamed in panic.

'Mother!'

'We've got to get out . . .' Anna gasped, but her legs seemed paralysed. The stinging smoke blinded her; tears streamed down her cheeks. Beside her, Liesel was clinging to her hand, coughing and choking and crying out for their mother.

Suddenly, a figure staggered out of the smoke towards them.

'This way,' Anna heard Tom's gruff voice calling to them. 'Cover your mouths, and try not to breathe too much.'

Next thing his hand was on her arm, pulling her into the nothingness. Anna resisted him.

'I need to find Mother first.'

'You need to get yourselves to safety.'

'Not without Mother!'

Tom was silent. 'I'll fetch her,' he said at last. 'You get yourselves out. The stairs are here . . . Just another step . . .'

Groping ahead of her, Anna found the banister rail. Pulling Liesel behind her, she slowly and carefully inched her way down. The heat seemed to rise to meet them, scorching her skin.

'We're walking into the fire!' Liesel screeched.

'Shhh, don't talk! Here, keep this over your mouth.' Anna pressed the blanket to her sister's face. 'Now, stay close to me. We'll get out through the kitchen . . .'

The smoke was acrid on the back of her throat as she pushed her way down the hall. Liesel had gone very quiet. Too quiet. When Anna glanced around, she saw her sister's eyes were half-closed, her body limp.

'Liesel! Try to stay awake, please.' Propping her up with one arm, Anna reached with the other hand to open the back door, but it wouldn't give. Then she remembered her mother had bolted it.

She fumbled in the darkness for the bolt, but couldn't quite stretch far enough to get her fingers round it while supporting her sister. And all the while the smoke was getting thicker, blacker. It seemed to have seeped into her brain, too, filling her head with fog. But this was a warm, comforting fog, like a cloud. She was so tired, all she wanted to do was close her eyes and surrender to it . . .

A sudden splintering crash from overhead brought her

back to her senses. Liesel woke up, screaming out for their mother. She pulled away from Anna and tried to run back towards the stairs, but Anna grabbed her by her hair, yanking her backwards until they fell in a heap on the tiled floor.

'We need . . . to get out . . .' she murmured. But even as she said it she knew escape was impossible. The smoke was filling her head like fog, making it harder and harder for her to breathe, to think . . .

Anna could smell the stench of charred wood and smoke in the air, even before they turned the corner into Chambord Street.

She stole a worried glance at her mother walking beside her. Dorothy Beck had aged overnight, face drawn and haggard, body stooped inside the borrowed clothes the Lady Almoner at the hospital had given her. She stared straight ahead of her, stumbling like a sleepwalker towards the wreckage of what had once been their home.

Anna steeled herself for what was to come, but nothing could prepare her for the sight of the bakery in the grey, chilly dawn light.

It was ruined beyond recognition, a blackened, splintered mess, dripping with water after the firemen had put out the flames.

Their neighbours stood in a huddle on the pavement, staring at the wreckage and talking amongst themselves. As Anna and her mother approached, they fell silent, parting to let them through.

'It's a bad business,' Mr Hudson mumbled, staring down at the pavement, his hands in his pockets.

Dorothy Beck didn't seem to hear him as she moved past, picking her way over the debris. She stood still, staring up at the ugly, jagged hole where once the shop doorway had been.

'I'm glad your father isn't here to see this,' she said, her voice barely above a whisper.

'Or Liesel,' Anna murmured. Her sister had recovered well, apart from her hacking, painful cough. She had been kept in hospital for observation.

This would have broken her heart, Anna thought. It was all she could do not to cry herself.

'Is there anything we can do?' Mrs Wheeler called out.

Anna turned to look at her and her husband. This was a couple who displayed a sign saying 'Proud to be British' in the window of their café. A couple who this time last year had drunk beer with their family to celebrate her engagement.

'Where were you last night, when we nearly died in our beds?' she called back.

Mrs Wheeler's face reddened. 'I – I'm sure I don't know what you're implying!' she spluttered.

As Anna turned away to follow her mother into the shop, she heard Mrs Wheeler muttering to her husband. 'Did you hear the way she spoke to me? I was only trying to be neighbourly.'

There was nothing left of their home, just a charred husk. Everything that hadn't been destroyed by the fire was soaked through. Anna could scarcely make out their furniture among the burnt remains that littered the floor. Only glimpses of her mother's cherished wallpaper remained on the walls, the rest consumed by creeping black stains.

Anna picked up the remnants of a photograph. 'It's all gone,' she said.

'Yes.' Her mother's voice was faint as she looked around her. 'Yes, it's all gone.'

'How will we tell Papa?'

'I don't know.' Dorothy was silent for a moment, then

she pulled herself together with an effort and said, 'But we're all alive, and that's the main thing.'

'Thanks to Tom,' Anna said.

'Yes.' Her mother put her hand to the wall, staring for a moment at the rose-patterned wallpaper she had loved so much. 'We owe him our lives.'

Don't trust Tom Franklin.

Edward's words came back to Anna's mind, startling her. She looked around at the blackened room.

'I wonder how it started?' she said.

'It must have been one of the ovens in the kitchen.'

'We don't light the ovens on Christmas Day.'

'A gas lamp, then.'

Anna watched her mother carefully. 'Liesel showed me the note,' she said.

Dorothy Beck's face paled. 'What note?'

'You know what I'm talking about, Mother.'

'That has nothing to do with it,' her mother said firmly. 'And I don't want you saying any different in front of your sister. She's upset enough as it is.'

'No, Mother.'

'And I certainly don't want you mentioning it to your father. He's worried sick, without all this.' She gestured with her hand then allowed it to fall by her side.

They spent a few minutes searching the rooms, looking for anything they could salvage. But there was nothing. Everything they owned had been destroyed. It was as if someone had tried to erase them, their memories and everything they had achieved, from the face of the earth.

As the enormity of their situation hit her, Anna's legs buckled and she sank down on the floor. First her father, then Edward, and now her family home. She felt as if she was deep in the bowels of the earth, with nowhere left to sink.

'What shall we do, Mother?' she whispered. 'Where shall we go?'

Dorothy Beck looked around the ruins of her home. She seemed utterly diminished, defeated.

'There is only one place we can go,' she said.

Chapter Twenty-Six

Rufus peered into the microscope. He was looking at the slide, but he was also aware of Kate's light scent as she stood behind him. She smelt of flowers, overlaid with the pungent chemicals of the Pathology lab.

'You see?' she was saying. 'I'm right, aren't I?'

He squinted down the lens. 'It's difficult to say.'

'That's what I thought. So I asked for a sample of the patient's sputum.'

He straightened up. 'You did what? You had no right.'

Kate ignored him, replacing the slide under the microscope with another. 'Have a look,' she said.

Reluctantly he bent to peer down the microscope. This time there was no mistaking the long, tubular strands he saw.

'I'm right, aren't I? They are tubercle bacilli?'

He couldn't meet her eyes. How she must be loving this, he thought.

'Yes,' he muttered.

'So the patient has phthisis.'

'So it seems.'

He looked back at the microscope, cursing himself. How could he have made such a simple mistake? He had been so sure the old man had a lung abscess, it hadn't even occurred to him to do the simplest sputum check first.

As if she knew what he was thinking, Kate said, 'I imagine the symptoms would be very similar, at first glance.'

He looked up at her. He expected to see gloating, but the serious grey eyes that looked back at him were free from any guile.

She moved to the microscope again, and he stepped back to let her look down the lens.

For a moment he stood watching her. She seemed to quite forget he was there, she was so fascinated by her discovery.

'I wonder you didn't go straight to Ormerod with this,' he spoke up finally.

Kate turned her head to look at him, genuinely mystified. 'But it's your patient, Dr French.'

Was she playing a game with him? It was hard to say. Her bland expression gave nothing away.

'It would have been an opportunity to prove yourself to him.' And get me into serious trouble at the same time, he added silently. 'I wonder that you missed such an opportunity.'

'Is that what you would have done?'

His gaze dropped. 'Probably,' he admitted, then added, 'but it's just the way everyone behaves at the Nightingale.'

Kate gave a slight smile. 'Yes, I've seen you all falling over yourselves to impress Dr Ormerod. But that isn't the way I like to go about things. I want to succeed on my own merits, not by bringing someone else down.'

A Carlyle, succeeding on their own merits? Rufus nearly laughed out loud.

'Perhaps you don't have to try as hard as the rest of us,' he said quietly.

'What do you mean?'

'I mean your name allows you certain – liberties.'

'Is that what you think? That I'm given an easy time because I'm a Carlyle? Have you seen the way I'm treated, Dr French? By Dr Ormerod, and the other students?' She looked around the dusty shelves of the lab. 'Look at me. Look at where I am. Do you really think I would be here if I were being given special treatment?'

Put like that, he couldn't deny the idea did seem foolish. 'Perhaps not,' Rufus conceded. 'But the fact that you're here, studying in this hospital at all, is surely because of your father.'

Kate laughed. 'Oh, Dr French, if only you knew!' She faced him squarely. 'My father didn't want me to come here. I had to fight against him to do it. And do you know why I defied him? Because I wanted to prove I was good enough. It wasn't some girlish whim, as you and the other doctors seem to think. I wanted to be tested, not just against other women, but against men too. I wanted to be a good doctor, the best I could be. And if I thought for a moment I wasn't up to it, then I would leave.'

Rufus stared at her. She stood before him, her hands on her hips, her face flushed with angry colour. Suddenly he felt deeply ashamed.

Kate seemed embarrassed by her own outburst. She turned away, shuffling through slides, dismissing him.

Rufus waited for a moment, but she didn't look back.

'Thank you, anyway,' he said. 'For the diagnosis.'

'I was only doing my job.' Her voice was sharp, the way he remembered it. 'Besides, I wasn't doing it for your sake. I merely wanted the patient to receive the correct treatment.'

Rufus turned to leave, then changed his mind. 'You know,' he said. 'This is why everyone finds it so hard to like you.'

Kate looked up, shocked. 'I beg your pardon?'

'You push people away, keep them at arms' length. You're too – abrasive.'

'Abrasive?'

'You never smile at anyone, or try to make conversation. All you ever do is issue orders in your usual brusque fashion.'

'I suppose you'd prefer me to simper and purr like a kitten?' Kate shot back angrily. 'Behave in a manner more fitting to my sex, is that it?'

It was all he could do not to laugh. Somehow he could not imagine Kate Carlyle simpering or purring at anyone. She was more like an alley cat, hissing and spitting at everyone who came near her.

'It wouldn't hurt you to be nice to people,' he said. 'A bit of charm wouldn't go amiss.'

'Oh, and you'd know all about charm, wouldn't you?' Kate's lip curled.

He folded his arms across his chest. 'What's that supposed to mean?'

'I've seen you on the ward, flirting with the nurses and the patients.'

'It's called being friendly. You should try it some time.'

'I'm sure I don't know what you're talking about. I'm perfectly friendly.'

'Are you? I don't think so. You know what they call you? The Ice Maiden.'

Kate coloured. 'They're entitled to their opinion.'

Rufus saw her set expression and sighed. 'Look, you'll never get anywhere until you learn to give people a chance. Not everyone's against you, you know.'

Kate raised an eyebrow. 'You could have fooled me.'

She had a point, he had to admit. 'All right, perhaps you haven't had the warmest of welcomes . . .'

'Least of all from you,' she murmured.

'But you haven't gone out of your way to be friendly either,' Rufus continued. 'And I'm not talking about purring or flirting or anything like that,' he said, as Kate opened her mouth to interrupt. 'I'm just talking about giving people a chance, treating them better. Let down those barriers, Miss Carlyle.'

For a moment she looked back at him, regarding him with those cool grey eyes of hers. Then she turned away.

'Thank you for your advice, Dr French,' she said coldly.

He nodded to the slide. 'And thank you for yours.'

As he went to walk away, he felt something under his foot and bent to pick it up. 'What's this?' He peered at the strange, crushed little sprig. 'It looks like mistletoe.'

Kate snatched it out of his hand before he had a chance to examine it further. 'Nothing,' she muttered, shoving it into her pocket. 'It's nothing.'

Rufus looked at her furiously blushing face and smiled. Perhaps Miss Carlyle didn't need his advice after all?

After he had gone, Kate took the mistletoe sprig out of her pocket and gazed down at it, crushed in the palm of her hand.

Poor Charlie Latimer, she thought. What must he have been thinking? She pitied his sore head this morning.

She was more confused than offended by his blundering attempts to kiss her. No man had ever shown any interest in her before, even when they were drunk, and it had all come as a bit of a shock to her. She hadn't known how to react.

Probably not by pushing him and sending him flying, she thought wryly, smiling at the memory.

Perhaps if she'd had sisters instead of brothers her life would have turned out differently, she thought. She would have learnt how to do her hair, and make small talk, and how to tell if a man was interested in her.

She might have learnt to play with dolls, to have tea parties and dress them up, instead of bandaging their wounds or treating them for mysterious illnesses. She might have fitted in with the girls at boarding school, been able to talk about hats and getting married. As it was, they'd all thought she was odd because she wanted to become a doctor.

And she got on with her brothers no better. They would never let her join in with them. Their games were for boys, they said, even though Kate taught herself to run faster and catch a ball far better than Leo ever could.

So she was left in the middle, the odd one out, not fitting in with anyone. And she had been that way ever since.

She could never explain that to Rufus, she thought. He was so sure of himself, his place in the world. He was a doctor, a man, and that gave him a certain position, one Kate struggled every day to achieve. He didn't need to try as hard as she did to win people's respect. She couldn't afford to allow her guard to drop, not even for a moment.

And yet . . . perhaps he had a point. Keeping her guard up had not served her very well so far, had it? Perhaps it was time to try a different tack?

She looked down at the sprig of mistletoe in her hand and smiled again at the thought of poor Charlie Latimer.

That morning she was assisting Dr Werner with a post-mortem on a nephritis case. As usual, he took gleeful pleasure in pointing out the affected organs, in this case the shrunken glomeruli and the tubular degeneration.

'Death would be inevitable with such a level of inflammation,' he said, with a smile that Kate had come to realise had nothing to do with the patient's demise. Dr Werner treated every PM as a kind of puzzle, and was always delighted when he could come up with a clear solution.

The patient had been one of Dr Ormerod's but it was Charlie Latimer who came down for the results. He stood sheepishly, clutching the patient's notes, not meeting Kate's eye as Dr Werner went through the results of the post-mortem.

It wasn't until Dr Werner left that Charlie whispered to her, 'Miss Carlyle . . . May I have a word?'

Kate turned to him. 'What is it, Dr Latimer?'

He blushed to the roots of his sandy hair. 'It's about last night.'

'Oh, yes? What about it?'

'I'm afraid I made rather a fool of myself. I'm sorry if I caused you offence, I didn't mean to, truly . . .'

Kate looked at him in silence. She had never known him to be tongue-tied, but now he seemed to be tripping and stumbling over every word.

'I feel terrible about it,' he went on. 'You're the last person I would ever want to offend. You know, I hold you in very high regard . . .'

He looked up at her, his green eyes meeting hers, full of contrition.

'It's all right, Dr Latimer,' Kate said. 'I understand. You were in rather – high spirits, as I recall.'

'Do you mean drunk? Oh, Lord, yes, I was. Very drunk indeed.'

'Dutch courage, you called it.'

'Did I say that? Oh, dear.' He ran his hand through his hair. 'Talk about *in vino veritas*.' He looked at her ruefully. 'I have to tell you, Miss Carlyle, that when I pay court to a young lady I usually do it with rather more decorum than I showed last night.'

Kate stared at him. 'Pay court?'

His blush deepened. 'Lord, I've done it again, haven't I? Put my foot in it, I mean.' He took a deep breath. 'What I'm trying to say, in my clumsy way, is that I like you. I like you very much. But surely you must have known that? You must have noticed me admiring you from afar, so to speak.'

'No. Indeed, I – I put it down to a drunken escapade.' She looked up at him. 'It never occurred to me you might be serious?'

'Well, I am. Very serious. Although I daresay you now think I'm a complete buffoon and will never want to speak to me again.'

You know what they call you? The Ice Maiden. Kate opened her mouth, then closed it again as Rufus' words came back to her.

It's called being friendly. You might try it sometime.

'What's this?' Charlie Latimer looked down at the object Kate pressed into his hand.

'Your mistletoe. You left it in the lab last night.'

'Oh, Lord.' He shook his head. 'I'm so sorry.'

'It would be a shame to let it go to waste.'

He looked at her, baffled. 'What? I don't understand . . .'

Give people a chance.

She smiled at him. 'I think you do, Dr Latimer.'

Chapter Twenty-Seven

Anna's mother rarely spoke about the house in Belgravia where she grew up. So Anna had no idea what to expect when they arrived at the house in Belgrave Square in the rain on Boxing Day morning.

'It's like a palace!' Liesel whispered as they stood at the foot of the steps, looking up at the grand, white-painted Georgian façade. Elegant pillars framed the glossy black front door. 'Did you really live here, Mother?'

'Once. A long time ago.' Dorothy was tight-lipped. Anna could see the tension on her mother's face as she stood there, staring up at the door.

For a moment none of them moved. 'Should we knock?' Liesel said, shifting restlessly from one foot to the other. 'I'm soaking wet.'

'Yes. Yes, of course.' Dorothy forced a smile.

As she followed her mother up the steps, Anna thought she saw a lace curtain twitch in one of the front windows. But as soon as she looked round, the curtain dropped.

At the top of the steps Dorothy paused for a moment to compose herself, brushing the rain from her borrowed coat. Anna felt for her. She would have liked her to be able to face her mother with more dignity, not in rough, ill-fitting clothes.

Dorothy tugged on the bell pull, and waited.

'There's no one at home,' Liesel whispered.

'Wait. Someone will come.' No sooner had her mother said it than the door opened and a man in butler's livery poked his head out.

'Hawkers are to use the servants' entrance,' he barked.

Dorothy stood her ground. 'We are not hawkers,' she said, lifting her chin. 'My name is Dorothy Beck, Grey as was, and this is my mother's house.'

The butler stared at her for a moment, then closed the door in her face.

'What's happening?' Liesel asked. 'Why won't he let us in?'

'Be patient,' Anna whispered back.

Sure enough, a few minutes later the door opened again and this time the man stepped aside to let them in.

He led the way down the hall and opened a door to their left. 'Wait in the library while I speak to your mother,' he instructed Anna and Liesel.

Anna looked at her mother. Dorothy nodded, and the girls went in.

The room was small and cold, with a fireplace that looked as if it had not been used in years. Thick velvet curtains shut out what meagre grey daylight there was. The book-lined walls gave off a smell of dust and damp.

But Liesel was still impressed. She stood before a gilt-framed painting of a severe-looking old man who frowned down on them.

'Do you think that's our grandfather?'

'I don't know.' Anna shivered. She looked around for a lamp to light.

'Look at all these ornaments on the mantelpiece. I've never seen so many lovely things.'

'It's like a museum.' No wonder her mother had wanted to escape it.

The door opened and her mother came in. Then the door closed again.

'What's happening, Mother?' Anna asked.

'We must wait for your grandmother to make up her mind whether she wishes to see us.'

'But why wouldn't she want to see us?' Liesel asked. 'We're her family!'

Her mother gave her a sad smile. 'That is not your grand-mother's way.'

After a few more minutes, the butler reappeared. 'Mrs Grey will see you now,' he said.

He led them back down the passage and through another door, and suddenly Anna found herself in the presence of her grandmother.

Hester Grey was like her house: stiff and formal, with no warmth. She was in her late sixties, as thin as a whip and fiercely elegant if old-fashioned in her heavily corseted Victorian dress. Anna searched her face to find some resemblance to her own mother's, but even though they had the same blue eyes and high cheekbones, Hester shared none of Dorothy Beck's warmth and kindness.

She surveyed them all in silence. 'Well,' she said finally. 'So here you are.' Her voice was dry but as clear as crystal.

'Hello, Mother,' Dorothy said.

Hester turned on her. 'I wonder you would still address me so, considering how long it is since I've seen you,' she said coldly.

Anna glanced nervously at her mother, but Dorothy only smiled.

'Yes,' she said. 'It has been a long time, hasn't it?'

'Twenty three years. Twenty three years since you ran off in the middle of the night.' Hester's thin mouth tight-ened. 'And now Morton tells me you have nothing?'

Dorothy lowered her gaze. 'It's true we have lost our home and all our possessions in a fire,' she said.

'And where is your husband? Surely he should be the one looking after you?'

'They've taken him away to an internment camp.'

'Indeed?' Anna saw a flash of malice in her grandmother's

eyes. 'And so you have come crawling back like a beggar? The proud girl who told me the man she loved was going to make a wonderful new life for her.' Her mouth twisted mockingly. 'How the mighty are fallen!'

Anna waited for her mother to retaliate, but Dorothy hung her head humbly and said, 'Will you help us?'

'I don't see why I should when you have ignored me for so many years. Ten years I've lived alone since your father died, and not once have I heard a word from you.'

'That's not true!' Anna protested. 'Mother wrote to you after our grandfather died. She begged you to let her come to the funeral but you refused. And Papa sent you a Christmas cake every year . . .'

She caught her mother's stricken expression and closed her mouth, but it was too late. Her grandmother turned slowly to face her.

'And who are you?'

'This is Anna,' her mother answered for her.

'And I'm Liesel,' her sister joined in, determined not to be left out as usual.

'You are impertinent!' her grandmother snapped. She lifted the *pince-nez* that dangled from a chain around her neck and peered at her younger granddaughter. 'How old are you?'

'Sixteen.'

'She looks like you did at her age,' Hester commented to her daughter. She turned to Anna then, her mouth turning down. 'I suppose you must take after him,' she said shortly.

Anna pressed her lips together to stop herself from speaking out again. She let her gaze wander around the room, taking in the dark, old-fashioned furnishings. It was dimly lit, with crimson walls and dark wood and the heavy, cloying scent of violets in the air.

Her grandmother lowered herself on to the couch. 'Of

course I knew it would happen eventually,' she said. 'The day you ran away with him, I knew one day he would let you down and you would have to come home.'

'He hasn't let us down!' Anna protested, but Hester ignored her.

'Come closer.' She held out her hands to Dorothy. 'Let me look at you.'

Dorothy approached cautiously and stood still as Hester looked her over.

'How he has dragged you down!' she murmured. She seized her daughter's hands and examined them. 'And look! My kitchen maid has prettier hands than yours.' She shook her head in sorrow. 'You have aged so much, but that is not surprising. I daresay you've led a hard life. Much harder than the one your father and I had hoped you might lead.'

Anna waited for her mother to say something, but Dorothy merely hung her head, the picture of contrition.

'Yes, Mother.'

Hester released her hands. 'I should turn you away, you know, after the cruel way you treated your father and me.' She sighed. 'But you are still my daughter, and I know my duty even if you don't. So I must find it in my heart to take you in.'

What heart? Anna thought. She was sure Hester had nothing more than a piece of flint under that stiff, high-necked gown.

She rang a small bell on the table beside her and almost immediately the door opened and the butler appeared.

'Morton, prepare some rooms for my daughter and her –' she waved her hand vaguely in the direction of Anna and Liesel '– to stay, if you please. And we must find you some clothes,' she added in an undertone. 'You cannot be allowed to live under my roof dressed as ragamuffins.'

'It's quite all right, you don't have to find a place for me,' Anna said. 'I have a room at the hospital.'

'Anna is a nurse,' Dorothy explained.

'Is she, indeed?' Hester stared at Anna over her *pince-nez*, her long nose wrinkling. 'How very modern.'

She took off her spectacles. 'Wait in the library until Morton has arranged some suitable accommodation for you,' she said.

The suitable accommodation turned out to be two narrow rooms up in the attic, just along the passage from the maids' quarters.

Anna was outraged. 'You'd think in a house as big as this she would be able to find you a decent room!' she said.

'Hush, we mustn't complain,' her mother said. 'At least we have a roof over our heads, which is more than we had this morning. I wasn't certain we would be allowed to stay at all.'

'How could she turn us away?' Liesel said.

Anna looked at her mother, but neither of them said anything.

'Besides, it's quite cosy,' Dorothy went on brightly. 'And it isn't as if we have to find space for any belongings.' She looked away, her lips trembling.

Anna went to the tiny dormer window and peered down to the street below. On the other side of the road was a large, leafy square, surrounded by wrought-iron fencing. Governesses and nannies pushed prams or walked their charges. She could hear squeals of childish laughter.

'I wish there were somewhere else we could go,' she said.

'Why?' Liesel piped up. 'I like it here.'

Anna glanced at her mother. Dorothy Beck looked even

more wretched than she had this morning, if that was possible.

'How will you bear it here?' Anna asked.

'I'll have to, won't I?' Her mother smiled wearily. 'We don't have any other choice.'

Chapter Twenty-Eight

The Christmas truce was on the front page of all the newspapers.

Eleanor heard the soldiers discussing it as she changed the dressing on a patient's shoulder wound. On the other side of the screen, one of the men was reading the story aloud.

'It says here they shook hands through the barbed wire in the middle of no-man's-land,' he said to his friend in the next bed. 'Can you believe it?'

'I'm surprised they didn't break their necks getting there,' one of the men said.

'Or drown,' another joined in. 'Some of those shell holes are sodding deep.'

'Our side heard the Germans singing carols from their trenches, so they joined in,' the first man read on. 'They started shouting to each other, then the next thing they'd gone over the top to meet.'

'I wonder who went over first?' one of the men mused.

'It wouldn't be me!' The man whose shoulder Eleanor was dressing muttered under his breath. 'You can't trust a bloody Hun further than you can throw him. Pardon my language, Nurse.'

The men on the other side of the screen were still discussing the matter.

'You know, something similar happened to me,' one of them was saying. 'The Germans stopped firing so the medics could collect our wounded from no-man's-land. Then we did the same for them. I reckon I wouldn't be here now if it weren't for them doing that.'

'Listen to him!' Eleanor's patient rolled his eyes. He was in his thirties, a tough-looking man with a square, scarred face. 'They sound like bloody collaborators.'

'That's what the newspapers call them,' Eleanor said. Her father had not been impressed with the stories about the truce, either.

'Those men are there to fight for their country, not hold hands with the Hun!' he had said. 'I hope I never hear of your brother doing anything of that sort.'

She had managed to get a couple of days off to go home to Hampshire over Christmas. Her father had read out Harry's latest letter to them as they gathered around the fire. He told them how he had marched into France from Belgium, and people had come from their houses to greet the British troops, waving and cheering as if they were heroes.

Then they had all raised a glass of sherry to him, but still Eleanor had felt his absence keenly. Her brother was always so full of life, the house had seemed quiet and empty without him.

She finished what she was doing and gathered up the soiled dressings on the trolley, ready for burning. As she headed for the sluice room she crashed straight into a second trolley, piled high with more dressings awaiting disposal.

She stormed into the sluice to find Anna standing at the sink, her face turned up towards the high metal grille. Seeing her standing there daydreaming made Eleanor's already fraying temper snap.

'What do you think you're doing?' she demanded. 'Did you leave that trolley outside?'

Anna turned slowly to face her, a dazed expression on her face.

'What if Sister had found it?' Eleanor cut her off before she had time to open her mouth. 'We would both have been in trouble then. You need to get it down to the stoke hole, *stat*.'

Anna didn't move.

'Didn't you hear what I said?' Eleanor sighed impatiently. 'I'm not going to end up with a black mark in the ward book because you're too lazy to—'

'Leave her alone.'

Eleanor swung round. Miriam Trott stood in the passageway. She looked past Eleanor at Anna.

'I'll take it down to the stoke hole for you,' she said.

Eleanor stared at her. 'But it's her job.'

'I said I'll do it,' Miriam cut her off firmly. She took hold of the trolley and marched off. Eleanor followed her, pushing her own trolley.

'What's going on?' she said. 'Why are you sticking up for her all of a sudden?' It wasn't like Trott to do anyone a favour.

Miriam looked back at her. 'Oh, I forgot, you've been away. You don't know, do you?'

'Know what?'

'Her father's bakery burnt down.'

Eleanor gasped. 'No! When did it happen?'

'Three days ago, on Christmas night. They were all there, Beck and her sister and mother. They could have died in their beds.'

'How awful.' Eleanor shuddered. 'Are they all right?'

'I think so. But Beck's still in shock, poor girl. We're all trying to be a bit nicer to her,' Miriam added pointedly.

There was no mistaking the meaning behind the look she gave Eleanor, who glanced away guiltily.

'Of course,' she muttered.

Eleanor watched Anna as she went about her work for the rest of the day. She moved slowly, like someone in a

250

trance, barely registering what was going on around her. Once or twice Eleanor thought about speaking to her, only to change her mind at the last minute.

She wanted to talk to Anna, to tell her how sorry she was, but how could she suddenly start speaking to someone she had pointedly ignored for so long? It seemed too awkward. But then so was staying silent.

She thought about it for a few days, wondering what to do. She watched the other girls fussing around Anna, sitting with her in the common room, having conversations in hushed tones. Eleanor was at a loss. She was hopeless at talking about feelings, or anything like that. It wasn't something her family ever did. They just got on with it, did what needed to be done, with no fuss.

'Actions speak louder than words,' her father always said.

And so Eleanor decided to take action.

It was another two days before she had the chance to speak to Anna alone. There always seemed to be someone with her at the nurses' home, and Eleanor didn't want an audience. But on the afternoon of New Year's Eve, Sister asked her to take some towels to the bathroom where Anna was running a mustard bath for a patient.

As she came into the room Anna looked up briefly at her, then turned back to what she was doing.

'Sister asked me to bring these,' Eleanor said over the sound of gushing water. 'I'll put them on the radiator to warm, shall I?'

Anna said nothing as Eleanor took her time arranging the towels. Eleanor watched her from the corner of her eye.

'I heard what happened,' she said. 'I'm sorry.'

Anna was silent. Eleanor risked a glance at her. She was still bending over the bath, her gaze fixed on the running taps.

Eleanor hesitated for a moment, then said, 'I have something for you.' She took a few steps towards her, reaching into her apron pocket.

Anna looked over her shoulder at her. Her gaze fell to the envelope Eleanor was holding out to her.

'I collected some money.' The words came out in a rush. 'It's from all of us. For your family.' She looked down at the envelope. 'I know it's not much, but it might help.'

Anna slowly lifted her gaze, and Eleanor found herself staring into a pair of cold brown eyes.

'Keep it,' she said.

Anna turned away, back to her work. Eleanor stared at her turned back. 'But it's for your family.'

'We don't need charity, especially from you.'

Eleanor was shocked. This was not what she had expected. 'But I collected it for you,' she murmured.

Anna reached over to turn off the taps. 'The fire was started deliberately,' she said. 'They destroyed everything my father worked hard all his life to make.' Her flat voice filled the bathroom, echoing off the tiled walls. 'They came in the middle of the night when they knew we would all be there. They wanted to kill us.' Anna looked up at her former friend. 'They felt we deserved to die because our father is German.'

Anna stood up slowly. 'So you can keep your charity,' she said. 'We don't need anything from you.'

As Anna went to brush past her, Eleanor said helplessly, 'But what shall I do with the money?'

Anna looked down at the envelope in her hand.

'Give it to your mother,' she said. 'She can buy more wool to knit socks for soldiers.'

Anna didn't know what made her return to Chambord Street on New Year's Eve, a week after the fire.

It was the last day of 1914, the year her whole life had changed. When it began she had been so full of hope, newly engaged and utterly content with her life.

She could never have imagined what was to come, how the war was to take everything from her, until there were not even the smallest shreds of her old life left.

Perhaps that was why she had felt compelled to return here, to prove to herself that this was really happening and not some horrible nightmare.

Turning the corner and seeing the blackened shell of her father's bakery was like a punch in the stomach all over again. The lingering smell of smoke still hung in the air. Someone had put planks of wood up at the broken windows, giving the shop a strange, blank look.

Anna went down the narrow alleyway that ran between Hudson's the butcher's and Herbert Morris' draper's shop, leading to the yards at the back. Mrs Hudson was bringing in the old tin tub for her husband's bath. She regarded Anna silently as she let herself in at the gate and in through the back door.

In the fading afternoon light she could just distinguish the blackened walls, and the sooty patches where the flames had licked across the ceiling. Her father's work table stood in the middle of the room, charred and blackened.

Anna ran her hand over it, feeling the hollows worn in its surface. It was the first thing Friedrich Beck had bought when he came to England. He loved it so much he'd always refused to replace it, even when its warped surface became bleached with age.

Tears spilled down her cheeks and she dashed them away.

Then a sound made her look up. Someone was moving about in one of the rooms overhead. As Anna froze, listening, the footsteps moved towards the stairs.

She snatched up a length of charred wood just as the door opened. She swung round, ready to fight, and came face-to-face with Tom, who was holding a brick in his hand.

She dropped the piece of wood. 'Tom! What are you doing here?'

'I thought I'd stay and guard the place.' He lowered the brick. His chin was dark with stubble, his clothes rumpled. There were deep shadows under his eyes.

Don't trust Tom Franklin. Once again, Edward's words came back to her.

'There's not much to guard, is there?'

'Even so, you don't want anyone getting in. This is your home.'

Anna looked around her. 'It isn't though, is it?' she sighed. 'There's nothing left. It's all gone . . .'

She felt emotion rising in her chest and fought against it, determined not to cry again.

Tom looked away. She had embarrassed him with her show of emotion, she could tell. 'I'll be on my way,' he muttered. 'I've no business being here.'

'No, stay. I'm not stopping long. I just wanted to have a last look round, before . . .' She couldn't finish the sentence.

She stepped past him into the hall, aware that Tom was following her.

'How's Mrs Beck and your sister?' he asked gruffly.

'They're staying with our grandmother.'

He nodded. 'It's good they've got somewhere to go.'

Anna thought about her bullying grandmother, and her mother's sad, defeated face. 'I suppose so,' she murmured. 'How about you? What are you doing for money now you're not working here?'

His chin lifted. 'I get by.'

I'll bet you do, Anna thought. Tom was a Franklin, after all. The less she knew about his activities, the better.

'I'm surprised you haven't enlisted,' Anna said.

His expression darkened. 'I ain't no coward if that's what you're thinking.'

'I didn't say you were.'

'I've tried twice. But they've turned me down on account of my punctured lung.'

'I didn't know you had a lung puncture?'

He nodded. 'Got into a fight when I was a kid.'

'It must have been a nasty fight.'

'It was.' Tom's face was grim. 'But the other kid came off worse than me.'

I'm sure he did, Anna thought. She had only seen glimpses of Tom Franklin's temper, but that had been enough for her to know she didn't want to see more.

As she headed for the stairs, Tom said, 'Be careful. It ain't safe up there. Some of the floorboards have burnt through.'

'I'll manage,' she said, then stopped dead at the foot of the staircase. The first few steps were missing, consumed by the fire.

'You have to go up the side, like this. Let me show you.' Tom picked his way up the broken staircase easily, then reached back and offered her his hand. Anna hesitated, staring for a moment at his grimy fingers. Then she took his hand and let him pull her up after him.

Upstairs was worse than she remembered. The cold December wind whistled through the broken windows, turning the room to ice. Anna shuddered at the charred remains of what had once been her and Liesel's bed. She hadn't realised how close they had come to dying. Just another few minutes, and it would have been too late.

'I never got a chance to thank you for saving us,' she said.

Tom shrugged. 'Anyone would have done it,' he mumbled.

Don't trust Tom Franklin.

'Why were you there?' she asked.

He didn't answer at first, his shifty gaze dropping from hers. Then he said, 'I was just passing.'

'In the middle of the night?'

Mottled colour flushed his throat. 'No law against being out, is there?'

Don't trust Tom Franklin.

'No,' she said. 'I suppose not. And it was a good thing for us you were passing, otherwise I don't know what would have happened . . .'

'Don't,' Tom said. 'Don't think about it.'

Anna looked around. 'I don't know how we're going to break it to Papa,' she said.

Tom said nothing.

Anna turned away. 'I've seen enough,' she said, gathering her coat more tightly around her. 'I want to go home.'

As she moved towards the door he suddenly said, 'I could put it right.'

Anna looked at him. 'What?'

'This place. I could rebuild it. Or I could try. I've done a bit of labouring work in the past.'

Anna gazed around her. 'It would take more than a bit of labouring to put this place right.'

'All the same, I'd like to have a go.'

'But we'd need wood, and bricks, and tools – I'm not sure we could afford it.'

'I could find what we need . . .'

Anna saw his evasive look, and realised she would be wise not to ask too many questions.

'Why would you want to do it?' she asked.

'For your father. He's a good man. He don't deserve any of this.'

For a moment their eyes met. The next minute Tom had

turned away, shuffling his feet. 'I'm sorry,' he mumbled. 'It's none of my business. I shouldn't get involved.'

He cringed like a whipped dog, Anna thought. One that expected a boot in its ribs for wagging its tail.

'I'd like you to try,' she said. 'Thank you, Tom.'

Chapter Twenty-Nine

'I, Sadie Lilian Sedgewick, swear to tell the truth, the whole truth and nothing but the truth, so help me God.'

As she rested her right hand on the leather-bound Bible, Sadie made sure she looked across the courtroom at Jimmy Clyde. He sat in the dock, flanked by police officers. He glared back at her with cold blue eyes. He was trying to frighten her, Sadie thought. But he was the one who should be scared. He was going to be locked away for a very long time.

She would make sure of it.

Where were his powerful friends now? she wondered. The public gallery was empty, except for Belle and Lily. Belle was grim-faced, done up to the nines as usual, her face powdered, a tattered fur around her shoulders. Lily sat beside her, thin as a wraith, staring down at her hands in her lap.

Sadie wished her mother would look up and meet her eye, just for a moment. *I'm doing this for you*, she wanted to shout across the courtroom at her.

After she had finished giving her evidence, Sadie stepped out of the courtroom to get some fresh air. Peter Machin had promised to come and find her before sentencing took place. He said it shouldn't be too long, but Sadie was determined to wait, even if it took all day. She wanted to see the moment Jimmy Clyde was taken away.

It was a freezing cold January day and people hurried by on the city streets, heads down against the cold. Sadie pulled her coat closer, her breath curling in the frosty air. Even after a couple of minutes, she could feel the tip of her nose stinging with cold.

She walked around the block, stamping her feet and rubbing her gloved hands together to help keep them warm. As she returned to the court, she saw Belle emerging from the building. She walked to the corner of the street and stood still to light a cigarette.

'Belle?'

She looked round sharply as Sadie approached her, the cigarette clamped between her lips.

'Oh, it's you.'

'What's going on? Have I missed the verdict?'

'Should be any minute, they reckon.' Belle exhaled, narrowing her eyes against the cigarette smoke. 'You did it, then? You stood up and gave evidence.'

'I said I would, didn't I?' She looked around. 'Where's Ma?'

'In the courtroom. She wanted to see it all.'

'Yes, I saw her weeping in the dock.' Sadie curled her lip.

Belle took another long drag on her cigarette. 'We ain't seen much of you lately.'

'Do you wonder, after she threw me out of the house at Christmas?'

'You know what your mother's like. She didn't mean it.' Belle paused. 'She misses you,' she said.

'Then why ain't she out here telling me that herself?'

Belle shook her head. 'Because she's too bloody proud, that's why.'

'Proud!' Sadie was scornful. 'What's my mother got to be proud about?'

As Belle opened her mouth to answer, the door swung open and Peter Machin appeared. Sadie hurried towards him.

'Peter?'

'There you are.' He cocked his head. 'They're ready.'

Sadie felt a quickening in her chest. She turned to Belle. 'Well, this is it.'

'This is it,' Belle repeated. Then, in a low voice, she added, 'Let's hope for all our sakes they lock him up and throw away the bloody key.'

'Five months? Is that all?'

'Five months' hard labour,' Peter corrected her, but Sadie wasn't listening.

'It ain't long enough,' he said. 'You promised me he'd be locked away for at least three years.'

'I know. I'm sorry.' Peter looked apologetic. 'But he had alibis.'

'Two thugs stood up and lied for him in court, you mean?'

'The jury believed them.'

'And what about the evidence? They didn't believe that, did they?'

Peter shook his head. 'They reckoned it could have come from anywhere.'

'They made it sound like I planted it, like I had a grudge against him.' Sadie pulled off her gloves and chewed on her thumbnail.

'He had a good solicitor. The best, thanks to his mate Billy Willis.'

'Billy Willis looks after his own, all right.' Hot tears of frustration pricked her eyes and Sadie blinked them back determinedly. 'So Jimmy'll be out by the summer?' she said.

'It looks like it. I'm sorry, Sadie.'

'And what good's sorry going to do?' She turned on him, then saw the hurt in his brown eyes. Being angry with him was like kicking a puppy. 'I'm sorry, Peter, I know it ain't your fault.' She sighed. 'I'm just a bit upset, that's all.'

'I know. And I really am sorry. Believe me, there's nothing we would have liked more than to see him behind bars for a long time.' He paused for a moment, then said, 'Look, I know this probably ain't the time, but I wondered . . .'

Just at that moment Sadie spotted her mother coming out of the courtroom, leaning on Belle's arm.

'Sorry, Peter, I've got to go.'

'Sadie, wait!' he called after her. But she was already sprinting down the stairs after her mother, one hand clamping her hat to her head, her coat flying behind her.

They had reached the street before she caught up with them. Belle spotted her first. She turned around and stepped between Sadie and her mother.

'Not now, love,' she said gently. 'Lily wants to go home.'

Sadie ignored her, shouldering past to face her mother. 'Ma? Ma, look at me.'

The minute Lily Sedgewick reluctantly raised her gaze, Sadie knew she had been drinking again. Her eyes were bloodshot in her haggard face.

Lily tried to turn away but Sadie grasped her arms, forcing her to stay still. They were thin as a child's.

'Ma, you've got to leave him,' Sadie said urgently. 'This is your chance. You've got to get away.'

Her mother stared at her. She looked lost, dazed, as if she was struggling to place her daughter's face.

'I've been saving,' Sadie went on. 'I've got some money put by. It ain't much, but it should be enough to set you up somewhere out in the country, far away from here. You could start a new life. You'd like that, wouldn't you?'

Lily shook her head listlessly. 'I can't.'

'Ma, listen to me. You've got to go. We ain't got that long, so we've got to make plans.'

'I ain't going anywhere, Sadie. I'm going to be here, waiting for Jimmy when he gets back.'

Sadie stared at her in despair. 'What are you saying? You want to stay with him, after everything he's done to you?'

'You wouldn't understand.' Her mother's voice was flat and tired.

'That's enough.' Belle stepped between them, gently extricating Lily from Sadie's grasp. 'Your mother's had a long day. She needs to rest.'

Sadie watched in frustration as Belle put her arm around Lily's shoulders, leading her away.

'No, you're right, I wouldn't understand,' Sadie called after them. 'I don't understand how you can turn your back on me, after everything I've done for you. I went to court for you, got him locked up. Now I'm offering you the chance of a new life, and you don't want to know. You're so bloody besotted by Jimmy Clyde, you'd rather stay and be a punchbag for him than learn to stand on your own feet. You're pathetic! Pathetic and weak—'

She didn't get to the end of the sentence before Belle was on her, slamming her backwards into the wall, so hard that it knocked all the breath from her body.

'You know nothing about it!' she hissed, her face so close Sadie could see the smudges of scarlet lipstick on her crooked teeth. 'If you understood what that girl's done for you . . .'

'What?' Sadie shot back at her. 'What has she done for me? Tell me, I'd like to know!'

'Belle.' Lily's voice drifted down the street, plaintive and pleading. 'Leave her, please.'

For a moment Belle held on, eyes fixed on Sadie, blazing fire. Suddenly she understood why those girls down at the docks were so afraid of her mother's friend.

Then Belle released her abruptly and Sadie fell back, gasping for breath.

'It ain't for me to say,' she muttered. 'But, believe me, one day you'll know. One day you'll know what you've done.'

Chapter Thirty

Anna's mother had told them they had to make a special effort when they visited the internment camp three weeks after Christmas.

'Your father is bound to be worried after everything that's happened,' she had said. 'We need to show him we are well and coping with everything.'

Anna scarcely recognised her mother and sister as they sat across the table from her in the recreation room that Sunday afternoon. Liesel was looking very grown-up in a stylish dress with a wide linen sailor collar, a neat little feathered hat tilted on her blonde head. Even Dorothy, who usually dressed strictly for practicality, looked soft and pretty in a pale pink silk blouse, her hair curling around her face.

Beside her beautiful sister, Anna felt like a frump in her shapeless winter coat, her dark hair drawn back off her face in a knot under her felt hat.

Not that her father noticed as he beamed proudly around at them all.

'My girls,' he said. 'You are all even more beautiful than the last time I saw you.'

Anna wished she could say the same. Her father had grown older and thinner since the last time they had met. His face was drawn, and his dark hair had turned grey at the temples. Even his bright brown eyes were etched with lines of anxiety.

He turned to his youngest daughter. 'Is that a new dress, Liesel?'

'Yes, Papa.' She smoothed the skirt proudly. 'Grand-mother had it made especially for me by her own dressmaker. She says a young lady should dress well if she wishes to be accepted in polite society.'

Anna hid a smirk behind her hand. Mother had warned her not to tease Liesel about her new clothes.

'She's never had a dress that wasn't a hand-me-down from you. She's bound to be excited,' Dorothy had said.

'Your grandmother is quite right,' her father agreed solemnly. 'You do indeed look like a very proper young lady.'

'Thank you, Papa.' Liesel preened herself. 'Grandmother says now we're living with her, I can have more new dresses. And she has arranged for me to have lessons in deportment.'

'That's very generous of her.' Anna caught the quick look her father sent her mother.

'Grandmother says a lady must know how to carry her-self well,' Liesel continued, oblivious. 'She says I must also have accomplishments. I am to learn to speak French and play the piano.'

'She'll be talking about presenting you at court next!' Anna burst out laughing.

Liesel turned on her. 'You're jealous,' she accused.

'I just think we've come to see Papa, not to listen to you boasting!'

'It's quite all right, my dear.' Her father laid his hand on Anna's. 'I'm delighted to hear you're all so well and happy.' He looked at his wife. 'It sounds as if your grandmother is treating you very well?'

Anna glanced sideways at her mother.

'Yes – very well,' Dorothy said.

'We have our own rooms now, in the main part of the house,' Liesel went on excitedly. 'You should see my room,

Papa. I think it must be nearly as big as the bakery kitchen and the shop put together!'

'Liesel!' Anna sent her a scowling look.

'Well, it is,' Liesel muttered, retreating into sullen silence.

'Tom is working hard on rebuilding the bakery, Papa,' Anna changed the subject. 'He's living there so he can spend as much time as possible on it.'

Her father smiled. 'Tom is a fine young man. A hard worker, too.'

Don't trust Tom Franklin.

'Have you heard any more about when you might come home?' Dorothy asked.

Friedrich Beck shook his head. 'Not yet,' he said. 'But I am sure it won't be much longer.' His face was full of sorrow. 'Believe me, I would like nothing more than to be with you. I have worried about you so much since . . .' His voice broke. 'When I think about what could have happened to you . . .'

'You mustn't worry,' Dorothy cut in. 'We survived and Mother is providing for us very well.'

Friedrich's thoughtful gaze took in all of them. 'You're quite right, my dear. It sounds as if you are being looked after. We are very fortunate to have her, *nein*?'

When they left later, Anna said to her mother, 'Is Grandmother really looking after you, Mother?'

Dorothy nodded. 'Yes,' she said. 'Much as it surprises me to say it, she has been very kind to us. It was difficult at first, of course, but now we have all grown used to the situation . . .' She paused for a moment, then said, 'The years certainly seem to have mellowed her, at any rate.'

'Perhaps she's glad of the company since Grandfather died?' Anna looked at her sister, hurrying on ahead of them. 'She has certainly made a pet of Liesel.'

'Yes, she has.' Her mother's expression darkened briefly.

'I thought perhaps she might become spoilt at first, but Mother says I'm fussing too much.'

Anna glanced sideways at her mother's determined smile.

'Anyway, Mother enjoys it, and so does Liesel,' Dorothy went on. 'Poor child, she so likes to feel special. And my mother likes dressing us up, so . . .'

'Us?' Anna said.

Her mother tugged self-consciously at the curls around her face.

'I don't mind,' she said. 'It's important to keep your grandmother happy. She is keeping us, after all.'

'But are *you* happy, Mother?'

Dorothy gave a sad little smile. 'I mustn't complain,' she said. 'We have a warm, safe place to live, and that's all that matters. Of course I miss your father, and the bakery. But I've found little ways to occupy myself. I write to him every day, of course, and my mother likes me to read to her. I talked to her about finding some kind of work, but she insists that it is not proper for a lady.' She smiled ruefully. 'Silly, isn't it? I remember those cold winter mornings when we had to get up before dawn to light the ovens, I used to long to be a lady of leisure then. But now . . .' she sighed. 'I have to admit, I wish I were busy again.'

'You will be soon.' Anna linked her arm with her mother's. 'Once Tom has finished rebuilding the bakery, we can move back in.' She grinned then. 'You wait, Mother. It won't be long before you'll be wishing you were a lady of leisure again!'

Anna called in to the bakery on her way back to the hospital. The back door was open and as she crossed the yard she could hear the rasp of wood being sawn. But there was another sound, too. Quiet but unmistakable.

Anna stopped to listen for a moment, smiling to herself. She could never have imagined Tom Franklin whistling.

She crept into the kitchen. The door leading to the rest of the ground floor was open, and Tom was working at the far end of the passageway. He had stripped to his vest; his braces hung loose around his narrow hips.

As if he knew he was being watched, he suddenly looked up and saw her.

'Miss Anna!' He quickly laid the saw down and hurried down the passageway towards her, shrugging on his shirt. 'I beg your pardon, I didn't know you were coming.'

'It's all right.' Anna turned her back on him, embarrassed. 'I didn't mean to disturb you. I just thought I'd call in and see how you were getting on.'

'Not too bad.' She risked a glance over her shoulder. Tom was slipping his braces back over his shoulders. 'It's nearly all dried out now the weather's turned.'

'You cleared everything out.'

He nodded. 'It was all ruined. I've left it in the yard, if you want to go through it?'

'No. As you say, it's all ruined anyway.'

They lapsed into silence, neither of them meeting the other's eye.

Anna spoke first. 'You've started replacing the window frames, I see?'

Tom nodded. 'Most of 'em was too burned to fix.'

'You've done a good job.'

He cleared his throat. 'I ain't no master carpenter, but I've done my best.'

The silence stretched again. Then Anna said, 'I forgot. I've brought you something.'

She held out the meat pie wrapped in brown paper, still warm from the pie-seller on the corner. 'I wasn't sure if you'd eaten?' she said. Then, seeing his wary expression, added, 'You don't have to have it if you don't want it.'

He took it from her with a grunt of thanks. He tore off the paper and took a big bite, like a ravenous dog. Anna looked away, back to the window frame. She ran her hand down the smooth, planed wood.

'This is very good work. Where did you learn to do it?' she asked.

'I've worked on a few building sites,' Tom said, his mouth full. 'You pick things up.' He swallowed, then took another bite. 'I like making things.'

'You've got a real talent for it,' Anna said. 'I wonder why you didn't get yourself apprenticed to a master builder, to learn the trade properly?'

Tom expression darkened. 'I'm a Franklin, miss. Who'd want to take me on as an apprentice?'

Don't trust Tom Franklin.

He finished the pie and screwed up the brown paper, crumpling it in his fist. 'Thank you,' he said.

Anna smiled. 'You must have been hungry.'

She knew it was the wrong thing to say as Tom looked away, embarrassed.

'Is there anything I can do?' she asked.

'In what way, miss?'

'I thought I might be able to help – not with the woodwork or anything complicated,' she said quickly. 'But perhaps I could do some cleaning?'

He looked her up and down. 'You're wearing your nice clothes.'

'I don't mind.'

He shook his head. 'I can manage, miss.'

He was dismissing her, she could tell. He wanted to do this alone.

'Well,' she said, 'I suppose I'd better go.'

As she turned away Tom suddenly said, 'Have you seen him, miss? Your father?'

'As a matter of fact, we went to visit him today.'

'How is he?'

Anna looked into Tom's face. The tenderness in his black eyes surprised her.

'You know Papa. He always tries to make the best of everything.'

Tom nodded. 'That sounds like Mr Beck.' He sounded almost affectionate, Anna thought. 'You'll be sure to give him my best wishes next time you see him?'

'I will.' Anna paused, then said, 'You know, you could always write to him. I'd be happy to take a letter for you.'

A deep flush spread up Tom's cheeks. 'I don't know about that,' he said. 'He wouldn't want to hear from me.'

'I'm sure he would. He was saying earlier what a fine young man you are.'

'He said that? About me?' For a moment she saw a spark in Tom's eyes, and then it was gone. 'All the same, I ain't much for writing letters,' he mumbled.

'Let me know if you change your mind, anyway.' Anna looked around. 'I'll come and see you again next week, if that's all right?'

'It's your house, miss.'

'So it is.' She nodded. 'I'll remember to bring my old clothes with me next time.'

'You do that, miss.'

As she closed the door and looked back, she wondered if she had imagined the faintest hint of a smile on Tom's face.

Chapter Thirty-One

'Monaghan, sir? But that's the Military ward.'

Dr Ormerod glared at Kate across his desk. 'I know what it is, thank you! And, believe me, I would not even think of this if there were another way. But we've lost several more students to the war effort in the past month, there are military casualties pouring in every day and we simply don't have enough doctors to keep up with the demand for them.'

He must be truly desperate, Kate thought, looking at his pained expression. She had not seen or spoken to Dr Ormerod in more than two months. She had begun to think she would spend the rest of her days buried away in Pathology until the Great Man had suddenly summoned her to his office that morning and instructed her to report to Monaghan.

'Thank you, sir,' she said.

'Oh, don't thank me.' Dr Ormerod waved his hand dismissively. 'As I said, I had no choice. Personally, I think it will all be too much for you. I daresay you'll be back in my office, weeping and begging for a transfer, by the end of the week.'

Kate sent him a level look. She made up her mind there and then that no matter how hard the work might be, she would find a way to endure it.

Kate soon realised why Dr Ormerod had sent for her. A fresh load of military patients had just arrived and there was a line of trolleys down the passage outside Monaghan.

Even from a distance, Kate could hear the animal cries and groans of the men. The air was thick with the smell of dirt and dried blood, and the sour stench of infected wounds.

Leo and Rufus French were there, going up and down the trolleys, assessing the men and issuing instructions to the nurses and orderlies who hurried back and forth.

Her brother looked up at her in surprise as she approached.

'What are you doing here?'

'She's come to lend a hand,' Rufus said, before Kate could open her mouth to reply.

Leo frowned. 'On whose instruction?'

'Dr Ormerod's. And if you have a problem with it, I suggest you take it up with him. But in the meantime, perhaps you could make yourself useful?' Rufus said to Kate.

Out of the corner of her eye, she could see Leo frown. 'What do you want me to do?' she asked.

'These casualties must all be assessed.' Rufus nodded at the line of trolleys. 'Some will need to go straight down to theatre, while others can go on to the ward. Sort out the most urgent cases, and deal with them first.'

'How do I know which are the most urgent?'

Rufus sent her a grim look. 'The ones who are dying,' he said.

As Kate turned to go, Leo said, 'Some of these men are in a very bad way. If you don't think you can cope . . .'

'If she didn't think she could cope, she wouldn't be here.' Once again Rufus answered for her, throwing the words over his shoulder as he headed down the line to the next patient.

Kate looked from him back to her brother's concerned face.

'I'll be fine,' she said.

In spite of what Rufus had said, he kept a close eye on Miss Carlyle as they worked their way through the patients.

Today's wounds were some of the worst he had ever seen. Sickening, filthy injuries: crushed faces, mangled limbs, and wounds that had healed so badly they had burst open, angry red, oozing pus and seething with infection.

It was almost more than he could bear to see, and he expected Kate to fall apart in the face of such horror. But every time he looked at her she was working steadily, her head down, checking respiration, cleaning out wounds and splinting limbs, making notes in that tiny, meticulous handwriting of hers. She worked tirelessly, going from patient to patient, and even the most grisly injuries did not seem to perturb her at all.

Only once or twice did Rufus see her faltering. The colour would drain from her face and she would turn away to compose herself. But each time, before he could go to her assistance, he saw her close her eyes and grit her teeth, as if willing herself to go on. The next moment she would be back, alert and ready to deal with whatever lay before her.

And to think he had once criticised her for being cold, he thought. Now her cool, unruffled presence seemed to be just what was needed to calm the men's terror and to cope unflinchingly with their terrible wounds.

The only one who didn't seem calmed by her presence was her brother. Late in the afternoon, Rufus was treating a patient in one of the private rooms when he heard Kate and Leo locked in an argument in the passage outside.

'I'm telling you, I believe he should be in isolation,' Kate quietly insisted.

'And I'm telling you, you know nothing about it!' Leo's voice was louder, full of suppressed anger. 'I don't even know why you examined him, since he's my patient.'

'Staff Nurse Hanley was concerned about him. He has a sore throat, vomiting, and his temperature is—'

'You don't have to tell me what his temperature is! I took it myself, not an hour ago.' Rufus heard Leo's angry sigh. 'Look, I know you think you're very clever,' he said, 'but you've barely been on the ward a few hours. Don't you think it's too early to start taking over?'

Rufus finished examining his patient and handed over to the nurse to finish dressing his wound, then went outside.

'What's going on?' he asked.

'Mind your own business!' Leo growled.

Kate kept her gaze fixed on her brother. 'I have reason to believe that a patient on the ward has developed erysipelas,' she said quietly.

'Reason to believe!' Leo mocked her. 'There isn't even a rash.'

'A rash can take up to forty-eight hours to—'

'It's all right, you don't have to quote your textbooks at me!' he cut her off angrily.

Rufus looked from one to the other of them. 'There's only one way to find out,' he said. 'Let's take a look at him, shall we?'

He was aware of Leo watching him with a mutinous expression as he examined the patient, a fusilier named Private William Pinder.

'He was admitted with a shell wound to his head,' Kate recited the notes. 'He had a temperature of one hundred and two degrees, and the wound was very dirty.'

'He can read the fellow's notes,' Leo hissed at her. 'Well?' he turned to Rufus.

'It's hard to be sure, but I suspect it may be traumatic erysipelas,' Rufus confirmed. 'I agree, he should be moved to solitary immediately.'

Kate looked up sharply, and he saw the surprise in her eyes. Leo let out an angry sigh.

'Waste of time,' he muttered. 'All he needs is rest.'

'It's better to be safe than sorry,' Rufus said. 'Will you speak to Sister about having him moved, or shall—?'

He didn't manage to finish his sentence before Leo stormed off.

'I suppose that means I'll do it,' Rufus murmured.

'I'll speak to Sister,' Kate said. She paused then added, 'Thank you.'

'What for?'

'Backing me up.'

Rufus frowned. 'But your diagnosis was correct.'

Kate's mouth twisted. 'That doesn't necessarily mean anyone will listen to me.'

Leo approached him later, as Rufus was checking on a post-operative patient. The ward was a great deal quieter and calmer now all the patients had been treated, their wounds cleaned and dressed, and the post-ops were all slumbering quietly behind their screens.

'You shouldn't have made a fool of me earlier, old man,' Leo said in a low voice.

Rufus stared at him. 'In what way – old man?'

'That chap – the suspected erysipelas. You should have taken my side.'

'Even if you were wrong?'

Leo's face coloured. 'Time will tell if I was,' he muttered. 'But in any case, you shouldn't have contradicted me in front of Kate. It sets a bad example.'

'So you think I should have let a highly infectious patient remain on the ward, just so you could save face?'

Leo looked at him uncertainly. 'I think you could have dealt with it differently,' he said. 'Perhaps you could have pulled me aside later, rather than pointing out my error in front of my sister.' Leo must have seen the rigid set of Rufus' face, because the next minute he was smiling. 'We're the same, you and me,' he said. 'We're both senior to her. We need to stick together.' He slapped Rufus on the shoulder. 'I think we understand each other, don't we, old man?'

Do we? Rufus looked at him. Leo Carlyle looked so sleek and sure of himself, it was all he could do not to punch that handsome jaw.

Just before his shift ended, Rufus looked for Kate to say goodbye to her. He wanted to thank her for all her hard work. But there was no sign of her on the ward.

'Have you seen Miss Carlyle?' he asked Miss Parker, who was writing up her report at her desk.

'She has just left, Doctor.'

'Already?'

Miss Parker eyed the clock. 'She was supposed to go off duty an hour ago. She stayed on to help with settling the infected shrapnel wound in bed three. He was having trouble sleeping.'

'I see. I just thought she might – but it doesn't matter. Thank you.'

As Rufus turned to go, Miss Parker said, 'She did very well, didn't she?'

'Yes,' he said. 'Yes, she did.'

'About time she's allowed to show everyone what she's made of, in my opinion.'

Rufus looked back over his shoulder at the ward sister.

Florence Parker's sharp blue eyes were full of warmth. At least there was one other person on Kate Carlyle's side.

'Indeed,' he agreed.

He took off his white coat, shrugged on his jacket and left the ward. Even though it was late February, there was still a frosty nip in the evening air. The plane trees in the courtyard were bare and black against the darkening sky.

He wasn't looking for Kate, Rufus told himself. It was of no particular concern to him whether she had said goodbye or not. He only had it in mind to offer her some words of praise, let her know she had done a good job.

He was still telling himself that when he heard her voice, coming from the other side of the Casualty block. He stopped to listen. She was with someone. A man. Rufus heard him laughing, and his heart sank.

A moment later they rounded the corner, and he found himself face-to-face with Kate and Charlie Latimer.

She had taken her hair out of its pins. It fell loose about her shoulders, framing her face and making her look younger, less severe.

'Dr French?' Kate looked as embarrassed as he felt.

Rufus felt hot with embarrassment. He knew that she and Charlie Latimer had been out several times – God knows, Latimer boasted about it enough – but this was the first time he had seen them together.

'Were you looking for me?'

'What? No.'

'I should think not!' Charlie grinned. 'It sounds as if you've already had more than your pound of flesh from the poor girl today.'

Kate looked up at Rufus, her grey eyes serious. 'There isn't a problem with one of the patients, is there?'

'No, not at all.' He cleared his throat. He couldn't seem to take his eyes from her hand, held in Charlie's. 'I just wanted to make sure you were all right after your first day?'

Kate smiled. 'Yes, thank you.'

'No need to worry, old chap. I'm looking after her very well.' Charlie Latimer slipped his arm around her shoulders.

'So I see.' Rufus glanced away. 'I'll bid you good night, then.'

'Good night, Doctor. I'll see you in the morning.'

Rufus turned on his heel and hurried away. As he strode off down the path, he heard Latimer murmur something to Kate. He couldn't catch the words, but then he heard a sound that he had never heard before.

Kate Carlyle was laughing.

Chapter Thirty-Two

For Sadie, one of the worst things about being moved to the military ward was doing the dressings round. The soldiers called it the Agony Wagon, and Sadie could see the fear on their faces as the time came for their wounds to be tended.

She really felt for them, but it had to be done. All she could do was grit her teeth and try to ignore their cursing and screams of pain as she applied hot poultices to raw wounds or pulled off blood-soaked bandages, taking flesh with them.

It was easier doing the dressings with Dulcie Moore, because she insisted on flirting with all the patients. It meant the round took ages and they invariably got into trouble with Sister, but at least it took the men's minds off their pain.

But this morning Sadie had no time for her friend's chatter.

'Can we get a move on?' she pleaded, as Dulcie laughed and joked with a young sapper. 'I'm supposed to have my off-duty time from ten till two, and at this rate it'll be lunchtime before we're finished.'

Dulcie pulled a face.'What's the hurry? Have you got a date or something?'

'No.'

'Are you sure?' Dulcie looked at her archly. 'You're blushing!'

'Leave her be,' the sapper joined in cheekily. 'So what if the lass has got a date? I wouldn't mind taking her out myself!'

'Why, Sapper Philipson!' Dulcie sent him a mock frown. 'I thought you only had eyes for me.'

Finally, Dulcie finished checking the young man's splint, and they headed off down the ward. 'Speaking of dates,' Sadie said, 'what time did you come in last night?'

Dulcie grinned, her cheeks dimpling. 'I can't remember, but it must have been gone midnight. Thanks for leaving the window open for me, by the way.'

'You're going to break your neck one of these days, shinning up that drainpipe!' Sadie folded her arms. 'Who was he, anyway?'

Dulcie tapped her nose. 'Never you mind.'

'A secret admirer, eh? Very mysterious. And there was me, thinking your heart belonged to Sam Talbot!' Dulcie had been head over heels in love with the handsome medical student until he had gone off to join the Army Medical Reserve.

'We're hardly engaged, are we? And if I know Talbot, he's not going to be turning his back on all those VADs while he's away!'

'True,' Sadie agreed. 'Hello, Gunner Hillary.' She stopped the trolley at the foot of his bed. 'Let's check those stitches, shall we?'

They made their way up the ward, changing dressings, checking and cleaning wounds and readjusting splints. Thanks to Sadie's urging, they finally finished the round with minutes to spare before ten o'clock.

'Looks like you won't be late for your date after all!' Dulcie winked.

'I told you, I ain't got a date.'

'Fine. Have it your way,' Dulcie said, then added, 'but if anyone asks me, I'm going to tell them you've got a mystery man!'

Sadie laughed. 'You've guessed my secret!'

*

What would Dulcie say if she could see her now? Sadie thought as she made her way through the grimy terrace streets of Bethnal Green to her mother's lodgings.

It was a sunny day in March, and a few women were hanging out washing on lines strung across the narrow alleys. Children played around them, chasing each other and rattling metal hoops made from old pram wheels over the cobbles.

The fine spring weather did not penetrate the gloomy stairwell of the tenement building where her mother lived. Inside, as ever, the air was stale and thick with the odours of cooking and unwashed bodies. A skinny cat toyed with a cockroach until it disappeared down a crack in the bare floorboards.

Sadie climbed the stairs until she reached her mother's lodgings. She took the money out of her pocket, folded it up and bent to push it under the door. Then she straightened her back and stood still for a moment, waiting, her eyes fixed on the peeling paintwork. Perhaps this time Lily would open the door . . .

But, as usual, there was no response. Sadie rested her hand on the doorknob, wondering if she should open it.

'She's gone out.'

Sadie turned to face the woman who stood behind her, a kettle in her hand. 'She still lives here, then? She ain't done a flit?'

The woman shook her head. 'She's still there.' She squinted at Sadie in the half-light. 'I'll tell her you called, shall I?'

'No, don't.' Sadie looked down at the crack under the door where she had pushed the money. 'She'll know I've been. And she'll know where to find me if she wants me.'

But her mother hadn't wanted her so far. It was more than two months since Jimmy's trial and Lily Sedgewick hadn't spoken to her since. Even Belle hadn't been near nor by.

Well, two could play at that game, Sadie thought. Whoever made the first move, it wasn't going to be her.

She returned to the ward, fresh in her uniform, her fair hair neatly tucked inside her cap, just as two o'clock chimed.

Staff Nurse Hanley looked pointedly at the clock then back at her.

Go on, Sadie thought. *Tell me I'm late. I'm just in the mood for an argument.*

But all Nurse Hanley said was, 'There are bandages in the linen room to be rolled, and splints that need padding. And the linen cupboard needs to be checked and counted.'

Sadie stifled a sigh. 'Yes, Staff.'

Out of the corner of her eye she saw Dulcie frantically waving to her from the other end of the ward. Nurse Hanley followed her gaze. 'And no gossiping!' she snapped. 'I've already had to report Moore today for talking when she should be working. I don't want to have to tell either of you again.'

'No, Staff.'

It wasn't long before Dulcie found her in the linen room. Sadie was trying to fix the broken handle on the bandage-rolling machine.

'This wretched thing's gone again,' she sighed. 'I keep saying it needs a screw or something to keep it in place, but no one listens.'

'Never mind that!' Dulcie's eyes were shining. 'I've got something to tell you.'

Sadie glanced at the door. 'Can't it wait? Hanley's in one of her moods, and if she catches us talking—'

'No, it can't wait.' Dulcie plonked herself down on the chair opposite Sadie. 'We've got a new patient,' she said.

Sadie looked up at her. 'And?'

'And you'll never guess who it is!'

*

282

'A bullet wound to the shoulder,' Matron said. 'Fortunately the bullet passed straight through, but it damaged the sub-clavian artery. Your brother is very fortunate to be alive, Miss Copeland.'

Eleanor stared at Matron and said nothing. She could see her mouth moving, but the words seemed to jumble inside her head.

None of this felt real. She had just spent two days in the sick bay with a septic finger. She was due to start back on the ward the following morning but this afternoon Matron had summoned her and told her that Harry had been admitted to Monaghan ward that morning.

Harry. Her darling brother. Lucky to be alive.

Matron was still speaking, her face grave beneath her elaborate starched headdress. 'It's a dreadful coincidence that he has been brought to this hospital, of course, but unfortunately it cannot be helped.'

'When can I see him?' Eleanor blurted out.

Matron's brows rose at the interruption.

'As soon as you wish,' she said. She paused, then went on, 'Although I wonder, Copeland, if under the circum-stances it might be better if you transferred to another ward?'

'I would like to nurse my brother, Matron.'

'Are you quite sure? There is a great deal of difference between nursing a stranger and a member of one's own family.'

Eleanor read the unspoken message in her eyes. If Harry were to die . . .

Eleanor straightened her shoulders. 'I want to do my duty, Matron.'

'Very well.' Matron regarded her with a look of grudg-ing approval. 'I must say, it would help us greatly. We are already overstretched on the military wards.' She sat back, resting her hands on the polished top of her desk. 'Very well, you may go.' She smiled thinly. 'I am sure you would like to see your brother.'

Eleanor did want to see Harry, but as she approached the ward she found her footsteps slowing. She paused outside the double doors for a moment, trying to compose herself.

But when she finally steeled herself to walk the length of the ward to Harry's bed, he was asleep.

'The doctor has given him morphia for his pain,' Miss Parker explained. 'You may sit with him if you wish.'

'Thank you, Sister.'

Eleanor was grateful when Miss Parker pulled the screens around them. She was already aware of the curious looks the other nurses were giving her.

She drew the chair closer to his bed and sat down to watch her brother.

He looked so different, she thought. Like Harry, but then not Harry. He had lost so much weight, she could see the bones and tendons standing out under his pale skin. What had happened to the big, muscular young man who'd rowed and played rugby for his college? His brown hair was cropped close, showing off the raw bones of his face, his eyes sunken in shadows. Looking at him reminded Eleanor of the photographs of corpses the Sister Tutor had shown them in an anatomy lecture . . .

'Oh, Harry,' she whispered.

His eyes snapped open, so wide his hazel-green irises were entirely circled with white. His body went rigid with panic, hands snatching up handfuls of bedclothes. Eleanor had seen that look of terror and confusion many times on the faces of wounded men when they woke up, not knowing where they were.

'Harry?' She reached for his hand. 'It's all right. You're safe.'

'Eleanor?' His voice was a hoarse whisper.

'Yes.' She smiled at him. 'Yes, it's me.'

'Oh, thank God!' He fell back against the pillows and burst into tears.

Eleanor watched him in dismay. She had never seen Harry cry before.

'Shhh.' She squeezed his hand, desperately trying to reassure him. 'It's all right, really. Don't cry.'

But Harry wouldn't stop. He sobbed, his body convulsed, his mouth twisted in a strange, ugly grimace. Eleanor gripped his hand, willing him to quieten, shocked and terrified by what she was seeing.

This wasn't Harry. Not her Harry.

She glanced over her shoulder, half expecting Sister to thrust aside the screens and demand to know what was going on. She could only imagine what the other nurses would be thinking.

Finally, after a long time, Harry seemed to settle. Relieved, Eleanor wiped the tears from his cheeks.

'Are you in any pain?' she asked.

'No.' He looked at her sheepishly, and she recognised her brother again. 'Sorry,' he muttered. 'I didn't mean to – you know. I was just so relieved to see you.'

'I know.' Eleanor filled up a glass with water from the jug at his bedside and helped it to his lips.

'Thank you.' He lay back, staring up at her. His eyes seemed huge in his drawn face.

Eleanor could feel his gaze on her as she set the glass down on the bedside locker.

'What happened to you?' she asked.

He glanced away. 'I don't know. Did I get shot? '

'In the shoulder,' Eleanor nodded. 'You're lucky to be alive.'

'Am I?' The bleakness in his eyes made her shudder. 'What about the others?'

'Others?'

'There were more of us . . . we were sent out into no-man's-land to search the dead Germans for intelligence.'

'I'll try and find out. But I think you were the only one from your unit brought in.'

'Only me.' He closed his eyes.

Eleanor stood up. 'I'll let you sleep,' she said. 'I'll write to Mother and Father tonight, tell them you're here.'

'No!'

Eleanor frowned. 'But they'll want to know you're safe.'

'I daresay they'll find out soon enough. The War Office will write to them.'

'Yes, but won't it seem odd if I don't tell them you're here?'

'Can't you leave it, just for a couple of weeks?' He looked up at her appealingly. 'Please, sis? I don't want them to know just yet. I'm not ready . . .'

She looked into his tear-stained face and she understood. Harry was too proud, he wouldn't want their parents to see him like this, a trembling shadow of the strapping young man he had once been.

She smiled. 'All right, I won't write to them for a while,' she said. 'But just for a week or two, mind. They'll be so worried otherwise.'

'Thank you.' He was already half-asleep, his eyelids fluttering closed.

Chapter Thirty-Three

'It seems I made the right decision, bringing Miss Carlyle to the military ward. She has certainly proved herself far beyond my expectations.' Dr Ormerod looked pleased with himself. 'It was rather a bold decision on my part, but it seems to have paid off richly, wouldn't you say?'

'Yes, sir,' Rufus replied through gritted teeth. How like the Great Man to take the credit, he thought. Ormerod seemed to have conveniently forgotten he'd been ready to dismiss Kate Carlyle a few months earlier. If it hadn't been for the huge numbers of military casualties they were receiving, she would still have been withering away among the specimen jars in Pathology.

He watched her now with one of the patients. She was listening to him, grey eyes intent, delicate hands clasped under her chin, a gesture he had come to notice when she was concentrating. Like Dr Ormerod had done, he had thought her far too fragile to survive on the military ward. But in the past three weeks he had seen her face horrific injuries that would have made even the most hardened male doctor flinch. She certainly worked harder and pushed herself further than most of the other medical students.

The men had taken to her, too. There was always some uncertainty when they first found out they were being treated by a woman, but that was quickly gone when they realised what an excellent doctor she was. They still liked to make jokes at her expense, but Kate took it in surprisingly good part, and even joined in sometimes.

She had not only survived, she had positively thrived. She had found a place for herself among the rough and ready soldiers. The cool reserve that had once made her seem so aloof was still there sometimes, but now Rufus recognised it for what it was. It wasn't that Kate was arrogant as he had first thought. If anything, she lacked confidence. She was so unsure of her position, it sometimes made her seem cold and defensive.

'Dr French?' Rufus snapped out of his reverie to see Dr Ormerod watching him over his spectacles. The Great Man tutted. 'Do pay attention, young man. Is there anyone else I should see before I leave?'

Rufus glanced at his watch. It was barely half-past nine. Dr Ormerod always liked to finish his round early on the days when Sir Philip Carlyle was due on the ward. If the two men ever did meet, there was a lot of posturing and wary eye contact, like two cats converging in an alley.

Besides, on such a fine spring day, Ormerod would probably want to spend as much time as possible on the golf course, improving his swing.

'No, sir. The only case giving real alarm is the post-op in bed seven.'

'Ah, yes. The cerebral compression.' Dr Ormerod looked grave. 'The hypertonic saline should do the trick. Just keep an eye on him for the next day or two, and give another injection if you think he requires it.'

After Dr Ormerod had left for the day, Rufus went over to join Kate. Thorough as ever, she was checking the chart of a suspected nephritis case, even though Dr Ormerod had seen him not fifteen minutes earlier.

The young man didn't seem to mind the attention, but chatted away happily.

'How are you feeling today, Private Hobson?' Rufus asked.

'Very chipper, thank you, Doctor.' The young man

waved an envelope at him. 'I've just had a letter from my sweetheart, Mary.'

'Mary, Mary, quite contrary!' His friend in the next bed, a tough Scotsman called Andy Mitton, sang under his breath.

'There ain't nothing contrary about my Mary, thank you very much,' Private Hobson said.

'She's probably no' your Mary nae more, neither!'

'Now then, Corporal Mitton.' Kate shook her head at him. 'You mustn't go around saying things like that.'

'Why not? Better the lad finds out the truth.' The grizzled corporal turned to his neighbour with a gap-toothed grin. 'You mark my words, laddie. She'll find herself someone else soon enough. I'd bet my good leg on it!'

'Take no notice of him, Private,' Rufus said. 'I'm sure your Mary is a delightful girl.'

'She is.' Private Hobson clutched his envelope defensively to his chest.

Corporal Mitton laughed. 'You should do yourself a favour, laddie, and find yourself a pretty nurse while you can. Or what about yon doctor here?' He winked at Kate.

Rufus shot Kate a look, expecting her to make some sharp retort. But to his surprise she simply smiled and said, 'I'm sorry, Corporal, but I'm spoken for.' He noticed the way her cheeks flushed delicately as she said it, the touch of pride in her voice.

She was in love, he realised. With Charlie Latimer, of all people.

'Is that right?' Corporal Mitton looked at her with interest. 'And who's the lucky man, might I ask?'

Kate smiled coyly. 'That would be telling.'

'It ain't you, is it, Doctor?' Private Hobson grinned at Rufus.

It was hard to tell which of them blushed harder. 'No,' Rufus said, in a clipped voice. 'No, it certainly isn't.'

He caught Kate's look of surprise and realised how

churlish that must have sounded. She was expecting one of his usual jokey comments, but for once the words stuck in his throat.

It wasn't that he was jealous, he told himself later, as he watched her from the other end of the ward. Far from it. He was disappointed.

How, he wondered, had a sensible girl like Kate Carlyle fallen so easily for someone like Charlie Latimer? Yes, he was good-looking, and he certainly knew how to flirt, but Rufus was disappointed that she hadn't seen through his shallow charm.

Their paths didn't cross again until some time later when Probationer Sedgewick approached him.

'Sister would like you to look at the patient in bed seven, Doctor,' she said. 'She's worried he still ain't woken up.'

When he pulled back the screen Rufus was surprised to see Kate with Miss Parker at the patient's bedside. He looked from one to the other.

'What seems to be the trouble?'

'The patient's level of unconsciousness seems to have deepened, Doctor,' Kate said. 'Earlier he was awake but disorientated. Now it's impossible to rouse him.'

Rufus checked his chart briefly then examined the man, lifting his eyelids to check for any signs of responsiveness. There were none.

'Dr Ormerod did say the hypertonic saline would take some time to work,' he said.

'Yes, but his pulse rate has increased,' Kate said.

'Which is a good sign,' Rufus pointed out. He was aware of Miss Parker watching them, her gaze going from one to the other as if she was watching a tennis match.

'It was rapid before,' Kate pointed to a figure on the chart. 'If you look here—'

'I can read a chart, Miss Carlyle.' Pride made Rufus' temper snap. 'What are you trying to say?'

'I'm saying, sir, that cerebral compression generally causes a slowing of the pulse.'

'And?'

'And I think we should consider the possibility of cerebral laceration.'

Kate looked at Miss Parker when she said it. Rufus saw the ward sister's slight nod.

'I see you've been discussing this already?' he said tautly.

Kate looked taken aback. 'I asked Miss Parker's advice,' she said quietly.

'I see. So my opinion and that of the consultant physician are not good enough for you, is that what you're saying?'

'No, I—'

'Really, Miss Carlyle, I'm surprised at you. You always have to have the last word. I think Dr Ormerod is right, it must run in the family.'

Kate flushed an angry scarlet. 'And you never want to admit you're wrong, even if a patient's life might be at risk because of it!'

For a moment they stared at each other in hostile silence. Rufus waited for Kate to back down, to apologise for her remarks. But her mouth remained closed in a tight line.

He turned to Miss Parker. 'Keep this patient under observation, as per Dr Ormerod's instructions.'

'Yes, Doctor.' Even the ward sister couldn't meet his gaze.

He snatched aside the screens and strode off down the ward. He could feel everyone's eyes following him, and felt sure they must have heard the angry exchange.

How dare she? She was a medical student, she had no

right to question his or Dr Ormerod's judgement. Just because her name was Carlyle, that didn't give her some kind of God-given authority.

And to accuse him of never admitting to being wrong! Well, she was a fine one to talk about that. Arrogance was ingrained in her family.

Anyway, he was willing to admit he was wrong about one thing. He'd been wrong about her. He had thought she was different, but she had proved herself to be every bit as conceited and high-handed as the rest of the Carlyles.

She and Latimer deserved each other, he thought furiously.

Just to make him feel worse, at that moment Sir Philip arrived for his round, trailing students and housemen behind him. He looked larger than life in his Savile Row suit, tall and upright, chin lifted so high he could only look down his nose at everyone.

Leo was at his side, a pale imitation of his father but just as supercilious.

Rufus groaned. This was just what he needed, all the Carlyles on the ward together! He looked for Kate, but she was nowhere to be seen.

Rufus tried to concentrate on his patient, a man with a leg wound that was not healing as it should. But it was difficult to ignore Sir Philip's stentorian tones carrying down the ward.

'He's got a voice like a bloody foghorn,' Rufus' patient put it succinctly. 'Likes the sound of it too, don't you think?'

'Indeed,' Rufus agreed grimly.

Kate's words still stung deep within him. But there was another part of him that wondered if perhaps they hurt so much because he knew they were true.

He did not like to admit he was wrong. Not because he was arrogant, but because he was afraid. Afraid that if he was ever found to be at fault then perhaps people would start to question whether he was good enough to be there.

He put down the patient's notes. 'I won't be a moment,' he said. 'I need to check on someone . . .'

The patient in bed seven was still unconscious. He barely stirred when Rufus tried to rouse him. Rufus felt for his pulse. It skittered under his fingers, so fast he could barely count the beats.

He was checking the man's blood pressure when he heard Kate's voice on the other side of the screen.

'May I have a word, please, sir?'

Rufus stiffened, listening.

'Yes, what is it?' Sir Philip's voice was clipped with irritation.

'There's a patient I'm concerned about. I wonder if you could have a look at him?'

Rufus felt his anger rising again. She was going behind his back! Of course, he should have known she would run straight to her father . . .

'Is it one of my patients?'

'No, sir. Dr Ormerod is in charge of his case.'

'Then why don't you speak to him?'

There was a long pause. Rufus could imagine the blush rising in Kate's face, her hands clenched together.

'Dr Ormerod is not here, sir.' Her voice wavered slightly. 'Please, I'm very worried—'

'I do not wish to hear any more,' Sir Philip cut her off. 'Frankly, I am extremely disappointed that you would even speak to me about another physician's case. You clearly have no idea how to conduct yourself.'

Rufus edged over to a crack in the curtains and peeped out. He could just make out Kate's profile, her head hung in shame. There was something so vulnerable about her, he promptly forgot his anger. All he wanted to do was go to her.

But he didn't. He forced himself to stand still behind the curtain until Sir Philip and his retinue had passed by. Only then did he continue with what he was doing.

Kate Carlyle had gone from the ward when he finally emerged. Rufus made himself wait for some time before he looked for her.

He finally found her in the sink room. He could tell straight away she had been crying.

She turned to him, dabbing her eyes with a cloth.

'I had some lint in my eye,' she muttered.

'Shall I look at it for you?'

'No.' She turned away from him sharply. 'No, it's all right now.' She turned back, her face composed. 'Can I help you, Doctor?'

There was something so heartbreaking about the way she stood there, it was all he could do not to comfort her.

'I've been thinking about the post-op in bed seven,' he said.

Kate dropped her gaze. 'I'm sorry, Doctor,' she said. 'I should never have spoken to you like that. You're right, Dr Ormerod said—'

'No, Miss Carlyle, I think *you're* right.'

She looked at him blankly. 'I beg your pardon?'

'I've taken another look at him, and I think his pulse rate and blood pressure would suggest cerebral laceration. I have sent him down for an X-ray. Hopefully that will tell us more.'

Kate nodded. 'Thank you, Doctor.'

'I'm the one who should be thanking you.' They looked at each other for a moment. 'You see?' he said ruefully. 'I can admit I'm wrong sometimes.'

Chapter Thirty-Four

'Your wound is healing nicely. It won't be long before it's mended.'

'That's good news.' Harry Copeland's smile didn't reach his hazel eyes.

Anna tried again. 'I daresay the doctor will let you start exercising it soon, to help the muscles grow strong again,' she said.

Harry did not reply. Anna studied his profile as she finished dressing his shoulder. He seemed even more withdrawn today.

She remembered what Sister had said when she handed out the work lists that morning: that they should keep an eye on him, make an effort to draw him out and cheer him up if they could.

'Is there anything else you'd like?' she asked, as she straightened his bedclothes and plumped his pillows. 'Would you like to read? We've had some new books donated. You never know, there might be something to interest you. Or perhaps I could help you write a letter?'

'No. Thank you, Nurse. I don't really feel like doing anything.'

Anna glanced towards the window. 'Would you like to sit outside for a while with the other men? It's such a beautiful day . . .'

'No!' he roared, startling her. 'I told you, I don't feel like doing anything. Just leave me alone, will you?'

'I'm sorry.' Anna turned quickly to gather up the soiled dressings.

'No, I'm the one who should apologise.' Harry looked up at her, his face contrite. 'I didn't mean to snap at you. I'm just tired, that's all.'

'What's going on?' Eleanor came bustling towards them, her accusing glare already fixed on Anna. 'I heard you shouting, Harry. Are you all right?'

'I was only asking your brother if he wanted to go outside,' Anna defended herself.

'If he wants to go outside he only has to ask me.' Eleanor reached over and plumped up the pillows Anna had rearranged not a minute earlier. 'Now, are you in any pain, Harry? Would you like me to ask the doctor to give you something?'

'I'm all right, really. I just want to be left alone.'

'Of course you do.' Eleanor stroked the hair back from her brother's face. 'But let me straighten your bed first, make you more comfortable . . .'

Anna watched Harry's face as his sister fussed around him, pulling and tweaking the already smoothed bedclothes, chattering all the while. He scarcely seemed to be listening to her, eyes closed as he patiently tolerated her ministrations.

'Don't take it to heart,' Grace Duffield said as she whisked past, her arms full of fresh linen. 'She's the same with all of us. No one can look after him the way she can. I suppose it's only natural that she'd be protective of him after everything he's been through, isn't it? I know I'd be just the same if it was my brother.'

'I know.' Anna looked back at Eleanor, carefully pouring out a glass of water for her brother. They might not have got on in the past, but Anna's heart still went out to her.

It had been more than a month since Edward had left for

France, and Anna worried about him constantly. At night she would lie awake, imagining him lying wounded in a clearing station.

In a way Eleanor was one of the lucky ones, she thought. At least she knew her brother was safe now.

The following Saturday was Anna's half-day off, so she went to Chambord Street to see Tom.

She found him up a ladder, replastering the sitting room. He had grown used to Anna's regular visits and now scarcely gave her more than a nod of greeting.

But today he stopped work, trowel in hand, and looked her up and down as she took off her jacket to reveal a man's shirt, the tails hanging almost to her knees.

'I've remembered to bring some old clothes this time,' she said.

'So you have, miss.' Tom turned away, but not before she saw the shadow of a smile at the corners of his mouth.

Anna rolled up her shirtsleeves and looked around. 'What's to be done?' she asked.

He nodded towards the planks of wood stacked up against the wall. 'You could start planning down that lot of skirting boards.'

'All right.' Anna picked up the heavy planing tool and turned it around in her hands, trying to make sense of it.

'Have you ever planed a bit of wood before?' Tom asked.

'No,' Anna admitted. 'But I'm sure I can manage it.'

'Here, let me show you.'

He set down the trowel and came over to take the plane from her hands. 'You run it along the length of the wood, like this. Keep it steady, and follow the grain, don't go against it.' He handed it back to her. 'Now you try.'

It was more difficult than Tom had made it look. It took Anna a while to get the smooth, sweeping motion right.

But she was determined to master it, conscious of him watching her from the other side of the room.

'You know, you don't have to help,' he said. 'I don't mind doing it all by myself.'

Anna smiled. 'You say the same thing every time I come. I'm beginning to think you don't want me here!'

Tom looked away, blushing. 'You may do as you please,' he muttered.

'Then I want to help,' Anna said. 'The more help you get, the quicker we'll be finished.'

'And the sooner you can come home?' Tom finished for her.

'That's right.' Anna looked around. She couldn't wait to show her mother and Liesel their new home.

'Mind, we ain't going to get finished at all with you planing great chunks out of that wood!' Tom said.

Anna looked at him. His face was unsmiling as usual, but there was a tell-tale glint in his black eyes.

'I can't help it. The wretched thing keeps sticking.'

'That's because you're pressing down too hard. Here, let me show you.'

Tom laid down his trowel and came over to her, wiping his hands on his trousers.

'Don't lean on it,' he said. 'Just guide it, and let it find its own way. Like this –'

He stood behind her, his work-roughened hands on top of hers, guiding the plane. His long fingers were caked in plaster dust, his fingernails bitten to the quick.

'It's working!' Anna grinned in delight as the plane glided along the length of wood. Tom went with her, his strong hands guiding hers.

'Told you. You just have to let it find its own way.'

Anna reached the end of the skirting board and straightened up to admire her handiwork. 'There,' she said. 'What do you think?'

It wasn't until she turned round that she realised how close he was to her, so close she could feel the warmth of his breath. His eyes weren't black at all, she thought, but a very dark grey, the colour of wet slate . . .

Tom released her abruptly. 'I reckon you can manage by yourself now,' he muttered. Before Anna could react, he was on the other side of the room, the trowel back in his hand, his broad back turned to hers.

He did not speak to her again, except for a gruff goodbye when Anna left.

Anna went straight from the bakery to her grandmother's house to visit her family. It had started to rain, but the butler left her on the doorstep for ages before he finally let her in.

'Miss Dorothy is out,' he announced as he took her coat.

Miss Dorothy? Anna winced. So her grandmother had decided her mother was to be a spinster again, had she? 'And my sister?'

'Miss Liesel is in the drawing room with Mrs Grey.' He looked askance at Anna's work clothes. 'I'll show you in.'

'Thank you, I'm sure I can find my own way.'

She heard laughter as she approached the drawing room. Anna pushed open the door and there was Liesel, pacing up and down with a book on her head while Hester Grey sat in her crimson plush-covered armchair, watching her.

'Put your shoulders back,' she instructed. 'Lift your chin . . . Keep your eyes forward, child!'

'What is going on?'

Liesel turned, and the book fell from her head with a clatter.

'Now look what you've made me do!' She bent to pick it up. 'Grandmother is teaching me to be a lady. Look!' She placed the book back on her head and demonstrated a few wobbling steps.

Hester watched her with approval. 'That is so much better,' she declared. 'You no longer slouch and stomp like a servant.'

She turned her cool gaze to Anna. 'My dear, what a pleasant surprise.' There was no warmth in her smile. 'But – good gracious – what are you wearing?' She lifted her *pince-nez* to peer at her. 'Is that a man's shirt?'

'And you've got bits in your hair!' Liesel joined in, laughing.

'It's plaster.' Anna picked a blob from her hair.

'Plaster, indeed!' Hester looked unimpressed. 'No, sit over there,' she instructed as Anna went to sit down on the couch. 'I'm afraid you'll mark the silk.' She picked up the small handbell by her side and rang it. 'I can see I'll have to teach you how to dress, too.'

Anna lifted her chin. 'I'm quite all right as I am, thank you.'

'That is a matter of opinion,' her grandmother muttered under her breath. Liesel giggled. 'Really, your education has been neglected for far too long,' Hester went on. 'I don't know what your mother was thinking of. But then, I suppose she had no choice.' She shook her head, her face sorrowful.

'I daresay our parents considered there were more important things in life than parading about with books on our heads,' Anna said.

'Like kneading dough and working in a shop?' her grandmother replied sweetly.

Anna gritted her teeth. 'We were happy to help with the family business.'

Hester turned to Liesel. 'Is your sister always this quarrelsome?' she asked.

'Yes, she is.' Liesel shot Anna a spiteful look.

Thankfully, just then their mother returned. She was wearing yet another new dress, Anna noticed, an old-fashioned style in a thick pale yellow fabric.

'Anna!' She greeted her with a warm hug. She was wearing a different scent, too. It was heavy, almost sickly, like violets.

The same scent Hester Grey always wore.

'Did the bookshop have the volumes I asked for?' Hester asked.

'Yes.' Dorothy handed her one of the parcels. 'And I bought you these gloves, too. I know how fond you are of Brussels lace.'

'Thank you, my dear. That's very thoughtful.'

Anna saw the way her mother smiled and felt a pang of something like jealousy. How well her mother and sister had settled in to life at Belgrave Square, practising deportment and shopping for trifles like proper ladies of society.

The butler arrived, bringing in the tea.

'Although I hardly think Anna is dressed for it,' Hester pointed out. 'Look at her, Dorothy. Quite a hoyden, don't you think?'

'I've been working at the bakery,' Anna defended herself.

'Have you? How wonderful.' Her mother turned to her, smiling. 'How are you getting on?'

'It's nearly finished,' Anna said proudly.

'What's this?' Hester asked. Her tone was pleasant but her gaze was sharp, passing from Anna to her mother and back again.

'The bakery is being rebuilt,' Dorothy explained.

'Really? You never told me?' Her smile masked the accusing note in her voice.

'Tom reckons we should be able to move back in within a month,' Anna said to her mother.

'I don't want to go back to Chambord Street,' Liesel announced.

'Liesel!'

'I don't care. I like it here.' She folded her arms mutinously.

'But Chambord Street is our home.'

'No, this is our home now.' Liesel pouted. 'I don't want to live over a shop anymore. Only common people live over shops.'

Anna noticed her grandmother hiding a smile behind her hand.

'I want to go to finishing school and learn how to be a young lady,' Liesel went on.

'And where will we get the money for a finishing school?' her mother said.

'Grandmother will pay. She said so.'

'I haven't discussed it with your mother, my dear,' Hester protested mildly. 'There is still a great deal to be decided.'

'There's nothing to be decided,' Anna declared. 'Papa would never allow it.'

'Papa might not be –' Liesel opened her mouth then closed it again.

'What?' Anna said. 'What were you going to say?' But her sister remained obstinately silent.

Chapter Thirty-Five

They had lost another patient during the night.

Private Norris, or Nobby as the other soldiers affection-ately called him, was a cheeky young man, brought in with severe bullet wounds to his arm and chest. By some miracle the doctors had managed to save his limb, but they could do nothing to stem the infection that weakened his chest.

Nobby had fought valiantly for more than a week, and even seemed to recover for a few days. But then the illness took over and after that he began to decline rapidly.

Sadie heard the sad news from the night sister when she and the other probationers came on duty that morning.

'I know he was a particular favourite,' the sister said. 'The other men are going to take it very hard, I think.'

Sadie looked around the ward. She had already felt the sombre atmosphere as the men woke up to the news that their brave little pal had lost his fight.

'He was so young,' she said to Dulcie, as they did the bed round together. 'Only seventeen. He told me he'd lied at the recruiting office so he could enlist and do his bit.'

Dulcie said nothing. Her usually smiling face was som-bre as she stripped off the bedclothes.

'At least he didn't suffer in the end,' Sadie went on. 'I'm glad Miss Carlyle was with him when he died. She didn't leave his side all night, so the night nurse told me. She sat with him, sponging his face and holding his hand and talking to him. And there we were, thinking she counted herself too good for nursing!'

'Any of us would have done the same,' Dulcie muttered, her head down.

'I know, that's our job, ain't it? But Miss Carlyle, she's a doctor. She could have just done a quick in and out, like most of the other students do. But not her.' Sadie pulled her corners of the bedsheet taut, the freshly starched smell rising up to greet her. 'I must say, I'm not surprised. I mean, I know she can be a bit sharp sometimes, but that's just her way. Underneath it all she's got a good heart.'

'Oh, she's an absolute angel!' Dulcie snapped.

Sadie looked up at her in surprise. 'You all right?'

'Of course.' The reply came out from between gritted teeth.

Sadie watched Dulcie punching a pillow into submission. 'It don't look like it,' she said. 'Come on, you can tell me.' Sadie straightened up and folded her arms. 'Man trouble, is it?'

Dulcie looked at her sharply. 'What makes you say that?'

'Because it nearly always is with you!' Sadie rescued the pillow from Dulcie's hands. 'Come on, out with it!'

Dulcie shook her head. 'I can't.'

Sadie saw her friend's look of distress and her heart sank. 'Here, you ain't . . .'

'No!' Dulcie shook her head. 'No, it's nothing like that.' She bit her lip. 'It's just – I've got a secret.'

'What kind of secret?'

But before Dulcie could reply, Nurse Hanley bore down on them, bristling with her usual efficiency. 'Hurry up, Nurses. Sister will be on the ward at nine, and she won't want to see half these beds unmade,' she bellowed.

'Yes, Sister.'

By the time the staff nurse had bustled off to bully someone else, Dulcie had fallen silent again.

'Well?' Sadie hissed.

Dulcie shook her head, her mouth a tight line. 'It doesn't matter,' she murmured.

Sadie looked across the bed at her friend's unhappy face. 'If this secret of yours is making you feel that wretched, then I reckon you should tell someone about it.'

Dulcie raised her miserable gaze to meet Sadie's. 'Even if it breaks someone else's heart?' she said.

Kate's sleepless night was beginning to tell on her.

She had managed to snatch a couple of hours' rest before she was summoned back to the ward to help with the new patients who had arrived that morning. But her brain was still foggy from the little sleep she had had, her limbs felt heavy and her eyes ached so much she could barely read the patients' notes in front of her.

But it had been worth it, she thought. Poor Private Norris had been so afraid, she hadn't wanted to leave him.

Kate had felt helpless. She had become a doctor because she wanted to make people better, to save lives. It always hit her hard when she failed. But there was no medicine she could prescribe, no procedure she could perform, that would have helped poor Nobby Norris. All she could do was sit there and watch him slip away.

She had still been sitting there, his cold, lifeless hand in hers, when the night sister came to check on them just before dawn. It was she who had gently guided Kate away to the kitchen and made her a cup of tea. Together they had stood at the window and watched as the pearly pink dawn rose above the rooftops.

'There was nothing I could do for him,' Kate said.

'You did more for him than you might think.'

'How?' Kate turned on her, raw from lack of sleep. 'I held his hand. What good did that do?'

The night sister smiled. She was a mature woman in her

fifties, with the wise, lined face of someone who had seen many nights like the one Kate had been through. 'Sometimes that's all that is needed, Miss Carlyle. Any good nurse will tell you that.'

As Kate moved from bed to bed, she was suddenly aware of one of the probationers trailing behind her. But whenever she turned around, the girl looked away and seemed to take a sudden interest in straightening a patient's bedclothes or rearranging their belongings on the bedside locker.

Befuddled by sleep as she was, Kate had begun to think she was imagining it, until she arrived at the bed of a new arrival, a gunner with auricular fibrillation. She was listening to the uneven stutter of his heart when, out of the corner of her eye, she saw the girl standing at the foot of the bed.

Kate pulled the stethoscope from her ears. 'Yes? What is it?'

The probationer bit her lip. It was the curly-haired girl, the one whose laughter could always be heard the length of the ward. Sister was continually telling her to be quiet but now she looked as if she was having trouble uttering a sound.

'Can I talk to you, miss?' she whispered finally.

Kate picked up the man's medical notes. They were blank apart from his name, age and rank. Corporal John Rayner of the Royal Field Artillery, twenty-nine years old.

'Isn't there someone else who could help you?' she said impatiently. 'I'm rather busy.'

'It's nothing to do with a patient.'

Kate looked up briefly from filling in Corporal Rayner's notes. The girl – her name had slipped Kate's mind – looked as if she might cry.

'What is it?' she sighed.

306

'It's about Dr Latimer.'

'What about him?'

'Is it true you two are courting?'

Kate's hand stilled briefly, then went on writing. 'I don't really see that's any business of yours—' she started to say, but the girl cut her off.

'He told me he loved me,' she said.

Kate stared at her. Suddenly the girl's name came back to mind. Dulcie. A silly, frivolous name for a silly, frivolous girl.

'I didn't know about you, I swear.' Dulcie's words came out in a rush. 'He told me I was the only girl for him.' She blushed. 'But then yesterday, I saw the two of you together outside the Casualty block, and you were holding hands, and you looked so in love.' She wrung her own hands, her face full of distress. 'But when I asked him about it, he said there was nothing to it. Said you were just friends, that you were useful to him.'

'Useful?'

Dulcie's blush deepened. 'On account of your father being important, miss,' she murmured.

All the blood drained to Kate's feet, leaving her light-headed. She could only stare at the girl in front of her.

'Anyway, I wanted to ask you,' Dulcie went on. 'I do like Char—Dr Latimer, but I wouldn't want to take it further if he's already spoken for.' She stared at Kate with wide, inno-cent eyes. 'I'm not that kind of girl, you see. I'd never go after someone else's young man, not if I thought they were serious.'

'I have no idea what you're talking about,' Kate cut her off. She finished writing Corporal Rayner's notes. 'Now please go away and find something else to do.'

'But, miss . . .'

'Go away, Nurse. *Stat!*'

Dulcie hurried off, her head down. Kate could feel the probationer watching her as she unlocked the medicine cupboard and measured out the digitalis. She was still watching when Kate finished administering the medication. Kate ignored her, forcing herself to walk calmly the length of the ward, straight through the double doors and out into the passageway that led to the private rooms.

It was only when she was out of sight that her legs began to shake and she leant back against the wall for support.

This couldn't be real. She was tired, not thinking straight. There was no other explanation for it.

Charlie Latimer. He had told her he loved her, too. They had even talked about getting engaged . . .

'Sis?'

When she opened her eyes again Leo was standing in front of her, his face full of concern.

'Kate, what is it? What's wrong?'

She held herself rigid, fighting the urge to burst into tears, and throw herself into the comfort of her brother's arms.

'Nothing. I'm just a bit tired. I was up all night with a patient.'

'You poor girl.' Leo was instantly sympathetic. 'You should go and get some rest.'

'I can't. There are no other doctors on the ward.'

'I'll take care of the rest of your round.'

'But they're not your patients.'

Leo patted her shoulder. 'Leave it to me,' he said gently. 'I'll sort it out. Now go and lie down before you fall down.'

'I shouldn't.' But as Kate turned her head towards the doors leading back to the ward, she could see Dulcie deep in conversation with Sedgewick, another of the probationers.

No doubt she would be the talk of the ward by lunchtime.

'Perhaps it might be best if I took a few hours off,' said Kate.

Leo nodded. 'Everything will seem better after a good night's rest.'

Tears prickled her eyes. If only that were true, she thought.

As soon as Kate saw Charlie Latimer's face a few hours later she knew the truth.

'That's utterly preposterous! My dear girl, who on earth told you such a story?' But underneath all the bluster and the wide grin, she could see the wary look in his eyes.

She glanced around the Students' Union bar. She had hoped to find a less public place to confront Charlie, but since it was early evening the room was nearly empty. There were only a couple of other students deep in conversation at a table on the far side of the bar.

'You know what these silly probationers are like.' Charlie was still talking, his words spilling out, smooth as honey. 'You only have to smile at them and they think you're besotted . . .'

'She said you'd told her you loved her?'

'Well, then. Now you must know she's making it all up!' He reached for her hand across the table. 'You're the only one I love.'

'And how many other girls have you said those words to? I wonder.' Kate drew her hand from his grasp.

Charlie sat back in his chair. 'Now don't go all cold on me. You know I adore you.'

'Do I?' Kate stared back at him.

They looked at each other in silence for a moment, then Charlie sighed.

'All right, I might have flirted with her a little.' He held up his hands. 'But it meant nothing, honestly. Boys will be boys, and all that.' He looked her in the eye. 'I love you, Kate. But sometimes it's very difficult for me. You can be so offhand, sometimes I wonder if you even care for me. Is it any wonder I succumb to a bit of attention now and again?'

Kate's brows rose. 'Are you trying to blame me?'

'No! No, of course not. I'd never do that. It was my mistake, I allowed my head to be turned briefly by a pretty girl. But that's all it was, honestly.' Charlie reached for her hand again. 'I love you,' he said. 'I want to spend the rest of my life with you, truly I do.'

Seeing the earnest expression on his face, Kate could almost have believed him. Then she remembered what Dulcie had said.

'Are you sure it's not my father who interests you more than I do?' she said.

Charlie's eyes flickered. 'I – I don't know what you mean.'

'I think you do. That's why you pursued me in the first place, wasn't it? Because of my father? You thought I might be useful to you, help you pursue your ambitions.'

'No! How could you even think that?'

'What was it you told Dulcie? That I was *useful* to you.' Kate spat out the word like venom. At the far end of the bar, the other students turned their heads to listen. 'Well, I'm sorry to disappoint you, but you're wasting your time. If you're looking to advance your career then I suggest a better way would be to spend more time on the ward and less in here!'

She stood up, pushing her chair back with an angry clatter.

'Kate?' Charlie said.

'What?'

He paused. 'You won't tell your father about this, will you?'

She opened her mouth to reply, then closed it again. 'Goodbye, Charlie,' she snapped.

As she walked away, he called out, 'Bloody cold-blooded bluestocking! And you wonder why I chased after little Dulcie Moore!'

Chapter Thirty-Six

'What do you mean, you can't come?'

'I'm sorry, my dear.' Dorothy Beck looked apologetic. 'But you must understand, I can't leave your grandmother. Not when she's so ill.'

Anna was silent for a moment, not trusting herself to speak in case her bitter disappointment got the better of her.

It wasn't fair. Today was supposed to be the day her mother and sister moved back to Chambord Street. But when Anna arrived that morning, her mother had met her with the news that Hester had been taken ill during the night.

'What's wrong with her?' she asked finally.

'The doctor thinks it might be her heart.' Dorothy looked sorrowful. 'Poor Mother, I didn't know she had heart problems.'

I didn't know she had a heart. But all Anna said was, 'Can I see her?'

Dorothy shook her head. 'Better not. We shouldn't disturb her while she's resting. The doctor says it's important for her not to have too much excitement.' She looked at Anna. 'You do understand, don't you? We must think of your grandmother's health.'

Anna nodded. 'I know. I'm disappointed, that's all. Tom has been working so hard to get the bakery finished for today, and I was looking forward to seeing you there again.'

'I'm sorry,' Dorothy sighed. 'But we couldn't leave your grandmother alone like this. The doctor says she could have another attack at any time.'

How convenient that she had this one, the very night before you left. Anna pushed the thought away.

'You do want to come home, don't you, Mother?'

'What a question!' Dorothy smiled. 'Of course I'm looking forward to going back to the bakery. Why would you even ask?'

Anna looked away. She could never voice her deepest fears, just in case she made them real.

'Liesel isn't,' she muttered.

Her mother smiled. 'You mustn't mind Liesel. You know how fanciful she can be.'

Anna looked around her. This house might seem austere and rather unwelcoming, but she could not deny it was far superior to their rooms over the bakery in Bethnal Green. And the longer her sister and mother stayed here, the harder it would be for them to leave.

'When do you think you might be able to come home?' she asked.

Dorothy frowned. 'I told you, when your grandmother is better.'

'And when will that be? Weeks? Months?'

'Anna!' Her mother was reproachful. 'I understand you're disappointed, but there is really no need to take that tone with me.'

'I'm sorry, Mother.' Anna looked down at her hands.

'I will speak to the doctor,' her mother promised. 'It may be that we can leave in a few days.'

'No, you must leave now.'

They both looked around. Hester Grey stood in the doorway, one thin hand pressed against the door frame for support. She looked a little paler than usual, but she was still dressed in her rigid, elegant style, not a hair out of place.

'Mother!' Dorothy Beck rushed to her side. 'What are you doing out of bed? You heard what the doctor said. You need to rest . . .'

'Do stop fussing, my dear. You know I have never been one for lounging about all day.' Hester's voice was brisk, in contrast to her frail appearance. 'I heard what you were saying,' she said, nodding to Anna. 'The child is quite right to be impatient. It's high time you and Liesel went home.'

'But I don't want to leave you while you're unwell.'

'Dorothy, I am an old woman. I have been unwell for years. I have managed quite well on my own for all these years, and I daresay I shall manage when you're gone. You must think of yourself and your family.'

Anna saw the flash of guilt in her mother's eyes. 'But you're my family too, Mother,' she said quietly.

Hester's expression softened a fraction. 'That's very kind of you, my dear, and I must say it has gladdened my heart to have you and Liesel here these past few months. It has been very pleasant to have some life back in this old house.' She gazed around her with a sigh. 'But I can't expect you to stay forever.'

'Surely I could stay until you're feeling better?'

'But you wouldn't want to disappoint Anna, would you? Not after she has worked so hard.'

'Anna understands. Don't you?'

She looked at her grandmother and wondered if she had imagined the gleam of triumph behind that bland smile.

'Yes,' she muttered. 'Yes, of course.'

Her mother followed her outside into the warm sunshine. It was the first day of May, and the trees in the square were heavy with frothy pink and white blossom.

'I'll come home soon,' Dorothy promised. 'Once your

314

grandmother has recovered.' She gave Anna a fierce hug. 'We will be a family again, my love, I promise.'

Over her mother's shoulder, Anna caught the twitch of a lace curtain.

Not if Hester Grey had her way, she thought.

Tom was waiting for them at the bakery. It touched Anna to see how he had spruced himself up for her mother's homecoming. His unruly dark hair was combed under his cap, and he was wearing a clean shirt under his shabby jacket. A vase of freesias stood in the middle of the table he had picked up from the rag and bone yard and lovingly restored.

He looked crestfallen when Anna walked in alone.

'Where's your mother?' He glanced behind her.

'She's not coming. Grandmother isn't well and she doesn't want to leave her.'

'That's a shame.'

'Yes.' Anna went to the window and stared out over the yard. Tom had cleared away the last of the building rubble and swept the cobbles carefully. It nearly broke her heart to see it.

'Still, at least it means I'll have time to find some more furniture,' he said bracingly. 'I saw the rag and bone cart going by with a couple of nice-looking chairs on it. I'll go down there later and see if he'll part with them. They're not exactly shipshape, but I reckon they could be all right with a bit of work.'

Anna went on staring out of the window, willing herself not to cry. But the tears still spilt down her cheeks.

'Miss Anna?' She could hear Tom behind her, shifting uncertainly. 'Are you all right?'

A moment later she felt a grubby handkerchief being pushed into her hand. Anna dabbed her eyes, breathing in the smell of sawdust and engine oil. Tom's smell.

'They'll come, y'know,' he said gruffly. 'They'll be home soon and then you can go back to how things were.'

'We can't though, can we? Things can never be the same. Papa's gone, and Edward's gone, and now my grandmother's trying to take the rest of the family away from me!'

'She what?'

'It's true. She wants to shut Papa and me out so she can have Mother and Liesel to herself.' Anna wiped away her tears. 'They're under her thumb now and I can't even make them see it.'

'I can't imagine your mother being under anyone's thumb,' Tom said.

'Well, she is. My grandmother's got her dressing and doing her hair to please her. And now there's this business with her weak heart. I know it sounds wicked, but I don't think there's anything wrong with her. It's all a trick to stop my mother leaving.'

'If it's a trick your mother will soon see through it,' Tom said. 'She ain't daft, is she?'

'I suppose not.' Anna sniffed.

'Of course she ain't. Your mother's got a kind heart, which is why she wants to make sure your grandmother's all right. But as soon as she can she'll be packing her bags and coming home. Because this is her real home, and you're her real family, you and your sister.' He laid his hand on her arm. 'It'll be all right in the end, you'll see.'

'Thank you.' For a moment neither of them moved. Anna stared down at his hand, resting on her forearm. His fingers were clumsy, his bitten-down nails rimmed with dirt. She could feel the warmth of it through the thin cotton fabric of her sleeve.

Then Tom seemed to recollect himself. He pulled his hand back and shoved it in his pocket as he turned away.

'I s'pose we should lock up,' he said gruffly.

316

'Aren't you going to stay tonight?' She had grown used to seeing his nest of blankets in the corner of the bedroom. Even when he managed to get hold of a couple of second-hand beds, he still slept on the floor.

Tom shook his head. 'It don't seem right. This is your place again now. Your home.'

'We wouldn't have a home if it wasn't for you.' Anna looked around the room, smiling. 'You've done so much for us, Tom. I don't know how we'll ever thank you.'

'You don't need to,' Tom said gruffly.

'But we owe you our lives.'

Tom looked away, and Anna realised she had embarrassed him.

'Anyway,' she said, 'we're all very grateful to you. And I want you to know there'll always be a place for you here at Beck's.'

'Even when Edward Stanning's running the place?'

Tom muttered the words so quietly under his breath, Anna wasn't sure she had heard them at first.

'What makes you say that?' she asked.

Colour rose in Tom's face. 'Nothing,' he said. 'I spoke out of turn.'

'This is my father's bakery,' Anna said. 'I suppose Edward will take over the business from him one day, but that won't be for a long time.'

Tom looked at her but said nothing.

Anna cleared her throat. 'Edward told me there was bad blood between you.'

'Did he now?' Tom's mouth lifted at the corner. 'And what else did he tell you?'

'Everything.'

'Everything?' His brows rose.

'He told me he'd been in trouble with the police, if that's what you mean.'

'Did he tell you why?'

There was something about the way Tom was looking at her that she did not like. It was almost as if he was taunting her.

'He said he'd fallen in with your brothers when he was younger. He said they led him into trouble.'

'He would say that, wouldn't he?' Tom muttered.

There it was again, that taunt in his voice.

'Why?' Anna asked 'What do you know that I don't?'

'I know Edward Stanning's a lying weasel.'

Anna gasped. 'How dare you speak about my fiancé like that!'

'You asked and I told you.' He faced her, his hands on his hips. 'You really want to know what happened? I'll tell you. Yes, he got involved with my brothers. But he wasn't some innocent little kid like he'd have you believe. Whatever they did, he was right in it too, up to his neck.'

Don't trust Tom Franklin.

'He used them,' Tom went on. 'It's true my brothers are villains, but they ain't too bright.' He tapped his temple. 'Edward was clever. Clever enough to let them do his dirty work and then make himself scarce and let them take the fall when things went wrong.'

'I don't want to hear this.'

'I'm only trying to warn you—'

'I said I don't want to hear!' Anna turned away from him. 'Edward told me this would happen. He warned me you might try to make trouble for him.'

'I just want you to know the kind of man you're marrying.'

'I know the kind of man I'm marrying, thank you very much!' Anna faced him angrily. 'My Edward is a hero. He's out there in France, fighting for his country, while you're here, making trouble for him.' She forced herself to calm down. 'I appreciate everything you've done for us,' she said quietly. 'But I can't have you speaking about Edward like that. If you can't be civil about him, then you should leave.'

Tom stared at her for a moment. Then, without a word, he snatched up his jacket and headed for the door.

Anna turned away, fighting the urge to call him back. She had to be loyal to Edward.

Don't trust Tom Franklin.

She heard the door open, then a long pause.

'I'll pick up my tools later,' Tom said. 'I won't trouble you again.'

'Please yourself.'

There was another long pause. Then Tom said, 'It takes more than a uniform to make a good man, you know.'

Anna turned round to answer him, but the door had already slammed shut.

Chapter Thirty-Seven

Kate was surprised to be summoned to Dr Ormerod's office first thing the following morning. She was even more surprised to see her father and Leo waiting for her there.

'Hello,' she greeted them, looking from one to the other. Neither of them looked back at her. Her father kept his rigid profile averted, while Leo stared down at his hands laced tightly in his lap.

Kate turned to Dr Ormerod. 'May I ask what this is about?' she asked.

'Sit down, please, Miss Carlyle.' Dr Ormerod gestured to the empty seat on the other side of his desk. Kate sat down, still eyeing her brother. Leo's face was the colour of whey.

Dr Ormerod cleared his throat. 'I am afraid we lost another patient on Monaghan last night,' he said.

'Oh, no. Which one?'

'Corporal John Rayner.'

Kate stared at him. 'Corporal Rayner, sir? The auricular fibrillation?' Dr Ormerod nodded. 'But I don't understand. He seemed quite well when I saw him yesterday . . .'

Dr Ormerod's eyes sharpened behind his spectacles. 'You saw this patient yesterday?'

'Yes, sir. He was a new admission.'

'And you treated him?'

'Yes, sir.' Kate glanced at her father. He was sitting up a little straighter in his chair. 'Digitalis. Two grains.'

Her father and Dr Ormerod sent each other significant

looks. Leo went on staring at his hands, his Adam's apple bobbing convulsively, as if he were trying not to be sick.

'And what time did you administer the drug?' Dr Ormerod asked.

'I can't remember precisely. Some time in the morning. But it will be in his notes, surely?'

'Ah, yes. His notes.' Dr Ormerod picked up a single piece of white card from his desk and peered at it over his spectacles. 'According to this, Corporal Rayner was given two grains of digitalis at ten-past nine yesterday morning.'

'Yes, that sounds about right, I suppose.'

'Except the signature on the notes is that of Dr Leo Carlyle.'

Kate flashed a look at her brother. 'I don't understand.'

'Neither do we, Miss Carlyle,' Dr Ormerod said gravely.

'But there must be some mistake?'

'Indeed there was.' Dr Ormerod picked up another sheaf of notes from his desk. 'We have just received the patient's post-mortem results. According to the PM, Corporal Rayner suffered heart failure following a large dose of digitalis.' He looked over his spectacles at her. 'Twice the recommended dose, I would imagine. Enough to stop a man's heart.'

Kate looked at Leo. 'Why would you give him digitalis when I'd already done it?'

'I didn't know.'

'But it was there, on his notes?'

Her brother looked up at her, his eyes meeting hers for the first time with a look of sorrow. 'There were no notes, Kate.'

'Yes, there were. I know there were.'

'Then where are they?' Her father spoke up, his voice rumbling like thunder.

'More to the point, why was your brother attending to one of my patients, Miss Carlyle?' Dr Ormerod put in.

Kate felt the heat rise in her face. 'I was unwell and Leo offered to finish the round for me.'

'Unwell, you say? In what way?'

'I was tired. I had been up with a patient all night.' She saw Dr Ormerod's knowing look. 'But not so tired I'd make a mistake like this,' she added quickly.

'Then how do you explain it?' Dr Ormerod asked.

'I – I can't.'

'I can,' her father interrupted her. 'It's perfectly clear to me what happened. You were distracted, not in your right mind, and you forgot to fill in this patient's notes. Then you abandoned the rest of the round to your brother, without even telling him which patients you had seen and which you hadn't. He then came upon this man, and finding no notes, quite understandably prescribed medication in the belief that he had not been treated. Isn't that what happened, Leo?'

He nodded. 'I suppose it must have been.'

'But I made the notes,' Kate insisted. 'I would never have prescribed anything for a patient without writing it up.'

'You said yourself, you were tired and feeling unwell,' Dr Ormerod pointed out.

Kate had a sudden mental picture of Charlie Latimer, and of that wretched girl talking to her while she was trying to deal with a patient. Had it been Corporal Rayner? she wondered. If it was, then she could imagine how it might have slipped her mind in all her mental confusion.

Dr Ormerod was watching her keenly. 'I can see from your face it is possible?'

'I suppose, but – I don't know,' she said.

Her father banged his fist down on the desk, rattling the inkwell and making them all jump.

'Do you realise what you've done, you foolish girl?' he thundered. 'Thanks to you, a patient has died. A man who should have expected to lead a full and vigorous life is now lying in the mortuary because of your stupidity!'

'Yes, Father.'

'Not only that, you have once again dragged the name of your family through the mud.' He shook his head. 'I am ashamed of you, Kate. Truly I am.'

'Yes, well. If we may proceed . . . ?' Dr Ormerod readjusted his spectacles. When he looked up at Kate she thought she saw a glint of sympathy in his eyes. 'Under the circumstances, I am afraid I have no choice but to place you before a disciplinary committee. With a recommendation for dismissal.'

Kate looked at Leo. His eyes were glistening with tears.

'I'm so sorry,' he mouthed back at her.

She took a moment to gather herself, then turned back to face Dr Ormerod. 'What will happen now?' she asked.

'What do you mean?'

'Should I report for duty?'

Sir Philip laughed harshly. 'Do you really think anyone would want a menace like you on the ward?'

'I think it would be better if you took some time off,' Dr Ormerod said kindly.

'Yes, sir. Thank you, sir.' She paused. 'I'm very sorry to have let you down.'

As Kate rose to go, she heard her father mutter, 'Sorry, she says! As if that's any help to that poor man lying in the mortuary.' He glared at her, his eyes cold. 'In God's name, why couldn't you have kept quiet and stayed at the Hampstead where you belonged?'

It didn't take long for word of Kate's disgrace to spread around the rest of the students. Rufus had stopped in at the SU bar for a swift drink after returning from a weekend visiting his mother, when he heard Evans, Gibson and Wallace discussing it.

'Well, I heard a fellow died in her care,' Evans was saying.

'No one seems to know what happened exactly. I asked Sister about it but she was rather tight-lipped.'

'All I know is Dr Ormerod's in a foul mood and no one's seen her since yesterday morning.'

'I say, you don't think she's been sacked, do you?' Gibson asked, eyes agog behind his thick spectacles.

'We can but hope, old boy!' Evans chuckled behind his pint glass.

Wallace nudged him. 'Her brother's just walked in. Doesn't look very happy, does he?'

'I'm not surprised. She's shamed the family name!'

Rufus approached Leo as he stood at the bar. Leo sent him a sidelong look then ignored him as he ordered a glass of whisky.

'What's this I hear about your sister?' Rufus said.

'What about her?' Leo downed the drink the barman put before him, then ordered another one.

'Is it true she's been suspended?'

'Who told you that?'

'It's all round the SU.'

'Bad news travels fast.' Leo downed his drink with a grimace.

'It is true, then?'

Leo turned on him. 'Yes, it's true. Happy now?' He slammed his glass down and gestured to the barman to refill it.

'Steady on, old man. You're drinking like a madman.'

'What business is it of yours if I am?' Leo stared down at the empty glass he gripped in his hand.

'So what happened?' Rufus asked him.

324

Leo was silent for a moment. Then he said, 'There was a mistake. A man died.'

'Not Kate's mistake, surely?'

Leo sent him a sharp look. 'What makes you say that?'

'Because she's too good a doctor.'

'Even good doctors make mistakes.' Leo spoke into his drink. 'Anyway, I thought you'd be celebrating. You never wanted her here.'

'That's not true.'

'Isn't it? None of you ever felt she deserved to be here.' His voice rose angrily. 'You all made it clear you wanted her gone. Well, now you've got your way.' He raised his glass in mocking salute to the students at the other end of the bar.

'What happened?'

'Ask him.' Leo nodded over Rufus' shoulder. Leo half turned to see Charlie Latimer had just walked in and was greeting a group of housemen who sat by the door.

'Latimer? What's he got to do with it?'

Leo looked at him wonderingly. 'You really don't know, do you? I thought he'd have run straight to you, bragging about it.'

Rufus felt an uncomfortable prickling up the back of his neck, as if he already knew what was coming. 'Bragging about what?'

'Your friend ditched my sister for a little nurse. Broke her bloody heart.'

'How do you know? Did she tell you that?'

Leo shook his head. 'Kate never tells anyone anything, that's her trouble. But a couple of the boys heard them having a big row about it in here.' He gulped down his drink.

Rufus glanced over at Latimer. He was laughing, slapping one of the housemen on the back.

'She was utterly besotted with him, poor little fool.' Leo

325

followed Rufus' gaze, his face bitter. 'She must have been in a terrible state about it. No wonder she forgot to write up a patient's notes . . .'

Rufus whipped his gaze back to Leo. 'Is that what she did?' Leo nodded. 'But that's not like Kate. Her notes are usually meticulous.'

'Not this time.'

Rufus paused for a moment, taking it in. 'But that can't be right,' he murmured. 'I know your sister. She would never be that negligent.'

'I told you, she was broken-hearted.'

Rufus shook his head. 'Zeppelins could be dropping bombs on Bethnal Green and Kate Carlyle would still be writing up her notes.'

'Well, she didn't this time, all right?' Leo snatched up his glass and downed the contents. 'So stop going on about it. You're only making everything worse.' He jerked his head towards the door. 'Go and bother your friends and leave me alone, would you?'

Rufus put down his empty glass and looked across at Latimer, his face grim. 'Oh, I will,' he said.

Charlie Latimer looked up with a grin as he approached. 'Hello, old boy. You're back, are you?' he greeted Rufus cheerily. 'How was sunny Leeds, or whatever God forsaken part of the world it is you come from?'

Rufus looked down at Latimer's hand, resting on his shoulder. 'Never mind me,' he said. 'What's all this I hear about you and Miss Carlyle?'

Charlie pulled a face of mock regret. 'Alas, I'm sorry to say, Miss Carlyle and I are no more.'

'What happened?'

'He got caught with his trousers down!' one of the young men said, and the others sniggered. Rufus looked at them, nudging and jostling each other like schoolboys.

326

'I was rather caught out, I'm afraid,' Charlie admitted. 'I thought it was just nurses who liked to gossip amongst themselves, but it seems even paragons of virtue like Kate Carlyle listen to tittle-tattle.' He sighed. 'It's a damn shame.'

'For her?'

'For me, old boy. I must say, I was having immense fun. But I suppose all good things must come to an—'

Rufus lashed out, felling him with a single punch before he reached the end of his sentence.

Charlie Latimer lay sprawled at his feet, nursing his jaw. 'Good God, what was that for?'

Rufus looked down at him. 'That', he said, 'was for Kate Carlyle.'

Chapter Thirty-Eight

On 7 May the ocean liner *Lusitania* was returning to Liverpool from a transatlantic voyage when it was torpedoed by a German submarine. The ship went down just off the coast of Ireland, with the loss of over a thousand passengers.

The tragic news caused shock waves all around the country. Eleanor listened to the men discussing it on the ward as she went about her work that morning.

'Just think, all those poor people dead,' one of the soldiers was saying to another. 'Women and children, too. They must have wondered what was happening to them, getting hit like that.'

'Evil German swine,' his friend joined in. 'It's one thing to have a go at us but killing innocent people!'

'There's already been riots on the streets, according to the newspaper,' a third man said. 'They went mad in Liverpool, smashing up German shops.'

'I don't blame 'em. Wait till this blasted leg of mine's mended, then I'll be back, making 'em pay!'

At last, Eleanor thought. She had been trying to tell people not to trust the Germans, but as time went by they seemed to forget who their real enemies were.

Well, at least this would remind them. It was just a terrible shame that so many lives had to be lost before they remembered.

And then she looked through the French windows and saw her brother sitting on the terrace with Anna Beck.

Eleanor pressed her face to the glass, watching them. They were playing chess, their heads bent together over the board. Harry looked up and grinned at Anna.

It gave Eleanor a jolt. She couldn't remember the last time she had seen her brother smile.

She pushed open the windows and stepped outside. 'Oh, hello,' she feigned surprise. 'I didn't see you out here.'

Anna sent her a wary look. Harry didn't even glance her way. He kept his eyes fixed on the chess board as if she hadn't spoken.

'What are you doing?'

'I'm painting Nurse Beck's portrait, what does it look like?' he snapped.

Eleanor looked at Anna, who coloured guiltily. 'Aren't you supposed to be cleaning the bathrooms with Trott?'

'She's busy,' Harry said.

'She has other work to do.'

'I thought you said I was supposed to be kept occupied?' He looked up at his sister for the first time, his eyes cold.

'I'll keep you company.'

'I'd rather spend time with Nurse Beck.'

Anna stood up, smoothing down her apron. 'Your sister's right, Harry. I should get on.'

She gave Eleanor a quick, embarrassed smile and then left, closing the French window behind her.

Eleanor turned on her brother. 'Really, Harry, I wish you'd stop being so childish' she scolded him.

'I might if you stopped treating me like a child!'

She flinched. Harry rarely raised his voice, especially not to her.

She busied herself, arranging the blanket around his shoulders in spite of the warm sun that bathed the terrace.

'You know, you shouldn't get too friendly with Nurse Beck,' she said.

'Why not? She's nice.'

'She's half-German.'

'And what's that got to do with anything?' Harry shrugged off the blanket. 'Do you think she's a saboteur, out to poison our cocoa?'

Eleanor stared at him. 'You may mock, Harry, but you hear stories—'

'Where? Where do you hear these stories?' He looked up at her, squinting in the sunlight. 'I suppose Father told you one of his yarns from the *John Bull*?'

The sarcastic edge to his voice rankled with her. 'I didn't hear about the *Lusitania* from Father. Or the *John Bull*.'

Harry looked away, scowling, but said nothing.

'Really,' Eleanor went on, 'I do wonder at your attitude these days. Especially after what the Germans did to you.'

'I don't want to talk about it.'

'They could have killed you, you know. If that bullet had been half an inch higher—'

'I said, I don't want to talk about it!'

Eleanor looked down at her brother's angry, set face. Harry always seemed to be irritable these days. Sister said it was because he was ill, but Eleanor refused to believe it. Her brother was not the kind to fall apart, not like those pale, trembling young men who howled in their sleep and cowered under their beds every time Grace Duffield dropped a bedpan.

He was just bored and restless, she told herself. It was bound to happen. Harry was too bold and outgoing to stay cooped up in a hospital bed for weeks on end. He needed to be taken out of himself.

She tried again. 'I didn't know you played chess?'

'Anna was teaching me.'

Eleanor winced. So it was Anna now, was it?

She sat down opposite him. 'Perhaps I could finish the game with you?'

He raised listless eyes to meet hers. 'Do you play?'

'No, but I'm sure you could teach me.'

'I don't feel like it.' He leant back in his seat and turned his face up to the sun. Eleanor watched him in frustration.

'Some of the other men are playing whist. Perhaps you'd like to join in?' she suggested.

'No, thanks, I'd rather be on my own.'

'Come on, Harry. You know you always used to love whist. It might help lift your spirits?'

'Do you know what would really lift my spirits? If you left me alone!'

Eleanor gave him a brittle smile. 'You seem to prefer Anna Beck's company to mine these days.'

Harry did not reply. The silence lengthened, broken only by the distant sound of men's laughter coming from the ward.

'I think I'll go inside.'

'Let me help you.' Eleanor made a move towards him but he brushed her off.

'For God's sake, leave me be! You're like an annoying fly, always buzzing round me.'

'I'm only trying to help.'

'Well, don't.'

She watched him struggle to his feet, leaning on his good arm to lever himself out of his chair.

'I wrote to our parents,' Eleanor said.

Harry froze. 'You did what?'

'They deserve to know,' she said. 'They'd already had a letter from the War Office letting them know you'd been injured. All I did was tell them where you were, that I was looking after you . . .'

Harry's face was a rigid mask. 'I asked you not to,' he said quietly.

'I know, but they were worried sick, Harry.' She paused, then said, 'They want to come and visit you.'

'No!' His eyes flew to meet hers, full of panic.

'Why not? They only want to see you, make sure you're all right.'

'I can't!' He was suddenly agitated. 'You'll have to write to them again, tell them not to come.'

'Why don't you want to see them?'

'I can't! I just can't. I'm not ready.'

She looked at him, his face drained of colour.

He wasn't ready. He had said that to her once before, on the day he was first admitted. She remembered the trembling, frightened young man who had clung to her hand then and made her promise not to tell their parents where he was.

'But you're so much better than you were,' she said. 'Your shoulder's almost healed, you've got your strength back . . .'

Harry shook his head. 'I can't,' he said, over and over again. 'I can't face them.'

Eleanor went over to him. 'Father wants to see you,' she said. 'Don't you understand, Harry? You're a hero.'

'No!' He looked up at her, pain flaring in his hazel eyes. 'Don't say that. Don't ever say that.' He dropped his gaze, his voice faltering. 'You don't know what it was like out there. It made cowards of us all . . .'

'Not you,' Eleanor said. 'You went into no-man's-land, took a German bullet—'

'For Christ's sake, Ellie!' he cut her off angrily. 'You don't see it, do you?'

'See what?'

'There was no German bullet.' He faced her, his expression bleak. 'I did this to myself.'

Chapter Thirty-Nine

'"Our Father, who art in heaven, hallowed be thy name . . ."'

Anna clenched her teeth together to stop them chattering. The summery weather had cooled, giving way to darkening skies and rain, and inside the church a damp chill seeped from the thick stone walls. The murky stained-glass windows kept out all but a dim light, casting a deep gloom over the pews.

'"Give us today our daily bread . . ."'

Anna opened one eye and looked around. Across the aisle from her in the front row sat Matron, very upright in her black dress and elaborate starched headdress. The ward sisters sat in a stern-looking line beside her.

'"And forgive us our trespasses, as we forgive those who trespass against us . . ."'

She shifted her gaze to Eleanor, sitting in the pew in front of hers. Her head was bowed, hands clasped. What was she praying for? Anna wondered. Forgiveness for the way she'd treated her room-mate? She doubted it; Eleanor Copeland was so self-righteous, she'd never believe she had any reason to reproach herself.

Anna stared at the back of her neck, the stray hairs escaping from underneath her cap. It was barely ten o'clock in the morning, and Eleanor had already snapped at her twice, once for leaving her shoe lying around where Eleanor could have tripped over it, and then for humming under her breath while she did her hair.

'Do you have to make so much noise?' she had snapped. 'I have a headache.'

Perhaps she was just spoiling for another fight, Anna thought. But Eleanor seemed different lately, tense and distracted.

She had been the same all the previous day. Sister had given her hell for emptying a patient's bedpan down the sink when they were supposed to be measuring his urine output.

It was the kind of mistake Grace Duffield might have made, but never Eleanor.

And then Anna had found her in the kitchen, the kettle in her hand, staring blankly at it as if she had completely forgotten what she was doing.

'Are you all right, Copeland?' Anna had asked her, but Eleanor had only turned on her and snapped, 'I'm fine. Just leave me alone, will you?'

Anna wondered if it had anything to do with her brother. Harry had been wretched all the previous day too, ever since she had left them together on the terrace. He had spent the whole day in bed with his face turned to the wall, just as he had when he was first admitted. And when Anna had suggested they resume their game of chess, his only response had been a listless shrug.

She hoped Eleanor had not upset him. It had taken Anna weeks to coax him out of bed. She had just started to encourage him into taking an interest in the world, and now they were back where they'd started.

Finally, the morning service ended. As usual, they waited for Matron and then the sisters to leave, and filed out after them, staff nurses followed by humble probationers. They hurried into the rain, pulling their thick navy blue cloaks around them.

And as luck would have it, Anna found herself beside Eleanor Copeland.

She sent her room-mate a sideways glance. As usual, Eleanor strode along, her chin lifted, presenting a confident face to the world. It was only when she looked closely that Anna noticed the tightly set lips, and the purple shadows like bruises under the eyes.

'Are you all right, Copeland?' she asked.

Eleanor shot her a glance. But before she could reply, Miriam Trott came up and started talking to her about the drive she was organising to sew sandbags for the trenches.

Eleanor turned away from Anna immediately. The next moment she had linked arms with Miriam and they were walking away, putting distance between themselves and Anna.

But she had seen the unguarded look of despair on her room-mate's face.

It was none of her business, Anna told herself. Whatever problems Eleanor had, she certainly didn't want to share them with the person she most despised.

Besides, Anna had better things to think about than Eleanor Copeland.

When they reached the Nightingale, most of the nurses headed back to the main hospital building. But Anna was lucky enough to have the day off and planned to spend it with her family.

She was looking forward to seeing her mother and sister again, but as she turned into the elegant Belgravia Square, Anna felt the familiar feeling of unease uncurling in the pit of her stomach. Liesel might love her grandmother's imposing house, but to Anna it seemed soulless, as if something dark and cold lurked within its walls.

It wouldn't be for long, she told herself. Now her grandmother was back on her feet again, there was no reason why her mother and sister couldn't move back to the bakery.

Then they would be a proper family again, back where they belonged.

Hester Grey was waiting for her in the parlour. She looked suspiciously well for someone who had so recently been confined to her bed. In fact, she seemed to be in better spirits than Anna had ever seen her. She even managed to greet her granddaughter with something like a smile.

'Hello, my dear. Would you like some tea?' She picked up the bell without waiting for an answer.

'Where are Mother and Liesel?'

'Your mother has gone upstairs to compose herself. I'm afraid she has had some unfortunate news.'

Fear washed over Anna. 'What sort of unfortunate news? Is it about Papa?'

'I'll let her tell you herself. Ah, Morton. Some tea, if you please.'

Anna stared at her grandmother. Hester Grey seemed to be enjoying herself, she thought.

'I need to see Mother.'

'All in good time. I told you, she has taken a moment to – ah, here she is now.'

Anna swung around. Her mother stood in the doorway. She seemed calm, but Anna could see the ashen pallor of distress in her face.

'Mother, what is it? What's happened?'

Dorothy Beck turned to her, her fragile composure crumpling.

'Oh, Anna! I'm so sorry, my love. It's the bakery . . .'

'I had word from Mrs Gruber, whose husband has the pork butcher's on Columbia Road. She said a gang of them went on the rampage yesterday afternoon with bricks and clubs.'

Dorothy reached for Anna's hand, her face full of sorrow. 'I'm so sorry, Anna. I know how hard you and Tom worked to put the place right.'

'How bad is the damage?' Anna asked.

'She didn't say. Poor woman was so terrified, she fled as soon as the trouble started. She really thought they were going to kill her . . .'

'I suppose you can't blame them for wanting to take revenge, after what the Germans did to the *Lusitania*,' Hester Grey said as she poured herself a cup of tea.

Dorothy Beck stared at her mother. 'You think it's right to put an innocent woman in fear of her life?'

'I didn't say it was right, did I? I merely said you couldn't blame people for being outraged.' Hester sipped her tea. 'Remember,' she said, 'innocent women died on that ship. And children, too.'

For once, her grandmother's barbed comment barely touched Anna. All she could think about was that they might never go home . . .

'I want to see it,' she said.

Her mother shook her head. 'Better not. It might be too upsetting.'

'I want to see the damage,' Anna insisted. 'I need to know.'

'Then I'll come with you.'

'Are you sure that's a good idea?' Hester interjected. 'It might be dangerous.'

'All the more reason not to let Anna go on her own. Besides, she's right. We need to see how bad it is. You never know, we might be able to repair it.'

'Repair it?' Hester's mouth curled in disdain. 'Why on earth would you want to repair it? They'll only come and destroy it again.' She set down her cup. 'Better just to board the place up and leave it, if you ask me.'

No one's asking you. Anna looked at her grandmother. It

was the first time Hester Grey had stopped smiling since she had arrived.

Anna's nerve failed her as they turned the corner into a rain-soaked Chambord Street. She clung to her mother's arm, sheltering under her dripping umbrella, eyes turned towards the ground.

'Oh, Mother, I can't look,' she whispered.

But as it turned out, the damage wasn't nearly as bad as she had feared. The front windows were smashed, and round the back someone had kicked the door in and thrown paint all over the kitchen.

'But it's still standing, and that's the main thing,' her mother said bracingly. 'It will be all right once we've cleaned up a bit. Perhaps Tom could help us.'

'No,' Anna said shortly. 'We can't ask him for more help.'

Her mother frowned. 'Why not?'

'I just think it would be wrong to impose on him any more.'

The truth was, Anna hadn't seen or spoken to Tom since their argument two weeks earlier. And she wasn't inclined to see him, either. She was still furious over what he had said about Edward.

Or perhaps you just don't want to know the truth, a small voice said inside her head.

'I'm sure he wouldn't mind . . .'

'I don't want to speak to him, Mother!'

Her mother sent her a long look, but she didn't press the point. 'I'm sure we can sort it out ourselves,' she said.

Anna put out her hand to touch the splintered wood where the back door had once been. 'How will we tell Papa?'

'We won't,' her mother said firmly. 'It would break his

heart.' She looked around. 'We'll get the door and the windows mended, and this paint cleaned up, and—'

'What's the point?' Anna said. 'Grandmother's right, they'll only come back and smash it all up again.'

'Anna—'

'It's true, isn't it? They don't like us here. In fact, they hate us.' She looked around the ruined kitchen. 'There's no place for us here anymore.'

Mr Hudson was sheltering in the doorway outside his butcher's shop, talking to Mrs Wheeler. They were looking over at the bakery, but as Anna's mother paused to put up her umbrella they turned away.

Anna stared at their backs and something inside her snapped.

'Had a good look?' she shouted. 'Don't stop on our account, will you?'

'Anna!' Her mother went to pull her away but she stood her ground.

'Where were you when this was happening? I bet you were standing out here then, weren't you?'

Mr Hudson shuffled his feet. 'We didn't see nothing.'

'No, I daresay you were looking the other way then, just like you were the last time it happened.'

She turned on them, rain running down her face. She could feel anger rising inside her, all the hurt and betrayal that had been building up finally spilling out of her.

'And to think my father considered you his friends.' She glared at Mr Hudson. 'You set up your shop at the same time as Papa did his, didn't you? I remember him telling me how you were both young men who worked hard to build up your businesses.'

Mr Hudson dropped his gaze and mumbled something Anna could not hear.

'What do you think he would do if it was your shop

being attacked? Or your café, Mrs Wheeler? Do you think he'd look the other way?' She shook her head. 'No, he'd be the first one out there, trying to stop them. Trying to help.'

'Come on, love. You're only upsetting yourself.' Her mother slipped an arm around her shoulders. 'I'll take you home.'

'Home?' Anna's laughter was hollow. 'We don't have a home anymore, do we?' She turned back, raking Mr Hudson and Mrs Wheeler with a look of contempt. 'I hope you're proud of yourselves,' she said.

Chapter Forty

They returned to the Belgravia house, where Hester was waiting for them.

Liesel was with her, perched on a stool at her feet, reading to her in a clear, piping voice. As soon as Anna and her mother walked in Hester gestured for her granddaughter to be quiet.

'How was it?' Her face was full of concern. 'You poor dears, you look so upset. I warned you, didn't I? I said you shouldn't go.' Her voice dripped false sympathy. 'Tell me, was it very dreadful?'

'There was quite a bit of damage,' Dorothy replied. 'But it wasn't as bad as we'd thought, was it, Anna?'

Anna couldn't answer her. She was still too choked with disappointment and rage to speak.

All her dreams of being reunited were shattered. Without their home, they no longer felt like a family.

And all the while there was her grandmother, hovering over them like a bird of prey, waiting to swoop.

'Well, it's a good thing you still have a roof over your heads here,' she was saying. 'I'm sure it must be a great relief to you, knowing you have somewhere safe to live.'

'Yes, it is,' Dorothy said. 'But we will still be moving back to the bakery.'

'Yes, of course. In due course.'

'Tomorrow,' Dorothy said.

Anna stared at her mother, shocked. She wasn't even

341

sure she had heard her say the words until she saw her grandmother's face tighten.

'But why?' Hester's smile looked forced. 'It doesn't make sense. You said yourself the house is badly damaged.'

'It isn't that bad. We can still live in it.'

'But why would you want to, when you can live here in comfort?'

'Because it's our home.' Anna caught her mother's sideways glance. 'It's where we belong.'

Hester pursed her mouth. 'I had hoped you would think of this as your home now. Haven't I made you welcome here?'

'Of course, Mother. You've been very kind to us.'

'And yet you can't wait to leave,' Hester said tightly. 'Even if it means being murdered in your beds.'

'I don't want to be murdered!' Liesel whimpered.

'You see? Look at the poor child, how terrified she is.'

'No one is going to murder you, Liesel,' Anna said quietly.

'And how do you know that?' Her grandmother turned on her angrily. 'They've already razed the place to the ground once. Who is to say they will not try again? And next time you might not be so lucky.' She put a hand to her chest. 'I can't bear to think about it,' she said faintly. 'I'm sure I will worry myself to death.'

Anna looked at her mother. She could see her weakening, her face anxious.

Hester must have seen it too. She sat up, pushing home her point. 'Can't you stay a little longer?' she wheedled. 'I've so enjoyed having you here. You have no idea how lonely I've been all these years, shut up in this house by myself. To have my daughter back, to be able to get to know my precious granddaughter . . .' She put out her hand to stroke Liesel's golden head, as if she were a pet. 'I can't bear to lose you now I've found you again.'

'But you won't lose us, Mother,' Dorothy said. 'Of course we'll still come and visit you, and I hope you'll come and see us, too. I'd love to show you the bakery. And perhaps when Friedrich comes home—'

'Don't be absurd, Dorothy. He isn't coming home!'

Her mother looked taken aback. Even Liesel was startled.

'Do you really think they will let him out of that internment camp?' Hester's voice was harsh. 'And even if they do, they'll probably send him straight back to Germany. Do you want to go and live there? I shouldn't think you'd be any more welcome over there than he is here!'

Liesel turned panicked eyes to her mother. 'Is it true? Papa's not coming home?'

'Of course he is,' Anna said, glaring at her grandmother. 'Take no notice of what she says.'

'Indeed you will take notice of me!' Hester pulled herself upright in her chair, her spine as straight and stiff as a poker. 'I watched you throwing away your life more than twenty years ago, Dorothy, but now you've been given a second chance and I refuse to allow you to make another mistake.'

'You refuse to allow me?' Dorothy's brows rose. 'Mother, I'm not a child anymore.'

Anna glanced at her grandmother. She could almost see the thoughts racing through her head, the calculation behind those narrowed eyes.

'I'm only thinking of you,' she said finally. 'Look at yourself, Dorothy. Look at what your life has become. He's dragged you down, just as I said he would. Now you have nothing, not even a roof over your head.' She forced a smile. 'My dear, you're a charming, beautiful woman, and still young enough to start again. Think of what your life could be, if only you allowed me to help you . . .'

Anna watched the two women staring at each other in silence. Then her mother shook her head.

'Oh, Mother, I really thought you'd changed,' she said sadly. 'When we first came here, you were so kind, I started to believe that things could be different between us, that we might be a family again. But you haven't changed, have you? You're still trying to control my life, just as you always did.' She took a deep breath. 'Pack your things, Liesel,' she said. 'We're leaving.'

'What things?' Hester mocked her. 'You came to me with nothing, remember? Even the clothes you stood up in were borrowed from the poorhouse.'

Dorothy stiffened. 'Very well,' she said. 'We'll leave with nothing.'

'And nothing is all you'll ever have!'

'That's where you're wrong, Mother. We have love, and we have each other.' Dorothy turned to her daughter. 'Hurry up, Liesel!'

Liesel didn't move. She perched on the footstool, knees drawn under her chin, looking from one to the other of them with wide eyes.

'You don't have to go, my dear,' Hester said to her. 'You can stay with me.' She smiled. 'You can live here, in this house, and you'll learn how to be a fine lady and have all the clothes your heart could desire.'

'Liesel?' Anna whispered. But her sister's eyes were on her grandmother, as if transfixed.

It seemed like an eternity before she spoke.

'I'm sorry, Grandmother,' she said. 'But I want to go home.'

They made their way back to Bethnal Green in subdued silence. Dorothy was particularly downcast, Anna noticed. She stared out of the window of the bus, lost in thought.

Anna felt the weight of her sadness. 'I'm sorry, Mother,' she said. 'About Grandmother, I mean.'

Dorothy turned to her with the smallest of smiles. 'She made her decision, my love. I wish things had turned out differently, that's all.'

The bakery looked worse than Anna had remembered. They stood in the street, the three of them sheltering under an umbrella as the rain poured down. A dull canopy of dark cloud seemed to press down on them, squashing their spirits.

'We can't live here,' Liesel whined. 'It's awful.'

'We have no choice,' her mother said grimly. 'Come on, I'm sure things will seem better when we're inside.'

The rooms were dark and cold. Anna found a penny for the meter and they went around the rooms, lighting all the mantles.

'Grandmother has electric lights in her house,' Liesel pointed out unhelpfully.

'Perhaps you should have stayed with her, then!' Anna snapped back.

Liesel glared sulkily at her, but said nothing.

Once the lamps were lit, they found some wood from the yard and used it to block up the gaping hole in the shop window. They stacked more wood against the broken back door.

'I wish we had a hammer and some nails, then we could seal it up properly,' Dorothy said.

Anna thought once again about Tom. She wondered if he was waiting for her to approach him.

He would have to wait a long time, she decided.

A hammer and nails weren't the only things they were missing. When they checked the coal cellar, it was empty. They had no way of making a fire.

'We don't have any food, either,' Liesel complained. 'And I'm hungry.'

'We could get fish and chips?' Anna suggested.

'It's Sunday,' Liesel said sulkily. 'There won't be anywhere open.'

Anna caught her mother's hopeless, helpless look as she sat staring into the empty fireplace.

'Then we'll just have to go without, won't we?' Anna shot a warning look at Liesel, who ignored it.

'But I'm starving!' she whined.

'Oh, no, you're not. You've got fat since you've been living with Grandmother.'

'I have not!'

'Yes, you have. No wonder you needed all those new dresses. You've—'

'Shh!' Liesel held up her hand. 'Did you hear that?'

'What?'

'That noise.'

Anna strained her ears to listen. 'You're imagining things.'

'I'm not. I heard something, I did.' Liesel's eyes grew wide with fear. 'You don't think it's someone coming to murder us again, do you?'

'I'll murder you myself if you don't shut up!' Anna said, but then she saw her mother's expression.

'Liesel's right,' Dorothy whispered. 'There is a noise. I think it's coming from the kitchen.'

The sudden crash made them all jump. Something, or someone, had pushed the wooden boards from the back door, making them fall with a clatter.

Dorothy shot to her feet. 'Stay here,' she said.

'No, Mother. We're coming with you.'

The three of them crept down the passageway towards the kitchen. Whoever was on the other side of the door was making no effort to be quiet. They could hear the sound of heavy breathing, and the scrape of the wooden boards being dragged across the floor.

Dorothy threw open the kitchen door and they all fell through inside, only to be confronted by the rotund shape of Mrs Wheeler from the corner café. She stood in the middle of the kitchen, holding one of the boards in her hands.

'Oh, hello,' she said. 'Sorry about the noise. I was going to knock, but—' She looked back at the shattered door.

'What do you want?' Terror still fizzed through Anna's veins, making her forget her manners.

Mrs Wheeler looked startled. 'I've brought you something to eat,' she stammered. 'Leftovers from the café.' She nodded to the box on the kitchen table.

'Thank you,' Dorothy said. 'That's very kind.'

'Like I said, it's only leftovers. A meat and potato pie, and some veg. There's some tea in there, too. And some milk and sugar. And a bit of seed cake.' She stared at the floor as she said it, the toe of her slipper scuffing against the bare boards.

'We're very grateful.'

Mrs Wheeler gave them a quick nod and then she was gone.

'Well, that was a nice surprise,' Dorothy said, picking up the discarded board.

'Wasn't it?' Anna muttered.

Liesel glared at her. 'There's no need to be so ungrateful.'

'I'm not ungrateful. It's just—'

Before Anna could finish her sentence there was a knock on the door frame. The next minute Mr Hudson's red face loomed through the splintered hole in the wood.

'All right?' he said. 'I saw your lights on, and thought I'd come round with this.' His meaty arms reached through the hole and dumped a sack of coal on the floor. 'The missus sent some old sheets and blankets, too. She wasn't sure if you had any?'

'We haven't. Thank you.'

'I'll leave them here, shall I?' He passed a stack of linen through the hole. 'Give us a knock if you need anything else.'

'Thank you.'

'No need for that. You'd do the same for us.' He looked uneasily at Anna when he said it.

Dorothy's mood seemed a lot brighter once they'd made up the fire. They gathered around the fireplace and drank hot tea and ate the meal Mrs Wheeler had provided for them.

'Wasn't that kind of them all to help us?' Liesel said through a mouth full of meat and potato pie.

Anna looked at her mother. 'More like guilty consciences if you ask me,' she muttered.

'You're probably right,' Dorothy said. 'But we have to be practical. It's better than nothing.'

'I don't know about that.' As far as Anna was concerned it was more a case of too little, too late.

Chapter Forty-One

When Dulcie first heard Kate Carlyle had been suspended, part of her was glad. She couldn't forget how high-handed the medical student had been when Dulcie tried to speak to her. She should have been grateful that someone had tipped her the wink about Dr Latimer, one girl to another. But instead Kate Carlyle had looked at her with loathing and contempt, as if she was nothing.

Typical of her, Dulcie thought. Kate had never been particularly nice, and now she was getting what she deserved.

But then all the other nurses had started going on about it, saying how sad it was, and what a good doctor Kate Carlyle had been, and wondering if it was true that Rufus French had knocked Charlie Latimer out because of it.

'They must have fallen out over something,' Grace Duffield said. 'They've always been such good friends before.'

'If you ask me, Dr French is rather sweet on Miss Carlyle,' Miriam Trott sighed. 'How romantic, don't you think, to have men fighting over you?'

And that had annoyed Dulcie even more because she had been every bit as hurt and humiliated as Kate and she didn't have anyone taking her side, let alone a knight in shining armour like Rufus French. None of the other nurses knew she was the other girl in Charlie Latimer's life, although she had heard them speculating about who it might be. They didn't seem to have a lot of sympathy for the mystery girl, whoever she was. If anything, they blamed her for causing so much trouble for Miss Carlyle.

'If it hadn't been for worrying about it, she would never have made such a mistake with that patient's notes,' Grace declared.

Dulcie knew she should speak up, but she was worried. She had left it too long, she was bound to get into trouble if she said anything now. And besides, who could she tell and what could she say? The damage had already been done. Kate Carlyle was gone and there was nothing Dulcie could do about it.

Then Grace Duffield returned to Lennox House one tea-time with the news that Miss Carlyle was back, working in Pathology. Dr Werner's latest assistant had gone off sick, and the Head of Pathology had particularly asked for her.

That was when Dulcie turned to her friend Sadie Sedgewick for advice.

It was almost a relief to get it all off her chest. Her secret had grown too heavy to bear alone. And of course Sadie was the right person to tell. She was kind and wise, and Dulcie knew she would never gossip about it with the other girls.

'You've got to talk to Miss Carlyle,' Sadie said, when Dulcie had finished telling her story.

'I was afraid you'd say that!' Dulcie sighed. 'But I can't. She'd never listen to me.'

'She will when she hears what you've got to say.'

Dulcie wasn't so sure, remembering the cold, contemptuous way Kate had looked at her before. 'I wouldn't know what to say.'

'Just tell her what you've told me.'

'Can't you do it for me?' Dulcie pleaded.

Sadie shook her head. 'This is your business, mate, not mine.' She paused, then said, 'Why don't you send her a note, if you're worried about facing her?'

'She'd never read it.' Dulcie bit her lip. 'You're right,' she said. 'I've got to speak to her, tell her the truth.'

Sadie smiled. 'That's the spirit,' she said. 'You know what they say. Tell the truth and shame the devil.'

Dulcie was still in two minds about it when she went off duty at ten o'clock the following morning. She longed to go back to Lennox House, or to walk through the hospital gates and keep walking, putting as much distance between herself and Kate Carlyle as possible. But instead she forced herself to walk down to the Pathology block.

She could feel her heart racing in her chest as she descended the steps and pushed open the door into the gloomy lab. All those dead bodies and bits of organs in jars made her nervous, but not half as terrified as Kate Carlyle made her feel.

Kate was alone in the lab, sitting at the table with her back to the door, writing up her notes.

'I'll be with you in a moment,' she said over her shoulder.

Dulcie cleared her throat nervously. 'Miss Carlyle?'

Kate turned round, scowled, then returned to her writing. 'You're not supposed to be here,' she said.

Dulcie stood her ground. 'May I have a word with you, please?'

'Not now, I'm busy.'

'But it's important—'

'I said, not now!' Kate cut her off. 'Besides,' she added, 'I don't think you have anything to say that I'd want to hear.'

Dulcie stared at Kate's turned back. She had a good mind to walk away and leave her to it. The rude, arrogant cow deserved everything that was coming to her.

But then she remembered what Sadie had said. *Tell the truth and shame the devil.*

'Not even if it saves your bacon?' she said.

Kate stopped writing and lifted her head. 'What did you say?'

'I've got something important to tell you. About that patient who died.'

Kate put down her pen and turned slowly to look at her. Her expression gave nothing away. 'Go on,' she said. 'I'm listening.'

'But that can't be!'

Leo paced restlessly back and forth over the rug in their father's study. His agitated movements were in sharp contrast to Sir Philip, who sat very still behind his desk, his fingers steepled in front of his face, deep in thought.

'But Dulcie Moore remembers it clearly,' Kate insisted. 'She was with me when I was examining the patient. She says she remembers me making out his chart.'

'Then someone must have taken it, because I definitely didn't see it.'

'Do sit down, Leo!' Sir Philip spoke up for the first time. Leo promptly stopped pacing and dropped into a seat, as if he was playing musical chairs. There was a sheen of perspiration on his brow, Kate noticed.

Her father turned to her. 'Should we trust the word of this young woman anyway? And why hasn't she come forward before?' he asked.

'I don't know.'

'It seems very convenient to me that she remembers this particular patient so clearly. Are you sure she's not making this up because she's your friend?'

Kate nearly smiled. No one could ever have described her and Dulcie Moore as friends!

'She remembers it clearly because we were arguing at the time.' Kate saw her father's gaze sharpen and realised too late what she had said.

'Arguing?' He pounced on the word. 'Why were you bickering with a student nurse?'

'I daresay it was about Dr Latimer,' Leo muttered.

'Dr Latimer? What does he have to do with this?'

Kate stared at her brother, willing him not to say anything more.

'Is this the young man you were – involved with?'

Kate's heart sank. Of course her father already knew about it. Rumours travelled fast around the Nightingale.

'Yes, Father.'

'And this nurse was the other young woman?'

'Yes. But that had nothing to do with—'

'So you were arguing, and it's probably fair to say you were both overwrought and not really concentrating on what you were supposed to be doing?'

'That's not true!' Kate looked up at her father's face and wondered if she'd imagined that glint of triumph in his eyes. 'I don't understand,' she said. 'I thought you'd be pleased? This evidence clears my name.'

'And casts a shadow over your brother's.'

Kate looked at Leo's downcast face and suddenly she understood. 'You know I'm innocent, don't you?' she murmured. 'You know because you were the one who made the mistake, not me.'

'Don't be absurd!' Leo's face flushed deep red. 'How can that be when—'

'Oh, for heaven's sake, Leo!' their father bit out. 'Look at you, blushing like a schoolgirl!' He stared at his son, mouth curling. 'You can't even save your own skin properly!'

Kate turned to her father. Sir Philip's jaw was rigid with rage, grey brows low over furious eyes. It was as if she could see it all unfolding before her, like the plot of a book.

'You knew too,' she whispered.

'Of course I knew!' her father dismissed this remark, his gaze still fixed on Leo. 'Do you think your damn fool of a brother could keep something like this to himself? He came running to me as soon as he realised what he'd done.'

Kate turned back to Leo. He was shrinking in his chair, his head hung so low she couldn't see his face.

'But you – you both sat in Dr Ormerod's office and let him accuse me.'

'I'm sorry,' Leo mumbled. 'It was a mistake, honestly. I found your notes after I'd given the patient the second dose. It wasn't my idea to destroy them, but Father said—'

'Oh, shut up, Leo!' Sir Philip cut him off angrily. 'I'm trying to save your career, in case you hadn't noticed.' He took a deep breath, calming himself. 'As you say, you made an honest mistake. You were under a great deal of pressure. Of course it's unfortunate that a man died, but there is no reason why you should lose a promising future over it.'

'And what about me?' Kate asked.

'What about you?'

Kate stared at her father's profile. He hadn't even looked her way once, she was so unimportant to him.

'What about my promising future? Or doesn't that count for anything?'

Sir Philip turned to her for the first time. His anger had gone, to be replaced by cold, implacable indifference. 'You and your brother are different cases,' he said. 'Oh, I know you think your career –' he said the word with disdain '– is the be all and end all of your life. But it isn't. One day you will marry, and then you'll give this up. But Leo . . .' He glanced at his son. 'This is his life we are talking about. He stands to lose everything.'

'Perhaps he shouldn't be a doctor if he makes so many mistakes?' Kate said quietly.

Leo looked up at her for the first time, his eyes wretched. How could she have not seen the guilt in them before? she wondered.

'Of course he must be a doctor!' her father snapped. 'He is a Carlyle.'

'So am I.'

Her father looked at her for a long time. Kate could see him calculating, weighing her up, choosing the right words to get the outcome he wanted.

'I know,' he said finally. 'And fortunately for you, that name still carries a great deal of weight in this hospital.' He sat back in his chair. 'I will speak to some people on your behalf,' he said. 'You will have to go through this unfortunate disciplinary, but I'm sure I can convince the panel not to dismiss you.'

'So I can stay here?'

'Well, no.' Sir Philip smiled thinly. 'I'm sure you can see that would be very – embarrassing – under the circumstances?'

'Of course.' Kate looked at Leo. 'You wouldn't want a Carlyle with a blemished record at the Nightingale.'

'Precisely.' Her father pressed his hands together. 'But you could go back to the Hampstead, start again there. I daresay they would be delighted to have you back.'

Kate stared across the desk at him. 'And if I don't agree?'

'Then you will be dismissed from the Nightingale with a stain on your record and you will never be able to practise medicine again.' Sir Philip regarded her with an even smile. 'You are a sensible girl, Kate,' he said. 'I'm sure I can trust you to do the right thing.'

Chapter Forty-Two

The fourteenth of May was Lily Sedgewick's birthday.

Sadie debated with herself for days about whether she should go and visit her mother. It had been months since they had last come face-to-face. Sadie still went round every couple of weeks to leave money for her, but she had never heard from her mother in all that time, not a single word of thanks nor anything else.

It was beginning to rile her, if she was honest. Why was she even bothering to look out for such a selfish, ignorant cow? Especially when it was so obvious Lily didn't give a damn about her.

But then at other times she would torture herself with worry that something dreadful had happened, that her mother had fallen ill or been murdered by a violent stranger down at the docks. Sadie would lie awake all night fearing the worst and make up her mind to go and see Lily, only to change her mind when morning came.

But as today was Lily's birthday and Sadie had one of her rare half-days off, she decided that she would finally swallow her pride and visit her mother. One of them had to make the first move, and since Lily didn't seem bothered, it was left to her daughter to make the effort as usual.

On the way, Sadie bought a bunch of peonies from a flower seller on the corner of Roman Road. Nothing fancy, she told herself, not like proper roses or anything. She didn't want her mother thinking she had gone soft.

As she climbed the stairs to her mother's lodgings, Sadie's nerve began to fail her. What if Lily didn't want to see her? What if she threw the flowers back in her face? She bent down and pushed the birthday card under the door, and propped the flowers against the door frame. That was enough, she thought.

She was just about to turn away when another impulse seized her. Without thinking about it, Sadie snatched up the flowers, turned the doorknob and walked in.

The curtains were pulled, shutting out the daylight and closing in the thick, warm air with its lingering aroma of stale cooking and cigarette smoke. Sadie put the flowers down on the table and went to draw the curtains back, letting in the May sunshine.

She turned to face the room. It was a mess, as usual, clothes strewn over chairs, the table littered with dirty cups and plates.

Sadie looked at the door to her mother's bedroom. It was firmly closed.

'Ma?' she called out. There was no reply. She was probably still sleeping off her latest binge.

Sadie gathered up the dirty crockery from the table and took it to the sink on the landing, then filled the kettle and set it to boil.

She searched through the cupboard and found an old jug for the flowers. Sadie paused for a moment, turning it in her hands. It was a sentimental-looking thing, decorated with flowers and a picture of two angelic children in matching sailor suits. Underneath the picture were the words 'A present from Southend' in curly script.

A memory came to mind of the three of them, her mother, herself and Belle, on the beach, paddling at the water's edge. Sadie couldn't have been more than six years old at the time. Lily and Belle had their shoes off and their skirts pulled up, shrieking every time the cold water lapped their bare ankles.

Sadie was arranging the flowers in the vase when she heard someone stirring in the bedroom.

'I've put the kettle on,' she called over her shoulder, as the door opened. 'Now, I know what you're thinking. Long time, no see . . .'

'That's just what I was thinking.'

Sadie swung round, and the jug fell from her hands in a crash of water and flowers and broken pottery.

There, standing in the bedroom doorway, was Jimmy Clyde.

'Hello, girlie.' He grinned, showing off nut brown teeth. 'Scare you, did I?'

Sadie forced herself to remain still, determined not to betray her fear. 'Not particularly,' she said. 'I just wasn't expecting you, that's all.'

'I daresay you weren't.'

She bent to pick up the shards of broken pottery from the floor. All the while she could feel him watching her.

'When did they let you out?' She struggled to keep her voice even.

'This morning. I came straight to see my girls.'

Panic surged through her. 'Where's Ma?'

'I thought you could tell me that.' His breath stank, even from across the room. 'Silly cow wasn't here when I got home. Not exactly what you'd call a warm welcome.'

'I don't know where she is. I ain't seen her myself in months.'

'Is that right? You two fallen out again?'

'You could say that.' Sadie carried the handfuls of broken pottery over to the table. The children's faces gazed up at her from a single piece, their blues eyes wide and innocent, framed by golden curls. Belle had laughed when her mother bought that old pot, but Lily had loved it.

And now it was gone.

'And why would that be? I wonder.' Jimmy's voice grated on her, jarring Sadie back to the present. 'It wouldn't be because you're a dirty little snitch, would it?'

She looked for an escape but Jimmy stood between her and the door, his face twisted with spite.

'You thought you were so clever, didn't you? Standing up there in that dock, telling that judge all about me. Wanted to put me away for a long time, didn't you?'

Sadie regarded him calmly. 'No,' she said. 'I wanted you to swing.'

The blow came from out of nowhere, knocking her off balance. Sadie fell sideways, into the table, her ear ringing, the side of her face blossoming with pain.

'You silly bitch, you're just as stupid as your mother.' Jimmy stood over her, stinking of stale sweat and rotting teeth. 'You should have known I'd want paying back for what you did. And to think I didn't even have to come looking for you!'

Sadie spat in his face. Jimmy put his hand to his wet cheek, eyes widening in surprise.

'You've got some bloody nerve, I'll give you that, lady. More spirit than your useless mother, at any rate.' He leered nastily. 'I like a girl with a bit of go about her. Makes things more interesting, if you know what I mean.'

He reached out, toying with the buttons on Sadie's blouse. 'Such a pretty little thing, too. I've always imagined what it might be like to have you—'

Sadie clutched the shard of pottery in her hand and swung it up against his face. Jimmy jumped back with a yell of pain, his hand to his cheek, blood trickling between his fingers.

She dodged past him and had almost made it to the door before his arms closed around her, bringing her down. They both fell to the floor, Jimmy on top of her, pinning her down.

'Bitch!' he hissed. 'Think you're so clever, don't you? Well, I'm going to teach you a lesson you'll never forget!'

'Leave her alone,' said a voice from the doorway.

Sadie twisted her head to one side. Her mother stood there, her eyes fixed on them.

Jimmy barely flinched, his weight still crushing Sadie, his face inches from hers. 'Hello, Lil.'

'Hello, Jimmy.' Lily's voice was oddly calm. 'I heard you was out.'

'Yet you weren't here to greet me?'

'I had some errands to run.' She nodded towards Sadie. 'What's going on here, then?'

'I'll tell you what's going on. Your bitch of a daughter attacked me, so I'm teaching her a lesson.'

'You're covered in blood. Come and sit down and I'll clean it for you.'

Jimmy hesitated for a moment, and Sadie held her breath. Then, slowly, he rolled off her and got to his feet.

Sadie sat up cautiously and looked at her mother. Lily looked different, she thought. Her high-necked blouse and carefully pinned hair were shabby, but almost respectable.

Her mother had poured some water from the kettle into a bowl and now she was dabbing carefully at Jimmy's cheek with a damp cloth.

'That looks nasty,' she said. 'It's deep, too. You might want to get it seen to.'

Sadie caught her mother's eye over Jimmy's shoulder. She jerked her head towards the door. Sadie stared back at her, uncomprehending, until she read the frantic message in her mother's eyes and realised she was silently signalling for her to go.

Her mother was fussing over Jimmy, distracting him, telling him how much she had missed him, how glad she was that he had come home. Still keeping her eyes fixed on him, Sadie slowly manoeuvred herself backwards across the floor away from them. She had nearly reached the door when Jimmy's voice stopped her in her tracks.

'And where do you think you're going?'

Sadie caught the look of fear in her mother's eyes, but Lily managed to keep her voice calm and steady.

'Oh, let her go, Jimmy,' she said. 'We don't want her around, do we? It's nicer when it's just the two of us.' She wound her arms around his neck. 'Besides, we've got a lot of catching up to do, ain't we?'

Jimmy pushed her off roughly. 'You think I'm stupid, woman? I know what you're playing at. You're as devious as your bloody daughter!'

He got to his feet, towering over Sadie. 'She ain't going anywhere. Not till I've finished with her.'

'Jimmy, please—'

'Shut it, Lil! This is between me and her.' He bent and grabbed a handful of Sadie's hair, yanking her to her feet. Sadie gritted her teeth, determined not to cry out.

He thrust his face close to hers, so she could feel his damp, sour breath. 'I did nearly six months behind bars because of you, you little cow. You cost me dear, and now you've got to repay me.' He twisted her hair so hard her knees buckled. 'And when I've finished with you, I'm going to carve up that pretty face of yours so no man will ever look at you again.'

'I've found someone else.'

Lily's words hung in the air. Jimmy froze, still looking down at Sadie. 'You what?' His voice was frighteningly quiet.

'You wanted to know where I was this morning? Well, I was with him.'

'Who is it?'

'No one you know.'

'You're lying to me!' He yanked Sadie's head back in a sudden, violent move that made her cry out in pain.

'All right! His name's Tommy Diamond, and he's a street bookie over in Bermondsey. Happy now?'

Jimmy was very still. 'You wouldn't,' he said quietly.

'Wouldn't I?' Lily threw back at him. 'He's twice the man you'll ever be, Jimmy Clyde. He looks after me, treats me right. I don't need you anymore.'

It all happened so fast Sadie barely knew what was happening. One minute Jimmy was holding her by her hair, the next minute he had released her and launched himself across the room to pin her mother over the kitchen table.

'Say that again, you whore!' he bit out.

Lily pushed him off, sending him flying across the room. He collided with a wall and seemed momentarily stunned. 'Go,' she said to Sadie.

'I ain't leaving you . . .'

'I said, go!' Lily turned on her. 'For gawd's sake, girl, do as you're bloody told for once in your life!'

She grabbed her daughter by the shoulders and shoved her out of the open door. Sadie tried to get back in, but Lily slammed it shut in her face.

Sadie clattered down the stairs and out into the cobbled alleyway, nearly colliding with a pair of kids in ragged clothes who were spinning an old pram wheel down the street. She pushed them aside, running down the alley and out into the street. Her chest was burning with the effort, but all she could see was a picture of Jimmy's face, twisted with anger, and her mother standing there, looking so oddly calm . . .

She had to get help, and she knew just where to go.

A girl answered the door at Belle's lodging house, pulling a faded silk robe around her. One of the night workers, by the way she yawned and blinked in the daylight.

'Is Belle in?' Sadie blurted out.

'Depends who wants – oi!'

By the time she'd reached the bottom of the stairs Belle was on the landing above her.

'Lil? Is that you?' she called down. Her expression changed when she saw Sadie. 'Oh, Christ almighty, what's happened?' She came running down the stairs, her feet thundering on the bare boards. 'He's back, ain't he?'

'She made me go . . .' The words rushed out, tumbling over each other. 'I didn't want to leave her but she made me . . .'

Belle's hands came down on Sadie, gripping her by the shoulders. 'Fetch the police,' she said.

Chapter Forty-Three

'I should never have left her.'

Sadie pressed her hands to her face, trying to shut out the images that crowded in every time she closed her eyes.

But it was the sounds that haunted her. The slam of the door in her face. The murmur of the crowd at the end of the alleyway, the thunder of policemen's footsteps up and down the stairs. Hearing someone screaming hysterically and realising it was herself as she struggled to break free from Peter Machin's arms wrapped tightly around her, stopping her from going inside the house . . .

And now here, in the hospital waiting room. The warmth of the summer sunshine pouring through the window, the smell of disinfectant tingling at the back of her throat. People moving to and fro across the waiting room, busy and purposeful, their lives continuing as normal around her while Sadie sat with Belle at her side, marooned on an island of misery and confusion.

'She wanted you to go,' Belle said in a low voice.

'But I should have stayed,' Sadie insisted. 'It was me Jimmy was angry with, not her. If I'd been there—'

'If you'd been there he would have killed you both!'

Sadie swung round to look at her reproachfully. 'Ma ain't dead!'

'I know, love. I spoke out of turn. I'm sorry.' Belle's scarlet slash of a mouth was turned down in her powdered face. She looked out of place in the waiting room, with her bright dyed hair and tattered fur stole.

'She's going to pull through,' Sadie murmured.

'Of course she is.' Belle put out a hand to cover hers. Her skin was rough, nails broken. 'She's a tough old bird, your ma.'

They sat in silence, each lost in their own thoughts.

The door swung open and Dr Latimer strode out into the Casualty hall. He caught Sadie's eye and grinned in recognition. Then his gaze flicked from her to Belle and Sadie saw his smile fade, to be replaced by a look of faint embarrassment. The next moment he turned on his heel and strode off in the other direction.

Belle must have noticed too, because she withdrew her hand and said, 'I should go.'

'I want you to stay.'

'But it don't seem right, what with you working here . . . What if one of your friends was to see us?'

'I don't care. I want you here. Besides, you're Ma's best friend.'

Belle smiled. 'Thank you, love. I must say, I wouldn't be able to settle if I had to sit at home and wait for news.' She stood up, craning her neck to look over the rows of benches. 'It's been a long time,' she said. 'You'd think we'd have heard something by now . . .'

'They have to wait for the swelling in her brain to go down,' Sadie said.

'And if it don't?'

Sadie raised her gaze to look at her. 'It will.'

Belle settled back into her seat and pulled her fur stole around her, in spite of the warm day.

'Lil came here, you know,' she said. 'To see you.'

Sadie turned to face her. 'When?'

'This morning. After she found out Jimmy was being released.' Belle pursed her mouth. 'She had word they were letting him out and wanted to warn you. She asked me to help her write a note for you.'

'I didn't see her.'

'No, you wouldn't have. I daresay she handed the note in at that Porters' Lodge and ran. She was that nervous.' Belle smiled. 'Got herself in a right old state about it, she did.'

'Why?'

Belle sent her an old-fashioned look. 'She didn't want to show you up, love.'

Sadie had a sudden recollection of her mother's high-necked blouse under her coat, her hair pinned up under a battered hat. Shabby but respectable.

Then another thought occurred to her. 'You say you saw her this morning?'

Belle nodded. 'She spent the night at my lodgings. Came round straight after she heard the news about – him.' Her mouth curled. 'I begged her to stay. She promised she was going to deliver the note here, then collect a few bits and pieces and come straight back. I was waiting for her when you arrived.'

'I thought she was with Tommy Diamond?'

Belle turned in her seat to face Sadie. 'And who's Tommy Diamond, when he's at home?'

'You know, Ma's new man? The bookie from south of the river? She must have told you about him?'

'She ain't said a dicky bird, mate. And you know your ma, she'd never keep a secret like that from me.' Belle shook her head. 'No, there ain't no new man. Believe me, I'd know about it.'

'But she told Jimmy she—' Sadie stopped talking abruptly. 'She made it up,' she murmured finally.

'Made what up?'

'Nothing.'

Sadie sat quiet for a moment, picturing the scene in her mother's lodgings, remembering the savage expression on

366

Jimmy's face as he bore down on her. He had intended to kill her, Sadie realised. Lily must have realised it too, which was why she had stepped in, drawn his fire.

She remembered the angry words Belle had flung at her outside the court.

If you understood what that girl's done for you.

'Why did she stay with him?' she asked.

'What?'

'Why did my mother stay with Jimmy Clyde?'

Belle shrugged. 'I don't know, do I?'

Sadie turned to look at her. Belle's face had turned a mottled scarlet. 'Yes, you do,' she said. 'You nearly told me once, the day of Jimmy's trial.'

Belle dropped her gaze. 'It don't matter now,' she muttered.

'I want to know.' Belle's mouth was a tight, obstinate line. 'She did it for me, didn't she?'

For a long time Belle said nothing. Then she said quietly, 'He said he'd kill you if she ever left him.'

Sadie nodded. 'I thought as much.' She paused, thinking about all the times she had called her mother weak and pathetic for staying with him.

Her thoughts must have been written on her face because Belle said, 'Don't be too hard on yourself, she never wanted you to know. I wanted to tell you, but she wouldn't have it. She wanted to protect you, Sadie. That was all she ever wanted to do, to protect her little girl.'

'Her little girl.' Sadie smiled wanly.

But she didn't have a chance to say any more because the next minute Belle was on her feet.

'About bloody time you showed your face!' she bellowed across the Casualty hall, ignoring the looks of the other people waiting on the benches. 'I hope you've come to tell us you've found the bastard?'

Sadie looked around and saw Peter Machin coming towards them, his helmet tucked under his arm. His face was bright scarlet under his neatly combed hair.

'No,' he said. 'But we've got people out looking for him. We'll find him, don't you worry.'

'You should never have let him out in the first place,' Belle muttered, sitting down again.

Peter turned to Sadie. 'How is your mother?'

She shook her head, tried to answer him, but the words wouldn't come.

'She's still unconscious,' Belle answered for her brusquely. 'And she's got three broken ribs, a fractured arm and internal bleeding where her organs ruptured.'

Peter's colour deepened. 'I'm sorry. Will she be all right?'

'What do you think?'

'We're waiting for her to regain consciousness,' Sadie managed to reply.

'I see.' Peter hesitated. 'I wondered if you'd be able to answer some questions?' he asked Sadie.

'Her mother's in there, fighting for her life, and you want her to answer questions?' Belle turned on him, jabbing her finger in his face. 'You should be out there looking for Jimmy Clyde, not in here waving your bloody notebook around!'

'It's all right, Belle. I don't mind answering questions if it helps.' Sadie turned to Peter. 'Shall we go outside? It'll be quieter out there.' She glanced back at Belle. 'I won't be a minute. Let me know if –' her voice faltered.

'– there's any news,' Belle finished for her with a nod.

She followed Peter outside, into the sunshine. Beyond the Casualty block, she could see figures dotted on the terraces and balconies of the main building, patients enjoying the sunshine.

'Are you all right?' Peter asked her.

'What do you think?'

'I'm sorry,' Peter looked embarrassed. 'Is there anything I can do to help?'

'You can find the swine who did this to her.'

'I meant as your friend, not as a policeman.'

Sadie looked into his soulful, puppy dog eyes. She didn't need a friend. She needed Jimmy Clyde caught.

'You said you had some questions for me?' she said.

'Yes – yes.' Fumbling, he took out his notebook and pencil. 'You say you were there when the attack happened?'

'Do you think I'd stand and watch her getting beaten senseless if I'd been there?' Sadie snapped, then took a deep breath. 'No,' she said more calmly. 'Ma sent me away before he went for her.'

'So you didn't see Clyde actually attack her?'

Sadie narrowed her eyes. 'Are you trying to make out he didn't do it?'

'I'm just trying to get the facts.'

Sadie watched his pencil scratching in his notebook and fought the urge to snatch it out of his hand.

'He's going to get away with it, ain't he?' she said.

Peter hesitated. 'It's your word against his that he was there.'

'And Ma's,' Sadie said.

'If she—'

'If she lives,' Sadie finished for him. 'And if she dies, he'll get away with murder. Is that what you're saying?'

'It'll be difficult to prove.'

'And you won't try very hard, will you?' Sadie said. 'I daresay you're not even bothering to look for him now, are you? I mean, why would you when he's got Billy Willis protecting him? Half you coppers are in the Willis family's pay anyway.'

'Sadie—'

369

'And besides, what does it really matter what he did to my mother?' Emotion clogged her throat. 'She's only a dock dolly, an old brass. Her life don't count for anything.'

'Shut up, will you?' Peter wasn't listening to her anymore. He was staring towards the Casualty block.

Sadie followed his gaze. There, in the doorway, stood Belle. As soon as Sadie saw her face she knew what had happened.

'The doctor's here,' she said. 'He wants to talk to you.'

Chapter Forty-Four

'Moore and Duffield, you will be doing beds and backs. Trott and Beck, you will be doing dressings. Copeland, you will be doing the massage round – Copeland? Are you listening to me?'

Eleanor looked up sharply. Miss Parker was staring back at her, blue eyes beady behind her spectacles.

'Yes, Sister. Sorry, Sister.'

'What did I just tell you to do?'

Eleanor glanced around at the other probationers. They all looked back at her sympathetically.

'Beds and backs, Sister?' she said hopefully.

Miss Parker shook her head. 'Really, Copeland, I'm surprised at you. You used to be such a hard-working, conscientious nurse, but lately you've really slipped. Any more of this behaviour and I will be mentioning your name in my ward report.' She sighed. 'You will be doing the massage round with Duffield. You will be doing the left-hand side, beds one to fifteen, and Duffield can do beds sixteen to thirty. Is that clear enough for you?'

'Yes, Sister.'

'Good. And when you've all finished the work you've been allotted, I expect you to make a start on cleaning. Visiting time is two o'clock, and I want this ward spotless.'

Eleanor's heart sank in her chest. As if she didn't know. The date had been marked in her diary for days now.

It was the date her parents were due to visit Harry.

Miss Parker finished handing out the work lists. As the

probationers dispersed, Grace said, 'I'll swop with you, if you like?'

'Why?' Eleanor looked back at her blankly.

'Your brother's name is on my list, and I know you like to nurse him yourself.'

'No!' Eleanor hadn't realised she had spoken so sharply until she saw the look of surprise on Grace's face. 'Better not,' she said. 'I'm already in Sister's bad books. I don't think she'd take kindly to me chopping and changing!'

'I suppose you're right,' Grace agreed.

Eleanor watched her heading off towards the sink room to prepare her trolley for the massage round. The truth was, she was glad Sister had not assigned her to look after Harry. She had been doing her best to avoid him, ever since he had dropped his bombshell.

Eleanor was still in a state of shock over his confession. It felt as if her world had been tipped on its axis, everything she trusted and believed in had been turned upside down by a few simple words.

I did this to myself.

At first she didn't believe him. It was simply too bizarre, the idea that anyone would turn a gun on themselves. Especially not her brother Harry, who never ran away from anything.

She had a sudden mental picture of him, marching at the head of his column of khaki-clad young men, so proud to be going off to war.

And those letters he had sent from France, full of stories about the miles they had marched, the villages they had passed through and the warm welcome they had received wherever they went. Even in the thick of the Front line he'd managed to make light of it all, joking about life in the cramped trenches, and the near misses they'd had.

But then his letters had stopped. At the time Eleanor had

assumed Harry was simply too busy to write to her. Now she knew it was because he could no longer bring himself to lie to his sister.

And yet he had done. He had come home wounded, and allowed everyone to think he was a hero. He'd concocted a story about being hit by a sniper in no-man's-land, when really the only shot was from his own gun.

Harry had tried to explain to her, but Eleanor couldn't bear to listen. She could hardly look at him anymore, let alone speak to him. She knew how much her silence hurt him, but she didn't care. He had hurt her, too. He had taken away from her everything she trusted, everything she believed in. Where once she had been so certain of everything, now she was filled with confusion.

She couldn't hate him. He was still her brother, even if she barely recognised him anymore. And besides, she had seen enough cases of shell shock on the ward to understand that the battlefield could do strange things to a man.

But she couldn't respect him, either. Just being his sister gave her a deep sense of shame and guilt. Sometimes she could scarcely face the other wounded soldiers on the ward, knowing what her brother had done.

She couldn't even speak to anyone about it, because Harry had made her promise not to say a word. Eleanor knew only too well that if his secret was to come out then he would have to face a court martial, might even be shot for his cowardice.

But she had insisted that he should tell their parents. And today was the day he had to do it.

He had pleaded with Eleanor but she had stood firm.

'You must tell them,' she said. 'They deserve to know.'

'I can't. You know what they're like. Don't make me do it, Ellie, please!'

'Oh, stop it. Don't be such a—'

A coward. The word hung unspoken in the air between them.

At first Eleanor had insisted out of spite, wanting to punish Harry for what he had done. But as the time of their parents' visit drew nearer and her brother grew ever more withdrawn and desolate, she began to pity him.

'What if they report me?' he said.

'They won't,' she tried to reassure him. 'You're their son, they'd never let anything happen to you. Of course they're bound to be angry at first, but they'll understand in the end.'

In spite of her assurances, her heart was in her mouth when visiting time came. Eleanor spotted her parents straight away among the throng of visitors that poured through the double doors. Her father stood tall and upright, holding himself proudly as he gazed around the ward. Her mother seemed more subdued as she looked from one bed to the next, taking in all the splints and heavily bandaged wounds and missing limbs.

Then she spotted Eleanor and gave her a little wave.

Eleanor went over to them. 'Hello, Mother. Father,' she greeted them.

'Hello, darling.' Her mother moved in to kiss her cheek. She smelt of powder and flowery perfume.

'Well? Where is he?' Her father scanned the ward eagerly. 'Where is my boy?'

'He's out on the terrace.'

Her mother frowned. 'In this weather? Surely he'll catch a chill.'

'He's well wrapped up,' Eleanor said. 'Besides, he likes it out there.' On his own, she added silently.

'Do stop fussing, Muriel!' Her father laughed. 'Harry's a soldier now. He's used to tougher conditions than this, I assure you.'

'How is he?' her mother asked.

'He's recovering well. His shoulder has healed very nicely.'

'You see? Tough as old boots. Even a Hun sniper couldn't stop him in his tracks.'

'But he's still very troubled,' Eleanor finished.

Her mother looked at her blankly. 'Troubled?'

'He finds it difficult to sleep.' Eleanor searched for the right words. 'And he can get – depressed – sometimes.'

'I'm not surprised, being in here!' Her father's confident smile reasserted itself. 'You know what Harry's like, Muriel. He always has to be up and doing, never likes to sit still. Being cooped up in bed for weeks on end is enough to drive any sane man to despair.'

Eleanor looked at her father and apprehension began to snake its way up her spine. 'I think you'd better see him for yourself,' she said.

She busied herself about the ward, making tea for the patients and their families. But all the time she kept craning her neck towards the terrace, trying to see what was going on.

Miss Parker must have noticed because she said, 'You may join your family if you wish, Copeland?'

'No! I mean, thank you, Sister. But I'd best leave them to it if you don't mind?'

'As you wish.' The ward sister sent her a puzzled look.

She was in the kitchen refilling the tea urn when Miriam Trott came in with a trolley laden with empty cups for washing.

'I say, Copeland, your father just nearly knocked me flying. And he didn't even bother to say excuse me!'

Eleanor looked back over her shoulder. 'Are you sure it was my father?'

Miriam nodded. 'Positive. He came in from the terrace

and marched out of the ward without a by your leave. I'm surprised you didn't hear the doors slam. Sister was not impressed, I can tell you!' She smiled slyly. 'I wouldn't be surprised if she had a word with you about it – where are you going? What about this washing up?'

'You do it.' Eleanor thrust the dishtowel into her hands and hurried out of the kitchen, just in time to see her mother coming towards her up the ward, her face pale and taut.

'Where is your father?' she asked.

'Gone, I think. What's happened, Mother?'

Muriel Copeland gave a slight shake of her head and hurried out of the ward. Eleanor followed her.

Once safely outside the double doors her mother took out a neatly folded handkerchief from her bag and dabbed her eyes.

'Oh, Eleanor, it was simply dreadful,' she whispered. 'The things Harry said, I could hardly believe it . . .'

'I know,' she said quietly.

Her mother's eyes narrowed. 'You knew? And you didn't think to tell us?'

'I – I didn't know what to do for the best.'

'Well, really, Eleanor, I think anything would have been better than being – ambushed in such a way.' Muriel Copeland blew her nose delicately. 'Your poor father, he was utterly beside himself.'

'I'm sorry, Mother.'

'Well, it's done now, I suppose.' She sniffed back her tears. 'I must find him,' she said, looking about her distractedly. 'He was so upset.'

She tucked her handkerchief back into her bag and closed it with a resolute snap.

'And how is Harry?' Eleanor asked.

Her mother sent her a look of pure ice. 'I don't know,' she snapped. 'And after what I've heard, I can't say that I care!'

Eleanor stared at her in shock. 'You can't mean that?'

'Can't I?' Her mother's voice was hard. 'Your brother has just confessed to us that he is a coward.'

'He's not a coward! He was scared—'

'You think all those other men weren't scared?' Her mother pointed a shaking finger towards the ward doors. 'Those boys, younger than him some of them, who've never been away from home in their lives? They're separated from their families and their loved ones, and sent off to a foreign country and given a gun and told to fight. You think they're not frightened out of their wits? But you don't see them turning a gun on themselves so they can be sent home, do you? No, they put their shoulders to the wheel and get on with it, like the real men they are.' She lifted her chin. 'They're the ones who make me proud. But Harry . . .' She glanced back towards the ward doors. 'I barely know him anymore. And I don't think I want to, either.'

'But he's your son!'

'Not any more. I'm ashamed to think about him.'

As she turned to walk away, Eleanor said, 'You won't tell anyone what happened, will you?'

Her mother looked back at her, stony-faced. 'Tell anyone? You think I'm going to go around boasting that my son is a coward?'

'I mean the authorities.' Eleanor swallowed hard. 'It could be bad for Harry if they find out what really happened.'

Muriel Copeland stared at her, tight-lipped. 'I don't know what your father will do,' she said. 'But whatever it is, you can be sure it will be no more than Harry deserves!'

Chapter Forty-Five

A week after Lily's death, Sadie returned to her mother's lodgings for the first time.

'You don't have to do this, you know,' Belle said, as they climbed the narrow, gloomy staircase. 'I don't mind sorting the place out by myself.'

'No, I need to do it,' Sadie said. 'I owe it to Ma.' She looked sideways at Belle. 'I'll be all right, honestly.'

But in spite of what she had said, Sadie's heart was in her mouth as she turned the doorknob. And as soon as she stepped into the room, her knees began to buckle under her.

Belle swept in, hooking Sadie's arm through hers. 'Come on,' she said, taking charge. 'Let's make a start, shall we? You'll feel better if you keep busy.'

She was right. For the next hour, Sadie didn't have to think as she swept and scrubbed and polished. They took down the curtains and stripped the bed, hung the rugs out of the window to shake the dust off, and cleaned out the ashes from the fireplace. All the time Sadie kept her eyes averted from the kettle on the stove, and tried not to think about the last time she had seen her mother standing there.

The only time her resolve nearly gave way was when she found a jagged fragment of pottery under the kitchen dresser. It bore the word 'South' in curly gold script.

'What's that?' Belle said, looking over her shoulder.

'It's a bit of old jug. It got smashed when—' Sadie stopped talking. Suddenly her chest felt very tight.

'Not that one Lily got from Southend?' Belle took the fragment and turned it over in her hand. 'She loved that ugly old pot. I remember the day she bought it. The three of us went on a charabanc trip to the coast. I daresay you won't remember, you can't have been more than four or five.'

'I do remember. You and Ma went paddling with your skirts up around your knees.'

'So we did!' Sadie chuckled. 'And your ma spotted a crab in the water. I've never seen her run so fast! Shot up that beach like the devil himself was after her! I don't think she went near the water again after that.' She shook her head. 'They were happy days.'

'Yes,' Sadie said. 'Yes, they were.'

Belle put her hand on her shoulder. 'Shall we sort out the wardrobe next?'

Lily didn't have many clothes, and what she had were shabby and threadbare.

Belle pulled them out and laid them on the bed. 'There's nothing here that's fit for a funeral,' she said. 'Nothing you'd call respectable, anyway.'

Sadie picked up her mother's favourite shawl, the one always wrapped around her shoulders on cold nights. It was old, faded pink and moth-eaten in places, but when Sadie held it up to her face she could breathe in Lily Sedgewick's faint scent. Tears prickled in her eyes.

'We should find something blue,' Belle said. 'That was her favourite colour.'

'Was it? I didn't know.'

Belle smiled. 'She always promised herself that if she ever got married she would have a sky blue dress, with a feather in her hat.' She caught Sadie looking at her and shook her head. 'It was when we were both young and fanciful,' she said.

379

There were a couple of hatboxes stacked on top of the wardrobe. Sadie pulled a chair over to the wardrobe and stood on it to lift them down. Behind them was another box, smaller and heavier than the others.

'What's this?' She passed it down to Belle.

'Gawd knows.' Belle put it on the bed and stood staring at it.

'Aren't you going to open it?' Sadie asked.

Belle shook her head. 'You do it,' she said. 'It don't feel right, me doing it.'

Sadie climbed off the chair and lifted the lid on the box. Inside was a jumble of papers.

'Blimey!' Belle laughed nervously. 'Don't tell me she left a will?'

'It doesn't look like it. Just a couple of old photographs and these.' Sadie picked up a handful of the papers and rifled through them. 'School reports. My old school reports.' She looked up at Belle. 'Why would she keep these?'

Belle laughed. 'Because she was proud of you, you daft ha'porth!'

Sadie looked back at the papers in her hands. 'I didn't know. She never said.'

'No, well, she wouldn't, would she? That was Lily Sedgewick all over. Too proud for her own good.' Belle looked at Sadie. 'Like mother, like daughter, I reckon.'

Sadie looked away sharply, delving back into the box. 'There's something else in here, too – it looks like a letter.'

'Who's it from?' Belle looked over her shoulder.

'Not from – to.' Sadie read her mother's scrawl on the envelope and handed it to Belle. 'It's to you.'

'Me?' Belle frowned at it. 'Why would your mother be sending me letters? I saw her practically every day!'

'Open it and find out.'

Belle hesitated for a moment, looking down at the letter

in her hands. Then she shook her head. 'I'll read it later on,' she said, tucking it into her pocket.

'But I want to know what it says!'

'And I'll tell you. When I've read it.' Belle picked up one of the dresses, a flowery print. 'What do you think of this one? It's got a bit of blue in it.'

'It's nice,' Sadie said.

'It'll have to do, anyway.' Belle folded it up. 'You'll take it down to the undertaker's, will you?'

'Why don't you do it?' Sadie said.

'Me?'

'I was thinking, it might be better if you sorted out the funeral arrangements.' The words came out in a rush. 'I'll pay for it all, of course, but you should sort it out.'

Belle sent her a shrewd look. 'What's brought all this on?'

'Nothing. I just think you'd know better than me what she would have wanted. You were her friend.'

'And you were her daughter.'

'A daughter who didn't even know what her favourite colour was!' A dam broke inside Sadie then and the next moment tears were spilling down her cheeks. 'I wish I'd had a chance to talk to her,' she sobbed. 'There are so many things I wish I'd said.'

'Oh, love.' Belle laid down the dress and gathered Sadie into her arms. 'Don't take on like this. You were a wonderful daughter.'

'I wasn't!'

'You were. Your mother wasn't an easy woman to love, I can tell you that. She was too prickly, too proud. But she knew how much you loved her. And she loved you too, with all her heart.'

'I don't know why,' Sadie mumbled. 'I ruined her life.'

Belle held her at arms' length. 'And how do you work that out?'

'If it hadn't been for me she would never have stayed with Jimmy Clyde. I was the reason she died.'

'Now you listen to me, lady!' Belle gave her a little shake. 'You weren't the reason Lily Sedgewick died. That murdering bastard Jimmy Clyde did that to her, not you. You were the reason she lived.' She stared at Sadie, forcing her to meet her gaze. 'Girls in our game don't make old bones,' she said. 'Especially girls as fragile as your mother. As soon as I met her on the streets, I didn't reckon her chances. I did my best to keep an eye on her, but I still thought she'd be chucking herself in the Thames before she was twenty. Then when she fell pregnant with you – well, I reckoned one of those backstreet doctors would soon finish her off.'

Her expression softened. 'But Lily went ahead and had you – well, it gave her someone to live for. You depended on her, and she had to keep going for your sake if not her own. She once told me that you were the only thing in her life that was truly pure and good. She didn't have much of a heart, but I reckon what she did have was because of you.'

Sadie sniffed back her tears. 'I loved her too,' she said. 'Only I couldn't always show it.'

Belle's mouth twisted. 'Like I once said to you, you were as bad as each other.'

Sadie remembered how she had bridled at that, taking it as an insult. But now the thought filled her with pride.

She looked down at the dress, folded on the bed. Lily Sedgewick deserved better, she thought. In life and in death.

And Sadie vowed to make sure that for once her mother would get it.

Chapter Forty-Six

The night before Kate was due to appear before the disciplinary committee she was summoned by Dr Ormerod and told she was to be on call on the military ward.

'Dr French is also working overnight, but he is covering four wards and needs assistance,' he said. 'Young Evans was supposed to be assigned to Monaghan, but the damn fool fell down a flight of stairs and fractured his ankle this morning. Horsing about as usual, no doubt.' He cleared his throat. 'I understand if under the circumstances you feel it would be too much for you to take on . . .'

'Of course I'll do it, sir,' Kate said. 'If I'm needed.'

Dr Ormerod peered closely at her from behind his spectacles. 'Needless to say, your work will be closely supervised,' he said.

'I understand.' Kate's face burnt with shame. There it was again, the cloud of guilt and suspicion that hung over her wherever she went. Even Dr Werner double-checked her work in Pathology these days.

She could feel it pressing down on her as she reported to Monaghan ward that night. She could see it in the wary looks of the night sister and the young probationer assigned to look after the ward overnight. She imagined the patients whispering about her, knowing her secret.

There goes that doctor, the one who killed Corporal Rayner . . .

And then there was Rufus French, emerging from behind a set of screens, his head down, preoccupied. Kate stood still, holding herself rigid.

He strode the length of the ward before he looked up and noticed her.

'Miss Carlyle!'

He looked shocked, Kate thought. Probably wondering, like the rest of them, why she had been allowed back on the ward.

'Dr Ormerod told me to come,' she blurted out. 'Mr Evans is in the sick bay.'

'Yes. Yes, of course. He told me about Evans. But he didn't mention that you—' Rufus stopped, gathering himself. He looked embarrassed, Kate thought. 'It's good to see you, Miss Carlyle,' he managed finally.

Is it? Kate thought. 'What would you like me to do, Doctor?' she asked.

'Well . . .' Rufus looked about him for a moment. 'Gunner Solomon in bed two needs more pain medication. And Night Sister says that Private Copeland in bed ten seems rather restless. Perhaps you could take a look at him, prescribe something to help him sleep if necessary?'

Kate paused. 'And will you be checking the prescription before I administer it?'

'I'm sure there's no need for that, Miss Carlyle.'

She studied the expression on Rufus' face. 'Yes, Doctor. Thank you,' she said.

'And then go up to the night corridor and get some sleep. It should be a fairly quiet night tonight, so you might as well rest while you can.'

As it turned out, Harry Copeland did not want any medication to help him sleep.

'I don't mind being awake, Doctor,' he said. 'I prefer it, as a matter of fact. I don't always like the dreams, you see. Beside, I like to watch the stars.' He nodded towards the window. 'It's a fine, clear night, isn't it? A good night for star-gazing.'

'Yes, I suppose it is.'

'I know all the different constellations, you know. I can pick out Orion, and The Plough, and Cassiopeia's Chair. My father taught them to me . . .' His voice trailed off.

Kate barely noticed his silence for a moment, she was so busy reading and rereading his notes, in case she had missed anything.

Finally she replaced them. 'Well, if there's nothing else I can do for you—'

'There is something. Will you sit with me, Doctor?'

'I beg your pardon?'

'Will you sit with me? Just for a few minutes. It gets a bit lonely on your own.'

'Well, I do have another patient to see –'

'Of course.' Harry settled back against his pillows. 'I'm sorry, Doctor, I didn't mean to be a trouble to you. You've got people who need you a lot more than I do.'

He looked so dejected, Kate said, 'Look, I'll just go and see to this other patient and then I'll come back and sit with you.'

'Will you?' He looked up at her, his face bright with hope.

'Of course,' Kate said. 'Give me a few minutes to see to my next patient, then I'll be back, I promise.'

As it turned out, the night proved to be busier than she had expected. No sooner had she administered pain medication to Gunner Solomon in bed two than another patient woke up from a nightmare, thrashing and screaming, and Kate needed to help the poor little probationer settle him. His cries woke another patient, who also needed help with his pain. Then another woke in a panic, tried to get out of bed and burst open his stitches.

'Looks like you've had a busy night?' Rufus French commented ruefully when Kate summoned him. 'And there was I, thinking you'd have turned in by now.'

'No such luck, I'm afraid.'

He sent her a considering look. 'I'm sorry,' he said. 'This is probably the last thing you need before—'

'My disciplinary hearing?' Kate finished for him. 'Actually, it's just what I need,' she said. 'I'd far rather keep my mind occupied. I'm not sleeping a great deal at the moment anyway.'

'No. No, I daresay you aren't.' He looked as if he was about to say more, then he changed the subject. 'I'll have to take this patient off to theatre and get him re-stitched. Will you be all right on your own for a while?'

'Of course, Doctor.'

As Kate turned away, Rufus suddenly blurted out, 'For what it's worth, I don't think you did it.'

Kate frowned. 'I'm sorry?'

'I don't know what happened,' he went on, his words spilling out. 'All I know is, you would never have made a mistake like that. It's just not like you.'

Their eyes met and held. Kate's heart swelled with gratitude, and for a moment she longed to tell him the truth about what had happened. But when she opened her mouth, all that came out was a hushed, 'Thank you, Doctor.'

He went on staring at her, and once again Kate had the feeling he wanted to say more. But then he recollected himself.

'Good luck, anyway,' he said. 'I shall be keeping my fingers crossed for you, Kate.'

'Thank you – Rufus.'

No sooner had Dr French left the ward than Kate was called to attend to another patient who had tried to get out of bed, stumbled and hit his head on the bedside locker. It took a long time for her and the probationer to wrestle the man's dead weight back into bed and then she had to check him over for signs of concussion.

She emerged from behind the screens, rubbing her weary eyes. She was surprised to see it was nearly one in the morning. Where had the last four hours gone? she wondered. It only seemed like five minutes since she had reported for duty.

She was halfway down the ward before she remembered her promise to Harry Copeland. Kate turned on her heel and headed back to his bed. The poor man would have given up on her by now, she thought. He was probably fast asleep, not waiting for her . . .

The sight of his empty bed stopped her in her tracks.

'Nurse?' she summoned the probationer. 'Where is this patient?'

Even in the dimly lit ward, she could see the colour drain from the young nurse's face. 'I – I don't know, miss,' she stammered.

They searched the bathrooms, and the kitchen, and the sink room and the sluice. They even looked in the linen cupboards and under the beds. But there was no sign of Harry Copeland.

All the while, Kate fought down a rising sense of panic.

I should have sat with him, she thought. If anything happens to him, it will be my fault.

The last place to look was the terrace. The probationer opened the double doors and they stepped out into the warm night air. The wide terrace was set with empty chairs, but there was no sign of Harry.

'I thought he might be out here.' The probationer's voice was barely above a whimper. 'I know he likes to look at the stars . . .'

The stars. Kate looked up, and that was when she saw the tiny figure silhouetted against the night sky.

'Up there,' she whispered, her mouth dry with terror. 'On the roof.'

'Oh my God!' the probationer gasped in panic. 'What's he doing there?'

'I don't know.' But even as she said it, Kate felt an uneasy stirring in her gut. *You know*, a voice whispered in her head.

'What shall we do?'

Kate took a deep breath, forcing herself to be calm. 'Go and find the night sister, let her know what's happened,' she said.

'And what are you going to do?'

Kate looked at her. 'What do you think?' she said.

Chapter Forty-Seven

Harry Copeland had his back to her and was looking up at the sky.

'Private Copeland?' Kate's voice sounded loud in the night-time quiet. 'Harry?'

He did not respond. Kate climbed cautiously out of the skylight. Outside the window there was a narrow ledge before the roof dropped away in a steep slope. Harry Copeland was perched on the parapet below, his legs swinging over the edge.

Kate took a cautious step in the darkness and felt her foot slide away beneath her. She stepped back, gripping the window frame to right herself.

'Don't move any closer,' Harry called out, not turning round. 'You might fall.'

'I was just about to say the same to you!' Fear made her voice tremble. 'Come back, Harry, please.'

'I can't.'

'You can. I'll lean down and put my hand out—'

'I can't because I have to die.' Harry looked up, scanning the rooftops on the horizon. 'I should never have come home,' he said softly. 'I should have died in France with the rest of my mates.'

'But you didn't. You were one of the lucky ones.'

'Lucky?' he echoed bitterly. 'Is that what you think?'

The night air was cooler on the roof, and every breath of breeze seemed to howl like a gale around her. Kate crouched down, scrabbling to find her footing on the sloping tiles, searching for a way down to Harry.

And all the time, a voice in her head nagged at her. *If only you'd sat with him when he asked you . . .*

'Please come back,' she begged. 'We can talk about this . . .'

'It's too late for talking, miss.' He glanced over his shoulder at her. 'Go back,' he said. 'It's not safe. I don't want your broken neck on my conscience too.'

'I don't want yours on mine, either.'

He turned away from her, his gaze moving restlessly around.

'Beautiful, isn't it?' he said. 'So peaceful. You can't imagine how I used to dream about seeing England again, when I was over there. I used to think if only I could get back here, everything would be all right.'

'Everything will be all right.' Kate edged down the slope towards him, inching her way, scraping her hands on the rough slate. 'You're nearly better, Harry. You'll soon be going home to your family.'

'Home?' His voice sounded bitter. 'I can't go home. I can never go home.' He reached up to dash a tear from his cheek. 'I'm an embarrassment to them. A coward.'

Kate's feet slipped and she slid the last few feet towards the low brick parapet. For a moment she could only lie there, her eyes squeezed closed, perfectly still, listening to the sound of her heartbeat crashing in her ears.

'I told you to go back.' Harry's voice came from close by. When she opened her eyes he was only a few feet away, still sitting on the parapet swinging his legs above the void.

A moment later there was a sound from above and she heard the night sister calling out to her.

'Miss Carlyle?'

Kate saw the panic and dismay on Harry's face and called back, 'It's all right, Sister. Harry and I are just talking.'

'Do you need help?'

'No, thank you, Sister. We're quite all right, aren't we, Harry?' she said in a low voice.

He turned away. Kate manoeuvred herself to sit up and peered over the edge of the parapet. The ground seemed to rise dizzyingly to meet her.

'Long way up, isn't it?' Harry commented.

'It is rather.'

He sent her a sideways look. 'I take it you're not keen on heights?'

'Hate them,' Kate said.

The faintest shadow of a smile touched his mouth. 'Then what are you doing up here?'

'I'm trying to keep you safe.'

He looked down at her, huddled beside him. 'I can see that.' Then his smile vanished and his eyes took on their old, dead look. 'Anyway, I don't know why you're bothering,' he muttered. 'I don't deserve it. You should be back on the ward, looking after those other brave boys. The ones who were wounded fighting for their country.'

'You were wounded too.'

'That's where you're wrong.' He lifted his arm, wincing at the pain in his damaged shoulder. 'See this? I did it to myself.'

Kate stared at him. 'I don't understand?'

'We call them Blighty wounds, miss. Wounds that are bad enough to get you sent home.' He put his hand to his shoulder. 'I went a bit too far with this one. Nearly nicked an artery and did for myself.' His mouth twisted. 'Might have been better if I had. Then my father and mother could have mourned their hero son.' He looked at Kate. 'Shocked you, have I? I suppose you're as disgusted with me as they were.'

'It isn't my job to judge you, Harry. All I do is treat your injuries and make you better, if I can.'

'Then you're the only one who isn't sickened by me!' Harry grimaced. 'My father says I'm a disgrace to the family. Even my sister can't bring herself to look at me. And to think how proud they were when I marched off to war in my new khaki uniform,' he said bitterly. 'That's all I've ever wanted to do, miss. Make my father proud.'

I know how you feel.

'Anyway, they're right to be ashamed of me,' he went on. 'When I look at some of those men on the ward . . . the terrible injuries they have, and the way they bear them. Some of them can't wait to be patched up so they can go back to the Front. And then there's me . . .' He shook his head. 'No, I don't blame my father for hating me. I've let him down. He can't hate me any more than I hate myself.'

'Would you hate yourself if it had been a German sniper who blew a hole in your shoulder?' Kate asked.

Harry frowned. 'Of course not. That would have been a war wound.'

'But don't you see? You do have a war wound. It's up here.' Kate tapped her temple. 'Just because you don't have a missing limb or shrapnel wounds doesn't mean to say you're not injured.' She edged closer to him. 'Think about those men on the ward: the ones who wake up screaming in the night, the ones who jump at the slightest noise or can't bear to be touched. They're wounded too, in their own way. We carry a lot of our greatest pain inside, where no one can see it.'

Harry was silent for a moment and Kate could see him weighing up her words.

'Please, Harry,' she said. 'Come back to the ward with me. I know you're upset about your family, but there's nothing we can't sort out, I promise.'

'Kate!' A man's voice calling from above shocked them both. Harry jerked away from her like a frightened animal.

Kate looked up. She could see Rufus French's head appearing from the skylight window.

'For Christ's sake, Kate! What the hell do you think you're doing?' he yelled.

'Go back inside,' she called back.

'I'm coming down—'

'I said, go back!' Kate swung round to face him and lost her balance. She felt herself toppling but a second later a pair of strong arms closed around her, holding her close.

'I've got you, miss.' Harry's voice was close to her ear. It took Kate a moment to realise he had jumped up to grab her.

She clung to him, helpless with terror. 'I could have fallen.'

'I know, miss,' Harry said gruffly. 'Come on, let's get you back to safety.'

Chapter Forty-Eight

Billy Willis ran his criminal empire from the back room of the Fallen Angel pub in Roman Road. Jimmy Clyde had often bragged about visiting his hideaway, concealed behind a secret door that Old Bill would never find even if they swarmed all over the place.

It was closing time when Sadie walked in. The pub was empty, chairs upturned on tables, sawdust swept from the floor. The landlord stood behind the bar, wiping glasses. He barely spared her a glance.

'Sorry, girlie, we're closed,' he said.

Sadie walked up to the bar. 'I don't want a drink. I've come to see Billy Willis.'

He frowned at her. 'Not sure I know that name.'

'You should do, he runs a gambling den in your back room. I'll go and find him by myself, shall I?'

She made a move to lift the bar flap, but the landlord blocked her way.

'Where do you think you're going?'

'I told you, I want to see Billy Willis.'

'And I told you, there ain't no one of that name here. Now push off.'

Sadie picked up one of the glasses from the bar and let it fall from her hands. It smashed at her feet.

The landlord stared at her. 'I'll call the police!'

'Go on, then.' Sadie grinned. 'I expect Billy will love you bringing Old Bill to his doorstep. I might even show them where to find him . . . that secret door behind the barrels in the cellar, isn't it?'

She picked up another glass. 'Or I can just carry on breaking these until you tell Billy I'm here.'

'I told you, there's no one—'

She let the glass drop and snatched up another one before the landlord had a chance to react.

'Give me that!' He tried to grab it from her hand but Sadie held on tight.

'Not until you tell Billy—'

'Tell Billy what?'

The landlord froze at the sound of the voice. Sadie swung around. A red-haired woman stood in the doorway behind the bar. She was tall, statuesque, smartly dressed – and very familiar.

'Ada?' Sadie's mouth fell open in astonishment.

'Nurse Sedgewick?' Ada's crimson mouth curved into a smile. 'Now what's a nice young girl like you doing in a place like this? And at this hour, too.' She glanced at the clock. 'Shouldn't you be tucked up in bed in the nurses' home by now?'

'I beg your pardon, Mrs Dixon, I didn't mean to disturb you,' the landlord stammered, rescuing the glass from Sadie's limp grasp. 'She says she wants to see Billy Willis.'

'My brother ain't here.'

Sadie blinked at her, struggling to take this in. 'Billy Willis is your brother?'

'Dixon is my married name.' There was no warmth in her narrowed eyes as she looked at Sadie. This Ada was nothing like the jolly, laughing woman Sadie had nursed at Christmas.

'So what's your business with Billy?' she asked.

'I want to talk to him.'

'What about?'

Sadie lifted her chin. 'That's between me and him.'

'Is it now?' Ada folded her arms across her bosom. 'Well, I reckon anything you want to say to my brother, you can say to me.'

Sadie pressed her lips together and said nothing.

Ada sighed. 'Look, go home, girl. You ain't got no business being here.'

She started to turn away but Sadie blurted out, 'It's about Jimmy Clyde.'

Ada paused, her back still turned. 'Who?'

'He works for your brother.'

'What about him?'

'He killed my mother Lily.'

Ada turned slowly to face her.

'The day he came out of prison he beat her up, broke her ribs, knocked her unconscious. The damage to her brain was so bad she never woke up.' Sadie paused to gather herself, determined not to falter. 'I never got to say goodbye,' she murmured.

'I'm sorry to hear that.' Ada's voice was distant.

'It was me he really wanted to kill. I was the one who shopped him to the police and got him locked up. My ma died trying to protect me.' The words clogged in her throat, nearly choking her.

Ada was silent for a moment. Then she said, 'I need a drink.' She gestured to the landlord. 'Two brandies, Arnold.'

'I don't want one,' Sadie said, but Ada ignored her.

They sat down at one of the tables. Ada did not speak until the barman placed two glasses in front of them. Ada picked up hers and knocked the contents straight back.

'Drink up,' she said.

'I told you, I don't want it.'

'I said, drink it!'

They stared at each other across the table. Then, reluctantly, Sadie lifted the glass to her lips and took a sip. It was fiery on her tongue, but the warmth that spread through her body was actually quite pleasant.

Ada leant back in her seat. 'And now I s'pose you're worried this Jimmy will come back for you?' she said.

Sadie shook her head. 'I ain't worried about myself.'

'Then what do you want?'

'I want revenge.'

This seemed to amuse Ada. 'What kind of revenge?'

'I want him to hang for what he did to my mother.'

Sadie gulped down the rest of her drink. Ada looked at the empty glass on the table, her brows rising. 'So why are you coming here? Why not go to the Old Bill?'

'They won't do anything.' Sadie wiped her mouth with her sleeve. 'They say they can't find him. And even if they did, I know they wouldn't do anything. Most of 'em are in your brother's pay anyway.'

Ada looked away, but not before Sadie saw her smile. When she turned back, her expression was bland. 'As it happens, I've heard of this Jimmy Clyde. But I haven't seen him around for a while.'

'That's because your brother's hiding him.'

'That's Billy's business, not mine,' Ada said shortly. 'I don't interfere. And neither should you,' she warned.

'I'm not afraid of your brother.'

'That's because you don't know him.' Ada rose to her feet. 'Look, I'll ask about, see if anyone's heard from Jimmy. But I wouldn't hold out too much hope.'

'Don't bother,' Sadie said. 'I'll find him myself.'

'And how will you do that?'

'I don't know. But I ain't going to give up.'

Ada sent her a long, considering look. 'You're a nice girl,' she said. 'I like you, which is why I'm giving you this advice.' She leant closer. 'Forget about getting revenge on Jimmy Clyde. You're in an ugly world, and you ain't got no business being here. Just forget about it all, and get on with your own life. I bet that's what your mother would have wanted.'

She was ready to go.

'You're right,' Sadie said, as Ada walked away. 'Ma would have wanted me to forget about it. She would have wanted me to stay safe, to protect myself. She wouldn't have thought her life worth anyone taking trouble over.' Ada did not turn around but Sadie knew she was listening. 'And perhaps it wasn't,' she went on. 'I mean, who was she anyway? Just some old brass. She wasn't even much of a mother most of the time. But her life was worth something to me. To me, she was everything.'

Sadie watched Ada, hoping that her words had sunk in. But the woman did not react.

The girl got to her feet. 'I'll go,' she mumbled. 'Thank you for your time.'

She was past Ada and halfway to the door before heard, 'I'll have a word with Billy.'

Sadie swung round. 'You do know where Jimmy is, then?'

'I'm not saying that. But if he does show his face—'

'You'll tell the police?'

'We'll deal with him,' Ada said firmly. She looked at Sadie. 'You have my word on that,' she said.

Chapter Forty-nine

Kate sat in the passageway outside the office where the disciplinary committee was meeting. Doctors and nurses bustled past, but Kate ignored their curious looks. Instead she kept her gaze fixed on the noticeboard opposite, where a notice for the Students' Union Midsummer Ball was pinned up alongside a list of that week's post-mortem demonstrations.

Once upon a time Kate would have been there, in the demonstration room, assisting Dr Werner. It all seemed like such a long time ago now.

It was a warm morning and Kate could feel perspiration trickling down inside the stiff collar of her blouse. She had dressed carefully that morning, trying to draw attention away from her face, still pale and haggard from lack of sleep.

Two students sat further along the passageway, whispering together. One of them, a lanky first year, was wringing his bony hands together while his friend did his best to reassure him.

'It was only a drunken escapade,' Kate heard him saying. 'I'm sure they won't throw the book at you for that.'

The door opened and Kate straightened up as a middle-aged woman appeared, carrying a piece of paper.

'Mr Burrell?' She looked at the first year. 'The committee will see you now.'

Kate watched as he was ushered in. A moment later his friend sauntered off. Kate turned back to the noticeboard and wiped her damp palms on her skirt. Today's PM was another demonstration of the effects of gas gangrene, she noticed.

'Miss Carlyle?'

She turned round to see Rufus French hurrying down the passageway towards her. Kate smiled at him without thinking, relieved to see a friendly face.

'Thank God,' he said. 'I thought I might have missed you.'

'Missed saying goodbye to me, you mean?' Kate said.

Rufus ignored her remark as he consulted his watch. 'I thought you were due in at ten?'

'They're making me wait. Apparently stolen test tubes and drunken high jinks and not turning up to lectures are more important than the accidental death of a patient.'

Rufus winced. He was silent for a moment, then he said, 'How are you? After last night?'

'Tired,' Kate said. 'But none the worse for my rooftop ordeal. How is Harry – Private Copeland?'

'Sleeping, at last. It took a lot to knock him out, I can tell you.'

'I'm not surprised, poor soul,' Kate said. 'He was in an awful state.'

'I wonder what made him do it?' Rufus said, then shook his head. 'What am I saying . . . It's this wretched war, isn't it? We can mend their bodies but not their minds.'

Kate thought about Harry's confession, but said nothing. 'What will happen to him now?' she asked.

'He's being taken to a convalescent home this afternoon.'

'Will they send him back to France, do you think?'

'I don't know.' Rufus frowned at her. 'Look here, why are you worrying about him? It's yourself you should be thinking about.'

Kate smiled. 'My problems seem very trivial compared to his.'

Rufus was silent for a moment. Then he said, 'Look here, do you want me to speak for you?'

The question took her by surprise. 'Speak for me?'

'Give you a character reference. You never know, it might help.'

Kate frowned at him. 'Why would you do that?'

'Because I think you're an excellent doctor.'

Kate stared at him, at a loss for words. 'You'd speak up – for me?'

'Of course.'

Their eyes met for a moment, then Kate shook her head. 'I couldn't ask you to do that.'

'You're not asking. I'm offering.' But then he said, 'Although I don't suppose you'll really need my help, will you? You're a Carlyle, after all.'

Before Kate had a chance to reply to this, the door opened and the first-year student stumbled out, looking dazed but happy.

The woman turned to her. 'Miss Carlyle?'

Kate rose to her feet. 'Well, here goes.' She turned to Rufus. 'Wish me luck,' she said.

'You won't need it,' he said.

Kate smiled weakly. *That's what you think.*

There were four doctors on the disciplinary committee. Kate was surprised to see her father was one of them. He sat behind the long table with Dr Bailey, a surgeon, Dr Dennys and Sir Patrick Jefferson, who were both orthopaedic consultants. With his broad, leonine head and his impressive height, her father seemed to tower over his colleagues.

Sir Patrick ventured to speak up. 'Sir Philip, I wonder, since this case is of a personal nature, if you would care to abstain? I'm sure we—' Kate's father cut him off.

'No need,' he said brusquely. 'I can deal with this matter impartially.'

I doubt it. Kate stared at him across the table. The other doctors looked uncomfortable, but none of them dared to argue with Sir Philip Carlyle.

'Very well.' Sir Patrick consulted the notes in front of him. 'Then we'll begin . . .'

Kate remained silent as he read out the charge against her. She kept her eyes fixed on her father, but he refused to meet her gaze.

Sir Patrick Jefferson finished speaking and sat back. 'Now we have heard the charge against you, Miss Carlyle, perhaps you would like to say something in your defence?'

Kate glanced at her father, and saw the imperceptible shake of his head.

How ironic, she thought bitterly, that this was her one chance to finally make him proud, to earn the respect she had always wanted him to feel for her.

'I would like to say something,' another voice declared.

At first she thought Rufus French had come in to speak for her after all, but when Kate turned she was surprised to see someone else standing in the doorway.

'Leo?'

'Hello, Sis,' he said quietly. He looked even more wretched than she felt, his dark hair tousled, deep shadows under his eyes.

'What is the meaning of this?' their father interjected. 'You can't come barging in here! We are in the middle of a disciplinary hearing.'

'Yes, I know, Father,' Leo said calmly. 'And I'm the one who should be facing it.'

The doctors all looked at each other, except for her father who was staring at his son with a look of pure thunder on his face.

'Leo, you don't have to do this,' Kate murmured.

'Yes, I do. For God's sake, let me do one thing right.'

'Could you explain what you mean, Dr Carlyle?' Dr Dennys asked him.

'I mean, Dr Dennys, that I am the one who made the mistake that caused Corporal Rayner's death.'

Kate could hardly look at her father as Leo stumbled through his explanation.

'So you're saying you gave the patient the medication before you saw Miss Carlyle's notes?' Dr Bailey said.

'Yes, Doctor.'

'And you then destroyed them to cover your own mistake?'

'This is absurd!' Sir Philip, who had been sitting in simmering silence, now exploded to his feet. 'Gentlemen, it's perfectly clear to me what is going on here. My son is acting out of some misguided loyalty, lying to protect his sister—'

As her father was speaking, Kate saw Leo take a piece of paper from the inside pocket of his jacket. He smoothed it out carefully and laid it on the table in front of the panel.

Kate recognised the writing on it immediately. 'My notes!'

'I was going to destroy them, but I couldn't bring myself to do it. Guilty conscience, I suppose,' Leo said.

The doctors mulled over Kate's notes, comparing them to Leo's. In the midst of it all, Sir Philip sat as still and upright as a statue, a fixed look on his face.

'Why are you doing this?' she whispered to Leo.

'I wanted to come forward before, but I was too afraid.' Leo flicked a glance at their father, then looked away. 'But then I heard what happened last night. That man up on the roof. The whole hospital is talking about what you did, Kate. And that made me realise that you're the one who deserves to be here, not me.'

'But you're a good doctor,' Kate protested.

'Perhaps. But I'll never be as good as you.' Leo's mouth twisted. 'I've always known that. That was why I didn't want you to come here, because I knew that sooner or later you'd show me up for the poor specimen I am.' He glanced at their father again. This time he did not look away. 'But it seems neither of us will ever be good enough for him, will we?' he murmured.

The other doctors finished reviewing the notes and sat back.

'In the light of this new evidence, we will have to consider the case further,' Sir Patrick declared. 'We will reconvene at a future date. You may go.'

He waved his hand to dismiss them, but Leo stood his ground. 'What about Kate?' he asked. 'Can she go back on the ward?'

The doctors looked at each other. 'I see no reason why not,' Dr Dennys said. 'What say you, Sir Philip?'

Kate looked at her father. His face was dark with suppressed rage.

'I have nothing at all to say on the matter,' he bit out.

Chapter Fifty

There was a game of cricket going on at the internment camp, inmates against the camp guards.

Anna and her father sat side by side on a grassy bank to watch it.

'It is such a British sport, I do not think the guards expected the Germans to be quite so good at it,' Friedrich Beck laughed. 'I think now they are rather sorry they challenged us!'

Anna shaded her eyes to look at him. It was a long time since she had seen him so content.

'It's good to see you so happy, Papa,' she said.

'I have learnt to be happy, *Liebling*.' Friedrich helped himself to another of the home-made biscuits Anna had brought with her. After six months, the guards no longer bothered to search them for contraband, and they were allowed to bring in whatever gifts they wished. 'Of course, I would be happier still if I was at home with you and your mother and sister. But we must all make the best of what we have, *nein*?'

'I suppose so.' Anna plucked disconsolately at a tuft of grass.

The umpire held up his hand and the crowd cheered.

'Look, another six runs!' Her father grinned. 'They are quite beating them at their own game, I think.'

He turned to her and his expression grew thoughtful.

'Listen to me, going on about a game of cricket when I should be paying attention to my beautiful daughter.' He reached out and stroked her hair. 'I am longing to know your news. How is your mother? She is well, yes?'

'Yes, Papa.'

'And Liesel?'

Anna pulled a face. 'Still complaining about everything, as usual.'

Friedrich smiled. 'I am glad to hear some things have not changed!'

'I think she misses the servants she had at Grandmother's house.' Anna snapped her mouth closed.

'Ah, yes.' Her father's mouth twisted. 'I can imagine your sister would have enjoyed that very much.' He paused, his gaze drifting back towards the match. 'Has your mother heard from your grandmother at all?'

'No, Papa.'

He shook his head sadly. 'It is a pity that things ended for them so badly. I know your mother cares a great deal for her. How I wish things could have been settled between them, then perhaps we could have welcomed Hester into our family.'

'I'm glad she's not part of our family!' Anna snapped. 'She's a horrible, selfish woman.'

'Anna!' Her father's brows rose. 'You must not speak of your grandmother like that.'

'But you don't know what she was like, Papa. She—'

'I will not hear anything against her.' He held up his hand to silence his daughter. 'Whatever you think of her, she took you in when you needed help. She must have a kind heart to do that.'

Anna pressed her lips together to stop the words of protest from spilling out. Hester had never had a good word to say about Friedrich Beck, had done her best to take his family away from him. He must have known that, and yet still he found it in his heart to forgive her.

But Anna couldn't. Hatred for her grandmother lay like bitter gall inside her heart.

Her father must have seen the resentment in her expression because he changed the subject. 'Anyway, at least you are home now. How are you settling in at the bakery? Things are going well, yes?'

'Yes, Papa.'

'It must be good to be home again, after everything that has happened. I am so grateful to Tom for helping you. You must give him my thanks when you see him.'

Anna plucked at the grass and said nothing.

'He is a fine young man,' Friedrich went on. 'I am pleased I put my trust in him. He has paid us back handsomely, I think.'

'Yes, Papa.' Anna put her head down so her father could not see her face.

She had not seen Tom for over a month – not since the night she'd sent him packing – but Anna still couldn't banish him from her mind.

As time had passed, she'd started to feel guilty about the way she had reacted. She remembered how hard he had worked, rebuilding their home. And what had he done that was so wrong? He had only spoken his mind, after all. Just because she didn't agree with what he had said, that was no reason to turn her back on him.

'Anna?' She looked up to see her father watching her curiously.

'Sorry, Papa. I was miles away.'

'I could tell. Is there something on your mind, *Liebling*?'

'No, Papa.'

He brushed aside a lock of her hair so he could see her face. 'There is something, I can tell. What is it, child? Tell your papa.'

Anna looked up at him. 'How do you do it?' she asked.

He frowned. 'Do what, *Liebling*?'

'How do you forgive all these people?'

She looked around. 'They keep you locked up when you've done nothing wrong, and yet you laugh and joke with them as if they're your friends.'

'They are my friends,' Friedrich said. 'It is not their fault this has happened to me. They are following the orders they have been given. And we are fortunate that they are kind to us. We are all just trying to make the best of the situation together.'

Anna glared across the cricket pitch. One of the guards had just bowled a German player out, and the spectators were applauding politely.

'Well, I can't forgive them,' she said. 'I can't forgive any of them. Not Grandmother, or the neighbours, or—' Or Tom, she was about to say, but stopped herself.

Her father smiled. 'What have the neighbours done to offend you? Your mother tells me they have been very helpful since you moved back to the bakery.'

'Oh, they have.' Anna's mouth curled. 'They're forever dropping in with bits and pieces for us. Mrs Wheeler brings us food, and Mr Hudson gives us wood and coal for the fire, and the Clancys from the hardware shop brought us a brand new kettle and some crockery.'

'Well, then.'

'But that's not the point, is it?' Anna turned on him angrily. 'Where were they when we really needed them? They looked the other way when the shop was smashed up, didn't they?'

'Perhaps they were afraid?'

'*They* were afraid? What about us? We were the ones who lived with all the threats and insults. I didn't see them offering us help then. They turned their backs on us, stopped buying our bread, put signs up in their shops boasting about being English. And now they've decided they want to help us,' she said bitterly. 'It's all very well for them to turn up on our doorstep with presents now, but where were they when we were nearly murdered?'

Her father was silent for a long time. 'So what are we supposed to do?' he said finally.

'I don't know!' Anna dug her fingers into the soft, bare patch of earth where she had plucked out all the grass. 'But it seems impossible for me to forgive them, that's all.' She looked up at him. 'I'm sorry, Papa, but I can't pretend none of this happened. They should be made to pay for what they did to us.'

Her father raised his eyebrows. 'Revenge, you mean?'

'Perhaps.'

Friedrich shook his head. 'Oh, Anna, what has happened to you? I am surprised my little *Liebling* would even think such a thing.'

'Perhaps I'm not your little *Liebling* anymore,' she said quietly.

Her father was right, the last six months had changed her. She had suffered humiliations and endured hardships she'd never imagined she would have to face. Everything she loved and cared about had been taken away from her; everything she believed in had been destroyed. She had been bruised, betrayed and battered, and had had to develop a hard shell to cope with it all.

Sometimes she hated herself for growing so tough and bitter, and longed once more to be the trusting little girl who kneaded bread dough and iced cakes in her father's bakery.

But that girl was long gone, never to return.

She flinched as her father stroked her hair.

'You are furious with the world,' he said softly. 'So am I, at times. When I think about what I have lost, what has been taken away from me . . .' His face filled with sorrow.

'I miss you all so much,' he said. 'I miss my friends, and my work, and the customers, and being able to walk in Victoria Park on a fine summer's day like today.' He turned his face up to the sun, basking in its warmth. 'But I cannot allow bitterness to get the better of me. I need to forgive, to make the best of what I have. For my own sake, not others'.' He looked back at her. 'In the end, being furious with the world only causes me more pain.' He put his hand to his chest. 'That is why I choose to forgive them, Anna, to see the best in people. I do it for myself.'

Anna looked at him, his angular features and dark eyes so full of kindness. Impulsively, she reached over and threw her arms around his neck, hugging him fiercely.

He laughed. 'What was that for?'

'I love you, Papa.'

'I love you too, *Liebling*.' He took her hand and kissed it. 'Now, let us finish watching this cricket match. Some of us have bet the guards a barrel of beer that we will beat them!'

Anna never would have ventured into the Hatcheries if she hadn't been so keen to see Tom again.

She knew the slums of Bethnal Green were bad, but nothing could have prepared her for the cramped, stinking warren of alleyways and cobbled yards hemmed in by crumbling tenement buildings.

Anna ducked beneath a sagging line of greying washing and tried not to stare at the thin, hostile-looking women who watched her from the open doorways as dozens of filthy children tugged their skirts. The stench of the open privies made her eyes water.

It took Anna a long time to find the Franklins' house. As she let herself into the yard, a scrawny dog went into a frenzy of barking, straining on the end of the rope that tethered it to the back door.

'Shut up, you noisy beggar!' A man's voice shouted from inside the house. Anna took a few cautious steps forward and the dog lunged at her, baring its teeth, its eyes blazing.

'I said shut—' A middle-aged man emerged from the open doorway, scratching his belly through his dirty vest. From across the yard, Anna caught the acrid smell of his stale sweat.

His eyes narrowed when he saw Anna. 'Who are you?'

'I'm looking for Tom Franklin.'

He smiled nastily. 'What's the little sod done now?'

Anna straightened her shoulders. 'I was told he lived here.'

'Who told you that?'

'Does he live here, or doesn't he?'

'Depends who's asking.' He leered at her, exposing a few brown stumps where his teeth should have been.

'I'm Anna Beck. My father runs the bakery—'

'The German?' The man spat on the cobbles in disgust.

Anna fought to keep her temper. 'Is Tom here, or isn't he?'

'What's it worth to you?'

She frowned. 'What do you mean?'

'You want something from me, so I want something from you.'

'You want money?'

'Unless you're offering something else?' He stepped closer, reaching out for her. She jerked away from his fat, dirty fingers.

The man's smile vanished. 'What's the matter with you? You'd be lucky anyone would want to touch you, bloody German bitch!'

'What's going on?' A woman appeared from the house, stout and belligerent-looking, with dyed yellow hair and thick black brows. 'Who's this?' she demanded.

The man looked cowed, and even the dog fell silent.

'She's looking for our Tom,' the man mumbled.

'Oh, him.' The woman's expression became even more sullen. She came across the yard and tucked her arm through the man's possessively. She wore no ring, Anna noticed. 'You've just missed him,' she said.

'What time will he be back?'

The woman's mouth curled, revealing the same brown stumps as the man. 'Depends.'

'On what?'

'On how quick he is at dodging them German bullets!' The man said, and the pair both roared with laughter.

Anna stared from one to the other. 'You mean he's been called up?'

'Blimey, she's quick, ain't she?' the man said. 'That's right, girlie. The army finally got desperate enough to take him, punctured lung an' all. And good bloody riddance to him, sulky little runt!'

Anna ignored her. 'When did he leave?' she asked the woman.

'I dunno, do I? Not long.' The woman screwed up her face in thought. 'About half an hour, I reckon. What d'you say, Bert?'

'Don't ask me. I ain't known what time it is since my watch went to the pop shop!'

They both roared with laughter again. They were still laughing as Anna hurried away.

Chapter Fifty-One

Bethnal Green had never seen a funeral like it.

Sadie was determined to give her mother the best send-off she could afford. There were flowers, a string of professional mourners in tall hats, and a carriage drawn by two black horses, their feathered plumes nodding as they plodded along.

Sadie walked behind the procession. She could see people stopping on the street to watch, doffing their hats and bowing their heads.

'Look at them,' Belle whispered beside her. 'They think it's a toff's funeral. I wonder what they'd say if they knew they were tipping their hats to a dock dolly?'

'And so they should,' Sadie said. 'It's about time Ma had the respect she deserved.'

Belle sent her a sidelong look. 'You've done her proud, mate,' she whispered. 'And that new blue dress you got her was beautiful. Just what she would have wanted.'

'I'm glad.'

Lily Sedgewick might not have worn sky blue on her wedding day, but Sadie had made sure she would go out of this world looking like a queen.

The church was full, and if the vicar realised that half his congregation were street girls he did not show it. Not that anyone would be able to tell. Out of respect for Lily, and under Belle's strict orders, the girls were dressed soberly, their faces stripped of make-up.

'Look at them, like a Sunday School outing!' Belle

413

grinned. 'I hope there ain't a ship due in today. Those sailors will be in for a shock!'

There was someone else in the congregation, too. As she took her own seat at the front Sadie spotted Ada Dixon in one of the back pews. She was looking very dignified in a black sable coat and neat feathered hat.

Sadie looked over her shoulder, trying to catch her eye. But Ada Dixon kept her gaze fixed firmly ahead.

Sadie sought her out in the churchyard after the burial.

'It was good of you to come,' she said.

'I wasn't sure I'd be welcome.' Ada glanced across the churchyard at Belle, who was watching them from a distance. 'But I wanted to pay my respects.' She turned to Sadie. 'It was a lovely service. You did your mother proud.'

'I hope so.'

'She sounded like a good woman.'

Sadie smiled. 'No one could ever call my mother good!'

'She didn't do a bad job of bringing you up.'

No, Sadie thought. She didn't. It was only now she had begun to appreciate how difficult it must have been for Lily.

Silence stretched between them. Then Ada said, 'There's another reason why I came. It's about Jimmy Clyde.'

Sadie tensed. 'What about him?'

'I've spoken to my brother, and – he's going to have a word with him.'

Hope deflated inside Sadie. 'What does that mean?'

'What I say.'

'Is he going to hand Jimmy over to the police?'

Ada lowered her gaze. 'That ain't the way we do things,' she said. 'But you ain't going to have any more trouble from him. All right?'

Sadie opened her mouth to argue, but Ada's forbidding expression stopped her. 'All right,' she said quietly. 'Thank you.'

'You've got nothing to thank me for,' Ada said briskly. 'My brother might not be an angel, but he knows right from wrong.' She paused. 'Right, well, I've done what I came for, so I'll be on my way.'

'Don't you want to stop for tea? We're having a little do in the Rose and Crown. Nothing fancy, but—'

Ada shook her head. 'I won't, if you don't mind? There's a bit of bad blood between us and a few of the locals in that pub. Besides,' she added, 'it's a family occasion. I wouldn't want to intrude.' She looked at Sadie. 'I don't suppose we'll have much call to see each other again.'

'Unless your gastric ulcer starts playing up again!'

'Blimey, let's hope not!' Ada smiled, the first trace of warmth she had shown. Then she looked hard at Sadie and said, 'You will be all right, won't you?'

'Of course.'

'If you need anything, you know you can always call on me.'

'Thank you.'

The next minute Ada had gathered her in a fierce hug. 'You're a good girl,' she said. 'I bet your mother was proud of you.'

The next minute she was gone, walking away down the path towards the lychgate, her head down.

Sadie was watching her go when Belle approached. 'What did she want?'

'She just came to pay her respects.'

'Is that all she said to you?'

'She said Billy was going to have a word with Jimmy Clyde.'

'What does that mean?'

'I don't know.' Sadie shrugged. 'The way she was talking, I thought it best not to ask too many questions.'

'You're right there, girl.' Belle stared down the path after Ada, her eyes narrowed.

415

'Right, we'd best head off to the Rose and Crown.' Sadie looked back at Belle. 'Are you coming?'

'In a minute. I'd like some time on my own with Lily first.'

'It ain't like you to miss a drink!'

'I just want to say goodbye.'

Sadie looked at her mother's best and oldest friend, Belle. Behind that hard expression, she could see there were tears waiting to be shed. Sadie wasn't the only one who had lost her family.

Belle didn't have to wait long. Minutes after the other mourners had left, she heard the sound of footsteps on the gravel path behind her.

Belle did not turn round. 'You came, then?' she said.

'I had to, didn't I? I wanted to pay my respects.'

'Bit late for that, ain't it? Where's the respect you should have given her when she was alive?'

'You watch what you're saying, lady! I ain't about to be spoken to like that by some old brass!' Ada Dixon snapped. 'Besides,' she said. 'I didn't know anything about her, did I? Not till you turned up.'

'I didn't know myself till I read her letter.' Belle shook her head. 'I still can't believe it. All this time she knew who the girl's father was, and she didn't say a dicky bird. I didn't think Lily had it in her to keep secrets.'

'Yes, well, we've only got her word for it, ain't we?' Ada said.

Belle turned to look at her. 'You don't think she's his daughter?'

Ada hesitated for a moment, then shook her head. 'She's his, all right. She's the dead spit of our Billy when he was a lad. Same blonde hair, blue eyes. Good-looking pig, he was. Still is, I s'pose.'

416

'I always thought he was too good for the likes of us. Shows how wrong you can be, don't it?'

'Oh, he was never fussy who he went with,' Ada dismissed. 'No offence,' she added.

If it had been anyone else, Belle would have decked them for the insult. But she knew better than to tangle with Ada Dixon. She was every bit as tough as her brother.

Besides, Lily had begged Belle in her letter not to make trouble.

Poor Lily. From what she had written there, she was once deeply in love with Billy Willis. Daft dreamer that she was, she had probably hoped that their affair might lead somewhere.

But Billy Willis had used her and thrown her aside, just like all the other men in her life had done.

'She don't know, does she?' Ada interrupted Belle's thoughts. She shook her head. 'Best we keep it that way,' Ada said. 'I dunno how Billy would take the news.'

'I dunno how his wife would take it, either,' Belle said. 'They've got no kids of their own, have they?'

'Leave Mollie out of this!' Ada turned on her, her eyes flaring. 'That's my family's business, and I won't have you sticking your nose in!'

'All right, keep your wig on. I ain't going to say nothing.' Belle held up her hands. 'I just want what's right for Sadie, that's all. Besides,' she added, 'I don't suppose she'd care to know she's Billy Willis' daughter either.'

Ada's face darkened and for a moment Belle thought she had offended her. But then she smiled and said, 'You're probably right, girl. She's well out of it. But that don't mean she won't be taken care of.'

'That's all Lily wanted. She wanted her girl to be looked after.'

'She will be,' Ada said firmly. 'She's under our protection now.'

'And Jimmy Clyde?'

'Dealt with.'

Belle saw Ada's forbidding expression and did not comment.

As Sadie had said, sometimes it was better not to ask too many questions.

Chapter Fifty-Two

Tom stood at the far end of the station platform, his kitbag at his feet, watching the other men saying goodbye to their loved ones. The platform was a mass of people, all talking, kissing, embracing, crying and smiling. There was so much raw emotion on display, it was almost too hard for him to watch.

Then he thought he heard someone calling out his name. He had swung round to look before he realised he was being foolish. Who would come to see him off? His brothers couldn't wait to see the back of him, and his father was too busy with his latest floozy to care where he went.

Besides, this had been a woman's voice. It had sounded like . . .

Tom shook his head. It was wishful thinking, that was all. Just his imagination playing cruel tricks on him.

The train came in and everyone started making their way towards it. Tom slung his kitbag over his shoulder and climbed aboard. He dumped his bag on the rack overhead then threw himself down in a seat, turning his face away from the platform so he wouldn't have to see the last-minute desperate embraces, the clutching hands and tears running down brave faces.

What must it feel like, he thought, to love someone so much you couldn't bear to leave them?

Suddenly he heard his name called again, more clearly this time. He looked up and by some miracle there she was, pushing her way through the crowd, calling out and looking this way and that.

Before he knew what he was doing Tom was on his feet and fighting his way back to the door so he could push open the window and call out to her.

'Miss Anna?'

She looked over her shoulder then ran down the platform towards him. Her hat had slipped and her hair had come loose. It streamed behind her like a bright auburn flag, and Tom didn't think he had ever seen anything so beautiful in his whole life. It was all he could do not to put out his hand and touch it.

Instead he said, 'What are you doing here?'

'Oh, Tom, thank heavens I found you! I didn't think I would, among all these people.' She was breathless, her face flushed. 'I couldn't let you go without saying goodbye.'

His chest tightened, making it impossible for him to breathe. He opened his mouth but as usual the words would not come out.

'How are you?' was all he could manage.

'I'm well.' She smiled up at him, that bright, heartbreaking smile. 'How are you?'

He nodded. 'All right.'

'I didn't know you'd been called up. I came looking for you, and your father said—'

'You came looking for me?'

'I wanted to see you. To say sorry.'

He looked away, embarrassed. 'There's no need . . .'

'No, listen to me, please.' Her brown eyes met his, full of sincerity. 'I had no right to send you away, not after everything you've done for us. You've been too good a friend to deserve that.'

A friend. He would hear her saying that word in his mind long after they had parted.

420

'I shouldn't have left it so long to say something.' Anna was still speaking.

'It doesn't matter. You're here now.'

'Only just!' She smiled. 'To think, if I'd left it a day longer I would have missed you completely.' She paused for a moment, looking down at her hands. 'I'm sorry you're going,' she said.

'I ain't. We've all got to do our bit.'

'That's true, I suppose.'

For a moment neither of them spoke. Tom willed his stubborn tongue to come loose and say something. Just a few words might make all the difference . . .

'We've reopened the bakery,' Anna said.

Tom brightened. 'Is your father home?'

'No.' Anna's face was wistful. 'Mother and Liesel are running the place, and I'm helping out when I can.'

'Liesel, in the bakery? I can't picture it.'

'I know.' Anna grinned. 'She spends most of her time admiring her reflection in the bottom of cake tins, but I'm sure she'll buckle down in the end.'

'And how is your father?'

'In good spirits.'

'I'm glad to hear it. I expect he'll be back soon.'

Anna nodded. 'I'm sure you're right.'

Men were pushing past them, trying to get on the train. They had to keep ducking back and forth, out of each other's sight. Tom was convinced that next time he looked she would have disappeared, a figment of his imagination.

They looked at each other, then they both started speaking at once.

'I just wanted to say—'

'Miss Anna, I—'

They stopped.

421

'You first,' Anna said.

'No, you.'

She hesitated for a moment. 'I've been thinking about what you said. About Edward.'

'I shouldn't have—'

'People can change, you know. Whatever Edward's done in the past, he's proved himself now. He's not the man he was, any more than you are. Everyone deserves a second chance, don't you think?'

'I suppose so.'

She bit her lip, and he could see her fighting to make herself speak. 'But if there's anything you know about him – anything you think I should know – I'd like to hear it.'

He looked down at her brave little face, staring back up at him. Those brown eyes, so full of hope and trust. She was steeling herself, he could tell. Those slender shoulders were rigid, bracing for the worst.

He opened his mouth to speak. He wanted to tell her what really happened. He wanted to tell her that he was the one who had scribbled the note warning her of what was to come. He wanted to explain how he had tried to persuade his brothers not to go through with it, how he had sat outside the bakery in the freezing cold all night so he could try to stop them, how they had set about him, knocking him out so that by the time he'd come round it was nearly too late . . .

But it hadn't been their idea. His brothers were stupid and greedy and easily led, but they weren't evil.

They would never have set fire to the bakery if Edward Stanning hadn't told them to do it.

Why Edward had asked them to do it, Tom didn't know. He could only guess that he wanted to give Anna a scare, a punishment for not marrying him when he'd wanted. Tom knew Edward did not like to be thwarted. Perhaps he wanted to frighten her so that she would fall in with his plans more easily next time.

Or perhaps it was just another example of Edward Stanning being a twisted, evil swine behind that handsome mask of his.

But Tom couldn't say this to Anna. He couldn't be the one to break her heart. All he could do was hope that fate would intervene so that Edward never came home – and then Anna would never have to face the truth.

'As you said, everyone deserves a second chance,' he said.

The sharp whistle blast startled them. At the far end of the platform the guard was waving his flag for the train to leave.

Tom took a deep breath. If he didn't speak now, he would regret it forever.

'Will you write to me?' he blurted out.

'Write to you?' She looked surprised.

'You don't have to if you don't want to, I know you're busy and all that. But I'd really like to hear your news, how you're getting on . . . if you can spare the time. I haven't got anyone else,' he murmured.

Anna smiled. 'Of course I'll write to you, Tom. And I'll send you presents, too. Socks, and chocolate, and cigarettes.'

'Steady on!' He felt himself grinning foolishly.

He craned out of the window as the train pulled out, watching her figure slowly receding, waving until she was out of sight. His heart was like a solid rock in his chest.

So this was what it felt like, he thought, to love someone so much you couldn't bear to leave them.

Chapter Fifty-Three

Christmas Eve 1915

'Bit of a rum do, ain't it, having Christmas Day on Christmas Eve!'

Belle set down her glass to throw another log on the fire. They had just finished eating a slap up Christmas dinner of roast chicken, crispy potatoes and a jug of bread sauce followed by a hefty plum pudding and thick cream. Belle was a dab hand in the kitchen when she wanted to be.

Had things been different, she could have made a lovely wife and mother, Sadie thought, looking around her. Her rooms might be humble but they were beautifully kept, with a handstitched quilt on the bed and lace-trimmed antimacassars on the armchairs. Belle had even made the colourful rag rug in front of the fire, where they rested their slippered feet.

'I tried to get tomorrow off, but Sister wouldn't have it,' Sadie said.

'I don't blame her. People don't stop getting sick just because it's Christmas Day, do they?'

'Will you be all right on your own?'

'Oh, don't you worry about me. I daresay I'll find some company!' Belle winked at her.

'Belle!' Sadie shook her head.

'What? Girl's got to earn a living, ain't she? Christmas or no Christmas.' Belle helped herself to another sweet from the box Sadie had bought her. 'I love parma violets,' she said. 'They were your ma's favourites, too.'

'I know.'

They sat for a moment, both gazing into the flames.

'Lil used to love Christmas, didn't she?' Belle said. 'Used to get as giddy as a little kid.'

'She was giddy last Christmas,' Sadie said. 'Remember that dinner she cooked us?'

'Lovely, weren't it?' Belle smacked her lips. 'She really tried hard. Wanted to make it so special for you.'

'I reckon it was the best Christmas I ever had.'

Belle smiled. 'She would have been very pleased to hear you say that.' She raised her glass. 'Here's to you, Lil. Wherever you are, mate.'

Sadie smiled. She could never have imagined how much she would miss her mother. But she had forced herself not to dwell on regrets or think about all the time they had wasted. As Belle always said, there was no point in living in the past and wishing things different. So she made herself think instead about the good times they had shared. Now when she thought about Lily, it was with warmth and love.

'Hark at us, all sorry for ourselves.' Belle put down her glass and stood up. 'Tell you what, I'll put some music on, shall I? We can have a dance.'

Belle set the gramophone going, and she and Sadie twirled around the room. They were laughing so much, it took Sadie by surprise when she turned round and saw Peter Machin standing in the doorway, stamping snow off his boots.

'Sorry,' he said, over the sound of the music. 'I did knock, but . . .'

Belle lifted the gramophone needle and the room fell quiet. 'What are you doing here?' she asked.

'I came to see Sadie.' He turned to her, colour rising above the collar of his tunic. 'I went to the nurses' home, but they said you had the day off. I thought I'd find you here.'

Belle laughed. 'Blimey, it's a wonder they ain't made you a detective with those powers of deduction. Regular little Sherlock Holmes, ain't you?'

'Shhh, Belle.' Sadie turned back to face him. She didn't know why, but her heart was suddenly hammering in her chest. 'What did you want me for, Peter?'

He cleared his throat nervously. 'They've found a man's body.'

Sadie heard Belle gasp. 'Where?'

'Washed up at low tide in Greenwich. Been in the water a while, they reckon.' He paused. 'It's Jimmy Clyde, Sadie.'

She had always wondered how she would feel when she heard the news. But once she did she seemed to go dead inside.

'Thank you for letting me know,' she said quietly.

Peter tilted his head to study her face. 'Are you all right?'

She looked up, her eyes meeting his calmly. 'Yes. Why shouldn't I be?'

'I dunno. I just thought you might—' He shrugged. 'I don't know,' he sighed.

He stood in silence for a moment, staring at her.

'Well?' Belle broke the silence. 'Ain't you got any more police work to do, Constable? I'll bet Roman Road's full of drunks you could arrest, this time of night.'

Peter hesitated for a moment, then wished them good night and left.

Belle closed the door firmly behind him and leant against it.

'Well,' she said. 'That's that, then.'

'That's that.' Sadie paused for a moment. 'What do you think happened?'

'Dunno. Probably had a skinful and fell in. That's what usually happens, ain't it?'

'You really believe that?'

426

'What other reason could there be?'

They looked at each other for a long time. 'You're right,' Sadie said. 'It was probably an accident.'

'He wanted to stay, you know.' Belle changed the subject.

'Who?'

'Him.' She jerked her head towards the door. 'PC Machin. I reckon he's sweet on you.'

'Come off it!'

'I mean it. I've seen the way he looks at you with those sad, little boy lost eyes of his.' Belle sent her a shrewd look. 'I reckon you could do a lot worse for yourself, too.'

'Do you now?'

'I do. Perhaps I should have invited him to stay. It's a perishing night, I reckon he would have appreciated a little warm by the fire . . .'

'You can stop your matchmaking, Belle. I ain't interested.'

Sadie went to the window and looked down into the street. Peter Machin had already disappeared, leaving a trail of boot prints in the thick snow.

'That would be something, wouldn't it?' Belle chuckled. 'Can you imagine it? Lily Sedgewick's daughter ending up with a policeman?'

Sadie looked back out of the window and smiled. 'Sounds like a match made in heaven,' she said.

Christmas morning on Monaghan ward began just after midnight with a ruptured appendix, an acute bronchitis, a couple of badly infected wounds and a vomiting and diarrhoea virus that spread like wildfire.

Kate had the misfortune of being the doctor on call, and spent most of the night trying to cope with it all. Probationers Copeland and Beck did their best to keep up, but in the end all three of them were rushing from bed to bed, administering bowls and changing sheets. By the time dawn broke they were so broken and exhausted they could scarcely speak, let alone wish each other a merry Christmas. Kate had lost count of how many clean aprons the nurses had gone through during the course of the night.

'I suppose this will be good training for you when you get to France,' Kate said to Eleanor Copeland when they stopped for a cup of tea just before six. The ward was still in darkness, silent but for the snoring of the men.

'I suppose it will, Miss,' Eleanor replied.

'It's your last week here, isn't it?'

'That's right, Miss. I leave New Year's Eve.'

'We'll be sorry to lose you. You're an excellent nurse.'

Colour rose in Eleanor's cheeks as she handed Kate her tea. 'Thank you, Miss.'

'Our loss is the Voluntary Aid Detachment's gain, I suppose.' Kate looked at her respectfully over the rim of her cup. Eleanor Copeland had all the makings of a fine nurse. Far too good to waste her talents making beds and scrubbing out bedpans with the VAD. But she had been so restless since the incident with her brother, no one was surprised when she announced she had enlisted.

'If only you could have finished your nursing training,' Kate said. 'Then you could have joined the Military Nursing Service.'

Copeland shook her head. 'I couldn't wait,' she said. 'I wanted to go as soon as possible. I talked about it with my father, and I felt it was my duty.'

Kate read the unspoken message in her eyes. She needed to atone for her brother's shortcomings. Honour required there should be a Copeland on the battlefield in France, and her father had decided it would be his daughter.

Kate knew all about domineering fathers.

'My brother has gone to France, too,' she said. 'He's joined the Army Medical Reserve.'

'Good for him,' Eleanor Copeland said.

Kate wasn't so sure. It wasn't Leo's decision to go but their father had insisted. Sir Philip had pulled strings and called in favours, and Leo had been quietly removed from the Nightingale and inducted into the military. Her father pretended he had done it to salvage his son's career, but Kate and her brother both understood this was Leo's punishment for letting him down.

Kate knew her father would have sent her into the military too, if he could. As it was, Sir Philip chose to ignore her presence completely. He never acknowledged or spoke to her if he could help it. If they met on the ward or in the corridor he would look the other way.

Kate was surprised by how little it troubled her. She had stopped looking for her father's approval. She knew she would never get it, and after the way Sir Philip had treated her over Corporal Rayner's death, she no longer wanted it anyway. His good opinion meant nothing to her.

'How is your brother getting on?' Kate asked.

'He's doing well, thank you, Miss.' Eleanor Copeland's gaze dropped.

'Still at the hospital in Scotland?'

'Yes. I'm hoping to see him before I go to France.'

'Be sure to give him my best wishes, won't you?'

'Yes, Miss.' Eleanor paused for a moment, pursing her lips. 'I'm very grateful,' she said. 'For everything you've done.'

Anna Beck came in to the kitchen and Eleanor fell silent. Kate understood why.

Only she and Eleanor knew about the Blighty wound. It had to be a secret, for Harry's sake. If anyone found out what really happened there would be a court martial. Harry Copeland could end up in prison, or even shot.

Kate was only grateful that his father had decided to keep quiet about it. Perhaps he had a heart after all, she thought. Or more likely the shame of having a coward for a son was greater than the desire to see justice served.

They finished their tea. Kate was washing up the cups at the sink when she heard a familiar voice ringing down the ward.

'Good morning, Gentlemen! Merry Christmas to one and all.'

Kate carried on with her washing up, annoyed to find herself blushing like a schoolgirl. She was even more annoyed that Eleanor Copeland and Anna Beck suddenly seemed to be watching her keenly.

By the time Rufus French stuck his head around the kitchen door a moment later, Kate had composed herself enough to turn around and face him.

'What are you doing here?' she demanded.

'Well, that's a nice greeting, I must say. And on Christmas morning, too.' He winked at the student nurses.

'I'm far too tired for your fooling about, Dr French,' Kate said. 'I've had a sleepless night.'

'As have I, Miss Carlyle.'

'Yes, but I've been looking after patients, not cavorting all night in the Students' Union bar.'

'The festive spirit has passed our Miss Carlyle by, it seems.'

The nurses giggled, but Kate didn't take offence. She had learnt not to take herself too seriously, especially where Rufus French was concerned.

'Unlike you.' Kate sniffed the air. 'You reek of whisky. What do you want, anyway? You still haven't told me.'

'To see you, of course.'

Kate turned away, knowing her rising colour would give her away.

'What's wrong? Have all the pretty nurses turned you down?'

'Alas, I only have eyes for you these days.'

Kate ducked her head, hiding her smile. 'Now I know you're drunk,' she said.

'They make a lovely couple, don't they?' Anna said to Eleanor as they left the ward an hour later. It was a relief to hand over to the day staff, although they still had to help with the breakfasts, sort the laundry and clean up the ward after their hectic night.

Eleanor looked up vaguely. 'Who?'

'Dr French and Miss Carlyle. There's definitely some romance there, don't you think?'

'Is there? I hadn't noticed.'

Anna sent her a sideways look. Eleanor Copeland had been changed by her brother's illness. She no longer bustled around so much, bossing everyone about. There was no more sewing of sandbags or knitting of socks. She seemed quieter, more reflective, as if nearly losing her brother had somehow rubbed off some of her sharp edges.

She was certainly less abrasive with Anna. No one could ever call them friends, but at least they were civil to each other now. Anna even thought she might miss Eleanor when she went off to France. Miss Carlyle was right, it would be a shame to lose her. For all her faults, Eleanor Copeland was an excellent nurse.

The sky was streaked with the first pale dawn sunlight as they returned to their rooms to change. Anna quickly set about putting away her uniform, while Eleanor flopped on to her bed and closed her eyes.

She was still there when Anna had finished getting

dressed. Anna watched her in the reflection of the dressing table mirror while she did her hair. 'What are you going to do today?' she asked.

'I don't know.' Eleanor's reply was muffled, her face buried in the pillow.

'You're not going home to visit your family?'

Eleanor was silent. She never seemed to talk about her father and mother anymore. There was certainly no more spouting from *John Bull*.

Anna hesitated. It was none of her business, she told herself. Eleanor had done nothing to earn her friendship.

She remembered her father's words.

Everyone deserves a second chance.

Anna cleared her throat nervously. 'You could always come home with me?' she said.

As soon as she had uttered the words she realised how stupid they sounded. Of course she would refuse. Why on earth would she do otherwise? Eleanor might have softened over the past months, but it was utterly foolish of her to expect her to change her heart that much.

'I'm sorry,' she said, 'it was stupid of me to even suggest—'

'Yes, please.'

Anna looked up sharply, her eyes meeting Eleanor's reflection in the mirror. Even then, she wasn't sure she had heard properly.

'I'm sorry?' she said.

Eleanor sent her a tremulous smile. 'I said I'd love to come,' she said.

Hear more from

Donna Douglas

The Nightingale Hospital, 1938

As Christmas approaches, the staff at the Nightingale Hospital have their own wishes for the festive season.

Ward sister **Frannie Wallace** is hoping she won't have to live through another war like the one that claimed her beloved fiancé while Staff Nurse **Helen Dawson** wants to find happiness again after the death of her husband.

Matron **Kathleen Fox** struggles to keep up morale and while everyone else worries about the future of the Nightingale, it's for her own future that Kathleen truly fears.

As the country prepares itself for war, one thing is for sure – by the time next Christmas comes, nothing at the Nightingale Hospital will be the same again . . .

arrow books

The Nightingale Hospital, 1941

Christmas is fast approaching and with shortages everywhere, and every news bulletin announcing more defeats and losses, the British people are weary and demoralised and the Nightingale Hospital is suffering too.

Millie is recently widowed and dealing with the demands of her family's estate. It's not long before her old world of the Nightingale begins to beckon, along with a long-lost love. **Jess** is struggling with her move from East London to the quiet of the countryside while **Effie** finds herself exiled to a quiet village. But the quiet doesn't last for long as Ellie soon finds excitement in the shape of a smooth-talking GI . . .

The Nightingale Hospital, 1944

With her husband Nick away fighting, **Dora** struggles to keep the home fires burning and is put in charge of a ward full of German prisoners of war. Can she find it in her heart to care for her enemies?

Fellow nurse **Kitty** thinks she might be falling for a German soldier, whilst Dora's old friend **Helen** returns from Europe with a dark secret . . .

arrow books

The Nightingale Hospital, 1945

The war is over, but its scars remain and **Matron Kathleen Fox** has the job of putting the Nightingale Hospital back together. But memories and ghosts of those lost fill the bomb-damaged buildings, and she wonders if she is up to the task.

In the name of festive cheer Kathleen decides to put on a Christmas Show for the patients. The idea is greeted with mixed feelings by the nurses, who are struggling with their own post-war problems.

As rehearsals begin however, it seems the show isn't just a tonic for the patients – could the Nightingale Christmas Show be just what the doctor ordered for the nurses too?

arrow books

FROM THE AUTHOR OF THE BESTSELLING
Nightingales SERIES

THE SUNDAY TIMES TOP TEN BESTSELLER

Donna Douglas

The Nurses of
Steeple Street

**Welcome to the district nurses' home on Steeple Street,
where everyone has a secret . . .**

Ambitious young nurse **Agnes Sheridan** had a promising future
ahead of her until a tragic mistake brought all her dreams
crashing down. Now she has come to Leeds for a fresh start as
a trainee district nurse.

But Agnes finds herself facing unexpected challenges as she is
assigned to one of the city's most notorious slums. Before she
can redeem herself in the eyes of her family, she must first win
the trust of her patients and fellow nurses.

Does Agnes have what it takes or will the tragedy of her past
catch up with her?

arrow books

West Yorkshire, 1926

After completing her training in Steeple Street, **Agnes Sheridan** is looking forward to making her mark as Bowden's first district nurse.

But when Agnes arrives, she's treated with suspicion, labelled just another servant of the wealthy mine owners. The locals would much rather place their trust in the resident healer – Hannah Arkwright.

And when the General Strike throws the village into turmoil, the miners and their families face hunger and hardship, and Agnes finds her loyalties tested.

Now it's time to prove whose side she is really on and to fight for her place in the village . . .

arrow books